DRAWN TO THE LIGHT

The History of Cape Canaveral

and its People

To: Allen
with Love all the
Best & Hope you
truly enjoy this
Book! My Respectfully
Sonny Wright
1-27-2011

Printed by

Central Plains Book

105 East 5th Avenue, 2nd Floor
Arkansas City, KS 67005

Cover design by Nancy D. Watts

Book layout by Nancy D. Watts

ISBN: 978-1-4507-1194-4

PRINTED IN THE UNITED STATES OF AMERICA

For the descendants of those

wonderful people who settled

South Florida and Cape Canaveral.

May their memories live on…

A promise kept

CONTENT

ACKNOWLEDGEMENTS

Many individuals and institutions assisted, pushed, chided, coached and gave moral support to me while making this book actually get completed. Well it took over five years.

First my undying gratitude goes to the wonderful people and descendants of those wonderful people that lived at Cape Canaveral between the years of 1847 and 1950. So many have given me pictures, stories, encouragement, support and their friendship.

A special acknowledgement must be given the Cape Canaveral Lighthouse Foundation, whose members and volunteers provided me encouragement, information, stories and just plain support. The Board of Directors provided me with unlimited access to the board and encouragement at every step of the way.

This book could never have happened without the help of Candace Clifford who is an author and researcher extraordinaire. Her work scouring the National Archives for letters, papers, journals and maps has been invaluable.

John Drebinger, an author, magician and lecturer gave me more books to read on how to write a book and how to get a book published, than I could read. He also has been a good friend and always gave me support and his ear.

 Rose Wooley, historian and author, was more help then I will ever be able to say in the few words here. Her work is quoted throughout this book. She helped with pictures, research, stories and just plain encouragement.

Nancy D. Watts helped me with research, editing, photography, offered advice, and used her magic to put the whole thing in a publishable format. I really don't think we would have gotten through the process without her help.

Neil Hurley, historian, retired Coast Guard leader and author whose work is quoted often in the book, offered his advice, friendship and encouragement.

Much credit for this book must go to Dr David Paterno. Dr Paterno, a historian, author and friend, gave me encouragement, advice, and opened a number of doors that I would have never been able to open or even know about.

G. Kay Witt, my wife, best friend, lover and biggest fan, I say thank you and promise that now I will spend less time in front of my computer and more time helping you in the yard and sailing. Without her support this book certainly would never have happened.

The history of Cape Canaveral from 500 - 1945 is very sketchy or non-existent. The Ais Indians controlled Cape Canaveral until their disappearance in about 1715. From that time, the Cape lay virtually uninhabited until about 1847 when the Lighthouse Establishment arrived to search for a location to build a lighthouse.

About one hundred and thirty years after the Ais Indians disappeared from Cape Canaveral, a hand full of settlers arrived. Their objective was to raise families, settle homesteads and operate the Cape Canaveral Lighthouse. Interestingly enough, the first lighthouse keeper left Cape Canaveral because of fears of raids by Indians and the third keeper came to the cape because Indians caused his family to leave their homestead near Fort Pierce.

Mills O. Burnham and his wife Mary should be credited for, all but completely, populating Cape Canaveral with the Burnham family members and the operation the Cape Canaveral Lighthouses between 1853 and 1939 when the Coast Guard took ownership.

Burnham or a member of his family saw the beautiful state-of-the-art Iron Lighthouse first assembled. He watched as it got its beautiful black and white day mark. His son-in-law became the first postmaster of Cape Canaveral. A cousin watched the Iron Lighthouse be disassembled and moved to its current location. After the lighthouse was moved to it's current location, a Burnham granddaughter lived in the Keepers home. The cause of and the route used for that move has been debated and sought for years. We will solve that mystery.

Every attempt has been made to be as accurate as possible and research included the use of original documents, letters, maps, drawings and copies of documents found in the National Archives, the Internet, and Descendant's records.

We start with the Ais' influence and their struggle to live on land that they had occupied for thousands of years. We will examine the first settlers and their settlements south of Apopka and what happened. Winding up at Cape Canaveral and its two lighthouses, hotel, four fishing piers, a couple of schools, three towns, and meet some of the wonderful hard working people who settled, lived, married, died, and are buried at The Cape.

The first inhabitants of what is now called Florida were referred to as Paleo Indians.[1] It's believed that those Native Americans were our first residents and migrated to the region about 10,000 years ago.[2] Most documentation about Florida's history starts around 1500 and even that history is ever so sketchy for the region of Cape Canaveral. In about 1513, the Indian population of Florida was made up of Indians from some fourteen different tribes. Those fourteen tribes were spread out all over Florida, starting with the Chacato in the west, the Timucua in the north east, the Mayaca and Surruque in central Florida, the Ais at Cape Canaveral, as well as the Calusa and Matecumbe in south Florida.[3] A number of authors have written on the subject of Cape Canaveral and its people. So many mysteries, so many secrets.

No story, book, or article about the settling of Cape Canaveral would be complete without some words devoted to the Ais Indians. For the most part, the Ais, pronounced eyees, were not farmers, they were hunter, gatherers. They subsisted by fishing, hunting and foraging in the area of the headwaters of the St. Johns River which is only 10 to 15 miles from the coast. The Ais probably fished and hunted in the St. Johns freshwater marshes and swamps, as well as the saltwater coastal lagoons. To supplement their fish diet, the Ais, more than likely, picked palmetto berries, cocoa plums, cabbage palm and sea grapes. "The Ais spoke an unknown language affiliated with the south Florida Tequesta or Calusa."[4] David M. Brewer, in his 1990 Thesis, advances the theory, supported by others, that the Surruque Ais controlled Cape Canaveral and that they may have practiced agriculture. He quotes Dickinson (1696) stating that just above the marshes of Canaveral was "an Indian plantation...being full of pumpion (pumpkin) vines and some small pumpions (sic) on them..."[5] Brewer goes on to suggest that "the Surruque, just north of Canaveral, were at least semi-agriculturist, using the marine resources of the Mosquito Lagoon and supplementing this with"[6] some cultivated plants and fruit. The previous assertions are supported by a paper by Tom Penders, presented to the Brevard Historical Society, providing evidence that the Ais may have established a village near or just north of the false cape.[7] Mysteries and more mysteries.

The Ais used spears made from the cane that grew along the river and in marsh areas and cast nets made from fibers.[8] They may have had another weapon, the "atlatl."[9] The "atlatl or spear-thrower is a tool that uses leverage to achieve greater velocity in dart-throwing. It consists of a shaft with a cup or a spur in which the butt of the projectile, properly called a dart, rests. It is held near the end farthest from the cup, and the dart is thrown by the action of the upper arm and wrist. A well-made atlatl can readily achieve ranges of greater than 100 meters and speeds of over 150 km/h. The atlatl dates back over 27,000 years."[10]

Picture of the atlatl courtesy WikipediA

The Ais built thatched huts of wood and palm fronds. These huts were furnished with wooden benches. A fire was usually built in the center of the hut with the occupants sleeping near the outer walls. The smoke from the fire tended to keep the flying bugs away and the fire deterred wild animal entry. They moved their camps and villages seasonally to avoid flooding and stinging insects. Dugout canoes were their primary means of transportation.[11] The Ais, both men and women, wore their hair long. Warriors would wrap their hair in a roll on top of their heads and fasten it in place using curved bone pins. The pins were sharpened like arrowheads. Bet no-one called any of them a girly-man. The Ais warriors wore loincloths made of moss or fiber. That must have really itched. Their shirts were made of deerskin, and of course, made by the women.

The adult Ais stood between 5 feet 8 inches and 6 feet tall, which made the adult Ais taller than the average Europeans they would encounter when the Europeans came to take the Indians as slaves. The Ais disappeared in the early 1700s.[12]

Picture of Ais Indian Chief courtesy Theodore Morris

The picture at left is of a painting by "Theodore Morris and is a representation of the Ais Cacique, or Chief," preparing for a ceremonial dance. Theodore Morris is an artist who uses oil paintings to tell the story of Florida's lost native cultures. Mr. Morris is a historian of Florida Indians and uses his research and work with archaeologists and anthropologists throughout the State of Florida gathering the latest information pertaining to artifacts and documentation for his oil paintings. He used descriptions of the Ais as documented by Jonathan Dickinson when Dickinson and his shipwrecked crew were captives of the Ais in 1696.[13]

There was no Starbuck's or Dunkin' Donuts on Cape Canaveral when the Ais were in control of the area. So how did the Indians get along without coffee? The Ais and other Indians learned the secret of the Yupan Holly. The Yupan Holly is one of a few plants in North America that contains caffeine.[14] Coffee from holly leaves? Yes, the Ais learned how to make coffee from the Yaupon Holly which is a plant native to the Atlantic Coast. This secret drink was made using Yaupon Holly leaves and known as the Black Drink. It was loaded with caffeine.

The Yaupon Holly was used as a substitute for coffee by the colonists and was called cassine or cassona. The Black Drink was consumed during village councils and was served at all other important council meetings. As a practice of tribute, it was prepared by special village officials and served in large communal cups, frequently made of whelk shell. Attendees were served in order of precedence, important visitors were served first. And the custom continues today.

The Creeks, Cherokees, Choctaws, and others believed it purified the drinker and purged him of anger and falsehoods. They consumed large quantities at a sitting. Afterward, they purged themselves by vomiting.[15] Thus the greek name of Ilex vomitoria.

"Two distinct Indian groups, the Timucua and the Ais, lived in the Cape Canaveral area at the time of Ponce de Leon's voyage. The Timucuans, a much larger group than the Ais, principally occupied the territory between the present border of Georgia and Cape Canaveral. The Ais lived in the Atlantic coastal region and Indian River area from Cape Canaveral south to the St. Lucie River. The Surruque Ais controlled Cape Canaveral."[16] It can be safely asserted that the Ais controlled the area of the east coast of Florida roughly from south of New Smyrna Beach to north of Fort Pierce Inlet and from the Atlantic Ocean, to west of the Indian River for at least 2000 years, and possibly much longer. Harriett Carr supports this assertion in her book Cape Canaveral Cape of Storms and Wild Cane Fields, with "Along the shores of Canaveral, and inland for twenty to thirty miles, the Ais were the ruling tribe."[17] How did they get to Cape Canaveral? From Texas?

From the <u>Handbook of Texas Online</u>: **AIS INDIANS**. The Ais Indians, an East Texas group associated with the Hasinais, spoke a language different from the Caddos of the region. For this reason, it has been suggested by some authorities that the Ais represented a culture older than the confederacy known to the French and Spanish.

Their early home was on Ayish Bayou between the Sabine and Neches rivers. In 1717 Nuestra Señora de los Dolores de los Ais Mission was founded for them in the vicinity of present San Augustine. According to historical accounts the Ais were distrusted alike by the Caddo and by French and Spanish authorities. In the later part of the eighteenth century they were placed under the jurisdiction of the officials residing at Nacogdoches. They were later placed on the Wichita reservation in Oklahoma.[18]

Although there is little evidence, the Ais "were reputed to be cannibalistic."[19] The accusation has been repeated so often that it has become fact. According to Harriett Carr, Missionaries wanted to convert the Ais. Some Missionaries "lived through the mercy of some convert who helped them escape told of hunger and cruelty. They saw their fellow priests tortured. Arms and legs were cut off and finally the suffering victims were beheaded, with only wild animals and wilder Indians to hear their cries of pain."[20] What a horrible story. If it were true, it might explain, why no one came onto Cape Canaveral for over 100 years after the Ais left.

Robert I. Davidsson, in his book <u>Indian River: A History of the Ais Indians in Spanish Florida</u>, tells us that the "Ais who controlled Cape Canaveral were known as Surruque Ais." He tells us on page 59 that; "The Surruque <u>Ais were not cannibals</u>, but as a rule they were not kind to shipwrecked victims."[21] In other words they had a bad reputation. The Ais were the first Indians that Juan Ponce de Leon encountered when he tried to land at St. Lucie Inlet in April of 1513. The Cape Canaveral Ais were encountered about this same time when "Captain Gordillo anchored off the coast of Cape Canaveral and sent a landing party ashore to capture the Indians."[22] Yes, he was a slaver.

It would appear that this same slaver may have been the person to give us the name for Cape Canaveral. Captain Gordillo called the cane arrows used by the Indians "canaveral-cane or reed" in Spanish. The area was known as Cape of the Canaveral or Cape Canaveral thereafter. This all took place between 1513 and 1520, some 45 years before St Augustine would be founded in 1565[23] thus making Cape Canaveral the oldest named or identified location in the United States. Sorry about the aside. More about the slavers and their intentions.

The Spanish laid claim to Florida as their territory even though people clearly had made homes and raised families long before the Spanish arrived. The Ais and other Florida Indians resisted the Spanish advance, and rightly so they were defending their homes. The Spanish captured Indians and transport them to such places as Santo Domingo and Cuba among other destinations.[24] Soooo, some of the first people the Ais met were there to enslave them!?

Eventually the Spanish recognized that they clearly had a problem. They couldn't convert or control the Ais. So what to do was the question. The answer came in 1573. The Ais must have done a pretty good job of defending their country causing Captain Mendez to, out of desperation, recommend that a solution to the damages and murders caused by the Ais, would be to attack them "with all rigor, a war of fire and blood, and those taken alive shall be sold as slaves, removing

Picture of Aviles Courtesy of the Library of Congress

them and taking them to Cuba, Santo Domingo, Puerto Rico."[25] Are you kidding me? Now we have an explanation as to how the Ais got to Cuba.

The Ais conducted raids on shipping by wrecking and plundering ships off the dangerous and unmarked waters of Cape Canaveral. The Ais set fires on the beaches near Cape Canaveral in order to draw ships onto the shoals of Cape Canaveral and the huge rocks, just north and east of the Cape, known as the Bulls. The Ais were feared and yet respected.

The wrecking and salvage operations of this tribe became such a major racket that, as much needed supply ships repeatedly failed to arrive at the Presidio, punitive steps had to be taken.

Menendez complained; "Then, too, the enemies of Spain - at first the French, and later pirating Dutch and English - were wont to deal with these Indians and use their inlets as their bases from which to harass her fleets."[26]

The relationship between the Ais Indians and the Spanish was not good. The Ais hated the Spanish who tried in vain to convert the Ais. The Spanish thought enough of them to name the river west of Marratt's Island after the Ais. Merritt Island was probably named after the Spanish surveyor Captain Pedro Marratt and was called for years Marratt's Island because he was the first to actually survey it. "Reo de Ais" - River of the Ais (Indians) was the Indian River's original name, given by Adelantado Pedro Menendez de Aviles in the 1560s. He also named the lagoon that lies just west of Cape Canaveral "bay of the Ais."[27]

In 1922, Ruby Andrews Meyers, writing for The Cocoa Tribune, provides the following: "The Seminoles called it "Eesta - chattee - hatchee" which translates to red-mans river."[28] "The suffix hatchee is Seminole for river, and eesta-chattee is classic for Indian for red-man."[29] By about 1819 the name was simply shortened it to Indian River. Imagine, how much history can be lost when "Reo de Ais" was economized to Indian River. It's almost like wiping out a complete people in the name of economy. Please note that there was no plan or plot to ignore the Ais by shortening the river's name. It was and is simply a part of our natural tendency to shorten long names of places or locations.

We have Jonathan Dickinson to thank for a glimpse into the life and activities of the Ais. He was among the first to describe the Ais and provides just about the only detailed description of this fierce and independent Indian. He, his wife, infant son, and the crew of the barkentine or barquentine, a sailing ship with three or more masts, and a square rigged foremast, *Reformation"* were shipwrecked during a hurricane on September 23, 1696. They came ashore near what is now Hobe Sound. Jonathan Dickinson was a Quaker merchant traveling from Port Royal, Jamaica to Philadelphia. He and his party of about twenty-five managed to reach the mainland, only to be captured by the Jeagas Indians.

On October 1, 1696, Jonathan Dickinson and his party were handed over to "Casseekey"

Chief of the very hostile Ais Indians. They were held captives in an Ais village for nearly two months. During that time, Dickinson observed, at first hand, and recorded in his journal an account of the Ais Indian's daily life, rituals, and their customs.[30] He described them as a primitive group that didn't plant crops but survived by collecting plants, hunting animals and catching fish. For some reason Dickinson and his group either, escaped, or were possibly allowed to - just leave.

The central village of the Ais in the Cape region may have been in the area of Ulumay located on the Banana River, and

Picture of Ais Hut, courtesy Brevard Parks, Ulumay

was surrounded by smaller camps. Their dwellings were rectangular thatched huts. In language, dress, and general culture, the Ais were similar to both the St. Johns Indians to the north and the Glades Indians to the South. Yet they were distinct from each other, adopting only parts of these other complexes. At the time of contact, the Ais were estimated to have numbered between 600-1,500. Introduction of European diseases rapidly decimated the Ais. By the late 1600s and certainly by 1700, the Ais had ceased to exist as an organized group in the Indian River area."[31] Ulumay is now the location of the Ulumay Wild Life Sanctuary on Marratt's Island."[32]

There is evidence that the Ais may have had villages in a number of locations near Cape Canaveral and the surrounding area. To identify only a couple: "Ais Indian town of Pentoaya, first mapped by the Spanish in 1605, was located in the area now called Ballard Park in Eau Gallie."[33] The Oak Lodge Area "located ¼ of a mile east of Mrs. Latham's home (Oak Lodge) 350 ft from the ocean."[34] This area may have been near Wabasso, Florida. "Mr. Charles N. Jenks describes the scene he found in an Archeology survey Publication, A Survey of Indian River Archeology, Florida, published by Yale University:[35]

> The chief was sitting on a throne, of bier of oyster shells. Two women sat at the bier
> at the feet of and facing the Chief in the same general positions to head and limbs.
> A shell pendant was between one woman's knees, having dropped in front. They
> had apparently been around her neck and her head and had dropped as time went
> on. I had failed to find any beads or ornaments on the second woman's body.[36]

Although some writers pinpoint the disappearance of the Ais from Cape Canaveral in about 1703, and to reappear in Cuba in 1763 where they were called Calusa,[37] the broader time frame of between 1710 and 1750 is more realistic and their appearance in Cuba may be attributed to them being sold there as slaves. Here it must be pointed out that a group of Indians called the Calusa lived in the southwestern part of Florida at about the time the Ais disappeared from Cape

Canaveral. Could it have been the Florida Calusa Indians that appeared in Cuba in 1763? Another mystery? Robert I. Davidsson offers an answer: "Captain Thomas Nairne: The agent of Death: The disappearance of the Ais Indians and the other native tribes in Spanish Florida during the early 18th century is no mystery. Their destruction was the outcome of a deliberate foreign policy by the British Royal Proprietary Colony of South Carolina based intertribal conflict and the Indian Slave Trade."[38]

The year 1711 was a turning point in the history of the Ais Indians. For nearly 200 years, after Juan Ponce de Leon landed on their shores in 1513, the Ais had resisted all European efforts to subdue or "civilize" the tribe. On February 26, 1711, an Indian leader who identified himself as Cacique of Ais, walked into the Spanish "Indios de la Costa settlement near St. Augustine and asked to join the village. With him came 16 warriors,"[39] perhaps the last of the free Ais from the Indian River region. Does this solve the mystery? Or, is it just another secret and another mystery yet to be completely resolved?

It is very interesting and a bit troubling that after the Ais left Cape Canaveral, we have found little evidence that anyone came to or lived on Cape Canaveral until 1847 when Stephen Pleasonton of the Lighthouse Establishment sent George Center to the Cape to find a good location to build a lighthouse.[40] There is some evidence that "Scobie" may have homesteaded the north region of Cape Canaveral prior to 1847. Was it the rumors of cannibalism, the harsh treatment of "visitors," fierceness in the defense of their homeland? Don't know.... There is still more to learn.

[1]The Florida Memory Project, (accessed December 16, 2007) <http://www.floridamemory.com/Timeline/>
[2]Lethbridge, Cliff ,The History of Cape Canaveral, Chapter 1, Cape Canaveral Before Rockets: (accessed December 16, 2007) <http://www.spaceline.org/capehistory/1a.html>
[3]Davidsson, Robert I. Indian River: a history of the Ais Indians in Spanish Florida, West Palm Beach Fl, s.n.: An Ais Indian Project Publication, 2001, pg 17
[4]David M. Brewer, An Archeological and Ethnohistorical Overview and Assessment of Mosquito Lagoon at Canaveral National Seashore, Florida, A thesis Submitted to Department of Anthropology in partial fulfillment of the requirements for the degree of Master of Science, Degree awarded: 1991, Florida State University Library, pg 55
[5]Ibid, pg 58
[6]Ibid.
[7]Tom Penders' 2009 letter to Brevard Historical Society
[8]Davidsson, Robert I. Indian River:a history of the Ais Indians in Spanish Florida, West Palm Beach Fl, s.n.: An Ais Indian Project Publication, 2001, pg 33
[9]Harriett Carr, Cape Canaveral Cape of Storms and Wild Cane Fields, Valkyrie Press Inc, St Petersburg, Florida, 1974, pg 7
[10]WikipediA, the free encyclopedia, (accesses 29 March 2009) <http://en.wikipedia.org/wiki/Atlatl>
[11]An Archeological Survey of Cape Canaveral Air Force Station, Brevard County, Florida, pg 30; Resource Analyst, Inc, Bloomington, Indiana, Prepared by Richard S. Levy, Ph.D.,David F. Barton, M.P.A., Timothy B. Riordan, M.A.
[12]Davidsson, Robert I. Indian River: a history of the Ais Indians in Spanish Florida, West Palm Beach Fl, s.n. :An Ais Indian Project Publication, 2001, pg 33
[13]THEODORE MORRIS: "AIS CACIQUE" painting (accessed July 12, 2007) <http://www.rootsweb.com/~flindian/ais.htm >
[14]Cassia The Black Drink, (accessed 28 August 2008) <http://pelotes.jea.com/NativeAmerican/blackdrnk.htm>
[15]WikipediA the free encyclopedia, (accessed 28 August 2008) <http://en.Wikipedia.org/wiki/Black_drink>
[16]Levy, Richard S., Ph.D., Barton, David F., M.P.A., prepared An Archeological Survey of Cape Canaveral Air Force Station, Brevard County, Florida, page 30; Resource Analyst, Inc, Bloomington, Indiana
[17]Harriett Carr, Cape Canaveral Cape of Storms and Wild Cane Fields, Valkyrie Press Inc, St Petersburg, Florida, 1974, pg 6
[18]Frederick Webb Hodge, ed., Handbook of American Indians North of Mexico, 2 vols., Washington: GPO, 1907, 1910; rpt., New York: Pageant, 1959 (accessed December 12, 2007) http://www.tshaonline.org/handbook/online/articles/AA/bma15.html
[19]Higgs, Charles D., Spanish Contacts with the Ais, (Indian River) Country, "The murderous wrecking and salvage operations of this tribe (who also were reputed to have been cannibalistic)..." (accessed December 12, 2007) <http://www.treasurelore.com/florida/ais.htm >
[20]Harriett Carr, Cape Canaveral Cape of Storms and Wild Cane Fields, Valkyrie Press Inc, St Petersburg, Florida, 1974, pg 6
[21]Davidson, Robert I. Indian River: a history of the Ais Indians in Spanish Florida, West Palm Beach Fl, s.n.: An Ais Indian Project Publication, 2001, pg 18
[22]Ibid. pg 18
[23]Ibid, pg 49
[24]Ibid, pg 18
[25]Ibid, pg 76
[26]Higgs, Charles D., Spanish Contacts with the Ais, (Indian River) Country, (accessed December 12, 2007) <http://www.treasurelore.com/florida/ais.htn>
[27]Davidsson, Robert I., Indian River:a history of the Ais Indians in Spanish Florida, West Palm Beach Fl, a.n.: An Ais Indian Project Publication, 2001, pg, 29
[28]Ruby Andrews Meyers, Indian River, a Streak of Silver Sea, That Charms and Holds Ever After the First Sight, The Cocoa Tribune, February 9, 1922
[29]Ibid
[30]Walker Andrews, Evangeline and McLean Andrews, Charles. (accessed July 26, 2007) <http://www.rootsweb.com/~flindian/jondick.htm> [from the dust jacket of Jonathan Dickinson's Journal, or, God's Protecting Providence: Being the Narrative of a Journey from Port Royal in Jamaica to Philadelphia between August 23, 1696 and April 1, 1697. (New Haven, CT: printed for the Yale University Press, 1961.)
[31]Levy, Richard S., Ph.D., Barton, David F., M.P.A., Riordan, Timothy B., M.A.. Prepared An Archeological Survey of Cape Canaveral Air Force Station, Brevard County, Florida, page 28; Resource Analyst, Inc, Bloomington, Indiana
[32]Brevard History, Ulumay, (accessed March 29, 2009) <http://www.Brevardparks.com/historic/hist_ulumay.php> Only the name Ulumay has survived as the name of the Ulumay Wildlife Refuge on Merritt Island (named by naturalist and local historian Johnnie Johnson). Quoting from Irving Rouse's survey of Indian River Archaeology, Mexia's diary says, "Here is the town of Ulumay, the first one of the province of the Ais. In back and adjacent to this town there are many camps." The Ais Indians remained in the area until their disappearance between 1715 and 1720. The shell mounds which were all that was left of these villages were used in the construction of early Merritt Island roads long before their archaeological significance was recognized. Recognition finally came on Dec 7, 1993, when

the Brevard County Historic Commission presented a plaque to the Board of County Commissioners dedicating Ulumay Wildlife Sanctuary as a Historic Landmark.

[33]The Brevard County Historical Commission, The Indian River Journal, Volume VII, Number 1, Spring/summer 2008

[34]Walter Obermayr, The Ais Indians, unpublished pamphlet

[35]Ibid.

[36]Ibid.

[37]Swanton, John R., The Indian Tribes of North America: The Smithsonian Institution Press, Washington

[38]Davidsson, Robert I. Indian River:a history of the Ais Indians in Spanish Florida, West Palm Beach Fl, s.n.: An Ais Indian Project Publication, 2001, pg 128

[39]Ibid, pg 137

Let us acknowledge here that St. Augustine was the first city or settlement in America. Spanish St. Augustine was founded some 55 years before the Pilgrims landed at Plymouth Rock. Therefore, St. Augustine is the oldest permanent European settlement in the United States.[1] It is believed that Cape Canaveral may be the oldest identified location in the United States. If it's not the oldest, it is most certainly one of the oldest.

Picture of Ponce de Leon, courtesy, WikipediA

As stated in Chapter 1, at some time between 1513 and 1520 Ponce de Leon arrived on the East Coast of Florida and came ashore near present day Melbourne Beach.[2] A member of his party, Captain Gordillo, sailed north looking for Indians to enslave and called the arrows used by the Ais Indians to defend themselves "canaveral." In doing so, he gave us the ultimate name for Cape Canaveral. In Spanish, canaveral translates into canes or reeds. From that time on the name Capo de Canaveral was used by the Spanish in reference to the Cape Canaveral. It is well documented that this all took place in about 1520 some 45 years before St Augustine was founded in 1565.[3]

Any conversation about the settling of Cape Canaveral must start with some discussion about the settlement of Florida, and something called the Armed Occupation Act. In the late 1830s, the Federal Government believed that an armed civilian population, willing to fight Indians to hold land that they had settled, would be much cheaper then sending an army to the area. The threat was the Seminole Indians during the Second Seminole War. So, on August 4, 1842 Congress approved the "Armed Occupation Act." Essentially the act gave 160 acres of land in the unsettled part of Florida to a person who was 18 years or older, provided they live on the land, clear five acres, build a house, and hold the land for five years. "Hold the land" meant not letting the Indians take it back. On the east coast, settlers looking to apply for land under the Act had to apply in St. Augustine.[4] The following is the short version of the act:

> The Florida Armed Occupation Act of 1842 (5 U.S. Statutes 502) was passed to encourage the settlement of Florida. The Florida District General Land Offices were responsible for the handling of claims made under this Act. The Act granted 160 acres of unsettled land south of the line separating townships 9 and 10 South (a line running East/West about three miles north of Palatka and about ten miles south of Newnansville) to any head of a family under three conditions: (1) the land selected could not be within two miles of a military post; (2) the settler must be able to bear arms and live on the land for five years; and (3) the settler must clear five acres and build a house.[5]

The serious settlement of the Florida Territory began in about 1842 with the establishment of two colonies. The Indian River Colony[6] on the east coast and the Manatee Colony,[7] on the west coast. Each was established under the Armed Occupation Act. The Manatee Colony settled on the Manatee River near where the city of Bradenton now stands. The colony was led by Major Robert Gamble and Colonel Samuel Reid. They and the colony contributed to the eventual settlement of the Manatee County and the Tampa Bay area.

The Indian River Colony was established with about forty families and heads of household.

Picture of
Major Robert Gamble,
courtesy, Florida Memory
Project Archives

The leaders of the Indian River Colony included Colonel Samuel H. Peck, a banker and cotton broker from Augusta, Georgia. Colonel Peck must have been wealthy because he had the only frame house in the settlement. He had the house built in Savannah and shipped to Florida on a schooner. A schooner is a type of sailing vessel characterized by the use of fore-and-aft sails on two or more masts. According to Ranson (1926) Colonel Peck sold his home to Mills Olcott Burnham in 1843. The settlement was established near what is now known as Ankona in St Lucie County near Fort Pierce, Florida.[8] Another leader of the Indian River Colony was Dr. Frederick Weedon.

Dr. Weedon was born in Maryland and moved to Alabama and then to Florida. He bought property in Leon County in 1829 and in St. Augustine in 1834. He even operated a drugstore and served as Mayor of St. Augustine in 1835. The Doctor was a leader in the Indian River Colony and was issued permit number 1 on October 11, 1842. The land, in permit number 1, included the deactivated Fort Pierce; the only structures in the area. The Doctor may have had influence and inside knowledge - the only structure in the area a deactivated Army Fort and with structures?? Dr. Weedon served in the Florida militia during the Seminole War and had been the physician in St. Augustine who cared for Chief Osceola. The doctor traveled with the chief to Ft. Moultrie in South Carolina.[9]

Picture of Dr Weedon,
courtesy, the Florida Memory
Project State Archives

Picture of Chief Osceola,
courtesy, the Florida
Memory Project
State Archives

After his (Osceola's) death, army doctor Frederick Weedon removed Osceola's head and embalmed it. He also persuaded other Seminoles to allow him to make a death mask and kept a number of objects Osceola had given him. Captain Pitcairn Morrison took the mask alongside other objects that had belonged to Osceola and sent it to an army officer in Washington. By 1885, it ended up in the anthropology collection of the Smithsonian Institution, where it currently remains. Later, Weedon gave the head to his son-in-law Daniel Whitehurst who, in 1843, sent it to Valentine Mott, a New York physician. Mott placed it in his Surgical and Pathological Museum. It was presumably lost when a fire destroyed the museum in 1866.[10]

Another very important member of the Indian River Colony was Ossian B. Hart who would become Florida's tenth Governor. Of Hart, Ranson, (1926) observed: "Among the aristocrats was a talented lawyer and fine musician who, with his delicate wife, seemed greatly out of place amid such rough and primitive surroundings."[11]

Although the Indian River Colony didn't survive, one of its leaders, Mills O. Burnham, would go on to leave his mark on the history of the East Coast of Florida and most importantly the area of Cape Canaveral. First we must meet and begin to know Mills O. Burnham.

Mills O. Burnham was born September 18, 1817 in Thetford, Vermont and mover, with his family, to Lansingburgh, New York. Burnham was not the only famous person to be associated with Lansingburgh. Chester

Picture of
Ossian Bringley Hart,
courtesy, the Florida
Memory Project

A. Arthur (1829-1886), 21st President of the United States, born in Fairfield, Vermont, spent part of his youth in Lansingburgh and Author Herman Melville penned his first two novels in Lansingburgh.[12] Burnham attended public school and later served an apprenticeship at the Watervliet Arsenal where he learned to be a gunsmith.

> Watervliet Arsenal, (Watervliet is pronounced water-vuh-leet) the nation's oldest, was Founded in 1813 to support the Second War for Independence, the War of 1812, the arsenal has been a valuable resource ever since. In 1887, the arsenal became America's "Cannon Factory." It is America's sole manufacturing facility for large caliber cannon in volume.

> Located along the Hudson River, just a few miles north of the state capital at Albany, Watervliet Arsenal continues to produce today's high tech, high powered weaponry. Cannon - the finest cannon manufactured in the world today - remains the principal product of Watervliet Arsenal.[13]

Pictures of
Mills Olcott Burnham
and
Mary McCune Burnham
Courtesy
of the
Florida Memory
Project Archives

Mills O. Burnham was barely 18 years old when he met and married 16 year old Mary Ann McCuen. Mary was born in Northern Ireland. The couple got married on September 9, 1835 in the Protestant Episcopal Church of Lansingburgh. The Reverend Phineas Whipple performed the ceremony. Just two years later, in 1837, Burnham left Watervliet for the Arsenal of the South, at Garey's Ferry, Florida. Today Garey's Ferry is known as Middleburg. Burnham moved to Florida because his doctor had diagnosed lung problems and suggested that he go south for a better climate. Mills Burnham sailed for Garey's Ferry onboard the schooner Perue.[14] The doctor was right. After about a year Mills Burnham's health had improved so much that he went back to New York, and in August of 1839 Mills returned to Florida onboard the brig Ajax. A "brig" is simply a large sailboat with two square-rigged masts. He brought his wife Mary Ann, daughter Frances and sons, George and Mills Junior to Florida - to stay. George was the couple's first born in 1836 with Mills Jr. following in 1837 at Lansingburg. The first girl was Frances Augusta born on August 29, 1838 in Albany, New York.[15]

Mills O. Burnham and his family settled in Florida and never again traveled to a destination north of Charleston, and Florida is all the better for his decision.

Beginning with the settling of the Indian River Colony, Mills O. Burnham has left his mark on Florida history. Mills O. Burnham was issued permit number 59 on April 16, 1842 for land 8 1/2 miles from Fort Pierce under the Armed Occupation Act of 1842.[16] According to People of Lawmaking in Florida, 1822-2005, Mills O. Burnham was a member of the Florida Territorial Legislature from St. Lucie County in 1847, 1848 and 1850. Florida, Brevard County, and Cape Canaveral owe so much to Mills O. Burnham. He is credited with naming the Banana River, one island and a point of land in that river, as well as the discovery and naming of New Found Harbor on the Merritt Island side of the Banana River. How did that happen? Great question!

At some time between 1840 and 1850, Burnham and his youngest son George went on a fishing trip up the Indian River. As they fished, they took the east fork of the river and entered the waters east of the tip of Merritt Island. Coming upon an island just west and north of what is now Patrick Air Force Base, George pointed it out and his father immediately dubbed it "George's Island." The pair saw a deer on a point of land just a bit north of the now George's Island and named it "Buck Point." They explored the waterway leading into Sykes Creek and named it "Newfound Harbor."[17] About 25 miles north of Newfound Harbor they came to Desoto Groves. The father and son noticed many banana trees along the banks of the river and named the river Banana, hence the name Banana River. Desoto Groves and Desoto Beach are 10 - 15 miles north of the Cape and the lighthouse. Bananas still grow along the river at the Cape.[18] Those names appear on navigational charts used today - 170 years later.

Picture of Mills O. Burnham Jr., courtesy, Florida Memory Project Archives

It was difficult for Burnham to provide for his family and being very resourceful he bought a schooner, named it Josephine, loaded it up with green turtles and sailed for Charleston. This wasn't new. Turtles had been shipped to Charleston before. However, Burnham made little wooden pillows for the turtles to rest their heads on and every morning he sponged their eyes with salt water. When Burnham's boat load of turtles arrived in Charleston in excellent condition they were promptly sold for export to England at a good price.[19] Wonder if he learned that at Watervliet?

"It was while he was on one of these trips, that Indians killed a trader named Baker, who had a store at Baker's Bluff. News rapidly spread through the colony that an Indian uprising was imminent and a massacre of all white settlers was feared. Major Russell, a Colony leader, advised all to leave."[20] Ranson speculates that had "Burnham been in the colony at that time they would not have left. Mrs. Burnham, with her family, left the colony with Capt. Pinkham bound for St. Augustine."[21]

The following letter, dated July 18, 1849, has been re-typed and printed here gives the story and details of the event that caused the Indian River Colony to disband and leave the area. The families left the Indian River Colony on or about July 12, 1849.

Brevet Maj.-Gen. R. Jones,
Adjutant-General, U. S. Army,
Washington, D. C.

General: As a pendant to my letter of yesterday, I have to report that this morning, a party of 27 men, women and children arrived in a small vessel from Indian river settlement (Fort Pierce) having been driven thence by Indian outrages on the 12th instant. Mr. Russell, the Inspector of the Customs at I.

R., is among the number; he is severely wounded in the arm by rifle bullets, fired by the Indians. From Mr. Russell and others of the party, I have gathered the following details.

On Thursday, the 12th inst., four young Indian warriors, armed as for hunting, made their appearance at the Indian river settlement, conducting themselves in their usual friendly manner, received from the families similar treatment, and in no wise (way) exhibited any hostile feeling. This was about 12 o'clock. Between two and three hours afterwards, the Indians left Mr. Russell's house, where they had dined, and proceeded towards Messieurs Russell and Barker (his brother-in-law) who were conversing in a field about a quarter of a mile distant. When within forty or fifty yards of them two of the Indians fired and wounded both R. and B., who immediately ran in different directions; the four Indians pursued Mr. Barker and killed him with their knives. This shooting and stabbing was witnessed by the greater part of Mr. Russell's household, in particular by an intelligent daughter of some 13 years old, with whom I have conversed.

The alarm was at once taken, and the remainder of the inhabitants fled to their boats, followed by the four Indians, who fired some ten or twelve vollies after them, without further damage.

On the succeeding day some of the males went on shore from the small vessel where the party had taken refuge, and found the house of Mr. D. H. Gattis burnt to the ground, and the houses of Messrs. Russell and Barker pillaged, furniture destroyed, etc. The remaining houses at the settlement they did not visit. They found Mr. Barker's body, stabbed in several places.

The settlement consisted of four families, viz.: those of Messrs. Russell, Barker, Gattis and one other person whose name has escaped me, and numbered, negroes included, some forty-five souls; twenty-seven of whom arrived here this morning. The remainder, consisting principally of Mr. Russell's family and negroes, (Negroes) endeavored to escape in boats by way of Indian river; whether they have been successful is thus far unknown. It was from some of Mr. R s negroes (who after crossing Indian river walked to the light-house at Cape Canaveral) that Mr. Scobie (the keeper there) gained the intelligence on which he founded his letter to Mr. Dummett.

I have endeavored to obtain from Mr. Russell, Mr. Gattis, and others of the party, such information as would tend to throw some light upon the causes of this outbreak. One and all disclaim any knowledge on the subject, and say they *cannot form any conjecture as to its cause; that up to the moment when the shots were fired they did not for a moment anticipate the slightest difficulty.*

Two of the Indians are known to the inhabitants, and could be identified the others were strangers. One of those known is called "Sammy" or "Sam," the other Eli.

I sent a trusty express rider this morning to Mr. Marshall, at Dunlawton, with the view of getting any fresh intelligence he might have; especially to know if this is an isolated case of outrage.

I shall send an express in the course of the day to the commanding-officer and Indian agent at Tampa, with the above account.

As soon as the surf-boat, mentioned in my letter of yesterday, is ready, I shall send a detachment under an officer to the light-house at Cape Canaveral, and to the Indian river settlement, to obtain information, and give such aid as may be necessary in that direction.

Very respectfully, your obedient servant,

C. F. Smith,
Capt. 2d Art. and Brevet Col. Commanding.[22]

Brevet means a temporary promotion to a higher grade but without the pay.

Mills O. Burnham played a major role in the settlement of Cape Canaveral when in 1853 he was appointed keeper of the Cape Canaveral lighthouse and would forever be addressed as Captain. The Captain and Mary Burnham had five daughters and two sons. Ranson (1926) tells us that George was just fourteen years old when he passed away.[23] In his book, Thomas L. Tucker has George's age at twelve when he passed.[24] It is very understandable that there could be some minor disagreement. We can conclude that George was twelve or fourteen when he passed away. Mills O. Jr. died during the Civil War and is buried in the Oakland Cemetery in Atlanta, Georgia.[25]

In 1850 six acres were set aside to be a public burial ground -- Oakland Cemetery. Oakland was designed as a rural garden cemetery, a 19th Century innovation conceived as an alternative to traditional graveyards which often were crowded and aesthetically unappealing.

The cemetery was originally called Atlanta Graveyard or City Burial Place. It was renamed in 1872 and had expanded to 48 acres, mainly due to pressures of the Civil War. During the war, the City and the Confederate government added land to bury soldiers who died in local hospitals. More burial space was needed as fighting drew closer and engulfed Atlanta. After the war, space was added to provide a proper final resting place for soldiers who had been hastily buried on area battlefields.[26]

The Burnham daughters were Frances, Katherine, Mary, Louisa, and Anna Dummett.[27]

Five daughters? Did Captain Burnham have a plan to populate Cape Canaveral with his family? One could make an argument that he did exactly that. Well, as each daughter married, Captain Burnham gave the newlyweds up to 60 acres of land and a position at the lighthouse, IF they would stay on Cape Canaveral. Henry Wilson was the first. As a result of the "plan" the Burnham family operated and maintained the Cape Canaveral Lighthouse in some capacity from 1853 until it was transferred to the United States Coast Guard in 1939 - 86 years; and populated Cape Canaveral.

Picture of Mills O Burnham, Jr's Grave Stone, courtesy, Oakland Cemetery Foundation

Four of the five Burnham sisters married and lived on Cape Canaveral. According to the U.S. Census only seven families lived on Cape Canaveral in 1885. They were (1) Mills O. Burnham, Lighthouse Keeper, (2) son-in-law and Assistant Keeper, Henry Wilson who married Frances Augusta Burnham; (3) son-in-law Orlando Adolphus Quarterman who married Katherine Jerusha Burnham, Fruit Grower; (4) son-in-law and George M. Quarterman who married Anna Dummett Burnham, Assistant Keeper; (5) son-in-law and Assistant Keeper, James Knight who married Mary Burnham.

Of the daughters only Louisa, who married David Cottrell, didn't stay on Cape Canaveral. However, Mills O. Cottrell, the son of David and Louisa Cottrell did become an Assistant Keeper in 1886.[28]

The sixth and seventh families living on Cape Canaveral included in the Census were (6) Nathan Penny, Fruit Grower and (7) John H. Hogan, Fruit Grower.[29] Of the last two, neither married a Burnham or held a position at the lighthouse.

Cape Canaveral grew slowly between the census of 1885 and the 1920's - just 106 persons or families lived on the Cape in 1920. The Census of 1910 listed only twenty four heads of household/families living on Cape Canaveral. Some of those families were: Mary Burns, Samuel L. Jeffords, Clinton Honeywell, George F. Quarterman, James Knight, Thomas J. Thompson, William G. M. Quarterman, Edward G. Praetorious and Nathan Penny; more on Nathan Penny in Chapter 8.

Picture of Louisa, courtesy, the Florida Memory Project State of Florida Archives

Of the original seven families, the following were living or had a residence on Cape Canaveral in 1910, Orlando A. Quarterman and his wife Katherine Burnham were still living on the Cape: O. A. Quarterman was appointed Keeper of the Chester Shoal House of Refuge, Florida on May 13, 1886.[30] He was transferred to Keeper of the Biscayne Bay House of Refuge, Florida on September 12, 1906.[31] James Knight and his wife Mary and working at the lighthouse. Clinton Honeywell had married Gertrude Wilson daughter of Frances Burnham - Wilson and was an Assistant Lighthouse Keeper from 1891 - 1904. He was appointed Keeper in 1904.

So far it has been established that the Burnham family contributed greatly to the settlement of Cape Canaveral. The obvious next step is to examine the role played by the Lighthouse Establishment in the settlement and growth of Cape Canaveral.

[1]NEH Landmarks of American History and Culture, Workshop for Teachers; June 18-23, June 25-30 2007, (accessed August 10, 2007) <http://www.flahum.org/sections/st_augustine/index.html>

[2]Brevard County Board of County Commissioners, Historic Interests, (accessed November 23, 2008), http://www.brevardparks.com/librarydocs/hist_juanponce.php>

[3]Davidsson, Robert I, Indian River:a history of the Ais Indians in Spanish Florida, p. 49, West Palm Beach Fl, s.n.: An Ais Indian Project Publication, 2001

[4]Ankona Bluff and Indian River Colony, St. Lucie Historical Society, Inc., (accessed August 12, 2007) <http://www.rootsweb.com/~flslchs/IRColony.htm>

[5]State Library & Archives of Florida, Armed Occupation Act permit files, 1842-1843, Online Catalog, Records Group Number 589, Series/Collection Number S 1305, (accessed October 2, 2008) <http://dlis.dos.state.fl.us/barm/rediscovery/default.asp?IDCFile=/fsa/DETAILSS.IDC,SPECIFIC=1276,DATABASE=Series>

[6]Kyle S. Van Landingham, Pictorial History of Saint Lucie County 1565-1910, 1988

[7]Joe Kmetsch, Manatee Colony settler Colonel Sam Reid (accessed February 15, 2007) <http://www.lib.usf.edu/ldsu/digitalcollections/S57/journal/v21n1_95/v21n1_95_029.pdf>

[8]Robert Ranson 1926, East Coast Florida Memories, 1837-1886, p 8, (Port Salerno, Fl: Florida Classics Library, 1989)

[9]Ankona Bluff and Indian River Colony, (accessed February 15, 2007) <http://www.rootsweb.com/~flslchs/IRColony.htm>

[10]WikipediA, the free encyclopedia, (accessed September 19, 2003)<http://en.wikipedia.org/wiki/Osceola>

[11]Robert Ranson 1926, East Coast Florida Memories, 1837-1886, p 10, (Port Salerno, Fl: Florida Classics Library, 1989)

[12]WikipediA, the free encyclopedia, (accessed September 19, 2003) <http://en.wikipedia.org/wiki/Lansingburgh,_New_York>

[13]U.S. Army's Watervlielt Arsenal, (accessed September 19, 2003) <http://www.wva.army.mil/ABOUT.HTM>

[14]Robert Ranson 1926, East Coast Florida Memories, 1837-1886, p 6, (Port Salerno, Fl: Florida Classics Library, 1989)

[15]Thomas L. Tucker, Florida Pioneers, The Tucker & Wilson Story, pg 51, n.s. 2003

[16]Roots Web Ancestry, (accessed June 16, 2007) <http://www.rootsweb.ancestry.com/~cenfiles/fl/stjohns/1850/notes2.txt>

[17]Robert Ranson 1926, East Coast Florida Memories, 1837-1886, p 21, (Port Salerno, Fl: Florida Classics Library, 1989)

[18]Robert Ranson 1926, East Coast Florida Memories, 1837-1886, p 22, (Port Salerno, Fl: Florida Classics Library, 1989)

[19]Robert Ranson 1926, East Coast Florida Memories, 1837-1886, p 14, (Port Salerno, Fl: Florida Classics Library, 1989)

[20]Ibid.

[21]Ibid.

[22] Google Books on line, Senate documents, otherwise Publ. as Public documents and executive documents, pgs 26-29 (accessed 19 July, 2009) <http://books.google.com/books?id=x3gFAAAAQAAJ&pg=RA1-PA26&lpg=RA1-PA26&d#v=onepage&q=&f=false>

[23]Robert Ranson 1926, East Coast Florida Memories, 1837-1886, p 22 (Port Salerno, Fl: Florida Classics Library, 1989)

[24]Thomas L. Tucker, Florida Pioneers, The Tucker & Wilson Story, pg 52, n.s. 2003

[25]Ruth Middleton, Historic Oakland Cemetery Foundation

[26]Historic Oakland Cemetery Foundation, (accessed September 24, 2008) <http://www.oaklandcemetery.com/history.html>

[27]Rose Wooley, History of Cape Canaveral and the Early Settlers, 1998, p 8

[28]U.S Census, 1885

[29]Ibid, p 4

[30]U.S. Coast Guard, Chester Shoal House of Refuge, (accessed July 23,2008) <http://www.uscg.mil/history/>

[31]Ibid.

Picture of Charles Downing,
courtesy, Florida Memory
Project Florida State Archives

harles Downing[1] was a Florida Territorial delegate when on May 21, 1838, he presented a request to have a lighthouse built on Cape Canaveral.[2] The request was made on behalf of captains of vessels and citizens of Florida. One of those who made a request was Lt. Commander Matthew Galbraith Perry, who served on the U.S. Schooner, Sharp in 1822.[3] Mr. Downing served as delegate from the territory of Florida from March 4, 1837 to March 3, 1841. It took almost ten years for the government to actually act on Mr. Downing's request. Familiar?

The first lighthouse on Cape Canaveral stood about 65 feet above the ground, and that 65 feet included a 55 foot tower topped with a 10 foot tall Lantern Room. The lantern room would hold fifteen lamps on twenty-one inch reflectors. The brick tower and a keeper's home had a price tag of just under $12,000.00. The Lighthouse and Keeper's home were built by Thomas C. Hammond who did the work for $8,465.00. The lanterns were installed by Winslow Lewis at a cost of $2,794.00. So how did we get here?

Cape Canaveral was selected as a location for a lighthouse for a couple of reasons; first, Cape Canaveral is approximately midway between Jacksonville and Miami, a road marker if you will, secondly and most importantly, a lighthouse at Cape Canaveral would warn mariners of the dangerous Bulls just north of the Cape, and the Hetzel, Chester and Southeast Shoals that extend some 4 or 5 miles out into the Atlantic Ocean. Mr. George Center, of the Collector's Office, District of St Augustine, Florida, received instructions to go to Cape Canaveral and find a site on which to build a lighthouse. The assignment came from Mr. Stephen Pleasonton,[4] Treasury Department, 5th Auditor's Office, Superintendent of Lights, Washington, D. C. in a letter dated March 12, 1847.

Picture of Stephen Pleasonton
Courtesy USCG

Stephen Pleasonton is remembered mostly for his work in establishing the Lighthouse Establishment. He was appointed to oversee operations of the United States Light House Establishment. Pleasonton was a bureaucrat and knew little about maritime matters. He delegated much of the responsibility of his office to local collectors of customs, district superintendents of lights, and had the authority not only to select the sites for lighthouses, but to also purchase the land to build them on. Superintendents were expected to oversee the actual construction of lighthouses, and ensure they were repaired when necessary. They would also mediate conflicts and deal directly, when necessary, with lighthouse keepers. Each superintendent was required to submit a yearly report detailing the status of light stations in his charge.[5]

In March of 1847, Pleasonton writes to George Center, "Congress appropriated at the late session Twelve Thousand dollars for the building (of) a Light House at Cape Canaveral, this Light is placed under your Superintendence." He goes on and directs Center to "...report to this place and select and purchase the most suitable site for the Lighthouse..."[6] What a responsibility for a person to delegate. It was probably Center's first trip to Cape Canaveral.

We just don't know how George Center traveled to Cape Canaveral. There were few roads from St. Augustine to even near Cape Canaveral in 1847.[7] He couldn't go to Titusville because it wouldn't be established until 1867, another 20 years. A U.S. Post Office was established at Sand Point, the site of Titusville today, in 1859.[8] He most probably traveled on board a ship owned by the Lighthouse Establishment, possibly a lightship or a tender.

After exploring Cape Canaveral, George Center wrote to Pleasonton on May 30, 1847, telling him that he had "selected a spot deemed most eligible..."[9] for building a lighthouse. How could he have known that in 1950, just a mere 103 years later, rockets would be launched and a few years after that men would go into space from the very land that he declared "...of no value whatever other than for the purpose of a light."[10] Imagine that, even the comic strip Buck Rogers was some 82 years away. "Buck Rogers in the 25th Century debuted on January 7, 1929. It ran consecutively until 1967, and at its peak was published in more than 400 newspapers throughout the world and translated into 18 languages."[11] Sorry for the deviation. Now back to the site selection and the building of a lighthouse.

With the site selected, Stephen Pleasonton wrote a long rambling letter to George Center on June 7, 1847. In that letter, he pronounced, "As the land belongs to the United States the jurisdiction is still in them, so that it will not be necessary to apply to the Governor for a cession of it." Now I'm no lawyer but, if Florida became a state, along with Iowa in 1845 – you would think that in 1847 they, Florida, would have jurisdiction. Pleasonton goes on the speculate that, "This (the Cape Canaveral Light) I shall make a revolving Light and have it of the 1st

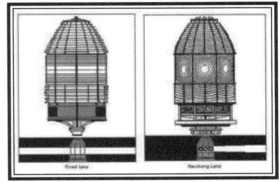

Picture of Fresnel lens, Courtesy WikipediA

order i.g. 65 feet from the ground to the lantern deck."[12] This guy must have had a lot of power over the Lighthouse Establishment. In the last sentence he must have misspoke the height; and meant the total height. Also, Pleasonton may have been referring to the Fresnel (fra-nell) lens that had been invented in 1822 by Augustin-Jean Fresnel (May 10, 1788 - July 14, 1827).

Fresnel was a French physicist who made significant contributions to the development of the theory of light wave optics. Had the Lighthouse Establishment installed a Fresnel lens at Cape Canaveral it would have been the first in the U.S. and sped up the eventual conversion to this extremely efficient and powerful lens. But he, Pleasonton, didn't.

With the site selected, things began to happen very quickly at Cape Canaveral. On July 7, 1847, the Collector's

Picture of Augustin-Jean Fresnel, courtesy WikipediA

Office of Boston sent out a Request for Proposals "for building materials and building a light-house and keeper's dwelling on Cape Canaveral, Florida." The proposals were to be "presented to the Collectors Office by noon on 19 July inst."[13] Note: The term "inst" or instant was often used in place of the current year, i.e. February 2 inst instead of February 2, 1939 assuming that 1939 is the current year.

Examination of the request for proposal shows that the lighthouse was to be constructed of brick, not wood. The building was, in fact, constructed using bricks as confirmed in 2006 when the remains of the original lighthouse were exposed. Remains?? What remains??

Picture of bricks taken by Author at the site of the first lighthouse on the Cape

It isn't even built and we're talking about remains. In case you are wondering why it had to be exploded, the September 1893 Cape Canaveral Lighthouse Keepers Journal has the following entry: "Sept. 26, 1893, The old brick tower was blown up with dynamite to be used in making concrete for the foundation of the tower at the new site."[14] New site? Much more on this later. Let's get back to the first lighthouse.

By reading the Request for Proposals, see Appendix I, we learn that the height of the lighthouse was to be 55 feet from ground level to the "top of the stone deck."[15] The stone deck would be the floor of the lantern room - a bit more about the lanterns later. The diameter at the base was to be 20 feet and 12 feet at the top. The walls were to be an amazingly 4 feet thick at the base and "regularly graduated" to 2 feet thick at the top. Pleasonton didn't want any wiggle or sway in this lighthouse! A soapstone deck 14 feet in diameter was to top off the lighthouse and would serve as a base for the lantern room. Note: Soapstone is a type of rock and has nothing to do with washing dishes or clothes. Soapstone is used for making counter tops and is virtually impervious to stains and marring. The last sentence in the Request for Proposals states: "The lighthouse is to be completed by the first day of January next "[16] - 1848. It was completed in January 1848.

On July 19, 1847, bids were opened in Boston for construction of the Egmont Key Lighthouse and the Cape Canaveral Lighthouse. In a letter to the Customs House Boston, dated July 20, 1847, Mr. Marcus Morton writes to announce the winning bidders. F. A Gibbson of Baltimore was the low bidder for building the Egmont Key Lighthouse with a bid of $6,250.00: Thomas C. Hammond of Mattapoisett, Massachusetts was the low bidder with an offer of $8,495.00 to construct the Cape Canaveral Lighthouse. Mr. Hammond must have lived nearby because he was present for the bid opening and witnessed that he was the low bidder.

In the same letter Marcus Morton tells the Collectors Office that "proposals were asked from Wess Hooper and W. Lewis for lighting the two lighthouses."[17] The letter continues to announce which would install the lights for the two lighthouses "...Winslow Lewis bid $2,794.00 for Cape Canaveral and $1,330.00 for Egmont Key."[18] The light for Cape Canaveral was to be a "revolving light with lamps."[19] So who was this Winslow Lewis person??

Winslow Lewis (1770-1850) was a sea captain, engineer, inventor and a contractor who was very active in the construction of many lighthouses during the first half of the nineteenth century. He lived in Wellfleet, Massachusetts, where he created a new lighting system based on Argand lamps; in 1812 the United States Congress purchased his patent rights for the system and got a sweetheart deal.

He was awarded a contract to equip all American lighthouses with the lamps. That took about four years. Then Lewis won another contract, this one allowing him to supply oil to all the stations and to visit them yearly to ensure their smooth operation.[20]

Now that's a deal.

Picture of Argand Lamp Courtesy WikipediA

When Stephen Pleasonton took over the responsibility for lighthouse contracts in 1820, he made a deal with Lewis, who was awarded most lighthouse construction in the United States. While demand for the towers was high, funds were short, and Pleasonton took great pride in the fact that Lewis was able to do cheap, fast work.

Lewis soon had a set of standard plans drawn up to meet demand; these plotted out five different sizes of lighthouses, at 25, 30, 40, 50, and 65 feet high. Many such towers were built; most were made of brick, but a few were constructed of stone. But Lewis knew little about proper engineering practices, and most of the lighthouses were either poorly constructed, or they were too short. Most had to be replaced; only a handful survive today.[21]

Picture of Winslow Lewis' patented lighthouse lamp that stole heavily from Argand's design, courtesy WikipediA

Notice that none were constructed of wood.

Stephen Pleasonton must have felt very comfortable with his relationship with Winslow Lewis. In fact the relationship was so close that it would probably be illegal today. Just two months after the bids had been opened, he, on September 20, 1847, wrote to Winslow Lewis, changing the specifications for the lamps at the Cape Canaveral Lighthouse. He directs Lewis to install "...5 lamps on a triangle with 21-inch reflectors."[22]

Although it probably was the practice of allowing local Superintendents to select overseers of construction, for some reason Mr. Pleasonton chose Mr. Charles Soran[23] to supervise the building of the Cape Canaveral Lighthouse. He informed Mr. Center of his decision in a letter dated September 17, 1847 and announced that Mr. Soran would be paid $3.00 per day, which would be a high for such work. Interestingly, he did not actually ask Mr. Soran until September 20, 1847. Soran would eventually decline the offer.

In a letter to George Center, Pleasonton told the Superintendent that Mr. Soran would not be the overseer and that he, Center, should appoint someone in the local neighborhood. The appointee should have "mechanical experience."[24] It's interesting that Mr. Pleasonton only authorized $2.50 per day for the local person, not the $3.00 that he had offered Mr. Soran.[25] Was that because the local person didn't have to travel or was it because he was willing to set a precedent for his friend but not for an unknown? Don't know.

At some time after the September 17, 1847 letter, Mr. Nathaniel C. Scobie was appointed to "oversee" the construction of the Cape Canaveral Lighthouse. Mr. Hammond was to start construction in mid October 1847. We don't know for sure, but Scobie probably took the job of overseer at about that same time. His duties would be to oversee the construction and to certify that Thomas C. Hammond had built the lighthouse in accordance with the contract and in a "substantial and workmanlike manner."[26]

The Proposal directed construction at Cape Canaveral to be completed on or before the first of January 1848. Thomas C. Hammond did complete the contract on time. George Center wrote to Pleasonton in a January 6, 1848, letter where he quotes a letter received from Nathaniel Scobie.

> The stairs are very narrow & difficult to get up but the contract says 10 inches Step & I suppose that was intended from the middle, but they have got it that width at the Extreme end. I can say nothing about it according [sic] to the reading of the specification. They have got the Octagon with the door in it made of small glass instead of having glass at c..... with the rest. The Scuttle has been made larger than the Contract Calls for but Mr. Hammond says it was done by Winslow Lewis order that he might get up his Lamps. The scuttle door has no Hinges & I do not see how it will be possible to open & close it. There are No Steps Mentioned in the Contract for Light House dwelling & Kitchen ... order to be raised two feet from the ground There is no .., No Shutters to the windows which are very necessary as I am sure that the wind there will blow any cover on (the) sash to pieces. The Copper on the Dome of the Lantern is I think entirely too lights [sic]. The contractor does not know the weights & being on the Dome I Cannot weith [sic] it. The Contractor has brought granite Stone instead of Mica Slate for the Lintels.[27]

Note: A Lintel is a support beam of wood or stone across the top of an opening, such as a window, door, or a fireplace.

Picture of First Lighthouse
Courtesy Florida Memory
Project, Florida State Archives

Even today, administering a construction contract can be confusing, and at times, contentious. Apparently a progress report was submitted by Scobie which included mention that the lighting contractor requested the construction contractor to change the size of the lantern room access door "the scuttle." Mr. Pleasonton writes in response "the Contractors had no right to enlarge it at the request of Mr. Lewis or any body else." As an aside, Pleasonton adds: "By the by, I do not believe he made any such request."[28] The "he" would be Mr. Peasonton's friend Winslow Lewis. The letter was written to George Center, St Augustine, Florida on January 17, 1848. The aside must have been directed at Nathaniel Scobie, implying that, Nathaniel Scobie, approved the contract change and that Winslow Lewis played no role. We will see this type of response later.

It can be easily lost here that the contract called for the building of a Dwelling House. The following are excerpts from the July 7, 1847 Request of Proposals: the house was to be "35 by 20 feet."[29] Seven hundred square feet. Now that's small.

The "foundation hard brick; wall one foot thick, laid 18 inches below the surface of the ground and carried up 2 feet above..."[30]

The dwelling was to have two rooms and another two rooms in the attic.

> ...the house to be divided into two rooms, with an entry between, 7 feet wide; a chimney in each end of the house, with fireplace in each parlor... The stairs to lead from the entry into the attic; closet back of the stairs; attic divided into two chambers, with an entry between 7 feet wide; one of the chambers to be sub-divided into two; a luthern window in the entry between the chambers, ten lights 8 by 10, collared with lead, as well as both the chimnies (sic); doors in front and back of the entry...[31]

Picture of first Lighthouse Dwellings,
courtesy Rose Wooley

A luthern window is a raised window sticking out from the roof.

There was to be, "...at a convenient distance from the dwelling house a frame kitchen, 15 by 12 feet to stand on six brick pillars, 2 feet from the ground;"[32] the wall would be "7 feet post; boarded and shingled..." "...one door; a chimney..."[33] The actual certificate of contract completion was not provided by Scobie until January 19, 1848. The following is a representation of the Letter of Certificate form Nathaniel C. Scobie, Overseer of the building of the Cape Canaveral Lighthouse, to George Center, Collector St. Augustine:

This is to certify that on this day Mr. T. C. Hammond has completed this contract on Cape Canaveral in a substantial and workmanlike manner, with the acception (sic) of furnishing granite stone in place of mica slate as the contract calls for, notwithstanding I consider the Granite a good Building material for a Fire proof Building.[34]
Signed by Nathaniel C. Scobie.
See Appendix II

With the lighthouse completed, all that was left to do was appoint a keeper and light it up. The logical choice of keeper would be the person that oversaw the construction. In a letter to Stephen Pleasonton dated February 7, 1848, the Collector at St. Augustine mentions that Nathaniel C. Scobie was appointed keeper of the Cape Canaveral light and we find in a Lighthouse Establishment Journal[35] an entry that on "January 27, 1848 Mr. Nathaniel C. Scobie was appointed Keeper of the Cape Canaveral Lighthouse."[36] His pay would be "$400.00."[37] In this same journal is a scrawled "Run away"[38] just to the right of his name. More on that later.

Although the Cape Canaveral Light was ready to be lit up, apparently in response to a January 3, 1849 letter from George Center, Pleasonton writes: "Jany (sic) 15, 1849 ...the Cape Canaveral Light House has not yet been lit up."[39]   He goes on to apologize and blame someone else with "...regret exceedingly that the supply of oil for this Light House had not been sent by the Collector at New York in March or April last"[40] he seems to defend himself by adding "as I wrote to him to forward them in March." Pleasonton then complains: "The Keeper ought to have informed you of the time of each revolution of the apparatus, as he could have ascertained that fact at any time..."[41] Notice the apparent displeasure with Keeper Scobie by Pleasonton. Although the Lighthouse was "certified complete" in January of 1848, it would not be lit up for at least a year after completion.

Pleasonton was so frustrated with not knowing the timing of the light that he wrote Winslow Lewis on "Jany (sic) 5, 1849" a letter requesting "...that you will immediately on the receipt of this letter, advise Mr. George Center...as to the time of revolving at Cape Canaveral."[42]

From the List of Light-Houses dated 1849, we learn that the light consisted of 15 lamps on 21 inch reflectors. It was a revolving lamp with a time of revolution set at 3 minutes and 15 seconds. The lamp was to be seen at a distance of 16 miles out to sea.[43] Pleasonton should have known this and given Scobie a break. The Timing of the lamp's rotation was "corrected" in 1854 to "Interval between flashes 1 minute."[44]

Wonder how and who Lewis provided details to within the Lighthouse Establishment without Pleasonton knowing. Guess we must blame the Washington Bureaucracy. Yes, a keeper could set the clock in motion and time the revolutions. However, we must remember, Scobie was neither an experienced keeper nor had he been appointed as keeper when the Lewis' work was completed, additionally there is no record of Scobie being appointed to oversee Mr. Lewis' work. To lay the entire responsibility for determining the timing of the revolutions of the Cape Canaveral Light on him is completely inappropriate. It may be that Winslow Lewis and Stephen Pleasonton's relationship was much too close.

Pleasonton knew the timing of the revolutions of the lamp or should have known because the following information was published in the "List of Light-Houses, Beacons, and Floating Lights, of the United States" "by order of Stephen Pleasonton - 1849"[45] The "height of the tower from base to center of lantern is 55 feet."[46] The 55 feet to the center of the lamp must be an error. The measurement would be more like 60 feet to the center. The lighthouse was to be 55 feet from the ground to the top of the soap stone deck.[47]

Nathaniel Scobie lit up the Cape Canaveral lighthouse for the first time on March 1, 1849, fourteen months after it was completed.[48] George Center wrote to Stephen Pleasonton on January 28, 1849 informing him "...that the Light House at Cape Canaveral will be lit up on the first day of March for the first time..." he goes on to mention that "...the communication between here & the Cape is very uncertain & difficult."[49] Now remember this statement about communication between the Cape and St. Augustine being "uncertain & difficult." It will soon become very very important.

Now to deal with the "Runaway"[50] statement in the Lighthouse Establishment's Keepers Journal. Yes. Nathaniel Scobie did leave his post as Keeper of the Cape Canaveral Light. However, it was only after he had petitioned the Lighthouse Establishment for protection from an indian threat.

Although the July 18, 1849 C.F. Smith letter said that he would dispatch troops to Cape Canaveral, there is no record of troops actually being sent to the Cape. Troops did go to Cape

Florida in late July 1849.[51]

 The following is an undated letter (note) from N. C. Scobie to Douglas Dummett begging for help. The note must have been written on or about July 14, 1849. This would be the note included in the letter that Pleasonton refers to in his August 1, 1849 letter to William Meredith. Scobie must have written a second letter in October 1849 or his first was resent by Sanchez of St. Augustine.

Dear Doc:

For God's sake come with your boat as soon as possible, and help us to get away. The Indians have broken out at Indian river, (sic) and I am obliged to take to the light house.

(Signed) N. C. Scobie. (Scobie)

Dear Col: I have this moment received the above from Mr. Scobie, (Scobie) by a black boy of Mr. Stamps.
The boy says, that this morning, four black women, one black boy and one white girl, came from Indian by way of the beach, and report that the Indians have broken out on Indian river, and are burning the houses. The boy can give no further information. What had we best do? Yours in haste.

(Signed) D. Dummett.[52]

The second letter here is from Douglas Dummett to the Commandant of St. Augustine.

Stephen Pleasonton acknowledges this in the following letter to William Meredith,[53] Secretary of the Treasury, dated August 1, 1849.

Sir,
 I have the honor to enclose a letter from Mr Sanchez, the Collector and Supt of Lights at St Augustine with one from the Keeper of Cape Canaveral Light by which you will perceive that Keeper considers himself and family in danger from hostile Indians, in his neighborhood, and request to be furnished with a guard of 10 men.
 As we have no money applicable to such a purpose, and this Light as well as that of Cape Florida, will be abandoned, if a guard is not furnished at each place. I respectfully submit the propriety (?) of call upon the War Department to furnish such a Guards.
 In the War of 1836 with these Indians the Light House at Cape Florida

was burnt by them, one keeper killed, and another badly wounded. Hence it is probable that neither this keeper nor the one at Cape Canaveral will remain at their respective Lights, if a guard sufficient to ensure their safety be not furnished.

I Have
S. Pleasonton [54]

Let us take note here that Nathaniel Scobie was issued permit number 40, under the Armed Occupation Act, on March 15, 1842 for land between the ocean and Indian River. He was designated a "Head of a Family" when the permit was issued.[55] Yes, he was a family man.

In the previous letter Pleasonton seems to be sympathetic to Keeper Scobie's fears and raises the probable fear of the Keeper at Cape Florida, and even predicts that each will leave their respective lighthouses for a safer location.

Stephen Pleasonton received a letter from James R. Sanchez, Superintendent of Lights, St. Augustine, Florida on the morning of October 10, 1849 along with a letter from Keeper Scobie. This was just two months after Scobie had asked for protection. Now, Pleasonton angrily responds to Sanchez the same day with the following:

I received this morning your letter of the 4th instant with one from Mr Scobie the keeper of the Cape Canaveral light by which it appears that he has abandoned the care of that Light House, in dread of attack by Indians.

His fears are perfectly groundless as you will see by a printed letter from General Twiggs, which I now enclose. You will direct the Keeper to return to the Light House without delay and perform the duties required of him. "[56] He goes on to write *"Should the Keeper decline to return you will send some other suitable man with an assistant, and nominate him to the Secretary for appointment. "*[57]

I Have,
S. Pleasonton

David Emanuel Twiggs (1790 – July 15, 1862) was a United States soldier during the War of 1812 and Mexican-American War and a general of the Confederate States Army during the American Civil War. Twiggs was born on the "Good Hope" estate in Richmond County, Georgia, son of John Twiggs, a general in the Georgia Militia during the American Revolution. Twiggs volunteered for service in the War of 1812 and subsequently served in the Seminole Wars and the Black Hawk War.[58]

Picture of Gen Twiggs
Courtesy WikipediA

It's very doubtful that Scobie would ever have seen any letter that General Twiggs wrote unless it would have been specifically delivered to him. Remember, Communication was "uncertain & difficult" with

Cape Canaveral. It was not until October 10, 1849 that Pleasonton did mail a "printed letter from General Twiggs, which I now enclose" to James R. Sanchez in St Augustine, Florida. It could have taken until at least December 1849 before that letter would get to Keeper Scobie as Cape Canaveral was so very remote from any civilization in 1849.

The tone of this letter is much different from the previous letter which clearly showed concurrence and some sympathy. The December 9, 1850 Census for St. Lucie, Florida has one Nathaniel Scobie, his wife and their three children Francis, Henry and Douglas living in St. Lucie. Believe it or not...two of Scobie's neighbors were Douglas Dummett and Mills O. Burnham.[59] Well maybe not exactly neighbors because St. Lucie stretched from about mid Cape Canaveral to below Jupiter in 1850. At the bottom of the 1850 Schedule of Free Inhabitants there is a disclaimer *("The Inhabitants of the County were driven from it on acct (sic) of the Indian hostilities and only a few of them have as yet returned")*[60]

Picture of grave marker, courtesy Jeffery Snively

Although they got the spelling wrong, the following chart is offered as some proof of Scobie's family: Mrs. Scobie may have passed away after her name was recorded in the schedule. A grave marker in the Huguenot Cemetery at St. Augustine, Florida had the following inscription on it: "Margaret Westray wife of Nathaniel C. Scobie - March 25, 1810 - December 6, 1850".[61]

SCOBIA N. C.	45	M	Merchant	Nova Scotia
SCOBIA Margaret	40	F		Nova Scotia
SCOBIA Francis	17	M	Merchant	Florida
SCOBIA Henry	16	M		Florida
SCOBIA Douglas	1	M		Florida [62]

Picture of Marie E. Scobie, 4th from left, courtesy Flossie Station

There, another mystery solved maybe... In this picture, the fourth person from the left is Marie E. Scobie, possibly a granddaughter or great granddaughter of Keeper Scobie. Scobie had a family. It is now left to the reader to decide whether Nathaniel Scobie abandoned his post without just cause.

My final comment about the Scobie matter is that the Indian River Colony, which Burnham helped settle, was broken up by an Indian attack in August 1849. So Scobie had good reason for concern. Pleasonton was safe and secure in Washington, not at the wild uninhabited and very isolated Cape

Canaveral. Nuf said!

Pictures of Ora and Antonia Carpenter's grave stones, courtesy, Bob Orrell

In February 1850, Stephen Pleasonton wrote to James Sanchez with "advise you to address a letter directly to the Secretary of the Treasury recommending Mr. Ora Carpenter for the appointment of Keeper of the Cape Canaveral Light House."[63] For some reason, in this case, Mr. Pleasonton didn't want correspondence to follow the chain of command - through him.

Mr. Ora Carpenter would become the second Keeper of the Cape Canaveral Light effective February 27, 1850 with a salary of $400.00. This appointment was announced in a letter from Stephen Pleasonton on February 28, 1850 as well as the appointment of James Sanchez to Superintendent of Lights, St. Augustine, Florida.[64]

Ora Carpenter was born on October 26, 1817 and passed away March 17, 1902. He and his wife, Antonia H., born on November 7, 1827 and passed away in May 1893, are buried in the Osteen Cemetery at Deltona, Florida. Very little more is known about Ora Carpenter. We do have evidence that, under the Armed Occupation Act, he was issued permit number 274 on July 21, 1842 for land 4 miles above Lake George. He was registered as a "single man" when the permit was issued.[65] He, in 1845, may very well have been the first postmaster of Enterprise, Florida. Enterprise was a railroad town in Volusia County and is located on the northern shore of Lake Monroe, it is flanked by DeBary and Deltona.[66] Mr. Carpenter must have gotten married after 1842, because the 1850 Federal Census has an "Ora Carpenter, from Vermont, married, working as a lighthouse keeper, with a pay of $300.00."[67] The census tells us that he was living in Volusia, was born in 1818 and married with three children. The 1860 Census lists his wife's name was Antonia H., age 34; children as Fanny F., age 15; Ora D., age 12; Amy W., age 10; Virginia Rosa, age 5; Jane M. Rosa, age 4; Charles C. Rosa, age 1.[68] The last three children may have been just living with the Carpenters at the time of the census.

Picture of two Dwellings at Original Lighthouse Site

We know that the original plan was to build a single keeper's dwelling at Cape Canaveral. However, in a letter of alarm on March 15, 1852, Keeper Carpenter informs Col J. M. Hanson, a new Superintendent of Lights, that "...the sand has blown away from about it" (the lighthouse) "to the depth of one foot and for several feet around, and unless something is done to prevent it the Light House will soon be undermined and fall down." The letter goes on to tell us that "as you are aware there are two families..."[69] Where the heck did that other family come from and when did the second dwelling get built? Well, he was authorized an assistant. The picture above was taken from atop one of the lighthouses. Study the picture carefully.

The record appears to show that an assistant, A. R. Rose, was appointed on October 1, 1851 at $30.00 per month. The 1870 U.S. Census has an Alexander Rose living at Sand Point, Florida, with an occupation of Assistant Lighthouse Keeper.[70] However, records appear to indicate that Mr. Rose resigned after Keeper Carpenter was replaced in 1853.[71] Note: Mr. Sanchez was replaced by Colonel John M. Hanson October 12, 1850 as Collector of Customs at St. Augustine.

Imagine how Pleasonton must have reacted! The lighthouse wasn't four years old, he has had one keeper leave and now this keeper is predicting doom! Keeper Carpenter had been given a $100.00 raise and an assistant in October of 1851, and now a letter of doom! Wonder if that letter had anything to do with Mills Olcott Burnham being appointed Keeper on July 30, 1853,[72] just 16 months and some 15 days from the date of Carpenter's letter warning that the lighthouse might fall over.

A very surprising letter from the "Superintendent of Lights, St. Augustine, Florida, dated 27 Aug 1853 reads, Cape Canaveral Lt Fl- reports delivery of dismissal of keeper, & of appointment of new keeper..."[73] This is surprising because according to the Keepers Pay Journal, Mills O. Burnham was appointed Keeper on July 30, 1853.[74] Okay, so much for the records agreeing.

Was Ora Carpenter dismissed? If yes, what for? Was he dismissed because of the letter predicting problems with the lighthouse? Don't know. We may never know because many records and letters pertaining to the Cape Canaveral lighthouse were burned in a 1920 Treasury Department fire. So much history lost.

Before we move on to other discussions we need to mention that Mr. Pleasonton wrote the first instructions for Lighthouse Keepers in 1835.

1835 INSTRUCTIONS

TO THE KEEPERS OF LIGHT
HOUSES WITHIN THE UNITED STATES

1. You are to light the lamps every evening at sun-setting, and keep them continually burning, bright and clear, till sun-rising.
2. You are to be careful that the lamps, reflectors, and lanterns, are constantly kept clean, and in order; and particularly to be careful that no lamps, wood, or candles, be left burning any where as to endanger fire.
3. In order to maintain the greatest degree of light during the night, the wicks are to be trimmed every four hours, taking care that they are exactly even on the top.
4. You are to keep an exact amount of the quantity of oil received from time to time; the number of gallons, quarts, gills consumed each night; and deliver a copy of the same to the Superintendent every three months, ending 31 March, 30 June, 30 September, and 31 December, in each year; with an account of the quantity on hand at the time.
5. You are not to sell, or permit to be sold, any spirituous liquors on the premises of the United States; but will treat with civility and attention, such strangers as may visit the Light-house under your charge, and as may conduct themselves in an orderly manner.
6. You will receive no tube-glasses, wicks, or any other article which the contractors, Messr. Morgan & Co., at New Bedford, are bound to supply, which shall not be of suitable kind; and if the oil they supply, should, on trial, prove bad, you will

immediately acquaint the Superintendent therewith, in order that he may exact from them a compliance with this contract.

7. Should the contractors omit to supply the quantity of oil, wicks, tube-glasses, or other articles necessary to keep the lights in continual operation, you will give the Superintendent timely notice thereof, that he may inform the contractors and direct them to forward the requisite supplies.

8. You will not absent yourself from the Light-house at any time, without first obtaining the consent of the Superintendent, unless the occasion be so sudden and urgent as not to admit of an application to that officer; in which case, by leaving a suitable substitute, you may be absent for twenty-four hours.

9. All your communications intended for this office, must be transmitted through the Superintendent, through whom the proper answer will be returned.

Fifth Auditor and Acting Commissioner of the Revenue
TREASURY DEPARTMENT
Fifth Auditor's Office
April 23d, 1835[75]

Number 5 is my favorite. As an aside, a review of Keepers Journals and a couple of quarterly reports reveals no record of collection of the data and information required by Instruction Number 4. Just in case you wondered what on earth is a gill, a gill is "in the United States defined as half a cup, or four U.S. fluid ounces."[76]

Here is the place to introduce Corporal Henry Wilson. Henry was born May 1, 1829 in Pen Yan, New York. He enlisted in the Army at age 16 and served in Mexico[77] with Zachary Taylor (the twelfth President of the United States).

The Mexican-American War was an armed military conflict between the United States and Mexico from 1846 to 1848 in the wake of the 1845 U.S. annexation of Texas. Mexico did not recognize the secession and subsequent military victory by Texas in 1836; it considered Texas a rebel province.

In the United States, the war was a partisan issue with most Whigs opposing it and most southern Democrats, animated by a popular belief in the Manifest Destiny, supporting it. In Mexico, the war was considered a matter of national pride.

The most important consequence of the war for the United States was the Mexican Cession, in which the Mexican territories of Alta California and Santa Fé de Nuevo México were ceded to the United States under the terms of the Treaty of Guadalupe Hidalgo.[78]

In 1846, after Texas was admitted into the Union, Polk sent militia under General Zachary Taylor to the Rio Grande to protect Texas,[79] Corporal Wilson also served with General William Jenkins Worth. Lake Worth in Florida is named for the General. Wilson served in the 3rd Artillery in Mexico with Lt Tecumseh Sherman.

In late 1853 two soldiers and a Sergeant were sent to protect the Cape Canaveral lighthouse families from Indian attacks.[80] Whoa, let's think about this. Soldiers were sent to Cape Canaveral,

Picture of Henry Wilson,
courtesy, the Florida
Memory Project

in late 1853, to protect Captain Burnham based on the same concerns that Keeper Scobie had. Scobie was denied protection and Burnham provided protection. Interesting....

One of the soldiers was twenty three year old Corporal Henry Wilson. He met and married Frances Burnham, the keeper's oldest daughter, and started a trend that would keep the Cape Canaveral lighthouse under the control of a descendant of Mills O. Burnham for the next eighty years.

Corporal Wilson took a discharge from the Army and returned to Cape Canaveral to become an Assistant to Burnham on March 12, 1855 when A. R. Rose resigned. Henry Wilson and Frances Burnham were married on March 30, 1856, in the Trinity Episcopal Church in St. Augustine, Florida. The trend, mentioned earlier, was that Mills O. Burnham would offer land and a job at the lighthouse to every man that married one of his six daughters. Henry Wilson was the first.

Picture of
Frances Burnham,
courtesy, the Florida Memory Project

During the era of the brick lighthouse, 1848 to 1868, the settlement of Cape Canaveral began with the building of the lighthouse. With the keepers came families and eventually a community.

There were only three keepers of the brick 65 foot Cape Canaveral Lighthouse, Nathaniel C. Scobie 1848 – 1950; Ora Carpenter 1850 – 1853; Mills O. Burnham 1853 – 1868 and two assistants - A. R Rose 1850 – 1853 and Henry Wilson 1855 – 1868.

In June of 1860, soil was being examined and tested to determine an acceptable location for the foundation for the new lighthouse.[81]

In 1868, a 151 foot tall Iron Lighthouse was assembled, as a replacement for the much shorter brick lighthouse. And the community began to slowly grow.

[1]Biographical Directory of the United States Congress at: (accessed January 27, 2007) <http://bioguide.congress.gov/scripts/biodisplay.pl?index=D000472>

[2]Journal of the House of Representatives of the United States, 1837 - 1838, Monday, May 21, 1838: pg 923

[3]Harriett Carr, Cape Canaveral Cape of Storms and Wild Cane Fields, Valkyrie Press Inc, St Petersburg, Florida, 1974, pg 18

[4]Stephen Pleasonton, WikipediA, the free encyclopedia, (accessed January 17, 2007) <http://www.wikipedia.org>

[5]Ibid.

[6]Letter from Stephen Pleasonton, Treasury Department, 5th Auditor's Office, March 12, 1847, Records Group 26, National Archives, Washington D.C.

[7]Casey's Florida Map Page: (accessed January 21, 2007) <http://www.luddist.com/map.html> Review of "Map of Florida, 1845" does show a road reaching south that ends at Ross. There is no information available about Ross. There may have been another road or trail west of the Indian River from New Smyrna through Delespines Grant and ending at Flemings Grant.

[8]City of Titusville History, (accessed May 23, 2009) <http://www.titusville.com/Page.asp?NavID=216>

[9]George Center, Letter to Collector's Office, District of St. Augustine, Florida, May 30, 1847, Records Group 26, National Archives, Washington D.C.

[10]Ibid.

[11]Buck Rogers in the 25th Century, Comic Strip (1929-67), (accessed 10 Oct0ber 1008) <http://www.buck-rogers.com/comic_strip/>

[12]Stephen Pleasonton, Treasury Department, 5th Auditor's Office, letter to George Center, Superintendent of Lights, St. Augustine, Florida, June 7, 1847, Records Group 26, National Archives, Washington D.C.: .

[13]Ibid, July 7, 1847.

[14]Journal of Light-hours Station at Cape Canaveral, 26 September 1893, Records Group 26, National Archives, Washington D.C.

[15]Request for Proposals, Records Group 26, National Archives, Washington D.C.

[16]Ibid

[17]Marcus Morton, letter to Custom House, Boston, July 20, 1847, Records Group 26, National Archives, Washington D.C

[18]Ibid

[19]Ibid

[20]WikipediA, the free encyclopedia, (accessed February 5, 2007) <http://www.wikipedia.org>

[21]WikipediA, the free encyclopedia, (accessed February 5, 2007) <http://www.wikipedia.org>

[22]Letter to Winslow Lewis, September 20, 1847, Records Group 26, National Archives, Washington D.C.

[23]Letter to George Center, September 11, 1847, Records Group 26, National Archives, Washington D.C.

[24]Ibid.

[25]Letter to George Center, October 12, 1847, Records Group, 26 National Archives, Washington D.C.

[26]Ibid.

[27]George Center, Collectors Office, St. Augustine, Florida letter to Stephen Pleasonton, January 6, 1848, Records Group 26, National Archives, Washington D.C.

[28]Letter to George Center, January 17, 1848, Records Group 26, National Archives, Washington D.C.

[29]Request for Proposals, Records Group 26, National Archives, Washington D.C.

[30]Ibid.

[31]Ibid.

[32]Ibid.

[33]Ibid.

[34]Nathaniel Scobie letter to George Center, January 19, 1848, Records Group 26, National Archives, Washington D.C.

[35]Lighthouse Establishment Journal of Correspondence, January 27, 1848, Records Group 26, National Archives, Washington D.C.

[36]Ibid.

[37]Ibid.

[38]Ibid.

[39]Pleasonton letter to Center, January 15, 1848, Records Group 26, National Archives, Washington D.C.

[40]Ibid.

[41]Ibid.

[42]Pleasonton letter to Winslow Lewis, January 5, 1849, Records Group 26, National Archives, Washington D.C.

[43]List of Light-Houses, Beacons and Floating Lights, 1849, Records Group 26, National Archives, Washington D.C.

[44]List of Light-Houses, Lighted-Beacons, and Floating Lights, Corrected, July 1, 1854, Records Group 26, National Archives, Washington D.C.

[45]List of Light-Houses, Beacons, and Floating Lights, 1849, pg 26 -27, No. 197, Records Group 26, National Archives, Washington D.C.

[46]Ibid.

[47]Ibid.

[48]George Center, letter to Stephen Pleasonton, January 28, 1849, Records Group 26, National Archives, Washington D.C.

[49]Ibid.

[50]Lighthouse Establishment Florida Keeper Journal; Records Group 26, National Archives, Washington D.C.

[51]Google Books Online, senate documents, otherwise publ. as public documents and executive documents, pages 34-39 (accessed 19 Jul, 2009) <http://books.google.com/books?id=x3gFaaaaqaaj&pg=ra1-pa26&lpg=ra1-pa26&d+v=one page&q=f=false>

[52]Ibid.

[53] William M. Meredith was 19th Secretary of the Treasury. President Zachary Taylor, appointed him on March 8, 1849, and served until July 22, 1850

[54]Pleasonton letter to William M. Meredith, Secretary of The Treasury, August 1, 1849; Records Group 26, National Archives, Washington D.C.

[55]Roots Web, (accessed Mar 2008) , <http://www.rootsweb.com>

[56]J. R. Sanchez letter to Pleasonton, Scobie abandonded Lighthouse, October 10, 1849, Records Group 26, National Archives, Washington D.C.

[57]Ibid.

[58]WikipediA, the free encyclopedia, (accessed February 2, 2007) <http://www.wikipedia.org>

[59]Ancestry.com, 1850 Schedule of Free Inhabitants in the 18th Division, St Lucie, Florida (accessed January 12, 2007) <http://www.ancestry.com>.

[60]Ibid.

[61]Jeffrey Snively

[62]ancestry.com, 1850 Schedule of Free Inhabitants in the 18th Division, St Lucie, Florida (accessed January 12, 2007) <http://www.ancestry.com>.

[63]Stephen Pleasonton, Letter dated February 6, 1850 to James R. Sanchez, Records Group 26, National Archives, Washington D.C.

[64]Ibid.

[65]Armed Occupation Act's land permits/Census, (accessed March 2007) <http://www.rootsweb.com/~cenfiles/fl/stjohns/1850/notes2.txt>

[66]WikipediA, the free encyclopedia, (accessed March 2007) <http://www.wikipedia.org> http://www.geocities.com/yosemite/rapids/8428/hikeplans/enterprise/planenterpris.html

[67]USGenWeb Archives by William Morgan, (accessed April 12, 2009) <http://files.usgwarchives.org/fl/orange/census/1850.txt>

[68]ancestry.com - 1860 United States Census (accessed April 12, 2009) <http://search.ancestry.com>

[69]Ora Carpenter letter to Col J. M. Hanson, March 15, 1852; Records Group 26, National Archives, Washington D.C.

[70]ancestry.com - 1870 United States Census (accessed April 12, 2009) <http://search.ancestry.com>

[71]Lighthouse Establishment Florida Keeper Journal; Records Group 26, National Archives, Washington D.C.

[72]Ibid.

[73]Letter, pg 432, Record of related correspondence from Bound in Letter Book No. 17, Records Group 26, National Archives, Washington D.C.

[74]Keepers Assignment and pay record for Florida, Records Group 26, National Archives, Washington D.C.: pg 115

[75]National Park Service; Maritime Heritage program, (accessed April 2007) <http://www.nps.gov/history/maritime/keep/keep19th.htm>

[76]Encyclopedia Britannica, (accessed November 23, 2008) <http://www.britannica.com/EBchecked/topic/233688/gill>

[77]WikipediA, the free encyclopedia, (accessed October 11, 2008) <http://en.wikipedia.org/wiki/Mexican-American_War>

[78]Ibid.

[79]WikipediA, the free encyclopedia, (accessed October 10, 2008) <http://en.wikipedia.org/wiki/Mexican-American_War>

[80]Robert Ranson, East Coast Florida Memories, (Port Salerno: Florida Classic Library) 20

[81]G. Caster Smith, Letter to Lighthouse Board, Bound in Letter Book No. 105 pg 141, Records Group 26, National Archives, Washington D.C.

ast iron lighthouse construction probably started in the early 1840s. A cast iron tower was built on Long Island Head in Boston Harbor in 1844. The 1848 tower at Brandywine Shoals was the first screw pile lighthouse in the United States and had a cast iron tower. The three Florida reef lights, Carysfort Reef light, Sand Key light, and Sombrero Key light, all built in the 1850s, incorporated a lot of cast iron in their construction.[1]

Why use cast iron as a construction material? The advantages of using Cast Iron were: it was light when compared to stone or brick, it was inexpensive, it was strong, it was water tight and it had a slow deterioration rate. All very good reasons for using cast iron. So what about safety? Engineers couldn't adequately calculate the stress loads on iron towers. To answer this need, bricks were used to line cast iron towers; the theory was that the bricks added to the tower's safety. As the towers were assembled each successive sheet of iron would rest on the one below and a brick liner, thus adding to the tower's safety and stability. The conventional wisdom at the time was that even though cast-iron lighthouses were cheaper to build than brick and stone lighthouses, they were not as structurally sound for exposed sites.[2]

Picture of Sombrero Key Light
Courtesy USCG

Picture of Carysford Light Courtesy USCG

The approval to build an Iron Lighthouse at Cape Canaveral was given at some point between 1858 and 1859. According to a memo of letters, in Records Group 26, National Archives, the 7th District Engineer, Hartman Bache, wrote on "Jan 19, 1860 with suggestions to build a tower of Iron"[3] for the lighthouse at Cape Canaveral. A request for proposals, to build an Iron Lighthouse at Cape Canaveral, was probably published shortly after that letter.

By June 1860, soil was being examined and tested to determine an acceptable location for the foundation of the new lighthouse. The site selected was about 95 feet from the base of the brick tower. How convenient. On June 7, 1860, Mr. G. Caster Smith, an Assistant Engineer for the 4th, 5th and 7th Light House Districts, reported on the selected site and "enclosed a soil sample to the depth of ten feet below the surface."[4] Imagine a ten foot deep sample of soil from Cape Canaveral. See Appendix I for a drawing of the foundation.

Picture of Robert P. Parrott
Courtesy Florida Archives

By October 1860, Engineer Turnbull had requested plans and specifications for the proposals for construction of the Iron lighthouse.[5] The Request for Proposals included the provision of materials and manpower for the construction. The Iron Lighthouse, like the Brick one, was built using an imported workforce.

More than twenty companies may have requested specifications and plans for the purpose of submitting bids to build the Cape Canaveral Lighthouse. R. P. Parrott of the West Point Foundry, Cold Spring, New York, made his request on November 13, 1860.[6]

Bids for constructing the Iron Lighthouse at Cape Canaveral were opened on December 3, 1860.[7] Bids from the Companies listed below were considered:[8]

Gage Warner & Whitney	Nashua	$69,600.00
Jas Bogardus	New York	65,756.00
Peoples Works	Philadelphia	63,800.00
Denio & Roberts	Boston	57,000.00
J. G. McPheeters	St Louis	55,521.87
Globe Locomotive Works	Boston	55,000.00
Wm Adams & Co	Boston	52,932.00
Pusey Jones & Co	Wilmington	49,500.00
Henry Steele	Jersey City	47,440.00
Atlantic Works	Boston	45,000.00
W. M. Ellis & Bros	Washington	45,000.00
J. P. Morris & Co	Philadelphia	45,000.00
Kittingen Cook & Co	Charleston	44,900.00
Hauzlehusrt & Co	Baltimore	39,900.00
Ira Winn	Portland	39.556.00
Trenton Loco. & Mach Mfg.	Trenton	39,450.00
Poole & Hunt	Baltimore	35,550.00
Knap Rudd & Co	Pittsburgh	32,000.00
J. Martin Pools & Co	Wilmington	31,985.00
West Point Foundry	Cold Springs	28,000.00

Even back then there was a bit of gamesmanship in submitting bids for government contracts. The low bidder and winner was the West Point Foundry with a bid of $28,000.00, which would equal approximately 28,000/.039 = $717,948.00 in 2006 dollars.[9] The Foundry had barely gotten started to work on the lighthouse before the government suspended the contract on February 5, 1861.[10] My goodness, why did they suspend the work? Did they know there would be a war? The Civil War started on April 12, 1861, and continued until the Confederacy collapsed with Lee's surrender to Grant at Appomattox Court House on April 9, 1865. Suspending the contract was going to cost the government, just like it would today.

The war had a profound impact on the community at Cape Canaveral; namely Mills Burnham and his family. At the beginning of the war, Stephen M. Mallory, Secretary of the Confederate Navy, ordered that all Florida, East Coast lighthouses "be extinguished."[11] In other words, turn

Picture of Stephen Mallory, courtesy Florida Memory Project, State Archives

the lights off. Mills Burnham, Keeper of the Cape Canaveral Lighthouse, learned about the order through Captain Douglas Dummett, Collector of the Port at New Smyrna. Dummett may have helped Burnham get the Keeper's job at Cape Canaveral. According to Ranson (1926), Keeper Burnham complied with the order by removing the lamp from atop the lighthouse, crated it, and then buried the crated lamp in his orange grove. At the end of the war Burnham returned the lamp to the government.[12] Well that's not exactly the way it happened.

On September 7, 1861, Douglas Dummett was paid $326.50 for the removal and transportation of "4 boxes for packing, 17 lamps and 15 reflection frames and transportation of same from Cape Canaveral" to St. Augustine, Florida.[13] Dummett started moving the lamps on June 7, 1861 from atop the lighthouse Cape Canaveral to the Indian river and then up the Haul-over Canal. Dummett arrived in St. Augustine on July 25, 1861 where he certified on a preprinted form by filling in the blanks. Note: Please notice that Dummett claims to have transported 17 lamps and frames. Burnham claims to have kept the reflectors.

"I herby certify that the above named Boxes for packing, hiring of hands animals and boats is for the Light-house Establishment; that they were actually necessary for and have been applied to the removal of and packing of the above mentioned Lamps and Frames from Cape Canaveral Florida to St. Augustine Florida and that they were obtained on the most reasonable terms."[14]

The form is signed by Paul Arnau, Collector and Superintendent and countersigned by Douglas Dummett as receiving the $326.50. See appendix I.

One year after sending the lamps to St. Augustine, Burnham requests to be paid. In a September 12, 1862 letter to C. G. Memminger, the Confederate Secretary of the Treasury, Mills Burnham explains that:

"at the time the light was ordered to be extinguished and the lighthouse property removed Mr. Arnau told me to still keep possession of the light house and all light house property for which I should receive half my former pay which was five hundred dollars per anum, (sic) all that I have received from Mr. Arnau since that time is sixty two dollars and fifty cents. The light house property in my possession is some two hundred gallons sperm oil, the reflectors fifteen in number with all the brushes and cleaning materials connected with the light, nothing was taken to St. Augustine but the lamps and clock, which I am told Arnau has given up to the enemy it has recently been reported that the Yankees ware (sic) going to light the lights at Canaveral. I have halled (sic) all the light house property in my charge to my place on the river distant

five miles from the light, but do not consider it secure from the enemy as we have traitors in this section."[15]

From a review of the 1862 letter from Burnham to Memminger, it looks like Burnham moved the lighthouse property to some distance in the woods where I think it will be safe from the enemy and also where the weather cannot damage it..."[16] Wish we knew where that safe location was.

At the end of the War, Burnham turned all the hidden lighthouse equipment over to the government. This very simple and patriotic act was probably why Mills Burnham served so long as the keeper and was given such deference by the Lighthouse Establishment. He and Henry were promptly re-nominated to their previous lighthouse keeping duties on April 9, 1866.[17]

Christopher Gustavus Memminger (January 9, 1803 - March 7, 1888) was a prominent political leader and the first Secretary of the Treasury for the Confederate States of America.[18]

Picture of Christopher G. Memminger, courtesy WikipediA

There was one other act that impacted the entire Burnham family and would for many years. Mills O. Burnham Jr. and brother-in-law Henry Wilson both enlisted in the Confederate Army.

The two joined the "Home Guard" in Gainesville. Now, the Home Guard was supposed to stay in and protect their local areas. Well, that didn't happen. Apparently the "Home Guard" was usually made up of very young boys and old men.[19] Captain Burnham remained at Cape Canaveral,[20] busied himself with looking after the family and just living. Not so for the two enlistees.

Mills O. Burnham, Jr. served as a Private in Company F of the 7th Infantry, 7th Regiment, Florida. Records indicate that he was killed in action on July 18, 1862 and is buried in the Oakland Cemetery, Atlanta, Georgia.[21] Robert Ransom (1926) has Mills Jr. buried in Chattanooga, Tennessee.[22]

Soon after Henry Wilson enlisted, he was transferred to Tallahassee and then sent to fight in Virginia. Near the end of the war, he got a furlough. Heading home, he hitched a ride to near the St. Mary's River[23] and then walked the last 200 miles to Cape Canaveral. The war ended before he was to report back. Legend has it (Ranson 1926) that, after the war, he never left Cape Canaveral except to deliver the mail by sailboat on the Banana River, and travel to Titusville, after becoming Cape Canaveral's first postmaster in 1881. He held that position for the next 31 years[24] and was followed as postmaster by his son-in-law Thomas Thompson.[25] Wilson held the position until his death in 1922. See more in, Cape Canaveral - Its People.

We need to point out here that the location of "Canaveral" or "Cape Canaveral" moved from the Banana River side of the Cape to further south on the Cape and then out near the ocean. Artesia appeared near the south part of Cape Canaveral, very near if not just north of where Port Canaveral is now. Some years later, Artesia is shown well south of the now Port Canaveral. There may have been four Post Offices on Cape Canaveral and three at the same time: Cape Canaveral,

Picture of Tomlinson Post Office, courtesy the Seidel Collection

Artesia, and Nathan.

The Nathan post office may have existed in about 1892. The fourth post office at Cape Canaveral was the Tomlinson Post Office at Lansing Beach. The 1945 census has Grace H. Tomlinson as the postmaster at Canaveral. Mr. Tomlinson's occupation is listed as an Electrical Engineer.[26]

According to Mrs. Helen Wilson Tucker, "The Jeffords family took over operation of the post office after Wilson passed."[27] Mrs. Tucker must have forgotten that Thomas Thompson took over when Henry Wilson died and then Jeffords followed him. As the population center of the Cape began to move more from the Banana River to the ocean, "the post office was moved to Lansing Beach where Mrs. Moore became Postmaster."[28] The Lansing Beach development was in full swing in the early 1900s. This is probably when the Canaveral Post Office disappeared. Now, back to the Iron Lighthouse.

> According to the May 1, 1862 issue of The Civil Engineer and Architects Journal, the designs, for the Iron Lighthouse, were prepared under the supervision of Captain Wm F. Smith, Engineering Secretary of the Lighthouse Board; the drawings were made by Mr. J. K. Whilldin, C.E. When assembled in 1868, the Cape Canaveral Lighthouse was the largest iron tower on the East Coast of the United States and an example of the state of lighthouse engineering in the United States.[29]

Apparently the Civil War didn't completely stop West Point Foundry's work on the Cape Canaveral Lighthouse, because parts for it must have been completed by January 1866 when the foundry asked to be paid for that part of the work. That was some eight months after the Civil War ended. Well, I suppose it could be that eight months would be enough of time for them to get the parts made.

Authors Comment: The designer of the iron lighthouse must have been a woman. She figured that men would be assembling the lighthouse and decided to make it somewhat full proof. Why? The answer is because men are wrongly accused of buying things that require some assembly, never reading the instructions and ending up with parts left over. It is told that, when questioned about the extra parts, most men almost always respond with "the manufacturer always ships some extra parts." Do wives believe it? She, the designer of the Cape Canaveral Light House, solved the problem by making it a put-together by-the-numbers lighthouse. She even took the precaution to prevent confusing inside parts with outside parts by numbering them; Roman numerals on the inside and Arabic numbers on the outside. Well maybe. A review of the specification under "Miscellaneous Items,"[30] we find two very interesting headings:

> *Iron work to be erected at workshop.* - All of the metal work must be fitted together and erected at the workshop, and inspected and approved by the agent of the Light-

house Board, before it will be received. All castings which are honey-combed, or otherwise imperfect, will be rejected.

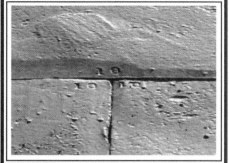

Markings. - All parts of the ironwork must be chisel-marked according to an uniform system, and a set of drawings also marked to correspond.[31]

Well no mention of the designer not being a woman.

The Iron lighthouse was planned to be assembled on-site with a minimal amount of supervision and probably without an engineer. The outside iron

Picture of numbered plates (#10), courtesy, Nancy D Watts

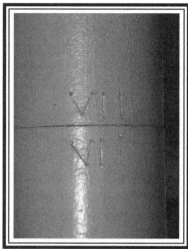

Picture of numbered spiral stairs (#7), courtesy, Nancy D Watts

plates do have Arabic numerals (numbers) at strategic locations on each plate. In each corner and at each center edge there is a number. Assembly is therefore by-the-numbers. When assembled correctly, the lighthouse has matching numbers at each point where two corners join. Also a matching number is in the center of the bottom edge of the upper plate and matched with the numbers on the joined corners of the lower plates. The process is repeated all the way up to the lantern deck. When assembled correctly, we simply see one number above two matching numbers forming a triangle or pyramid.

The outside steps leading to the living room and the entrance, except the bottom step, are numbered with Roman numerals in order of assembly. The bottom step has a different number because it had to be made after the lighthouse was fully assembled. A new bottom step was requested in a December 4, 1867 letter from M. C. Dunnier.[32]

The inside spiral stairs are all identical with only one exception: each has a Roman numeral stamped on the bail where a pipe travels though it to the top of the stair case. With the numerals lined up in sequence, the 167 steps, taking up approximately a six foot section up the center of the lighthouse, spiral in a perfect circle reaching each landing and the watch room in perfect order.

Inside the lighthouse outer cast iron wall is what appears to be a brick liner. There is approximately a one inch, or so, air gap between the bricks and the iron plates. As stated earlier, the liner provides outer plate support adding strength. The air gap

Picture of Lighthouse foundation taken by Author

42

may act somewhat as a crude thermos bottle and help to maintain inside temperature. The brick liner is approximately 16 - 18 inches thick at the bottom and tapers to about 4 - 6 inches where it ends in the Lamp Room.[33] Okay now let's build the thing.

The original 65 foot lighthouse came alive after the civil war when a "temporary light was established atop the old tower on April 3, 1867."[34] The light was a Fourth Order fixed lens. It would remain there until construction the new tower was completed.

The 6th District, acting engineer, M. C. Dunnier reported, in a letter on February 2, 1867 that the "Schooners Archer & Reeves were ready to leave with materials (and) Implements for..."[35] the Cape Canaveral Iron Lighthouse. It sailed on February 4, 1867.

Engineering Secretary O. M. Poe wrote to Joseph Ledrele on February 15, 1867 that "A course of cut stones for the foundation of the Cape Canaveral Lighthouse, now ready for shipment at Saco, Maine, will be landed at the Light House Depot at Staten Island and you will please receive, and have these stones cared for."[36]

Picture of O. M. Poe, courtesy Library of Congress Prints Division

Following a successful military career as chief engineer under General W. T. Sherman during the Civil War, Orlando M. Poe assumed the position of engineer secretary of the U.S. Lighthouse Board and was charged with supervising building projects in the upper Great Lakes. Accountable for all aspects of lighthouse construction in the area, Poe was largely responsible for the design of several tall, conical lighthouse towers that gently tapered from bottom to top.[37]

We have little information on the shipment of the stones. They probably came from the Andrews Quarry[38] of Saco, Maine and were transported to Staten Island, deport, New York to await shipment to Cape Canaveral. On February 27, Dunnier wrote referencing the "shipment of steam engine for hoisting purposes at Cape Canaveral."[39] About this same time, the Tender Du Pont was sent to the Cape for use as a "dispatch boat for parties constructing the lighthouse."[40] By May 1867, the foundation work was well underway. At last, we now have a date on which the work actually started - May 1867.

There must have been a problem or possibly a second ship was used to deliver the Iron Work to Cape Canaveral. The Third District Acting Engineer, Joseph Lederle, wrote on May 20, 1867 "reporting charter of Schooner Yankee Doodle for shipment of iron work"[41] to Cape Canaveral. The actual ship date most likely was May 30, 1867. Either way, we can safely say that the Iron Works for the Cape Canaveral Lighthouse was being shipped in May 1867 and on the good ship Yankee Doodle.

Records indicate that in July of 1867 there were some employee relations problems at the Cape. We have no idea what the problems were. M. C. Dunnier on July 24, 1867 reports that the "Schooner L. E. Jayne unloaded provisions & material (for the lighthouse) & discharged L. H. employe's (sic) shipped by Schooner."[42] M. C. Dunnier's report of July 26, 1867 mentions "...work complaints of L. H. Employees..."[43] The report doesn't clarify whether the complaints came from construction employees, the keeper, or an assistant keeper. It must have involved construction employees. A review of the keeper payroll and assignment journal indicates that no keeper or assistant keeper left during 1867. Well, it appears the problem was solved.

Engineer Dunnier apparently assumed supervision of the construction on or about April 1, 1867 when he wrote that he was "in Charge of the Cape Canaveral Works" and took over the day-to-day supervision of the project because on November 6, 1867, he wrote in a progress report that "there is no further necessity for the services of Forman..."[44] Sure would like to have that person's name. According to an April 16, 1866 letter from Acting Engineer Lederle to the Lighthouse Board, Mr. John A. Bailey, the Clerk of Works at the West Point Foundry, was offered the job of supervising the assembly of the Iron Lighthouse at Cape Canaveral.[45] Mr. Bailey would have been a very good and logical person to oversee the work, simply because he had, as the Clerk of Works, overseen or was a part of the original assembly team at the West Point Foundry site as required by the contract. Apparently, John A. Bailey never reported and eventually declined the job in a May 1866 letter.[46]

Picture of the Fresnel Lens, courtesy, Ponce de Leon Lighthouse Preservation Association

On September 7, 1867 more building materials and supplies were being shipped to Cape Canaveral on board the schooner J. H. Burnett.[47] The Burnett must have had some problems on the trip. It arrived at Cape Canaveral on October 22 "in damaged condition - & loss of part of cargo."[48] That didn't seem to slow things down much because the lighthouse was coming along nicely when in December 1867 they had to order one more "step" and some "bricks."[49] M. C. Dunnier apparently wrote to the Lighthouse Board on Christmas day 1867. He recommends that, the "old L. H. and other useless building be pulled down..."[50] That didn't happen for about 26 years.

In a February 15, 1860, the French manufacturer acknowledges the order of a "gilt-edged machine (of the best quality) for the lighthouse at Cape Canaveral Lighthouse." Please take note of the following sentence. "We conform ourselves exactly to the information contained in these instructions and we will ship everything toward the coming month of June." See letter in Appendix I.

In 1867, the lighthouse was nearing completion and its 1st order lens was being shipped from France. The lens planned for use at Cape Canaveral was "made by Barbier et Fenestre for the Light House Board, and exhibited at the 1867 Exposition at Paris..." Yes. The lamp *planned* to be used at Cape Canaveral was exhibited in Paris.[51]

"In 1864 it was decreed by Emperor Napoleon III that an international exposition should be held in Paris in 1867. A commission was appointed with Prince Jerome Napoleon as president, under whose direction the preliminary work began. The site chosen for the Exposition Universelle (1867) was the Champ de Mars,..."[52]

The lens was shipped to New York on the Steamer Atlanta in December 1867.

In a February 3, 1868 letter, to Acting Engineer Lederle, in Tompkinsville, New York, O. M. Poe, Engineering Secretary, wrote that "from drawings just received from the manufacturer, it is evident that the lens heretofore designed for the Cape Canaveral Light House cannot be used there, and the shipment heretofore directed will not be made until further orders."[53] So the lens originally planned for Cape Canaveral was put on hold. It seems that the pedestal that was to hold the Paris lens was three and one half inches too short for the planned lens. Go Figure! Unfortunately that lens never made it to Cape Canaveral. Instead of shipping the Paris lens to the Cape, another lens marked *Mandacius* was approved for shipment on or about February 14, 1868.[54]

The lens that was delivered was made by the Henry-Lepaute et Fils (and sons) Company. The lens is now at Ponce de Leon Inlet Light Station in Florida and may be inspected to find markings as follows: "The upper cat panels are stamped Henry-Lepaute. A Paris at the bottom of each panel. The dioptric panels have stamps at the upper and lower supports. The lower cats are stamped on the upper support frames. Each panel is marked by a number that matches with the adjacent panel. The letter A is used to indicate the first panel to the right of the entrance opening."[55]

The Henry-Lepaute factory was a combination of two clock-making families, the Henrys and the Paute family. After 1820, the Paute family was generally known as Lepaute. In 1838 the Henry lens factory was founded and built next to the old Lepaute clockwork manufacturing buildings. Augustin Henry made his first Fresnel lens in that same year. Through the marriage of Augustin's father, Pierre Henry, and Elizabeth Paute, the family had merged and between 1854 and the 1860s, their Fresnel lenses were stamped Henry-Lepaute A Paris. Sometime after the 1860s, the company became known as Henry-Lepaute et Fils (and Sons).[56]

Picture of Iron Lighthouse & homes LEIB Image Archives, York, PA
(taken between 1887 and 1894)

On March 13, 1868, the schooner Yankee Doodle was again chartered to deliver the lens to Cape Canaveral.[57] How about that? Captain Hiram Waudel or Mandel may have been the skipper. At least he received payment for the charter.

The lens planned for Cape Canaveral may have been sent to Germany and installed in the Amrum Lighthouse. Another mystery.

The Amrum lighthouse is located in the southern part of the German island of Amrum. ... workers and some additional auxiliary hands were able to finish the brick building in November 1874, and to install the first order Fresnel lens with its Argand lamp of five wicks. The lens had been displayed at the Paris Exposition in 1867.[58]

Picture of Admiral Shudrick,
courtesy U.S. Navy

A notice to mariners announcing the relighting of the Cape Canaveral Lighthouse was sent on/or about April 21, 1868.[59] The new lamp was lit with a signature of one flash every minute[60] and construction thereby completed May 11, 1868.[61] As an interesting side note here, we learn that Mills O. Burnham was sworn in, for the second time, as keeper of the Cape Canaveral Lighthouse on May 1, 1868.[62] Payroll records show Burnham being reinstated effective June 5, 1868. There is no explanation the disparity.

With the Iron Lighthouse construction completed, it was time to dispose of unnecessary equipment. So on June 20, 1868, Acting Engineer Lederle of Tompkinsville reports an acknowledgement letter that the "Steam Engine and Hoisting gear (was) authorized for use at Little Gull Island, Light Station, N.Y."[63]

Remember the Copper Dome that was removed from the brick lighthouse? Somehow it got stored in a buoy shed at Fort Johnson, South Carolina. In a letter dated September 1, 1868, C. G. Anderson, Master of the Tender Dupont, informs E. E. Stone, Lighthouse Inspector that he had "discovered that the shed had been entered and robed of 365 lbs. of Copper belonging to dome of Cape Canaveral, L. H."[64] And so it goes.

Col. Henry T. Titus
1825 - 1881

Picture of Henry Titus,
courtesy North Brevard
Historical Society

With equipment being disposed of, life of the keeper at Cape Canaveral was about to settle down to the everyday duties of tending the light and keeping the lighthouse clean and painted. Or was it? Interesting times were about to come to the tiny Cape Canaveral community. For one thing, work on the beach erosion would take up much of the keeper's time and attention for the next twenty-five plus years. Erosion was used as the reason for moving the lighthouse to its current location.

Talk about interesting times! Now here's something that is amazing! Inspector Edw. E. Stone of the 6th District in Charleston sent a letter, dated October 13, 1868, recommending the removal of Keeper Mills O. Burnham, "as I find him to be unfit to perform properly the duties of that function. His returns have never been properly made out and are still behind for two quarters."[65] This letter was sent to Rear Admiral W.B. Shubrick, USN, Chairman, L.H. Board, Washington, D.C. Could it have been that the "quarterly returns" were sent to the wrong District? Or, the officer didn't know to which District the Cape Canaveral Light Station was assigned. We find the following as a partial answer. Inspector B. M. Dove of the 7th District, Key West writes "Cape Canaveral & other L. Houses in 7th District, (FL) Transmits Quarterly Returns..." to Key West. That letter was written on November 4th 1868.[66] No record of an investigation could be found. We will probably never know for sure, but I'm betting the quarterly "returns" from Cape Canaveral were sent to Key West not Charleston.

The call for Burnham's removal reared its ugly heard some nine years later. Alex B. Rose wrote to the Lighthouse Board with accusations that Mills O. Burnham "had used lighthouse oil for personal use in his orange grove"[67] and that Burnham had "misrepresented, in a report, that he had complied with all specification in the building of a storage shed."[68] He, Burnham, was also accused of being derelict in his duties by "not performing his watches, and for not keeping the lamp mechanism clean and oiled."[69] That's quite a list.

In December 1877, Mr. Rose, Mr. Meyer, and a person named B. Thomas signed a statement attesting to the above charges at Sand Point, Florida in the presence of Henry T. Titus, Notary Public.[70] Henry Titus got the name of Sand Point changed to Titusville.

How about that? "Colonel" Henry T. Titus, the namesake of Titusville. Titus was a postmaster, a liquor dealer, a part-time "Special Agent" for the Board of Underwriters and the owner of Titus House Hotel. The "Colonel" was apparently a self-proclaimed title.[71] Before he settled in Sand Point, Col Titus made a trip to Kansas and built "Fort Titus" near Lawrence, Kansas.

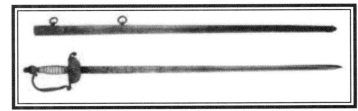
Picture of Sword, courtesy the Historical Society of Kansas

On August 16, 1856, Samuel Walker and a group of Lawrence, Kansas men attacked Fort Titus and forced Colonel Titus to leave the state after surrendering his sword. The sword and scabbard were donated to the Kansas Historical Society by the widow of James Harvey in 1883. They are in the collection of the Society's Kansas Museum of History.[72]

Back to the charges against Captain Burnham; In February 1878, Lighthouse Engineer E. A. Benham investigated the allegations. His report must have concluded that the allegations were unfounded. This finding prompted Assistant Keeper, John M. Meyer to write another rambling statement, in which he resigned. Assistant Keeper Rose also resigned and still nothing about the B. Thomas person.

How about this? There is some evidence that in the 1870s, the infamous Boss Tweed, of the Tammany Hall investigations, may have visited Cape Canaveral before leaving on a trip to Cuba. Robert Ranson (1926) refers to Tweed as being a visitor to the Cape Canaveral Lighthouse.[73] Sorry for the diversion.

Picture of Joseph Henry, courtesy Smithsonian Institution Archives

The Cape Canaveral Light House got its beautiful black and white stripes in June of 1873. The following Notice to Mariners (NOTM) was issued:

Notice to Mariners No 17 of 1873

Notice is hereby given that, for the purpose of making it more readily discernible in the daytime, the light-house tower at Cape Canaveral, Florida will in the month of June 1873, be painted in horizontal bands, alternately black and white, there being three white and three black bands, the upper one or next to the lantern, being white.

By order of the Light-House board:
Joseph Henry
Chairman[74]

Joseph Henry served on the U.S. Light-House Board from its inception in 1852 to his death in 1878.

Joseph Henry became the "first Secretary of the Smithsonian Institution in 1846. Prior to that Henry taught natural philosophy at the Albany Academy in New York and the College of New Jersey (Princeton). During these years, Henry designed the most powerful electromagnets of his day, showed that magnets could make a basic telegraph, invented the electric motor, and discovered the concept of the transformer. He constructed am electromagnet, which could support a weight of more than 2,000 pounds, for Benjamin Silliman of Yale to exhibit before his students.[75]

Although, for the most part, though it is a very boring read, it is amazing what one may find in the Journal of a Light-House Station. The following are some selected Cape Canaveral Lighthouse Journal entries:

Mills O. Burnham tells us when the fuel for the lamp was changed from lard to mineral oil. The Journal entry of December 18, 1885 reads: "Steamer Fern, U.S Supply Ship arrived (with) Capt Wm. Wright Master and changed the Lamps from Lard oil to mineral oil..."[76]

Mills O. Burnham's next entry in the Journal is on December 31, 1885, documenting the arrival of "Capt Brown and Capt B. P. Lamberton, U.S. Navy bringing paint and oil for painting the tower..."[77] This entry was his last.

First Assistant Keeper George M. Quarterman made the following entire dated April 17, 1886: "The Keeper of Station, Mills O. Burnham died at the station this day at 4 pm...[78] We learn the cause of death from Thomas L. Tucker, "The measles was spreading like a major epidemic. Mills Burnham contracted the measles."[79]

George M. Quarterman was Captain Burnham's cousin and First Assistant Keeper at the time Captain Burnham's death. George M. Quarterman was promoted to Keeper on April 27, 1886. James M. Knight moved up to First Assistant from Second Assistant.[80]

James M. Knight was born in about 1848 in Georgia.[81] He came to Florida and married Mary Burnham,

Picture of George M. Quarterman, courtesy Florida Memory Project

the daughter of Mills O. and Mary Burnham in about 1876. Mary was born in about 1855 and was seven years younger than James. Keeping the trend going, James was appointed Second Assistant Lighthouse Keeper of the Cape Canaveral Lighthouse on May 21, 1880 just a few years after marrying a Burnham daughter.

The Knight's raised two boys, F. E. Knight, born in about 1878 and Thomas J. Knight, born in December 1880. Thomas would become an Assistant Keeper of the Cape Canaveral Lighthouse on April 16, 1902 and served until August 24, 1911.

Thomas Knight married Bernice Bedell, April 3, 1894 - July 1972, of McLean, Illinois, in about 1920. The couple and their two daughters Lucia and Rebecca were living in Polatka, Florida and Bernice's mother Della Bedell was living with the Knights at the time of the 1930 Census.[82]

The Keepers Journal, for the date of August 31, 1886, reflects that "at 9:30 pm. Experienced quite a shock causing the lens and tower to shake so much as to shake out quite a lot of putty out of the frame of the lens and stopping the time piece for about two minutes... ...weather clear..."[83] It took 20 minutes for the quake to travel the four hundred miles from Cape Canaveral and be felt in Charleston.

"The Charleston Earthquake of 1886 was the largest quake to hit the Southeastern United States. It occurred at 9:50 p.m. on August 31, 1886, and lasted just under a minute. The earthquake caused severe damage in Charleston, South Carolina, damaging 2,000 buildings and causing $6 million worth in damages, while in the whole city the buildings were only valued at approximately $24 million."[84]

When George M. Quarterman's resignation became effective on March 14, 1887, he turned the Cape Canaveral Lighthouse over to James M. Knight. Journal entry: April 1, 1887 "George M. Quarterman turns over all the property belongings to the Light House Establishment to James M. Knight taken his receipt thereof."[85]

How about this entry dated May 12, 1887. "Heavy hale storm comencing (sic) East and shifting to South East then to South and South West and wind blowing very heavy banking up the hale (sic) stones against the buildings and fences ten inches in thickness many of which ware (sic) three inches in diameter which broke thirteen lights of glass in the dwellings and kitchen."[86] So, NASA thought they had problems with hail. Note: The term "lights of glass" is refereeing to the windows. Seems they called windows lights back then.

This entry is dated December 25, 1887: "Christmas. Hoisted oil up to oil room." The word Christmas is written in above the word Hoisted.[87] Almost as if he wrote the entry and then remembered it was Christmas. Christmas day and here this poor guy is out there dragging oil to the top of the lighthouse.

Mary Burnham passed away in January 1888. She is buried at Cape Canaveral beside her husband Mills O. Burnham. A white cross marks her grave.

Picture of the White Crosses taken by the Author

The following Keepers Journal entry records her passing: "at 7:30P M Mary M Burnham the wife of the former Keeper of this Light Station the late Mills O. Burnham Died at this L-S January 25 AD 1888 in the 68th year of"[88]

On December 10, 1888, R. D. Hitchcock was at the Cape Canaveral Lighthouse to investigate the death of large brown Hawk. The bird was found on the beach in front of the lighthouse. In his 1888 letter to the Lighthouse Board, Hichcock, reports that the bird having been seen alive on the previous day, but in a disabled condition.

Upon examination, a small metal Percussion Cap-box was found wired about its neck and inside was the following attached slip of paper. This species of Hawk feeds principally upon Quad-pipers, to catch which requires considerable alertness and the box and wires had so infected bird in his pursuit of food that he had starved to death.[89]

49

So what was on the slip of paper? It's like a puzzle or mystery that must be solved and we must keep asking and looking for the answers. The answer is found in the December Keepers Journal. "The keepers son found the above tide (sic) to the neck of a fowl hawk"[90] Okay Okay the Slip of Paper saysss: Authors translation.

> Oct 10/88 the Schn You Wall
> Frying Pan Let Ship
> WSW 7 mile
> Wind NE GE overcast
> and moderate
>   John Cone (Cone)(Corne) Jr
>   516 Lenden (Lunden)
>   (Lurden) St
>   Camden N J[91]

Frying Pan Shoals are located in North Carolina, off the outer end of the extensive shoals marking out nearly 17 miles south and east of Cape Fear. The Light Ship served as a guide for passing clear of the shoal area in the approach to the Cape Fear River which accessed Southport and Wilmington. The Light Ship was eventually replaced by the Frying Pan Shoal Light Tower which was established 1.7 miles and 309 degrees from the final position of the lightship station.[92]

Keeper John L. Stuck apparently was the first to bring a teacher to Cape Canaveral. "In the fall of 1890, Janet Wilson Martin Packard came to teach at the Cape Canaveral Lighthouse."[93] Ms. Packard was to teach Captain Knight's three boys and her son, Roy at the lighthouse. The trip from Cocoa to the lighthouse took about eight hours. The pair crossed the Indian River on a little steamer and walked across Merritt Island to the Banana River. They were taken on a round bottom rowboat equipped with a small sail to make the trip up the Banana River to Canaveral, a distance of six or seven miles. From Canaveral the teacher and son were hauled the five miles to the lighthouse in a small wagon pulled by a mule.[94] Now where did that mule come from?   They didn't stay long and left for Cocoa in December 1890.

As if they needed more distractions, just before the lighthouse was to be moved the Journal of Light-House Station at Cape Canaveral has the following journal entry: May 26, 1893 "Keeper Knight was discharged." [95]

In a letter from the Naval Secretary, Commander R. D. Evans to the Secretary of the Treasury asking for:

> the immediate dismissal from the Light House Service, of Mr. James M. Knight, Keeper of the Cape Canaveral Light Station, Fla. Mr. Knight has been guilty of most disgraceful conduct while drunk and is totally unfit for retention in the Service. He has been drunk in uniform in public; he has treated his wife with cruelty and brutality, and plied his youngest boy with whiskey in a public bar room.[96]

From the July 1894, Keepers Journal, we learn the exact date and time the move of the Cape Canaveral Lighthouse was completed. Keeper John L. Stuck or 1st Assistant Keeper Clinton

P. Honeywell wrote, "The 4th order beacon was discontinued at 5:14 AM and the 1st Order was lighted at 6:58 pm to-day the 25th"...[97]

The Florida Star reports that the "Government schooner Pharos, with twenty workmen on board arrived in the Bight, Friday morning..."[98] The Pharos returned in August and got caught anchored during a severe storm. During the high tide and surge created by the August 1893 storms caught the Pharos at anchor in the Cape Canaveral Bight. The high winds coupled with the high tide and storm surge caused the Pharos to "narrowly escaped being driven ashore after parting the chains of three anchors which she had down at the time."[99] The only mention in the keeper's journal is that of "Rain Gale U.S.L.H. Tender Pharos got underway on account of heavy seas. Barometer 29.3."[100]

Two lighthouses stood within some ninety-five feet of each other for twenty five

Picture of the two Lighthouses, courtesy Rose Wooley

years at Cape Canaveral. Yes, from 1868 to September 26, 1893,[101] they stood side by side until the short one was blown up. Blown Up!!?? Yes, its bricks were needed to make concrete for the foundation of the Iron Tower when it's moved to a new location.

Whoa!!! Moved?? What move?? How did it get moved and why??

[1] Dr Robert Browning, <u>Lighthouse Evolution & Technology</u>, Historian, U.S. Coast Guard, (accessed October 12, 2008) <http://www.uscg.mil/history/weblighthouses/LHevolution.asp>

[2] Ibid.

[3] Letter, Bound in Letter Book No. 105 pg 75 Records Group 26, National Archives, Washington D.C.

[4] G. Caster Smith, Letter to Lighthouse Board, Bound in Letter Book No. 105 pg 141, Records Group 26, National Archives, Washington D.C.

[5] Letter, Bound in Letter Book No 115 pg 100, Records Group 26, National Archives, Washington D.C.

[6] R. P. Parrott, Letter to Lighthouse Board, Bound in Letter Book No 112, Pg 101, Records Group 26, National Archives, Washington D.C.

[7] Letter, Bound in Letter Book No 21, Pg 181, Records Group 26, National Archives, Washington D.C.

[8] Minutes, Lighthouse Board, Volume 14, pg 588, Records Group 26, National Archives, Washington D.C.

[9] Consumer Price Index and Conversion Table for previous year dollars to 2006 dollars, 2008 Robert C. Sahr, Political Science Department, Oregon State University, Corvallis

[10] Letter, Bound in Letter Book No 65, Pg 229, Records Group 26, National Archives, Washington D.C.

[11] Robert Ransom, <u>East Coast Florida Memories</u>, (Port Salerno: Florida Classic Library) 24 -25

[12] Ibid.

[13] Confederate States light-house establishment, appropriations certificate for Douglas Dummett, dated September 7, 1861, National Archives, RG 365

[14] Ibid.

[15] Mills Burnham letter to C.G. Memminger, dated September 12, 1862, record group 365 (Confederate States Light House Board) National Archives

[16] Mills Burnham letter to Confederate Lighthouse Board dated January 15, 1863, record group 365 (Confederate States Light House Board) National Archives

[17] Neil E. Hurley, <u>Florida's Lighthouses in the Civil War</u>, Middle River Press, Oakland Park, Florida

[18] WikipediA, the Free Encyclopedia, (accessed January 28, 2008) <http://en.wikipedia.org/>

[19] Neil E. Hurley, <u>Florida's Lighthouses in the Civil War</u>, Middle River Press, Oakland Park, Florida

[20] Ann Hatfield Thurm, <u>The History of The City of Cape Canaveral and The Cape Canaveral Area</u>, Publication made possible by the City of Cape Canaveral, Florida 1995: Online Associates of Brevard, pg 131

[21] ancestry.com (accessed January 28, 2008)

[22] Robert Ransom, <u>East Coast Florida Memories</u>, (Port Salerno: Florida Classic Library) 21

[23] Ann Hatfield Thurm, <u>The History of The City of Cape Canaveral and The Cape Canaveral Area</u>, Publication made possible by the City of Cape Canaveral, Florida 1995: Online Associates of Brevard, pg 131

[24] Robert Ransom, <u>East Coast Florida Memories</u>, (Port Salerno: Florida Classic Library) 21, 23, 25

[25] K. Denise Donovan, Virginia, Copy of Appointment Certificate, Grand Daughter, Mechanicsville, Tennessee

[26] ancestry.com, 1945 census (accessed January 27, 2008) <http://www.ancestry.com>

[27] Helen Wilson Tucker, <u>The story of Cape Canaveral as Long as I have lived on it</u>, (Unpublished, hand-written manuscript) IX

[28] Ibid.

[29] <u>The Civil Engineering and Architect's Journal</u>, May 1, 1862, Pgs 131 - 169

[30] <u>The Civil Engineering and Architect's Journal</u>, May 1, 1862, Pg 169

[31] Ibid.

[32] Dunnier, Letter, Records Group 26, National Archives, Washington D.C.

[33] <u>The Civil Engineering and Architect's Journal</u>, May 1, 1862, Pgs 131 - 169

[34] Letters, Journal Record of Letters, 1867-1868, pg 22, entry date April 3 1867, Records Group 26, National Archives, Washington D.C.

[35] Letter, Bound in Book No 198, Pg 512, Records Group 26, National Archives, Washington D.C.

[36] O. M. Poe letter to Joseph Lederele, dated February 15, 1867, Records of the United States Coast Guard, Records Group 26 E-1, National Archives, Washington D.C.

[37] National Parks Service, Maritime Heritage Program, (accessed April 28, 2009) <http://www.nps.gov/history/maritime/keep/architect.htm>

[38] Raymond Gaudette, Beddeford Historical Society

[39] Dunnier Letter, Bound in Letter Book No 198, Pg 516, Records Group 26, National Archives, Washington D.C.

[40] Dunnier Letter, Bound in Letter Book No 198, Pgs 416 ½, 426, 428, and Pg 482, Records Group 26, National Archives, Washington D.C.

[41]Lederle Letter, Bound in Letter Book No 194, Pg 724, Records Group 26, National Archives, Washington D.C.

[42]Dunnier, Letter, Bound Letter Book No 213 Pg 135, Records Group 26, National Archives, Washington D.C.

[43]Dunnier Report, Bound in Letter Book No 213, Pg 95, Records Group 26, National Archives, Washington D.C.

[44]Dunnier, Progress Report, Bound in Letter Book No 213, Pg 259, Records Group 26, National Archives, Washington D.C.

[45]Acting Engineer Lederle April 16, 1866 letter to the Lighthouse Board, Recorded in Bound in Letter Book No 181 page 487, Records Group 26, National Archives, Washington D.C.

[46]John A. Bailey May 15, 1866 letter to Acting Engineer Lederle, Bound Letter Book No 181, Pg 557, Records Group 26, National Archives, Washington D.C.

[47]Dunner, Letter to Lighthouse Board, Bound Letter Book No 213, Pg 140, Records Group 26, National Archives, Washington D.C.

[48]Dunner, Letter to Lighthouse Board, Bound in Letter Book No 213, Pg 247, Records Group 26, National Archives, Washington D.C.

[49]Dunner, Letter to Lighthouse Board, Bound in Letter Book No 213, Pg 307 and Pg 309, Records Group 26, National Archives, Washington D.C.

[50]Dunnier, Journal Record of letters 1867-1868, entry date December 25, 1867, Records Group 26, National Archives, Washington D.C.

[51]Journal Record of Letters 1867-1868, entry date December 28, 1867, Pg 104, Records Group 26, National Archives, Washington D.C.

[52]WikipediA, the Free Encyclopedia, (accessed January 28, 2008) <http://en.wikipedia.org/wiki/Exposition_Universelle_(1867)>

[53]O. M. Pose letter to Lederle, dated February 3, 1868, Records Group 26, National Archives, Washington D.C.

[54]Lederle, Letter, Journal Record of Letters 1867-1868, entry date February 14, 1868, Pg 121, Records Group 26, National Archives, Washington D.C.

[55]Ellen J. Henry, MFA, Curator, Ponce de Leon Inlet Light Station

[56]Ibid.

[57]Lederle, Letter, Letters Sent to District Inspect by Engineer 1852-1910, Vol 66, Pg 71 and 117, Records Group 26, National Archives, Washington D.C.

[58]WikipediA, The free encyclopedia, (accessed April 12, 2009) <http://en.wikipedia.org/wiki/Amrum_Lighthouse>

[59]Notice to Mariners, Bound in Letter Book No 213, Pg 497, Records Group 26, National Archives, Washington D.C.

[60]U.S. Light-House Board, Bulletin No 30, Pg 3, Item 6, Records Group 26, National Archives, Washington D.C.

[61]Notice to Mariners, Bound in Letter Book No 210, Pg 754, Records Group 26, National Archives, Washington D.C.

[62]Andrew Goss, Letter, to the Lighthouse Board, Dec 1868, Records Group 26, National Archives, Washington D.C.

[63]Lederle, Letter, Journal Record of letters 1867-1868, entry date June 20, 1868, Records Group 26, National Archives, Washington D.C.

[64]C.G. Anderson, Report, Bound in Letter Box 230, Pg 89, Records Group 26, National Archives, Washington D.C.

[65]E. W. Stone, Letter, Bound in Letter Box 230, Pg 139, Records Group 26, National Archives, Washington D.C.

[66]B. M. Dove, Letter, to Lighthouse Board, Records Group 26, National Archives, Washington D.C.: Bound in Letter Book 234, Pg 215

[67]Alex B. Rose, Personal Letter, Bound in Letter Book 446, Pgs 417, 435, Records Group 26, National Archives, Washington D.C

[68]Ibid.

[69]Ibid.

[70]Ibid.

[71]James D. Snyder, A Light in the Wilderness The Story of Jupiter Inlet Lighthouse & The Southeast Florida Frontier, (Merritt Island, Fl: Pharos Books) pg 203

[72]Kansas State Historic Society: <http://www.kshs.org/cool3/ titussword.htm> (accessed August 22, 2008)

[73]Robert Ransom, East Coast Florida Memories, (Port Salerno: Florida Classic Library) pg 31

[74]Notice to Mariners No 17, Bound in Volume 761, Records Group 26, National Archives, Washington D.C.

[75]Smithsonian Institution Archives, (accessed April 12, 2009) <http://siarchives.si.edu/history/jhp/joseph12.htm>

[76]Keepers Journal, December 18, 1885, Records Group 26, National Archives, Washington D.C.

[77]Ibid.

[78]G. M. Quarterman, Keepers Journal, April 17, 1886, Records Group 26, National Archives, Washington D.C.

[79]Thomas L. Tucker, Florida Pioneers, The Tucker & Wilson Story, pg 55, n.s. 2003

[80]G. M. Quarterman, Keepers Journal, April 27, 1886, Records Group 26, National Archives, Washington D.C.

[81]ancestry.com. James M. Knight (accessed August 24, 2009) <http://trees.ancestry.comtree 5170623/person-775653774>

[82]ancestry.com, 1930 US census, (accessed August 24, 2009) <http://ancestry.com>

[83]Keepers Journal, August 31, 1886, Records Group 26, National Archives, Washington D.C.

[84]WikipediA, the free encyclopedia, <http:en.wikipedia.org/wiki/Charleston_earthquake> (accessed Jaunuary 22, 2008)

[85]Keepers Journal, April 1, 1887, Records Group 26, National Archives, Washington D.C.

[86]Keepers Journal, May 12, 1887. Records Group 26, National Archives, Washington D.C.

[87]Journal of Light-house Station at Cape Canaveral, December 25, 1887, Records Group 26, National Archives, Washington D.C

[88]Journal of Light-house Station at Cape Canaveral, January 25, 1888, Records Group 26, National Archives, Washington D.C.

[89]Hitchcock Letter to the Lighthouse Board, December 29, 1888, Records Group 26, National Archives, Washington D.C.

[90]Keepers Journal, December ?, 1888, Records Group 26, National Archives, Washington D. C.

[91]Ibid

[92]U.S. Coast Guard History, (accessed June 20, 2009) <http://www.uscg.mil/history/weblightships/Lightship_Station_Index.asp>

[93]Roy McDougall Pacard; Autobiography

[94]Ibid.

[95]Journal of Light-house Station at Cape Canaveral, records group 26, National Archives, Washington, D. C., May 26, 1893

[96]Naval Secretary Evans letter to Secretary of Treasury, dated May 15, 1893, records group 26E-31, National Archives, Washington, D. C., marked 103

[97]Journal of Light-house Station at Cape Canaveral, July 25, 1894, 25 July, Records Group 26, National Archives, Washington D.C.

[98]Florida Star, July 7, 1893

[99]Report of the Lighthouse Board 107

[100]Journal of Light-house Station at Cape Canaveral, August 27, 1893, Records Group 26, National Archives, Washington D.C.

[101]Journal of Light-house Station at Cape Canaveral, entry September 26, 1893, Records Group 26, National Archives, Washington D.C.

CHAPTER FIVE
The Iron Lighthouse Gets Moved

The Iron lighthouse stood, for some 25 years, just a few feet from the Atlantic Ocean at Cape Canaveral before it was moved. The cause for the move was fear of encroachment by the ocean. We must remember that Ora Carpenter warned of the ocean's encroachment and warned that the brick lighthouse may fall over in 1852. That was sixteen years before the Iron Lighthouse was erected. Well, as of 2009, just 157 years after Mr. Carpenter's warning, the foundation at the location of the original site is still there, it is not under water and the shoreline has now extended further away from the site.

By the time the iron lighthouse was erected at Cape Canaveral, moving lighthouses was not a novel idea. The move was probably considered when the original design and specifications were developed and the request for proposals was sent out. It would appear that cast iron lighthouses were designed with the possibility of being disassembled, moved, and then reassembled at a new location in mind. Apparently the Cape Canaveral Lighthouse was the third cast iron lighthouse to be moved. The first was the 1852 Matagorda Island Lighthouse in Texas, moved in 1873. The second cast iron lighthouse to be moved was the 1875 Hunting Island Lighthouse, South Carolina which was moved in 1889.[1]

Picture of the Matagorda Island Lighthouse, courtesy, Dewey A. Stringer

Picture of Hunting Island Lighthouse, courtesy, Hunting Island Parks

As early as October 1872, the sea's encroachment at Cape Canaveral was a concern. That concern was raised in the October 12, 1872 "Description of Light-House Tower, Buildings, Premises at Cape Canaveral Florida"[2] report. The report is a preprinted form in book format. It has fourteen pages with fill in the blank items down the left side of each page. Richard Gowers, Assistant Light House Engineer (L.H.E.) filled in the blanks. On the unmarked page 1 to the right of the Question: "By Whom Described."[3] The entry is "Richard Gowers, Asst. L.H.E."[4] On page 3 we find a clue for the motivation or impetus to move the lighthouse to a safer location. In response to the statement Miscellaneous remarks upon tower and site, we find: "Keeper states that during the severe gale of August 1871 - the entire site was overflowed and about 50 feet of beach in front of the lighthouse was washed away. During that gale the water in the tanks of the tower was spoiled by the salt water washing into the gutters at the base of the tower and carried into the cistern..."[5] Now that would probably be a reason to move the lighthouse or at very least protect the water supply. We have no evidence that the lighthouse had a cistern, however the dwelling did. A hurricane in 1876 destroyed all of the outbuildings. The keeper's dwelling was rebuilt in 1883 with the assistant keeper's quarters being built later in 1883.[6] Hurricanes, yet, another potential reason for moving the lighthouse to a safer location.

Again concern for sea encroachment on the lighthouse was noted. In a letter to the Light House Board, John C. Mallery wrote that: "...During a visit of inspection made in March 1885, by Mr. B.B. Smith, Assistant Light House Engineer, (observed) the sea's encroachment... and the keeper instructed to report any subsequent advance."[7]

By April 1886 continuous protection of the Iron Lighthouse at Cape Canaveral was seriously underway. In August, Engineer Mallery, responded to a request from the Light-House Board to provide "views and recommendations for further protection"[8] ...of the Cape Canaveral Light Station and recommended the following: "The substitution of stone jetties for the present wooden structure would be a great improvement which can be secured however only at a great cost."[9] Now where did that come from? He goes on: "The present structure has held the site without loss for a year and is practically in as good a condition as when first built. It is therefore unadvisable in my opinion to take any steps to give additional protection until it is demonstrated that the present structure is inadequate. It may, however, become necessary to substitute stone for wood in the near future and respectfully recommend that an appropriation of $10,000.00 be asked for from the next congress for the protection of the site, the amount to be expended when additional protection is necessary."[10]

So how about that Mallery? He says all looks good and then launches into discussion about replacing the wooden jetties with stone. Wonder why he didn't recommend stone in the first place?

In a May 1886 letter, Major Gregory, Light House Engineer, submitted: "...a project for the protection of the site which was adopted and executed during the summer of 1886."[11]

Well according the Keepers Journal for 10 October, 1887 "The sea runs high and the Breakwater is Breaking of (off) very fast."[12] Engineer Mallery sends a letter to the Light House Board on the same day October 10, 1887 announcing: "I have the honor to report that the keeper at Cape Canaveral Lightstation (sic)..."[13] in his report, states that "the jetty has washed out and gone and 150 feet of the planking along the beach has washed out on the south end and that the beach ... has cut away 30 feet, and that the distance from houses to the seas high water mark is 192 feet. The distance of the tower from the sea is the same as it has been for the past year."[14]

From the forgoing it appears that the southern portion of the revetment which was constructed in July, 1886 "has carried away and that the sea has advanced their way nearer to the dwellings, which are in rear of the tower."[15] If one were to face the towers from the northeast standing with back to the ocean the dwellings would indeed be behind the towers. In the August 1893 MONTHLY REPORT OF THE CONDITION OF THE Cape Canaveral LIGHT-STATION, John Stuck reports, the distance of the dwellings to be "approximately 350 feet from the tower."[16]

Chief Engineer, John C. Mallery wrote a rambling six page letter to the Light House Board reporting the findings of a November 15 and 16, 1887 inspection. The following are excerpts taken from that letter: "The high water mark was 165 feet from the tower. ....All but about 200 feet of the beach timber protection constructed in 1886 and the wooden jetty had been carried away. The 200 feet remaining was twisted and out of line. This revetment failed because it did not have sufficient footing in the sand and because the sea got in behind one of its ends and

Picture of Amelia Island Lighthouse, courtesy WikipediA

Picture of Ponce de Leon Lighthouse, courtesy Nancy D Watts

washed out."[17]

He goes on to tell of his visit to Mosquito Inlet, St. Augustine, now known as the Ponce de Leon Inlet Light Station; The St Johns River, the Amelia Island, Fl, and Huntington Island, S.C. stating that "At all...there are marked evidence of the recent advancement of the high water mark."[18] He goes on the remark that the encroachment at Amelia Island "took place in spite of stone ...jetties."[19]

Some may find this interesting: "There used to be a narrow channel of about 10 feet at low water close to the shore and along the Cape. This channel was formerly used by small vessels. It has shoaled up so that it can be used no longer. At the point about 1400 feet north of the lighthouse there is but 2 or 3 feet at low water."[20]

Next, Engineer John C. Mallery describes exactly what has actually happened over the years and why. "This is a favorable feature, as the shoal increases at this place and the point of land advances seaward, further erosion opposite the lighthouse would be prevented."[21] He pretty much nailed it and goes on the point out that, "Cape Canaveral is a remote and isolated place."[22] Ya think? "There is no harbor...unless the anchorage under the lee of the Cape can be called one. All materials have to be landed on the beach 2 1/2 miles from the lighthouse and transport would be along the beach."[23] There was no wharf or road to the lighthouse. In 1925 the lee of the Cape described above and known as the bight was touted as a great East Coast Harbor.

All of this was a prelude to Engineer Mallery's following statement and recommendation. "A beach protection to be effective should be watched, damages repaired and changes made to meet changes as they occur."[24] Almost unbelievably, Mallery, has just made a case for not moving the lighthouse.

Now for the recommendation "...In view of the foregoing considerations, I have the honor to recommend that an appropriation of $60,000.00 be asked for moving and establishing the light upon another site..."[25] Engineer Mallery continues with a technical description of the lighthouse reservation and recommends reserving more land for lighthouse purposes and finishes the description with: "This land is of little or no value but has higher ground suitable for a lighthouse."[26] Now we haven't heard that since George Center wrote it in 1847. We still have 63 years until a rocket launch at Cape Canaveral. He finishes the letter by recommending another "$6,000.00"[27] to rebuild the revetment.

On a roll! Engineer Mallery, followed up the November letter with another on December

7, 1887 recommending "that a landing near the Anchorage Buoy and on a right of way through the southern quarter of said section 29 and also a right of way from the present site to the above right of way through section 29 as far as may be necessary along the road which runs between the lighthouse and the Burnham home on Banana River reserved by executive order for lighthouse purposes..."[28] A government wharf would eventually be built at the exact spot near the Anchorage Buoy.

Mallery's recommendations are acted upon in December 1887 when the Engineering Committee wrote to the Light-House Board stating: "...relating to the encroachment of the sea upon the light-house reservation at Cape Canaveral, Fla., has had the same under consideration, and returns them with the following report: The committee recommends that for the temporary protection of this site, the sum of $6,000 be allocated, as recommended by Engineer of the 6th Light-House District in his letter of 29 Nov. '87, and that the matter of asking for an appropriation of $60,000 for permanent protection be considered."[29] As far as we know, this was the first time that serious protection, moving the lighthouse and work to prevent the encroachment was formally discussed and monies allocated.

The following is a short version of the time line for protecting the lighthouse from the ocean's encroachment: In December of 1887, Capt John C. Mallery, USA, Engineer of the 6th District, Baltimore wrote several letters: He wrote to the Lighthouse Board recommending "... the reservation of North half of Section 29 Township 23 South Range 38 East be by Executive Order for Lighthouse purposes..."[30] A second letter requested "$6,000.00 for immediate protection and recommends $60,000.00 be considered for moving the lighthouse."[31] Engineer Mallery's request was approved on December 8, 1887[32] and on December 31, 1887, Mallery was directed to "advertise and work the plan for protecting the Lighthouse"[33] The protection effort was mostly continuous from early 1888 for about five years until the lighthouse was moved in 1893.

On January 3, 1888, a request for proposals was issued for protecting the Cape Canaveral Lighthouse. The request consisted of proposals "for furnishing lumber, hardware, and steam pumps, boilers, etc., required for the revetments and jetties for the shore protection of the Cape Canaveral Light Station."[34] Bids were opened and the bid of "Messrs Bailey and Lebby, of Charleston, S.C. accepted and rejected the bid of the Steinmeyer Lumber Manufacturing Company, of Charleston."[35] The bid was "rejected because the Tender Pharos could haul only about one third of the lumber required in one trip. The board felt it would be cheaper to purchase the lumber in Jacksonville, Florida."[36]

The above decision was countermanded by the Lighthouse Board, the board on January 19, 1888, sent a letter instructing that Steinmeyer Lumber Manufacturing Company be given the contract to "supply sufficient lumber to load the Light-House Tender Pharos to be used in construction of the revetment and jetties for shore protection..." The board also directed that additional lumber requirements be "advertised and purchased at Jacksonville and Fernandina, Florida."[37]

Mallery responded to the Light House Board's direction to purchase lumber in Florida for the shore revetment with: "Mr. B. B. Smith, Assistant Engineer, Sixth District, traveled to Jacksonville to obtain terms for all lumber before the receipt of the Boards letter."[38] Covered his tail there. Mallery continued: "He visited all the lumber dealers there and succeeded in getting four offers...two of the bids include the delivery of the material... those [bids] of Geo. A. De Cotter and T. V. Cashen, that of Mr. De Cotter in the sum of $19.75 being the lower. Both of these bidders rely on the schooner Emily B to take the lumber to the light station and as she can carry only 22,000 feet, B.M. at one load...I therefore recommend the offer of Mr. De Cotter..."[39]

In the February 4, 1888, Abstract of Bids for lumber for Cape Canaveral shore protection opened in the Office of the Engineer of the 6th District at Charleston, S.C., February 1, 1888, as per poster and Circular letter dated January 26, 1888.[40]

Names of Bidders	Residence	Price	Deliver
Geo. A. De Cotter	Jacksonville	12.75	19.75
Thomas V Cashen	"	13.00	
Henry Clark	"	14.00	
Dexter Hunter	"	13.00[41]	

If all the above has you confused, just imagine the researcher trying to make sense out of all these letters. The following letter on the subject of revetments and jetties may bring some clarity.

Major Gregory wrote a January 19, 1888 letter to Engineer John C. Mallery directing the following: "Under authority granted by the Honorable Secretary of the Treasury, in his letter of 18 Jan'y '88, the Board authorizes you to employ Messers. Bailey & Lebby to furnish lot No. 2, Hardware, and Lot No. 3, Steam Pumps, Boilers, & in accordance with the terms of their bid, the formality of a written contract being waived."[42] That's fairly clear.

Gregory continues, "With reference to Lot 1, Lumber, I have to say that the Board Authorizes you to procure (from) Steinmeyer Lumber Manufacturing Company, sufficient lumber to load the tender Pharos, and as to any additional lumber....you are requested to invite proposals ....at Jacksonville and Fernandina, Florida..."[43] Enough, now let's move the thing.

While protection of the site continued, Mallery did not forget that moving the lighthouse was always an option. In January 1888, Mallery wrote that "Mr. Smith made an examination of the vicinity for the purpose of selecting a site should it become necessary to move the light-tower and decided tht (sic) the best location was on the N. ½ of S. 29, T23 S. R. 38 E. ...Attention is respectfully invited to the fact that the work of protection was in 1886 while the homestead entries on Section 29 were made by Robert Ranson and Frank Kline. On Feb. 19th and July 27th, 1887."[44] The 1900 Census of Brevard County, Precinct 15, Canaveral, indicates that a Frank Kline was living on the Banana River south of the Burnham homestead and it lists Kline as a farmer and from Austria.

Yes!! Now we know that Mr. B. B. Smith was the person who selected the site where the Cape Canaveral Lighthouse now resides. And, in a February 15, 1893 letter to the Secretary of the Treasury, we learn when the money in the amount of $80,000.00 was approved to move the lighthouse by The Sundry Civil Act on August 30, 1890.[45] Just a bit more then was originally estimated.

So how did they do it? On 3 March 1893, "Mr J. R. Mew was employed to superintend the removal of the Cape Canaveral Light-station."[46] In a search of the 1880 U.S. Census a record for a J. R. Mew was found indicating that he may have come to Cape Canaveral from Coosawhatchie, Hampton County, South Carolina.[47]

Work must have started in earnest by July of 1893, because a mule and a cart were delivered to the Superintendent of Construction, Mr. Mew, on June 24, 1893 by Mr. B. J. Pacetti.[48] This mule would be used to pull a cart loaded with lighthouse parts over a tram road to its new location.[49] Tram road: "A road prepared for easy transit of trams or wagons, by forming the wheel tracks of smooth beams of wood, blocks of stone, or plates of iron."[50] The mule "was first employed in 1873 at Charleston Lighthouse-Station, S. C. from which place she was taken and did service for the construction party at Amelia Island and Mosquito Inlet Light-Stations, Florida."[51] Did you notice the she? Her name was "Nancy Hanks."[52] We don't know if she came to the lighthouse with that name or she was named, Nancy Hanks, later. "Nancy Hanks Lincoln (February 5, 1784 – October 5, 1818) was the mother of Abraham Lincoln."[53]

Picture of Lighthouse & Tracks, courtesy Rose Wooley

The Star Advocate reported on July 7, 1893 that "The government schooner Pharos, with twenty workmen on board arrived in the Bight, Friday morning; and before long the work of moving the Lighthouse will be underway."[54] These workmen must have built the tram road. We get a misleading hint that the tram road may have followed the ocean from an article presented the Star Advocate dated October 30, 1893: "...long stretches of loose sand thrown up from the tram road, were washed away."[55]

Although, there is little definitive documentation that describes the exact route that was used to move the lighthouse, we do have a March 29, 1971 interview of the 89 year old Mrs. Oscar Floyd Quarterman (Florence Wilson). Mrs. Quarterman was interviewed and provides the following: "The Cape filled in after they moved the light. They built the tram road to move the lighthouse. It was moved in pieces with one mule. I remember where they buried the sailor. It was a mile or so doen (sic) (down) the tram road from the lighthouse."[56] There you have it right from a person who lived on the Cape. It, the lighthouse, was moved in pieces along "rail road tracks" or a tram road.

The interview with Mrs. Quarterman would lead us to believe that the tram used to move the lighthouse pieces ran from or past the cemetery where sailor, Harry Osman, more on Harry later, is supposed to be buried. A tram road did in fact run past a cemetery but it was constructed to be used to deliver parts, construction equipment and materials to the new location. It is most

Picture of Bergland, courtesy U.S. Corps of Engineers

probable that the lighthouse was moved over a part of that tramway.

Just in case you are not convinced the following analysis and evidence is provided for your review: The study of a picture of tracks leading to the current lighthouse,[57] a 1922 survey of "Cape Canaveral Lightstation, Fla."[58][59] as well as 1943 and 1950 aerial photos, the 1971 Mrs. Quarterman interview, and now believe that it must be concluded that: a "Tram Road" with tracks was laid generally southwesterly, along the eastern edge of the swamp on the original Burnham Road from the original site to a point near the western end of the swamp where the tram road joined a second tram road coming from the government wharf leading to the current location. In a December 20, 1892 letter from Captain Eric Bergland titled, "Report giving estimate of cost and proposed method of carrying on the work of moving Cape Canaveral Light station to the approved new site supports the conclusion."

Major Eric Bergland, born April 25, 1844 in Helsingland, Sweden, was the son of Anders Berglund who emigrated to the United States in 1846. The Bergland family settled in Illinois where Eric spent much of his youth working at the Bishop Hill Colony printing office. At the outbreak of the Civil War, Bergland, then aged seventeen, joined the 57th Illinois Infantry, organizing in Henry County. He took part in the capture of Fort Donelson, the Battle of Shiloh, Corinth, and Resaca. While in the field at Rome, Georgia, Lt. Bergland received his appointment to the United States Military Academy at West Point, New York[61]

In 1878, Bergland married Lucy Scott McFarland, daughter of Mary Eppes Scott and William C. McFarland of Lexington, KY. Lucy was a cousin of Lucy Webb Hayes, wife of President Rutherford B. Hayes. The Berglands were frequent visitors to the White House while Hayes was president from 1877 to 1881[62]

The Bergland letter confirms that there were two tram roads or tramways. From the estimate of cost lists on page 1 we find: "WHARF cost $1,650."[63]

On page 2 we find:
TRAMWAYS (Earthwork 1 3/4- Trestle 1/4 mile).
2,000 cubic yards Earthwork at 10c $220.
Trestles 130 lineal feet at 1.25   1625. [130 x 1.25=162.50]
10 tons 30-pound Iron for curves, etc., at $35.   350.
50,000 feet B.M. Lumber at $20. per M (B.M.)   1000.[64]

Captain Bergland's final cost estimated for moving the lighthouse was "$79,367"[65] which equals about $1,763,711.11 in 2006 dollars. $80,000 had been appropriated.[66] Now that's some good estimating. Notice the plural word "tramways."

In a research report submitted in July 2002, Mr. Al Hartman and Dr. Lori Walters provided documented agreement with the above stated assumptions and the track in general. With the permission of Dr. Walters and Mr. Hartman that report and analysis is provide in its entirety below:

Cape Canaveral Lighthouse Movement Theory
Researched by: Al Hartman and Dr. Lori C. Walters
Draft prepared by: Dr. Lori C. Walters

Overview: The following materials have been prepared to resolve the Cape Canaveral Lighthouse movement path between 1893 and 1894.

Table Cloth – View #1 and "Trail" view
A tablecloth acquired from Johnny Johnson provides a rough map to the Cape Canaveral region. While the precise date of origin is unknown – it does predate the

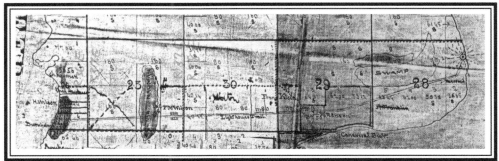

Picture of Table Cloth Map Courtesy Rose Wooley

movement of the Cape Canaveral Lighthouse. The route of the lighthouse keeper's trail from the original lighthouse placement to the Burnham and H. Wilson sites along the Banana River is provided. The trail bends southwest from the lighthouse until reaching the southernmost point of an area labeled "swamp" from this point the trail angle repositions but maintains a southwest direction until reaching the R. Ranson site where it heads due west to Burnham and H. Wilson sites. The tablecloth map provides an early record of the lighthouse keeper's trail and its proximity to the swamp area east of the present day CCLH location. When superimposed as an overlay over a contemporary USGS map - the regions and natural landmarks closely match - further reinforcing the validity of the hand drawn tablecloth map.

1951 Aerial View

The path appearing in this aerial view follows the lighthouse keeper's trail as depicted in the tablecloth map. From the original CCLH location, the path detours beneath the marsh-like area to its immediate north. Magnification of the trail reveals a northwest spur in the trail to the current location of the CCLH compound. When viewing this region, place a straight edge on this path - it reveals direct alignment with the current location of the CCLH tower. This suggests the Cape Canaveral Lighthouse transport occurred along the existing lighthouse keeper's trail to reduce required clearing of the dense brush. Expanded for this effort, the trail would have provided a solid dry bed to support the lighthouse structure. Upon reaching the western most point of the swamp region, the lighthouse transport

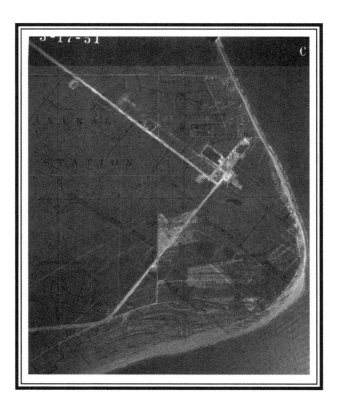

path would have been redirected to facilitate the shortest route to the intended location just to the northwest. This photo supports the northwest redirection path.

Negative reversal of 1951 Aerial View

The utilization of the photo negative option on a computer photo program, such as Corel Photo House, provides additional clarification of the lighthouse keeper's trail. The path in the photo at right, has been highlighted in red. Compare this red highlighted path to the loop contained in the 1913 map provided below.

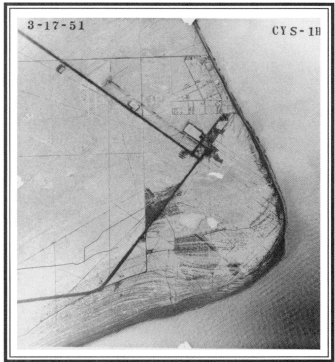

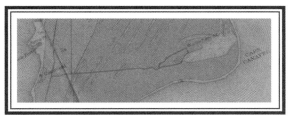

1951 Aerial Overlay

At right, an overlay of a current USGS map superimposed over the 1951 aerial photograph provides overall perspective of the site. Special notation should be given to the swamp region to the immediate southeast of the current location of the Cape Canaveral lighthouse. Again, a move involving a weighty structure such as the lighthouse components would seek to skirt the swamp region and upon locating a solid path proceed to move in a straight line to the newly prepared lighthouse location.

1950 Overlay USGS

This item (below) provides a differing perspective from the previous 1951 Aerial Overlay - it is comprised of a 1950 USGS survey map as the primary document with a current USGS map superimposed over the earlier USGS Map. The 1950 document provides detail to the original lighthouse keeper's trail skirting the swamp region to the south, angling at the western most point of the swamp region and proceeding west. It is at this angling juncture where the proposed northwest movement path to the current lighthouse location began. Again - it is clear the point of embarkation for this theorized path would have begun on the western most reach of the swamp area - the first solid ground and then head northwest to the current location.

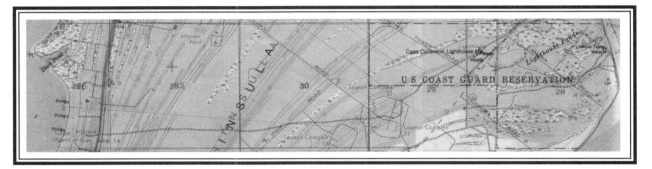

1955 Aerial View – John Carden Photo

Tracing back from the original Cape Canaveral lighthouse location, the lighthouse keeper's trail is clearly visible. The path proceeds westward, skirting the marshy swamp-like area immediately to the north. The marsh area appears reduced in this aerial photo. This condition could be attributed to drainage efforts since the inception of the JLRPG. The photograph could also have been taken during the dry winter months.

Magnification of this trail reveals a northwest spur path near the end of the

dense march area. The spur path though marsh edge and brush heads directly to the current location of the Cape Canaveral lighthouse compound - in direct alignment with the Cape Canaveral lighthouse tower. As with the previously analyzed 1951 aerial photo, this photo also supports the northwest redirection path theory.

Light 02 Aerial Photo
The southeast perspective of this aerial photo (right) provides a closer view of the actual path in question. Headed southeast from the Cape Canaveral lighthouse tower, a dark trail-like image can been seen skirting the western boundary of the swamp region. This trail links into the lighthousekeeper's

1943 Aerial photograph, courtesy, Brevard County Florida Engineering

trail and proceeds in a northeast direction toward the original Cape Canaveral lighthouse location.

I suspect the reason as to why the believed path from the lighthouse trail to its current location appears to be darker than the surrounding vegetation and permits visibility from aerial photography is the base materials (crushed shells) laid for the move are providing a greater source of nutrients for the vegetation - thus appearing a rich darker color.

1913 Map
This map, dated 1913, is a US Coast Survey Charts Base Map, developed by the Bureau of Soils - the original can be found at the Alma Clyde Field library of the Florida Historical Society. While the map makes no mention of the original location of the Cape Canaveral lighthouse, it provides strong support to the proposed lighthouse movement path. The current lighthouse location is provided with the entire lighthouse keeper's trail through

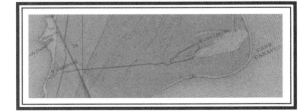

to the West Side of the Cape. Note the loop on the East Side of the trail - the easternmost portion of the loop as documented on this map is the precise location of our proposed movement path. Clearly the movement path on the western edge of the swamp was maintained for several years after the move as an alternate pathway. Without sufficient need for use, the path was abandoned sometime between the date of this map and the 1940s and subsequently reclaimed by Cape vegetation.[67]

Actual work on the tram road must have started on or about June 30, 1893. The Keepers Journal has the following entry: "U S. L. H. Tender Pharos anchored in the Bight and work started to remove the station under the direction of Mr. Mew supt (sic) of construction"[68] They must have been building the tram road between June and November when the first parts were removed from the tower. That's it another mystery solved!?

On September 26, 1893 "The old brick tower which was built in 1847 was blown up with dynamite to be used in making concrete for the foundation of the tower at the new site."[69] They must have hauled the rubble from the old tower to the new site over the tram road in the cart pulled by the mule that was delivered in June 1893, by Mr. Pacetti.

With the route prepared and apparently tested, work on the lighthouse started with the lens being removed and another beacon being established. A Notice to Mariners, No. 111 announced the intention of a light change at Cape Canaveral and records its implementation.[70] In the Keepers Journal the follow entry dated October 19, 1893 "Mr. Hy Wilkinson visited the station to put up the lens in the beacon and remove the lens from the tower."[71] Just four days later a Journal entry states: "The 4th order beacon was lighted at 5.21 PM for the first time and the 1st order light was discontinued at 6.8 (could be 6.08, or 6.18, or 6.28, or 6.38, or 6.48, or 6.58) AM"[72] Probably 6:58.

Actual disassembly of the lighthouse began when "The ball and first Iron work was lowered from the tower on November 2, 1893."[73] The Keepers Journal also lets us know that "Mr. L.C. Demaree, acting 2nd Asst received a notice of transfer and promotion to 1st Asst at the Mosquito Inlet Light Station to take effect Dec 1st."[74] A severe storm hit Cape Canaveral on November 27, 1893 and played havoc on the new lighthouse site. From the Keepers Journal, "At 2.15 PM today the 27th Inst a whirlwind past from the west destroying a building at the new site, and injuring three men, Supt of Construction Mew, and injured Mr. Hitchcock leg broken Mr. Gohandlern (?) badly bruised."

The last piece of the tower was moved to the new site on February 11, 1894. From the Keepers Journal: "The last plates of the Tower were taken to the new site today."[76] Just three days later, February 14, 1894, assembly of the lighthouse must have started because we find this entry in the Keepers Journal. "Work started at the new site to rebuild the tower."[77] Assembly of the Iron Lighthouse must have gone well and with few problems because in less than three months, on May 4, 1894 "the ball was placed on (top of) the tower."[78] The lighthouse got a new keeper on May 16, 1894, "John L Stuck was appointed Keeper today"[79]

During the move of the lighthouse, a wharf was constructed in the Cape Canaveral Bight. From the July 1894 Keepers Journal, we find the following Journal entry: The "Sch (Schooner) Wade

Picture of Keeper Stuck, courtesy the Memory Project Florida Archives

Hampton, Capt Issac Relyea, laid alongside discharged and loaded at the dock in the bite being the first vessel to do so."[80] This wharf was connected to the lighthouse by an extension of the tram road used to move the pieces of the lighthouse to its new site. The wharf was located east and just south of the grave of the sailor Harry Osman and north of Stinkmore.

We repeat ourselves. We learn the exact date and time the move of the Cape Canaveral Lighthouse was completed: from the July 1894, Keepers Journal. Keeper, John L. Stuck or 1st Assistant Keeper, Clinton P. Honeywell wrote, "The 4th order beacon was discontinued at 5:14 am and the 1st Order was lighted at 6:58 pm to-day the 25th"...[81] Amazing, we now have the exact time and date that the Cape Canaveral lighthouse move was completed with the light being relit at 6:58 pm on July 25, 1894.

With the lighthouse moved and in operation, the keepers and their families would settle down to living and working at Cape Canaveral and just letting stuff and life happen.

[1]Candace Clifford, Moving Lighthouses, CRM No 9—1999, pg 36

[2]Description of Light-House Tower, Buildings, Premises at Cape Canaveral Florida, October 12, 1872, the original in a private collection

[3]Ibid, page 1

[4]Ibid, page 1

[5]Ibid, page 4

[6]Candace Clifford - Mary Louise Clifford, Nineteenth-Century Lights, History Images of American Lighthouses, Pages 194, 195

[7]Capt J.C. Mallery, Letter to the Lighthouse Board, dated March 1885, Records Group 26, National Archives, Washington D.C.:

[8]Mallery, Letter to the Lighthouse Board, dated August 13, 1887, Records Group 26, National Archives, Washington D.C.

[9]Ibid.

[10]Ibid.

[11]Major Gregory, Letter to the Lighthouse Board Records, dated May 1886, Group 26, National Archives, Washington D.C.

[12]Keepers Journal, Light-Station at Cape Canaveral, entry October 10, 1887, Records Group 26, National Archives, Washington D.C.

[13]Mallery, Letter to the Light-House Board, dated October 10, 1887, pg 174, 176, Records Group 26, National Archives, Washington D.C.

[14]Ibid.

[15]Ibid.

[16]Monthly Report, Cape Canaveral Light-Station, dated August 1893, Records Group 26, National Archives, Washington D.C

[17]Mallery, Letter to Lighthouse Board, dated November 29, 1887, pg 226, 228, 232, 234, 236 and 238, Records Group 26, National Archives, Washington D.C.

[18]Ibid.

[19]Ibid.

[20]Ibid.

[21]Ibid.

[22]Ibid.

[23]Ibid.

[24]Ibid.

[25]Ibid.

[26]Ibid.

[27]Ibid.

[28]Engineer Mallery, Letter to the Light-House Board, dated December 7, 1887, page 264 Records Group 26, National Archives, Washington D.C.

[29]Letter, dated December 5, 1887, pg 366, Records Group 26, National Archives, Washington D.C.

[30]Mallery, Letter to Lighthouse Board, dated December 7, 1887, pg 264, Records Group 26, National Archives, Washington D.C.

[31]Mallery, Letter to Lighthouse Board, dated December 8, 1887, Records Group 26, National Archives, Washington D.C.

[32]James N. Gregory, Engineering Secretary, dated Letter to Capt. J.C. Mallery, December 8, 1887, Pg P 228. Records Group 26, National Archives, Washington D.C.

[33]Lighthouse Board, Letter to Capt Mallery, dated December. 31, 1887, Pg marked P 230, Records Group 26, National Archives, Washington D.C.

[34]Record of letters, in Record Group 26 E1 Vol 13, National Archives, Washington D.C.

[35]Ibid.

[36]Ibid.

[37]Letter from Lighthouse Board Secretary to The Light-House Board, December 31, 1887, Pgs 372, 374, Records Group 26, National Archives, Washington D.C.

[38]Mallery, Letter to Lighthouse Board, dated January 23, 1888, Records Group 26, National Archives, Washington D.C.

[39]Ibid.

[40]Abstract for Bids, Pg 384, Records Group 26, National Archives, Washington D.C.

[41]Ibid.

[42]Major Gregory, Typed letter to Capt Mallery, dated January 19, 1888 pg 2, Records Group 26, National Archives, Washington D.C.

[43]Ibid.

[44]Mallery letter to Lighthouse Board, dated January 18, 1888, Records Group 26, pg 362, National Archives, Washington D.C

[45]Letter the Secretary of the Treasury dated February 15, 1893, Records Group 26, Book RG26E31, National Archives, Washington D.C.

[46]Light-House Board, Treasury Department, Form 153, Index Slip, Letter Box No. 980, Pg 540, Records Group 26, National Archives, Washington D.C.

[47]1880 United States Census, Ancestry.com

[48]Clinton Honeywell entry, Journal of Light-house Station at Cape Canaveral, June 24, 1893, Records Group 26, National Archives, Washington D.C.:

[49]Journal of Light-house Station at Cape Canaveral, entry July 3, 1893, Records Group 26, National Archives, Washington D.C.

[50]The Free Dictionary, http://www.thefreedictionary.com/

[51]Letter to the Lighthouse Board, dated April 28, 1906, Records Group 26 E 58, Box 16, National Archives, Washington, D.C.

[52]Raymond Swanson, Descendant of Keeper Clinton Honeywell

[53]WikipediA, the free encyclopedia (accessed April 26, 2009) <http://en.wikipedia.org/wiki/Nancy_Hanks_(passenger_train)>

[54]Star Advocate, Article, Canaveral, July 7, 1893, Library at Titusville, Florida

[55]Star Advocate, Article, Canaveral, Sepember 29, 1893, Library at Titusville, Florida

[56]Rose Wooley, Historian, Titusville, Florida, Interview with Mrs. Oscar Floyd Quarterman, 29 Mar 1971

[57]Picture of tracks at the lighthouse, provided by Mrs. Rose Wooley

[58]Cape Canaveral Lightstation Brevard Co. Fla, DR. No. G-104, Sheet 1 of 3, performed for First Assistant Superintendent T. H. Greg, by W. G. Wallace and approved by H. L. Beck.

[59]Survey of Cape Canaveral Lightstation, Brevard Co. Fla.: Township 23 S. Range 38 E., September 1921, Approved March 11, 1922, Book S-1, Pgs 30 - 37

[60]Estimate of cost, Records Group 26, E, 7, National Archives, Washington D.C.

[61]Rutherford B. Hayes Presidential Center, (accessed April 26, 2009)
<http://www.rbhayes.org/hayes/mssfind/274/Berglandwebpage++.htm>

[62]Eric Berglans, USMA 1869, (Accessed April 27, 2009) <http://www.math.usma.edu/people/Rickey/dms/02273-Bergland.htm>

[63]Ibid.

[64]Ibid.

[65]Ibid.

[66]Letter the Secretary of the Treasury dated February 15, 1893, Records Group 26, Book E 31, National Archives, Washington D.C.

[67]Dr. Lori Walters and Mr. Al Hartman, Research in an Unpublished Document for the author

[68]Journal of Light-house Station at Cape Canaveral, entry June 30, 1893, Records Group 26, National Archives, Washington D.C.

[69]Journal of Light-house Station at Cape Canaveral, September 26,1893, Records Group 26, National Archives, Washington D.C.

[70]Inspector Mackerrqie Letter to the Lighthouse Board referencing Notice to Mariners No. 111, Bound in Letter Book No 997, pg 596, Records Group 26, National Archives, Washington D.C.:

[71]Journal of Light-house Station at Cape Canaveral, entry October 19, 1893, Records Group 26, National Archives, Washington D.C.

[72]Journal of Light-house Station at Cape Canaveral, entry October 23, 1893, Records Group 26, National Archives, Washington D.C.

[73]Journal of Light-house Station at Cape Canaveral, entry November 2, 1893, Records Group 26, National Archives, Washington D.C.

[74]Journal of Light-house Station at Cape Canaveral, entry November 6, 1893, Records Group 26, National Archives, Washington D.C.

[75]Journal of Light-house Station at Cape Canaveral, entry November 27, 1893, Records Group 26, National Archives, Washington D.C.

[76]Journal of Light-house Station at Cape Canaveral, entry February 11, 1894, Records Group 26, National Archives, Washington D.C.

[77]ibid, 14 February

[78]Journal of Light-house Station at Cape Canaveral, entry May 4, 1894, Records Group 26, National Archives, Washington D.C.

[79]Journal of Light-house Station at Cape Canaveral, entry May 16, 1894, Records Group 26, National Archives, Washington D.C.

[80]Journal of Light-house Station at Cape Canaveral, entry July 9, 1894, Records Group 26, National Archives, Washington D.C.

[81]Journal of Light-house Station at Cape Canaveral, entry July 25, 1894, Records Group 26, National Archives, Washington D.C.

eeper John L. Stuck, 1st Assistant Clinton P. Honeywell and Acting 2nd Assistant Frank M. Wilson were faced with what could be described as an exciting task, that of starting over and reestablishing a life at the newly relocated lighthouse. Frank Wilson reported for duty on the very day that the lamp was relit, July 25, 1894. Not often does one get to start over with what could be called a new town center and for all practical purposes Keeper John L. Stuck was the Mayor. The lighthouse was the center of just about everything that happened on Cape Canaveral until the 1920s.

All work associated with moving the lighthouse must have been completed on or about November 30, 1894 when Engineer Bergland reports that the "Services of J. R. Mew, Supt. of Construction discontinuance."[1] With his job completed, "J. R. Mew, Superintendent of Construction, boarded the Lighthouse Tender Pharos[2] on the 2nd of October and left for Charleston at 9 o'clock A. M."[3]

The last sailing lighthouse tender to see service was the Pharos. She was originally built as the private schooner H. H. Talman. She was purchased for service on 30 April 1854 and was renamed Pharos. She saw service as a supply tender in the 2nd Lighthouse District, delivering supplies along the east coast. In 1873 she was sent to the 8th Lighthouse District. She was then laid up for sale but that was cancelled and she was instead rebuilt and was assigned to the 5th Lighthouse District. She transferred to the 6th Lighthouse District in 1890. She was declared unseaworthy in 1907 and sold the following year.[4]

So why do we call boats she? One theory is that boats are called she because they are traditionally given female names, typically the name of an important woman in the life of the boat's owner. Although male captains and sailors historically attributed the spirit of a benevolent female figure to their ships, actually women were considered very bad luck at sea.[5]

The little community around the Cape Canaveral Lighthouse was coming together when "A new 1st Assistant Keeper's dwelling was completed on September 5 & 6, 1884 a New L. H. Road cut and xxxxx completed."[6] The Keepers

Picture of Pharos, courtesy U.S. Coast Guard

Journal tells us approximately when another building, the Oil House, was completed with the following September 22, 1894 entry, "Oil was stored in the new oil house."[7] The oil house still stands and has been refurbished with a new roof, door and a general cleaning.

Of all the things needed at the lighthouse was certainly not a door bell; exactly what they got. The Keeper's Journal tells us that on September 28, 1894 a door bell was "put up a

Picture of the Oil House, courtesy, Nancy D Watts

(sic) electric call bell in the new tower"[8] and on October 2 we learn that a "Lampest started up the electric call bell in the tower and got it to work on October 16."[9] Wish we knew how the "electric" bell was powered, batteries, generator or electricity? Today we would call a "Lampest" an electrician.

The people on Cape Canaveral suffered a severe freeze in December of 1894. This would have been the Great Freeze that almost ended citrus as an industry in Florida. Extremely cold temperatures reached as far south as Palm Beach. In Tampa, it dropped to 18 degrees. Fruit simply froze and dropped off trees and covered the ground resulting in farmers losing the year's crop. That freeze surely caused the agriculture industry to diversify.[10] It got really cold on Cape Canaveral, the Keeper's Journal, of December 27, 1894 records that there was a "Heavy frost causing pipes freezing. Thermometer 21 out of doors."[11] The temperature at Titusville dropped to 18 degrees and stayed below freezing for about 24 hours. The Indian River fruit growers lost almost all their fruit.[12] As if December's freeze wasn't enough, just a couple of months later there was another freeze on Cape Canaveral. On February 8, 1895, the keeper writes in the journal, "Heavy frost, Ice on plate glass of the lantern at 5 o'clock A.M."[13]

On January 11, 1895 the "Supply Vessel Armeria, Capt W. Wright landed years supply."[14] Wonder if Alfred B. Wilson, 2nd Assistant Frank Wilson's brother, was on board? Nope, he didn't serve on the Armeria until after 1904. More about Alfred B. Wilson in Chapter 8.

The Armeria was a lighthouse tender built in 1890 at Camden, New Jersey. The

Picture of Armeria, courtesy, Rose Wooley

boat cost just over $178,930.00. Armeria served the Third Light House District out of New York. On March 24, 1898 Armeria was transferred to the U. S. Navy for service in the Spanish American War her commanding officer was LCDR Leavitt Curtis Logan.

Armeria's service in the Navy was short. She made two voyages from the United States to Cuba carrying ammunition. On August 9, 1898 Armeria went to Key West, Florida and two days later was returned to the Lighthouse Service.

The U.S. Lighthouse Service tender Armeria, assigned to Ketchikan, Alaska, ran

Picture of Armeria in 1910 Courtesy the U.S. Coast Guard

aground off Cape Hinchinbrook on 20 May 1912 while delivering supplies for the construction of the Cape Hinchinbrook lighthouse. She was declared a total loss but fortunately there were no casualties.[15]

In 1898, there was a plan to move Florida lighthouses into the age of telecommunications by bringing the telephone to East Coast Florida lighthouses and the Cape Canaveral Lighthouse by "connecting to a point near Oak Hill on the Florida East Coast Line"[16] was proposed. That phone line wouldn't happen for a few years but it would happen.

The telephone was supposed to come to the Cape Canaveral Lighthouse shortly after 1898 when the sum of $50,000,000.00, which equals $1,219,512,195.00 in 2006 dollars,[17] was appropriated for installation of telephone lines, from lighthouse stations within the 6th Lighthouse District to the nearest telegraph station. This money was appropriated for National Defense purposes. A contract was made to connect the Cape Canaveral Lighthouse with the Florida East Coast Railway in the vicinity of Oak Hill, Florida.[18]

According to a letter, dated June 20, 1898, the Corps of Engineers, U.S.A. Engineer Secretary, to Maj. E. H. Ruffner, Engineer, 6th Light-House District, Charleston, S. C. informs the Light House Board that bids had been "forwarded to the Board with your letter for construction of telephone lines in the 6th District."[19] The telephone did come to Georgetown Lighthouse when "the bid of Mr. Laurens Mouzon, of Georgetown, S. C. in the sum of $225 for line No. 1 between Georgetown, S. C., Light Station and Quarantine Station at South Island, S.C. has been accepted..."[20] In that same letter it was announced that; "The bid of Messer's Hunter & Heyward, of Charleston, S. C. in the sum of $2,790."[21] "for line No. 2, between Cape Canaveral Light-Station, Fla. and Florida East Coast Railway in the vicinity of Oak Hill, Fla., has been accepted..."[22] $2,790.00 would be about $60,652.17 in 2006 dollars; pretty good money in those days. Hunter and Heyward

Picture of Clinton Honeywell, courtesy, Yvonne Thornton

did not perform, which is bad - cannot find a record of them having been paid, which could be good.

By June 23, 1899 the phone line for the Cape Canaveral Lighthouse had not been completed and the contractors Messrs. Hunter and Heyward, of Charleston, S. C. were sent a notice to return all parts and material to the government. The contractors didn't return the materials. The materials had to be reclaimed at government expense, which was $190.24.[23] A law suit was then filed against Mr. R. G. O'Neil. Mr. O'Neil was the bondsman who guaranteed the contract that was awarded to Hunter and Heyward. After more than 25 letters between the Lighthouse Board, the U. S. Attorney of South Carolina, and Mr. O'Neil, an offer of compromise was accepted from Mr. O'Neil in the sum of One Hundred Dollars. The suit wasn't settled until 1902.[24] Well, that took long enough. The telephone did eventually make it to the Cape in 1917.

Changes in keepers happened in 1904[25] when Keeper John Stuck resigned

Picture of Cistern taken by the author

on September 30, 1904 and Clinton P. Honeywell was promoted to Keeper on November 4, 1904.

Another improvement, pressure water, was about to come to the lighthouse. In April of 1906, the Light-House Board sent G. P. Howell, the 6th District Engineer a letter authorizing "an Artesian well sunk at the Cape Canaveral Light-Station at a total estimated cost of $700.00"[26] about $15,909.09 in 2006 dollars. The only water supply at the lighthouse was from a cistern built under each of the keepers dwellings.

A cistern is simply a container that holds a liquid, usually water. The cistern dates back to about 840 BC.

An artesian well allows water to rise to the surface that has traveled through porous rock from a higher elevation. This pumpless well seems to defy gravity because the pressure that builds up between layers of rock gets relieved when the water finds a path to the open air. For nearly a thousand years, people have drilled wells to drink such cold, filtered water that doesn't need to be hauled up from the depths.[27]

The three cisterns, if full, would supply approximately 14,000 gallons of water via pitcher pumps. There was a 4,000 gallon cistern under both the Keeper's and the 1st Assistant's dwellings, and a 6,000 gallon cistern under the 2nd Assistant Keeper's dwelling.[28] These cisterns were deigned to catch rainwater and provide drinking/fresh water inside the dwelling and not intended for fire-fighting. A well was requested to provide water needed for fire-fighting because the cisterns just did not provide enough water.

The final approval for the well came in a letter from the Light-House Board in November 1906 stating that "The bid of Mr. Alex Near, of Eau Gallie, Fla, at the price stated therein, $625.00, has been accepted, and the Board authorizes you to employ the person named to perform the work specified without formal contract."[29] Notice that it took seven months to get the well approved. Good thing they didn't need a formal contract. Getting it in a contract could have taken another year.

The well had a four inch casing, was 328 feet deep and would provide pressure water for fire fighting and eventually provided low pressure water into the dwellings.[30] Drainage from the indoor plumbing was routed to a cesspool which was eventually replaced by a septic tank.[31] How 'bout that? Indoor plumbing! Moving into the big time. All that was needed now is that telephone.

Things were about to get interesting at the lighthouse. John Belton Butler was appointed 2nd Assistant Keeper for the Cape Canaveral Lighthouse on June 17, 1909 replacing Thomas Knight. Keeper Butler and his wife Mamie Wilhelmina Witzel were married in 1902. They raised six children mostly at the Cape Canaveral and the Ponce de Leon Lighthouses. They were: John B. 1904; Myrtle V. 1906; Charles W. 1902; Grace E. 1909; James H. 1911; William E. 1913. See Pictures of the Cape for their group picture. One son, Harold Wetzel Butler was born June 8th 1914. He passed away August 13, 1914 and is buried in the Burnham Cemetery on Cape Canaveral.[32] Although Butler did not get along with Keeper Clinton Honeywell, they would work together for twelve years.

The 2nd Assistant Keeper's dwelling was just too small and Captain Butler needed more room. Keeper Honeywell contacted the 6th Light-House District Engineer requesting expansion of the 2nd Assistant Keeper's dwelling. In an April 3, 1909 letter to the Light-House Board, the Engineer provided his rational for the work: "the dwelling in which 2nd Asst. Keeper is quartered consists of two rooms only. That 2nd Asst. Keeper's family consists of himself, wife and two babies. One room is utilized as a bed room; the other as a kitchen and dining room. I request authority to construct an "addition to be 15' X 20'; to be utilized as a kitchen and dining room: permitting to two rooms of the present structure to be utilized as bed rooms. The cost will be $1500.00; payment

Picture of Grave Stone taken by Author

Picture of John B. Butler & Wife, courtesy Ponce de Leon Inlet Lighthouse Preservation Association

to be made from Appropriation Repairs & Incidental Expenses."[33] The lumber and materials "1 lot of Moulding, (sic) sash, doors, lead, brick, cement, lumber, and shingles"[34] for the upgrade to the dwelling was purchased from the East Coast Lumber Co. of Cocoa, Florida for $355.50.[35] The $355.50 equates to 7,900.00 in 2006 dollars.

The East Coast Lumber buildings were facing Willard Street, which today is the west-bound lane of Highway 520 in Cocoa. The lumberyard

Picture of East Coast Lumber Company, courtesy, Brevard Historical Commission

office was a single-story square topped building set just in front of a two story steep roofed building. The two story building over the years served as the police station and a firehouse and no longer exists. G. F. Paddison was one of the original founders of the company back in 1902.

The truce between Keeper and Assistant Butler lasted about five years. In 1914, Honeywell sent a list of problems that he had with Butler to H. D. King, the Assistant Superintendent of the Sixth Lighthouse District in Charleston. Among other things, Honeywell accused Butler of not working in harmony, of ignoring Honeywell's instructions, of not keeping his quarters clean, and of trying to bring goats onto the reservation to add to his herd of cows and pigs. Honeywell felt Butler had prevented the station from receiving a commendation that would have given it the "Inspector's Star." However, Honeywell did not feel Butler deserved to be dismissed from the service but only transferred to another station.

To promote efficiency and friendly rivalry among lighthouse keepers, a system of efficiency stars and pennants was established during Fiscal Year 1912. "Keepers who have been commended for efficiency at each quarterly inspection during the year are entitled to wear the inspector's star for the next year, and those who receive the inspector's star for three successive years will be entitled to wear the Commissioner's star. The efficiency pennant, being the regular lighthouse pennant, is awarded to the station in each district showing the highest efficiency for a year, and may be flown during the succeeding year."[37]

The District Office, however, investigated the case and felt that Butler should remain at Canaveral and that the two keepers should just try harder to get along. Apparently, the keepers did just that, for inspectors a year later reported that the relationship between the two keepers was harmonious. Although problems would continue to occasionally flare between the keepers at this very isolated station, the two men would end up working together for twelve years. During his service at Cape Canaveral, Butler received several commendations for services in saving shipwrecked people.[38]

The Butlers were very concerned about the education of their six kids and hired a teacher. Although there is some disagreement, Miss Elizabeth F. Evrard would be the second teacher to teach at Cape Canaveral Lighthouse.

In 1922, Butler hired Miss Elizabeth F. Evrard to tutor the children. According to regulations, the Federal Government would

Picture of the children and teacher, courtesy, Ponce de Leon Inlet Lighthouse Preservation Association

reimburse keepers for the subsistence that was provided to schoolteachers. However, one day when Keeper Honeywell was driving Miss Evrard to the town of Cape Canaveral, Miss Evrard told Honeywell that the Butlers were charging her $10 per month for her subsistence. Honeywell thought that Butler must have been charging the schoolteacher illegally for rent for a room which was government property and encouraged her to report Butler to the District Office. Her letter got Butler into a lot of trouble in the form of an official investigation. Butler claimed that he had informed the teacher that the government would provide him with 45 cents per day ($23.50 per month) towards her subsistence (room and board). Miss Evrard, Butler claimed, had decided she wanted better meals and had offered to pay Mrs. Butler $10 per month to provide her with more substantial meals. The arrangement had been made strictly between Miss Evrard and Mrs. Butler and had been done willingly on the part of Miss Evrard. However, after eight months of questions and interrogation into the matter, Superintendent Henry L. Beck finally decided that Butler had been guilty of irregular conduct, and recommended that Butler be reprimanded by the Department and transferred to Jupiter Light Station, where, in the words of Beck, School facilities are perhaps the best in the 6th District.[39]

Butler was eventually transferred to Ponce de Leon Inlet Light in July 1923.

It was inevitable that the Lighthouse wouldn't stay the center of focus and became obvious with the arrival of Samuel L. Jeffords. Mr. Jeffords was a business man whose first project was

Picture of Samuel L. Jeffords
Courtesy John Whitney, Descendant

to attempt to establish a fish fertilizer plant at Cape Canaveral in the very early 1900s. He must have been fairly well connected politically. He apparently contacted Senator James P. Taliaferro, a Democrat from Jacksonville, requesting the Senator's assistance in getting the use of ten acres of lighthouse reservation land. Senator Taliaferro responded with a June 8, 1906 letter to Victor H. Metcalf, Secretary of Commerce and Labor with:

Hon. Victor I. Metcalf

My dear Sir:

I am sending herewith a letter from Mr. Samuel L. Jeffords, of Canaveral, Florida, in which he expresses a desire to obtain revokable (Sic) license for ten acres of land in the light-house reservation at Cape Canaveral, Florida.

I shall appreciate it if you will give the matter consideration and let me know if it would be practicable to grant the license requested.

Very truly yours,

Jas. P. Taliaferro [40]

Victor Howard Metcalf was appointed United States Secretary of Commerce and Labor by

Picture of Taliaferro,
courtesy, Florida Memory Project, Florida State Archives

Picture of Victor Howard Metcalf,
courtesy, National Archives

President Theodore Roosevelt, serving until December 12, 1906, when he became United States Secretary of the Navy.[41]

The Secretary responded to the Senator on June 13, 1906 stating that the matter had been referred to the Lighthouse Board. He went on to tell the Senator that the Board had reported that it was customary, when issuing a revocable, the Secretary spelled it correctly, license, for such a large area to "invite proposals by public advertisement, with the award going to the highest bidder."[42] Now, ten acres is really not a large tract of land. You think the Secretary is being a bit mean to the Senator for getting his name wrong? The Senator addressed the letter to Victor I when it should have been Victor H. Metcalf. The following is part of the letter, referring to advertisement of the request and is presented as written:

It would hardly seem necessary to take this step in the present instance, for the reason that the applicant for the revocable license, according to his own statement, proposes to establish what might be regarded as more or less a nuisance: to-wit, a fish fertilizer plant, which is always accompanied by a more or less disagreeable odor, and this near present landing used in connection with the Cape Canaveral light station, and not so far from the lighthouse itself and not to make its presence felt under favorable conditions.

In view of this report of the Lighthouse Board this Department states that it is not deemed best to lease any portion of this lighthouse reservation for the purpose in question.

Victor H. Metcalf[43]

Picture of Fletcher
Courtesy U.S. Senate Historical Office

The turn down for the fertilizer plant didn't stop Mr. Jeffords. He let only a few years go by before he again tried to get a license for lighthouse reservation land. This time he applies for 20 acres offers the use of his wharf and enlists the help of U.S. Senator Duncan A. Fletcher. Senator Fletcher wrote a December 31, 1909 letter to Rear Admiral Adolph Marix, Chairman of the Light-House Board. Admiral Marix served in the US Navy during the Spanish American war and served on the battleship USS Maine.[44] The 20 acres was to be fenced and used for pasture purposes a map of the area requested was included with the letter. See map in appendix II.

The Senator reminds the Admiral that Mr. Jeffords "allows the government to use his privately owned pier without charge."[45] In his request he also reminds the Light-House Board that the government wharf is not usable and condemned. The Senator makes certain that the Admiral knows that "no building, or other improvements are to be made on the 20 acres."[46] The last sentence was probably because of a legal action known as adverse possession, which basically would give the user ownership of the land after a certain period of time when improvements are made unless there was a deal or the owner

Picture of Jefford's Place at his pier, courtesy, John Whitney

complained.

In March of 1910, the Lighthouse Board sent a letter including a hand-written letter and the map provided to the Sixth Light-House District Engineer directing him "to make a joint report and recommendation of the subject, as soon as practicable."[47] It didn't take long to get a response - less than two weeks. On April 11, 1910, the Joint report was rendered, "we recommend that a revocable license be issued to Mr. Jeffords." The recommendation is signed by the Inspector and the Engineer of the Sixth Light-House district.[48] You think Senator Fletcher had anything to do with the quick decision? Bet they never studied the request or the maps?

The April 11th letter elicited a hand-written response from someone with the initials HBB. HBB was familiar with the Jeffords requests and must have studied this request and the accompanying map. HBB writes:

Picture of J. J. Jeffords,
courtesy, John Whitney, Descendant

I respectfully ask attention to the fact that the size and location of the tract as described by him on the back of the map accompanying his letter of Mar 22/10, contains 23 acres not 20, and lies straight across lot 5 and into lot 4, and over the boardwalk or roadway from the light station, as shown in pencil lines on the map. Apparently everyone going to and from the LH will have to pass thru 2 gates of Jeffords enclosure & what ever stock is within for pastorage.[49]

Pastorage?? That's probably not a word. HBB finished the Memo with: "It would be better to repair our own wharf rather than make the arrangement recommended"[50] It's pretty obvious that this person objected and equally obvious that HBB was ignored.

Before we leave Mr. Jeffords it must be pointed out that the Julius J. Jeffords who was appointed Second Assistant Keeper on December 17, 1929[51] was Samuel Jeffords' son. More on Jeffords family in the Chapter, Cape Canaveral - It's People.

The keeper on duty never knows what might happen during his or her watch, a quiet non-eventful watch or explosions on board boats. Well...an explosion on board a boat is almost always a disaster. The evening of January 5, 1913 was no exception when the Huntress anchored only a few miles just north of Cape Canaveral. Early the next morning, a fire and explosion below decks threw three people overboard. A cook, steward and deck hand, Harry Osman. The trio were asleep on the fore deck when the explosion happened. Only the body of Harry Osman was found. The children of Lighthouse Keeper Clinton

Picture of the Albert Sopher Crew, courtesy, Ponce de Leon Historical Preservation Association

Honeywell found his body on the beach somewhere near Stinkmore.

The owners of the Huntress were William and Henrietta Chesebrough of the Chesebrough-Ponds family. According to an affidavit dated Tuesday January 7, 1913; We find:

I Reinold Ekshom, Master of the Yacht Huntress, hereby certifies that Harry Osman, a sailor of aforesaid vessel was acciedently (sic) drowned by been (sic) blown overboard by the explosion and fire occuring (sic) Monday morning at halve past four Jan 6th 1913 on said vessel, when about twelve miles N E of Cape Canaveral.

The body of said Harry Osman has this day been buried here on Cape Canaveral in presence (sic) of the following witnesses who also were present at the drowning of said Harry Osman.

Signed by
William Loden C.E.;
Edward Larson A.B.;
XXman Y. Brimmenas A.B;

Witnesses to signatures
Samuel L. Jeffords;
Clinton P. Honeywell,
Keeper of the LightHouse [52]

Three people died in that accident, Harry Osman, a cook, and a steward. For a bit more about the Huntress, see the Chapter: Cape Canaveral - Factoids, Information and Stuff that Happened.

Shortly after the Huntress sank, Albert the cat showed up at the Lighthouse. The good ship Albert Sopher struck the cape and jettisoned some lumber and a cat. The crew made their way to the lighthouse for help. Florence Honeywell tells us that (summarized); some men, they would be Captain Pappas and the crew of the Albert Sopher, came off the beach and through the woods down to the lighthouse. Clinton Honeywell put the men up in the storehouse for the night and the next morning Mrs. Honeywell cooked oatmeal for about 10-15 people. A crew member had with him a big white cat that had a yellow tail and yellow on his head - the classic markings of the Turkish Van.[53] He gave the cat to Gertrude, sister of Florence Honeywell. The cat was named after the boat - Albert Sopher. The cat now had a home at the lighthouse.[54] Albert lived at the Cape Canaveral Lighthouse with the lighthouse keeper's family. Gertrude Honeywell took care of and played with Albert.

Albert's original cat family came from the Lake Van region of Turkey. The Turkish Van is an ancient breed from the Middle

Picture of Albert the Cat,
courtesy, Yvonne Thornton

East, kept as domestic pets for hundreds of years. The first record of white, semi-long haired cats with ringed tails and color on their heads were carvings on jewelry. (1600-1200 BC). The Turkish Van Cat is called the "swimming cat" because they swam and caught fish in the shallow streams and in Lake Van. Lake Van is the largest lake in Turkey.[55]

How about that? A Turkish Van Cat on Cape Canaveral in 1913 when they weren't recognized as a breed until about 1954.

According to the Cocoa Tribune, a front page article entitled, Canaveral Peninsula Now Has Phone Line to Mainland, tells us that "Work is being rushed, Tuesday marked completion of the circuit to Lighthouse." The article goes on: "Tuesday evening Cocoa wall? called up and the other end of the line proved to be Canaveral Light Station, finally enclosed in the Atlantic Telephone circuit that now girdles the southeast coast of Florida, connecting with the main line by way of Chester Shoals House of Refuge to Titusville."[56] Well that only took long enough.

New era, how about this for seeing the future? The Cocoa Tribune had an article "Resolutions of Needed Inlets in Brevard County" on April 5, 1917. Notice that it refers to inlet not harbor. Oops "The people of Brevard County by their votes on Tuesday last, put to rest the matter of an inlet construction under the so-called Rhodes Inlet Act."[57] The inlet, Port Canaveral, had to wait some 30 more years.

The Cape Canaveral bight has always been a natural harbor, and as early as 1917 development, of the harbor, was getting high level attention. A headline in The Cocoa Tribune states "Secretary of War Orders a preliminary (sic) survey Harbor. ...This is good news--big news--to people interested in that section of Brevard County, some of whom have been waiting to hear it for many years."[58] The "Order for the Harbor was reported in associated press dispatches early in the week along with news of river and harbor appropriations for other parts of Florida. No time was set for operations to begin..."[59] The article goes on: "A recent order of the government issued this spring that-the-entire government reservation in the vicinity of Canaveral light-house be put under cultivation, looking

Picture of Canaveral Harbor sign, courtesy, Florida Historical Society

to the increase of food supplies..."[60] World War I was still going strong and the government was looking at all options and possibilities.

Between 1920 and 1949 a number of changes, mostly economic, occurred that would impact Cape Canaveral including the development of a number of commercial operations and residential subdivisions. Although Brevard County was considered to be the fastest growing county in Florida, Cape Canaveral's population fluctuated from a low of 91 in 1920 to a high of 148 in 1930.[61] The number of people living on the Cape remained at less than 150 prior to the government acquisition in the 1940s.[62]

By the 1920s, Cape Canaveral appeared to be growing with the arrival of Captain Charles Lansing. Lansing was former New York newspaper publisher and a retired Army Captain. In "1925 Capt Lansing, the owner and developer of Canaveral Beach Park, truly opened Cape Canaveral to settlement as a seaside bungalow colony without frills... Canaveral Beach Park already has running water, electric lights, telephone connection, a store and filling station"[63] and the lighthouse was no longer the center of commerce. The paper goes on the say: "The observer here feels that soon this entire country will be thickly populated by people moving in from the north and other sections."[64]

Picture of Charles Lansing, courtesy Ponce de Leon Inlet Lighthouse Preservation Association

Almost every year people in Central Florida talk about a rail line from the Port to Orlando, an old and long running discussion. According to The Cocoa Tribune, "A charter was issued by the State of Florida about a year ago (1924) to the Orlando-Canaveral Harbor Railroad Company. This charter permits the crossing of the tracks of the East Coast Railway and is in Perpetuity."[65] In perpetuity, means forever. "Mr. J. F. Ange, president of the company, visited Canaveral Harbor and looked over various sites that are under consideration for the terminal."[66]

Exactly what Cape Canaveral needed - A Hotel? In April of 1928, the Canaveral Harbor Corporation started construction of a hotel. The hotel "was to be a 10 room structure but by December 1928 it had grown into a two story, twenty one room hotel, the Canaveral Inn. The hotel included two 10-foot glass enclosed porches, a barber shop, post office, dining room, and a ball room. The cost is reported to be $25,000. Mr. George Burgess leased the hotel and officially

Picture of early Canaveral Beach Home, courtesy Advertisement by Apollo Land Company

opened for business December 31, 1929 with a party on New Years Eve with 200 attendees. A local orchestra, the Merry Makers, which has been playing at dances in the county for several weeks, was to furnish the music."[67] The final name of the Hotel was the Harbor Inn.

Just a few months after hotel construction started, work began on a 315 foot boat landing pier and breakwater at Canaveral Harbor, in August of 1928 on the property owned by Mr. Henry Ewing of Chicago. The pier being constructed by W. D. Joyner was intended for use by the boats of Johnson & Sons Fish Company. The pier was located approximately 300 feet north of the Canaveral Harbor Inn. It extended into the bight to water depths of 15 feet.

Picture of Harbor Inn, courtesy, Rose Wooley

The pier was to be 12 feet wide and with a T-head of 40 by 50 feet with a warehouse for packing fish and shrimp. Some 75 to 150 fishing boats were expected to operate out of the harbor by the first winter of operation. The pier was open to full operation on or about October 15, 1928 and work started on a 100 foot V-shaped breakwater which will provide protection for boats while loading and unloading at the pier.[68] By October 1929 the fishing pier was getting an upgrade: it was reported that "Henry Ewing is building four cottages at Canaveral, to take care of deep sea fishermen. The four buildings are to be used by the men who work in the fishing vessels and at the dock."[69]

Picture of Pier, courtesy, Ponce de Leon Inlet Lighthouse Preservation Association

Mr. Glenn Shockey, a former resident, provides verification of the pier and its location in a map showing a generator house near the road on the left (shown in the picture of the pier) as one turns into the road leading to the pier. He shows two rows of one room sleeping quarters on the right side of the road, supported by the picture. The map also indicates that several four-room houses were set back from the generator building and are also shown in the picture. The road was a Tar and Grit W.P.A. Project.[70] Glenn Shockey is the grandson of Thomas and Addie Hardin.

Mr. Shockey also provides a very accurate description of the pier: "the pier is out in the ocean approx. 150 yds long 14 ft wide constructed of creosote pilings heavily cross braced 2 x 12 plank surface."[71] This description compares favorably with the description provided by the Cocoa Tribune. See Mr. Shockey's map in Appendix III.

The pier must have been an interesting place to go and have a meal at Reba's Restaurant or Reba's Place. Reba Nelson and Al Praetorious were the operators. According to Shockey's hand-drawn map, the two story building (shown in the picture of the pier) at the pier housed a restaurant and kitchen, bed rooms upstairs, and dance hall with a jukebox.[72] Reba Nelson had two children,

Barbara and Leo. She married Al Praetorius and together they operated the establishment until the area was closed.[73]

Construction at Cape Canaveral was in full swing by 1929. The Cocoa Tribune reported on April 19th that "a new building was being built by Dr. Whidden and his sister Miss Lena Whidden. When finished the building will be occupied by a drug store and a grocery store to be operated by the owners. The building, Whidden's Store was to be 26 feet by 54 feet",[74] about 1400 square feet and "occupied a location on Ocean Drive."[75] Today we know Ocean Drive as Pier Road. "Whidden's Store was to cost between $4,000 and $5,000 dollars"[76] about $58,000.00 in 2006 dollars. "This is to be a general store carrying a variety of merchandise. The building is to be of stucco finish on the outside while the interior will be conveniently arranged to meet the needs of a store of this kind. Miss Lena Whidden was the manager

Picture of Grace Schokey, Reba Nelson, and Betty, Reba's Daughter, courtesy Darlene Kosko

of the Canaveral branch of the Wholesale Drug Corp. of Pensacola."[77]

Picture of Al Praetorious, courtesy Rose Wooley

A new First Assistant Keeper, Arthur Franklin Hodges transferred from the Ponce de Leon Lighthouse where he served from February 4, 1920. He left on January 30, 1930 and arrived at Cape Canaveral at least by June 1, 1930. Along with Assistant keeper Hodges came his wife Wilma, daughter six year old Myrtle V.; sons three year old Rufus W.; and two and a half year old Crawford L. Hodges. Arthur and Wilma were both born in South Carolina and were married in 1919 when she was just 16 and he was 27.[78]

According to Neil Hurley's, Keepers of Florida Lighthouses, Quincy Edward Atkinson was appointed Second Assistant Keeper at the Cape Canaveral Lighthouse on April 15, 1925.[79] Very little is known about Quincy Edward Atkinson. Records show that he was born January 21, 1895 in North Carolina and passed away September 15, 1963 in Brunswick, North Carolina.[80]

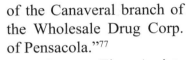

Picture of Whidden's Store, courtesy, Rose Wooley

The 1930 United States Census records Atkinson at "Canaveral, Brevard, Florida as a head of house"[81] with no Household members identified. He records, on the death certificate of his stillborn son, his birthplace as Supply, North Carolina. His wife's maiden name is recorded as Bernice Booker, of Decatur, Alabama.[82] They may have married between 1930 and 1932.

The Atkinson's baby boy was stillborn on June 16, 1933 in the Melbourne, Florida Hospital, and according to a memorandum signed by Ernest I. Jandreau, "This child is buried on the south side of the Jandreau family plot in the Cape Canaveral

Community Cemetery." A white cross marks his grave.

Atkinson may have been "employed as a teacher in Lockwoods, Folly Township in Brunswick Co., N.C."[83] before coming to Cape Canaveral. On June 22, 1933, the Cocoa Tribune published the following: "Friends of Mrs. Quincy Atkinson, of the lighthouse, who has been seriously ill in the

Picture of Keeper Hodges, courtesy Ponce de Leon Preservation Association

Picture of Baby Atkinson grave marker, taken by author

Melbourne Hospital, will be glad to learn that Mrs. Atkinson is much improved and on the road to recovery."[84] It could very well be that she was in the hospital because of the stillbirth of her baby. Assistant Keeper Atkinson was transferred to the Jupiter Light in 1935.[85]

Keeper Honeywell must have gotten himself a car after the mule died. The Cocoa Tribune reported that "a three-car garage is being erected at the Canaveral lighthouse by the U.S. Government for Captain Honeywell. W. A. Norsworthy, of Canaveral, has the contract and hopes to have the building finished in a short time."[86] The papers go on to tell us "...the only garage had by Captain Honeywell was the old stable erected for the lighthouse tender."[87]

Picture of Garage, courtesy, Ponce de Leon Inlet Lighthouse Preservation Association

Little is known about the Norsworthy's. From the Cocoa Tribune:

William A. Norsworthy, age 80; died at home on Monday after a long illness. He was a native of Greenville, Alabama. He was a retired cabinet maker. Rev. T. A. Hayes, Pastor of the Seventh Day Adventist Church performed services. Interment was a Pinecrest Cemetery.

Mr. Norsworthy came to this area about 22 years ago and first lived at Canaveral. Later moved to Cocoa.

Surviving are his wife, Mrs. Mary Ellen Norsworthy of Cocoa, five sons: George and Ralph, Miami; Brooks, Arthur and Jared, Cocoa. One stepson, W. B. Lewis of Canaveral; one daughter Willie May of Columbus Georgia.

His occupation is listed as Carpenter.[88] The 1935 Florida State Census has a W. A. Norsworthy and wife Mary living in Rockledge. His employment is listed as an upholsterer and records indicated that he had a college degree.[89]

The following announcement is found in The Cocoa Tribune: "T.A. McKee, radio expert, is at the Lighthouse this week."[90] Now we know about when, August 17, 1933; the lighthouse had radio and weather equipment installed on the third level. Although the lighthouse was designed to be lived in, it was never used as a residence. The third level of the lighthouse was designed to be the living room. The second level was to be used as a kitchen and a bedroom and the forth level to be used as a very small bedroom. Although the keeper or possibly a guest may have spent some nights in the lighthouse it was never used regularly.

The Fresnel lens got electrified in 1931. The Keepers Journal of April 1931 has the following entry: "The Electric light was put in Lens for regular operation on April 11th - 1931 at 6:45 PM."[91] The light was originally fired using whale oil that was replaced by kerosene and then the electric light bulb.

Picture of electric light bulb in Fresnel lens, courtesy, Ponce de Leon Inlet Restoration Association

One of the remaining questions (mystery) that needs to be solved here is; when did the door at the bottom of the lighthouse get cut in? The door was not part of the original design. Electrification came to the lighthouse in 1931 for sure when the lamp was converted from fuel oil to electricity.

A review of a picture of Clinton Honeywell astride a 1916 Harley shows us proof that the door was not there in about 1919. Another picture taken in the mid 1920s, is one of Capt Charles Lansing, who came to the Cape in about 1924, at the lighthouse shows no door at the bottom of the Lighthouse. See both pictures in Pictures from Cape Canaveral.

On "May 24, 1924 two 750 gallon kerosene storage tanks were installed in the oil house, H. L. Beck approved Drawing number C-120"[92] setting the stage for electrification of the lamp.

A notation in the Keeper's Journal March 29, 1931 tells that a generator may have been installed in the lighthouse, "painted in engine" April 7, 1931. By the time of the electrifying of the lamp, April 11, 1931, a generator or generators must have been installed, in an engine room, on the first floor of the lighthouse. Based on this we can draw the conclusion that the door was cut in between 1924 and 1931. A review of U.S. Coast Guard Drawing Number B-132 Sheet 1[93] of 1, entitled Eng. Gen. 1 & 2, tells us that the door and generators were approved February 4, 1930.[94] Well that mystery is solved; the door was cut-in between 1924 and 1930.

By 1933, business at the Cape appears to have been booming and apparently the community was growing. In February "T. L. Broughton, former resident of Cocoa, but now a resident of New York City, has let a contract to Ivan Crowder, of Canaveral for improvement of the Canaveral Harbor Hotel, which Broughton owns. The improvements include a new roof, walls and ceilings of the hotel redecorated and the woodwork of the exterior and interior repainted."[95] Now that sounds like the hotel was getting a major face lift and the hotel was being "operated under the management of Mr. and Mrs. John Spies."[96] And, there was a booming business at the hotel: The Cocoa Tribune reported on October 19, 1933 that "The Harbor Hotel was filled to capacity with guests over the weekend."[97]

Picture of Pier, courtesy,
Ponce de Leon Inlet Restoration Association

By October, things were really looking up at the Cape. A second fishing/seafood operation may have been established north of the Canaveral Pier closer to the location of current day Camera Road A. Notice this operation was established "at the Point"[98] which would be well north of the Hotel and its Fishing Pier. Could this place be eventually called Stinkmore or Stink Town? "Dr. G. A. Ciccone and son, who are operating the Canaveral Sea Products Co. at the point and Mr. and Mrs. R. H. Welsh have taken the Jeffords' place for their home. Mr. Welsh is superintendent for the Industry."[99] Yep! We can conclude that, this small operation would eventually be called stink-more or stink-town. The Jeffords' place was located just south of the Cape and south of what is now called Camera Road A.

You know you have made the big time when your community builds a golf course. Apparently that was happening at Cape Canaveral in 1933. From the Cocoa Tribune: "The Canaveral Ocean Golf course is about completed. It is nine holes, covers nineteen hundred yards, and a par game of eighteen holes is estimated at sixty. The course is free to those desiring to use it."[100] How about that a golf course at the Cape? See Factoids, Information and Stuff that Happened for a bit more.

Cape Canaveral received major attention in December 1933, when The Cocoa Tribune reported that "Money was allocated for exploration of secrets of Mounds by Smithsonian Man, Mr. M. W. Starling."[101] From the Cocoa Tribune: "The secrets held in the Indian Mounds of the Canaveral Peninsula in the vicinity of Artesia will be unearthed by representatives of the Smithsonian Institute with the aid of labor furnished by the Civil Works Administration, it has been announced from Washington and Tallahassee."[102]

The CWA was established as a works program during the Great Depression. The Civil Works Administration was established by the New Deal during the depression. Harry Hopkins was put in charge of the organization. President F. D. Roosevelt introduced the program November 8, 1933.[103] The Tribune continues:

Authorization of the use of money for exploring the secrets of the mounds in Brevard County and some in Manatee and Palm Beach counties was made by Harry Hopkins who designated it as federal project.

F. H. McFarland, Brevard County Civil Works administrator, has been authorized to furnish 100 laborers, 10 skilled laborers and four technical men to dig into the mounds. M. W. Starling, representing the Smithsonian Institute for Washington, will select the mounds to be investigated and will direct the work.

Mounds on the peninsula from time to time have been dug into by private individuals, who have taken out skulls and bones of an Indian race unknown to modern civilization. Pottery and stone weapons and household articles have been taken from them. The window of R. M Packards's Transfer has a display of some of the articles taken from the mounds.[104]

According the Keepers Journal, "Keeper O. F. Quarteman retired on Saturday, Jul 1, 1939."[105] The next day we find the following entry: "Additional Keeper Mr. L. G. Owens arrived at sta 1130 AM to assume charge, and all responsibility of Sta."[106]

It appears that the Coast Guard actually took charge of the lighthouse on July 3, 1939 when "L. G. Owens changed over all property and signed for same. Mr. T. L. Willice (sic) [Willis] was retired from duty."[107] From the same Journal we have verification that the telephone did come to the lighthouse. A July 11, 1939, Keepers Journal entry reads "...routine duty, and paid the Telephone bill..."[108]

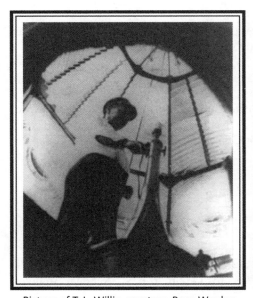

Picture of T. L. Willis, courtesy, Rose Wooley

Picture of Oscar F. Quarterman, courtesy, Florida Memory Project, Florida State Archives

[1] Engineer Bergland, Report to Light-House Board, Treasury Department, Form 153, Index Slip, Letter Box No. 1056, Page 106, Records Group 26, National Archives, Washington D.C.

[2] United States Coast Guard History, (accessed January 27, 2007) <http://www.uscg.mil/history/WEBCUTTERS/Pahros_1854.html>

[3] Journal of Light-house Station at Cape Canaveral, entry October 2, 1894, Records Group 26, National Archives, Washington D.C.

[4] United States Coast Guard History, (accessed January 27, 2007) <http://www.uscg.mil/history/WEBCUTTERS/Pahros_1854.html>

[5] Wisegeek, (accessed May 14, 2008) <http://www.wisegeek.com/why-are-boats-called-she.htm>

[6] Journal of Light-house Station at Cape Canaveral, entry September 28, 1894, Records Group 26, National Archives, Washington D.C.

[7] Ibid.

[8] Ibid.

[9] Journal of Light-house Station at Cape Canaveral, entry October 2, 1894, Records Group 26, National Archives, Washington D.C.

[10] My Florida History, Adventure with history and culture in the Sunshine State, (accessed 21 May 2007)<http://my-floridahistory.blogspot.com/2008/01/its-cold-outside.html>

[11] Journal of Light-house Station at Cape Canaveral, entry October 2, 1894, Records Group 26, National Archives, Washington D.C.

[12] Historical Society of North Brevard, Inc, (accessed 20 July 2008) <http://www.nbbd.com/godo/history/NBrevHist/index.html>

[13] Journal of Light-house Station at Cape Canaveral, entry Feb 8, 1895, Records Group 26, National Archives, Washington D.C.

[14] Journal of Light-house Station at Cape Canaveral, entry Jan 11, 1895, Records Group 26, National Archives, Washington D.C.

[15] United States Coast Guard, History, (accessed 21 February 2009) http://www.uscg.mil/history/articles/arcticphotogallery.asp

[16] Light-House Board, Treasury Department, Form 153, Index Slip, Letter Box No. 1257, Pages 12, 56, 58 and Letter Box 1272, Page 912, Records Group 26, National Archives, Washington D.C.

[17] Robert C. Sahr, Political Science Department, Oregon State University, Consumer Price Index Conversion Factors 1774 to estimated 2019 to convert to 2006, (accessed 26 August 2008) <http://oregonstate.edu/polisci/faculty-research/sahr/cv2006.pdf >

[18] Department of Commerce and Labor, Letter to the Light House board, dated July 22, 1907 and signed by the Inspector 6th L.H. District and the Engineer 6th L.H. District, Records Group 26, National Archives, Washington D.C.

[19] Engineering Secretary Letter to E. H. Ruffner to the Lighthouse Board, dated June 20, 1898, Records Group 26, National Archives, Washington D.C.

[20] Ibid.

[21] Ibid.

[22] Ibid.

[23] Treasury Department, Light-House Board. Form No. 220 1049 record of correspondence, Apr 3, 1902, Records Group 26, National Archives, Washington D.C.

[24] Ibid.

[25] Letter from Launeuce O. Murray, Acting Secretary of the Department of Commerce and Labor to The Light-House Board accepting resignation of Keeper Stuck, dated 1 October 1904, Records Group 26 E 31, National Archives, Washington D. C.

[26] Light-House Board to the Engineer, Sixth District, Letter dated November 12, 1906, Records Group 26, National Archives, Washington D.C.

[27] wiseGEEK. <http://www.wisegeek.com/what-is-an-artesian-well.htm> (accessed 26 March 2009)

[28] Drawing # 1056, United States Coast Guard, 7th Naval district, Miami, Fl

[29] Light-House Board, Letter to the Engineer, Sixth District, dated November 12, 1906, Records Group 26, National Archives, Washington D.C.

[30] Repairs to 1st Asst Keepers Dwelling, Plot Plan Drawing 1056, U.S. Coast Guard 7th Naval District, Miami, FL.

[31] Ibid.

[32] Mrs. Rose Wooley, History of Cape Canaveral and The Early Settlers

[33]6th District Engineer to Light-House Board, Letter dated April 3, 1909, Records Group 26, National Archives, Washington D.C.

[34]Purchase Order for repairs dated May 22, 1909, Records Group 26 E48, File 1047, National Archives, Washington D.C.

[35]Ibid.

[36]Short Biography of John Belton Butler, written for Rose Wooley by Tom Taylor, Ponce de Leon Inlet Lighthouse Organization

[37]U.S. Coast Guard History, (accessed February 2, 2009) <http://www.uscg.military.mil/history

[38]Short Biography of John Belton Butler, written for Rose Wooley by Tom Taylor, Ponce de Leon Inlet Lighthouse Organization

[39]Ibid.

[40]Senator Taliaferro, letter, dated June 8, 1906, to Victor I. Metcalf, Secretary of Commerce and Labor, Records Group 26, E 58, Box 17, National Archives, Washington D.C.

[41]WikipediA, the free encyclopedia, (accessed 25 August 2008) <http://en.wikipedia.org/wiki/Victor_H._Metcalf > (accessed 25 August 2008)

[42]Secretary of Navy, Letter, dated June 13, 1906, Records Group 26, E 58, Box 17, National Archives, Washington D.C.

[43]Ibid.

[44]WikipediA, the free encyclopedia, (accessed 25 August 2008) <http://en.wikipedia.org/wiki/Adolph_Marix>

[45]Senator Duncan A. Fletcher Letter to Rear Admiral Adolph Marix, dated December 31, 1909, Records Group 26, E 58 Box 17, National Archives, Washington D.C.

[46]Ibid.

[47]Lighthouse Board Letter to the Sixth District Engineer, dated March 29, 1910, Records Group 26 E 58 Box 17, National Archives, Washington D.C.

[48]Sixth District Engineer Letter recommending Jeffords lease, dated April 11, 1910, Records Group 26, E 58 Box 17, National Archives, Washington D.C

[49]HBB Memo Objecting to Jeffords Lease, dated May 12, 1910, Records Group 26, E 58 Box 17, National Archives, Washington D.C.

[50]Ibid.

[51] Neil Hurley, Keepers of Florida Lighthouses, An Illustrated CD-ROM database, Jeffords is shown as 2nd Assistant at Ponce de Leon Inlet on 24 Feb 1930

[52]Reinold Ekshom, Affidavit; Filed in the County Judges Office, January 7, 1913, B. R. Nelson Ct Judge. County Court House, Titusville, Florida

[53]Turkish Van Cat Club, (accessed May 23, 2004) <www.turkishcancatclub.co.uk/index2.htm>

[54]Roz Foster, A Tribute to Florence Honeywell Patrick, A Reflection in Time of the Good Ole' Days, Bad Days, and Some in-between Days As recalled by Florence Honeywell Patrick, Transcribed April 25, 2002

[55]Turkish Van Cat Club, (accessed May 23, 2004) <www.turkishcancatclub.co.uk/index2.htm>

[56]The Cocoa Tribune, Canaveral Peninsula Now Has Phone Line to Mainland, 1917

[57]The Cocoa Tribune, August 23, 1917

[58]The Cocoa Tribune, May 16, 1917

[59]Ibid.

[60]Ibid.

[61]Richard S. Levy, Ph.D., David F. Barton, M.P.A., Timothy B. Riordan, M.A.; An Archeological Survey of Cape Canaveral Air Force Station, Brevard County, Florida, U.S. Air Force, Eastern Space and Missile Center, March 16, 1984, pg 52 table 6

[62]Ibid.

[63]The Cocoa Tribune, February 12, 1925

[64]Ibid.

[65]Ibid.

[66]Ibid.

[67]The Cocoa Tribune, October 18 and December 28,1929

[68]The Cocoa Tribune, August 23, October 4, 1928

[69]The Cocoa Tribune, December 28, 1929

[70]Glen Shockey, hand-drawn map, provided by Evelyn (Evie) Grose

[71] Ibid.

[72] Ibid.

[73] Flossie Staton, descendant and former resident

[74] The Cocoa Tribune, April 19, 1929

[75] Ibid.

[76] Ibid.

[77] The Cocoa Tribune, Canaveral, March 29, 1929

[78] ancestry.com, 1930 US Census (accessed February 22, 2009) ,ancestry.com> Arthur Hodges

[79] Neil Hurley, Keepers of Florida Lighthouses, An Illustrated CD-ROM database

[80] Ancestry.com - North Carolina Death Certificates, 1909-1975 (accessed April 12, 2009) <http://ancestry.com>

[81] Ibid.

[82] State of Florida Office of Vital Statistics, Certificate of Death., file # 8666

[83] Neil Hurley, Keepers of Florida Lighthouses, An Illustrated CD-ROM database

[84] The Cocoa Tribune, June 22, 1933

[85] Neil Hurley, Keepers of Florida Lighthouses, An Illustrated CD-ROM database

[86] The Cocoa Tribune, January 31, 1929

[87] Ibid.

[88] The Cocoa Tribune, William A. Norsworthy, Obituary, March 22, 1945

[89] ancestry.com, (accessed February 22, 2009) http://content.ancestry.com/iexec/?htx=View&r=an&dbid=1506&iid= CSUSAFL1867_089266-01056&fn=W.A&ln=Norsworthy&st=r&ssrc=&pid=2605056

[90] The Cocoa Tribune, August 17, 1933

[91] Journal of Light-house Station at Cape Canaveral, entry April 11,1931, Records Group 26, National Archives, Washington D.C.

[92] U.S. Coast Guard Drawing, DC120, Sheet 1 of 1, Brevard Historical Commission

[93] U.S. Coast Guard Drawing, Dr No B132 Sheet 1 of 1, Brevard Historical Commission

[94] The Cocoa Tribune; February 2, 1933

[95] Ibid.

[96] The Cocoa Tribune; October 19, 1933

[97] Ibid.

[98] Ibid.

[99] Ibid.

[100] The Cocoa Tribune, March 2 1933

[101] The Cocoa Tribune, December 14, 1933

[102] Ibid.

[103] Ibid.

[104] The Cocoa Tribune; "Indian Mounds on Canaveral, Peninsula to the Explored," December 14, 1933

[105] Journal of Light-house Station at Cape Canaveral, entry July 1, 1939, Records Group 26, National Archives, Washington D.C.

[106] Journal of Light-house Station at Cape Canaveral, entry July 2, 1939, Records Group 26, National Archives, Washington D.C.

[107] Journal of Light-house Station at Cape Canaveral, entry July 3, 1939, Records Group 26, National Archives, Washington D.C.

[108] Journal of Light-house Station at Cape Canaveral, entry July 11, 1939, Records Group 26, National Archives, Washington D.C.

This chapter is devoted to a compilation of items/stuff the author has found during researching this book and didn't know where to put them. Some may be of interest to the reader and some are here just for fun. You just cannot make this stuff up.

Let's start with Florida

Florida and its counties have evolved over the years with names being changed and county names being replaced by others. In 1810, Florida had only two counties East Florida and West Florida.[1] Very original? The two counties were on either side of the Suwannee River. In 1821 the two counties were renamed, the East Escambia and the West St. Johns. The Suwannee River was still the dividing line.[2] By 1840, things were-a-changing. Florida was rearranged into seventeen counties with Cape Canaveral being located in Mosquito County. Florida joined the union, becoming a state in 1845. Guess what? Yep. The state reorganized again in 1850 into twenty six counties with Cape Canaveral ending up in St. Lucie County. Well that lasted about 30 years. In 1880, Florida again did the county shuffle and came up with thirty nine counties with Cape Canaveral now in Volusia County. In 1975 the State made another reorganization regrouping into sixty seven counties. This time Cape Canaveral wound up in Brevard County.[3]

The First Lighthouse (Pharos)

The lighthouse of Alexandria, or The Pharos of Alexandria, was a tower built in the 3rd century BC, between 285 and 247 BC, on the island of Pharos in Alexandria, Egypt to serve as that port's landmark, and later, its lighthouse.

With a height variously estimated at between 115 - 150 meters (377 - 492 ft) it was among the tallest man-made structures on Earth for many centuries, and was identified

Picture of Pharos, courtesy WikipediA

as one of the Seven Wonders of the World by Antipater of Sidon. It may have been the third tallest building after the two Great Pyramids (of Khufu and Khafra) for its entire life. Some scholars estimate a much taller height exceeding 180 meters that would make the tower the tallest building up to the 14th century.[4]

The U.S.S. Peacock

"The capture of HMS Epervier was a naval action fought off Cape Canaveral, Florida on April 29, 1814 between the sloop-of-war USS Peacock and the brig HMS Epervier in which the Epervier was captured and sent to Savannah."[5]

Picture of the USS Peacock and Epervier Courtesy the Florida Memory Project

The U.S.S. Beauregard Patrols Cape Canaveral Waters

On "August 12, 1863 the U.S.S. Beauregard was on station at the Haul Over Canal, thirteen miles north of Cape Canaveral. The U.S.S. Pursuit was stationed off the coast at Jupiter Inlet. Confederate blockade-runners were suspected of using the Indian River area to land contraband cargoes.

The U.S.S. Beauregard was back on November 5, 1863 to seize the British schooner Volante off Cape Canaveral. The Volante was carrying a cargo of salt and dry goods."[6] Again on "January 28, 1864, the U. S. schooner, Beauregard, captured the British blockade-runner Racer about ten miles north of Cape Canaveral. The English vessel had left New Smyrna bound for Nassau with a cargo of cotton. On a roll, "the Beauregard captured the English schooner Spunky April 7, 1864 off Cape Canaveral. The Spunky was enroute to the Bahamas with a cargo of cotton."[7] Just one month later, "the U.S.S. Beauregard captured the British sloop Resolute while the sloop was at anchor off Cape Canaveral on May 12 1864."[8]

The Florida Star

The Florida Star was first printed in New Smyrna, Florida and has been a very important source of information and facts used in this book. The paper was "established on February 20, 1876 by W. H. & C. H. Coe and W. A. Cook and was the first newspaper published south of St. Augustine. It was issued as a monthly paper for over a year and moved to Titusville in 1880."[9]

Cape Canaveral gets a Seawall

In 1888, a "500 ft seawall is completed to protect the Cape Canaveral Lighthouse. The seawall was 500 ft long, 8 feet high, and formed of two courses of 1 1/2 inch plank, supported by piles 12 inches square driven into the sand 12 feet deep and 8 inches apart. Stringers, 6 X 8 inches, are bolted to the piles and diagonal braces 6 X 8 inches, 16 feet long are bolted to the piles and stringers and braced against another row of piles sunk to the level of the sand: a wing is run landward 50 feet at each end and the wall supported in the same manner. From it extend 7 jetties, each 70 feet long and built of 12 inches square. The work cost about $4,500 and 140,000 feet of lumber was used. The project was supervised by Capt Anderson of the Lighthouse Service."[10] We still don't know exactly where it was located. The seawall cost about $95,744.68 in 2006 dollars.

Turtle Climbs Seawall

The seawall was supposed to keep the ocean in check and one would think that turtles in search of a nesting spot wouldn't climb over it. Well one did. "A huge sea turtle climbed over the sea wall and was found fully a hundred feet back in the yard of Mrs. W. H. Moore. The turtle became entangled in the brush and would have died but for the aid of Mr. Quarterman of the Lighthouse, who cleared the brush and piloted the turtle back to its ocean home."[11]

French Boots: None that matched

In August of 1870 a French Steamer, the Ladona, was caught in a storm off the Cape. The boat was carrying a load of French boots and shoes. The boots were washed overboard and wound up on the beaches of Cape Canaveral. Being resourceful, the residents of Cape Canaveral put the new found shoes to good use and "for years people could be seen wearing mixed pairs of expensive French shoes and boots. There was a rumer that one person did find a matched pair of shoes."[12]

Snake oil or Medicine?

"Women as Well as Men are Made Miserable by Kidney Trouble."[13]

Something called Dr Kilmer's Swamp-Root oil was sold to residents of Cape Canaveral and advertised in the Florida Star:

> "The mild and the immediate effects of Swamp-Root is soon realized. It is sold by druggists, in fifty cent and one dollar sizes. You may have a sample bottle by mail free, also a pamphlet telling all about it, including many of the testimonial letters received from suffers cured. In writing Dr Kilmer & Co. Binghamton, N. Y., be sure and mention this paper."[14]

So who was Dr Kilmer?

Pictures of Bottle & Dr. Kilmer, courtesy, Digger O'Dell Publications

Dr. Andral S. Kilmer, the inventor of the Swamproot, set up business in Binghamton, New York in the 1870s. There, he developed a line of proprietary medicines, pills and ointments. Dr. Andral S. Kilmer graduated from Bennett College of Eclectic Medicine and Surgery. He received his diploma in 1875 from that Chicago Institution. He received more medical training in Wisconsin, where he studied botanic practices. He set up practice and a medical dispensary around 1878 in Binghamton, New York.

Kilmer was joined by his younger brother, Jonas M. Kilmer and together they expanded sales locally to the point where they had to rebuild their dispensary around 1882. A five story building with laboratory was constructed and fitted with the most up to date bottling equipment available capable of filling over 2,000 bottles an hour. In 1886, son of Jonas Kilmer, Willis finished courses in modern business advertising at Cornell. Willis embarked upon a national advertising campaign. Back woods folks might not be able to read, write or identify the president of the United States, but they instantly recognized the image of Andral Kilmer.[15] His likeness was printed on every box, pamphlet and advertising sign.

At sometime after the passage of the Food and Drug Act of 1906, the word "CURE" was dropped in favor of the word, REMEDY.[16]   A word about this and other cures?

> The vast majority of patent medicines were alcohol-based, many containing opium
> or morphine as well. Virtually none contained the ingredients they claimed to have,
> and none could heal. Vital Sparks, promising to revitalize masculine virility, was
> made by rolling rock candy in powdered aloe. Tiger Fat, a cure-all balm touted
> to be rendered from Royal Bengal tigers' backbones, was concocted of Vaseline,
> camphor, menthol, eucalyptus oil, turpentine, wintergreen oil, and paraffin. Liver
> pads, promoted as a cure for liver diseases, were nothing more than small fabric
> swatches with a spot of red pepper and glue; when the body heat melted the glue,
> the sting of the red pepper was perceived as a healing sensation.[17]

You decide.

Tobacco as a Cash Crop

From the Florida Star, dated August 9, 1887, we learn that an experiment in growing tobacco on Cape Canaveral was conducted. "A somewhat out of the usual line of crops now growing on Cape Canaveral and worth of mention, is Mr. Harrison's experiment in tobacco culture in the Burnham's grove. He has two acres, Sumatra, Persioan, (sic) and Havana and is carefully testing these kinds."[18]

A bottle floats up on the Cape Canaveral Beach

On January 19, 1900 "Capt. Henry Wilson found a drift bottle which according to the paper corked up inside, was thrown overboard on Nov. 4th, 1889, in latitude 26 minutes north, longitude 85 minutes, 18 seconds, west, from the American S.S. Louisiana, with a request to forward it to the U.S. Hydrographic Office."[19]   Assuming the person writing the note got confused with the latitude and longitude, and meant 26 degrees North Latitude and 85 degrees West Longitude, the bottle was dropped in the Gulf of Mexico approximately 190 miles West of Sanibel Island, Florida and approximately 160 miles North West of the Dry Tortugas[20] and took eleven years to get to Cape Canaveral.

A Steamboat named Canaveral

The Florida Star reported that "the steamer Canaveral, which was purchased by Capt. Ramsey a few weeks ago, having had necessary repairs made, steamed down the river to Eau Gallie Sunday. The Canaveral will go on the Banana river mail route on July 1, 1900."[21]

Nathan, Florida

A check of "Maps of Florida" shows that the small town of Nathan, Florida appeared on the east shore of the Banana River on Cape Canaveral at some point around 1899.[22] Nathan existed only a few years and was originally established as a steam boat water station and presumably named after Nathan N. Penny who is buried just a few hundred yards from the spot where the town of Nathan was located. There may have been a Post office at Nathan at about that time.

"A quiet wedding occurred at Nathan last Thursday, June 21, 1900. The contracting parties were Miss Fanny Penny, of that place, and Mr. Charley Gifford, of Vero. Only the immediate relatives were present at the ceremony."[23] Fanny Penny was the "first teacher at the first school in Oslo, in 1898. She boarded with the O. O. Helseth's for $8.00 a month and was paid $25.00 per month for teaching."[24] $25.00 equates to $595.24 in 2006 dollars.

"The town of Oslo, as it was once called, was first established by some of Indian River County's first pioneers, which included the Helseth, Gifford, and Hallstrom families. The area was given the name Oslo by the Helseth family, and was named after the Norwegian capital city."[25]

On April 19, 1901, the community of Nathan announced that Nathan N. Penny had been shipping peppers and Beans during the past week. It was also announced that he had killed a fine bear and his "neighbors were regaling on the bear meat of the finest kind."[26]

Not only did Nation O. Penny, son of Nathan N. Penny at Cape Canaveral have the first automobile in the area; he was the second Post Master of Vero being appointed July 24, 1905. Henry T. Gifford was the founder and first Post Master.[27]

Picture of Nathan O. Penny
Passport Courtesy Ancestry.com

Picture of Nathan N. Penny's grave
marker taken by author

The Cape Canaveral Lighthouse Mule

Apparently in 1906, concerning the mule, there was a "...recommendation that she should be shot..."[28] Keeper Clinton P. Honeywell, saved the mule, Nancy Hanks, from being shot with the following letter to the Lighthouse Board:

Sir, in reply to your letter of the 14th in regard to work done and cost of feed for mule, I will say that the mule (mare) was delivered at this station on June 21st, 1893, by the keeper of Mosquito Inlet station,... ...and turned over to the keeper of this station by the construction party on Oct. 20th 1894.

Since October 20th 1894, the mule has hauled all the oil used in the light-house, our fire wood (drift) from the beach, and made on an average of two trips a week to the post office (about 4 miles from station) for mail and household supplies for the keeper and two assts.

We have to use a ground feed, for the mule's teeth are so bad that she can not eat whole grain or hay, the only grass here that the mule can eat is the thin at the station, the growth in the surrounding country is Saw Palmetto and Saw Grass.

I will say that the feed for a year will cost about $50.00.

Respectfully
Clinton P. Honeywell
Keeper [29]

On June 2, 1906 the Inspector 6th L. H. district wrote to the light-House Board that the Cape Canaveral Light-Station's "...old mule at that station died May 16, 1906."[30]

The Huntress sinks off Cape Canaveral, 1913

The East Coast Advocate reported that "The fine power yacht, Huntress, of the New York Yacht Club, was completely destroyed on Monday morning at 4 o'clock, about fifteen miles to sea, east of Cape Canaveral, entailing a loss of three lives. There was an explosion and the boat was enveloped in flames, and the owner, Mr. F. W. Cheesebrough and wife and four men had time to get in the power dory. The ship-wrecked party made their way to Canaveral and were brought to Titusville by Capt. Peterson. The Huntress was about 90 ft. long and cost about $20,000.

The cook and the steward were asleep in the forecastle and must have been instantly killed by the flames which started in that part of the boat and soon became a roaring furnace, while a sailor (Harry Osman) asleep in a life boat on the bow of the ship was blown overboard and drowned: his body being rescued and buried at Cape Canaveral."[31] Notice here we have three deaths but only one body found. Harry is buried in one of the two graves located in the dunes of Cape Canaveral.

Picture of Harry Osman's grave marker taken by author

Canaveral or Cape Canaveral

The town or possibly a location called Canaveral and later Cape Canaveral appears on maps of Florida in 1890.[32] On subsequent maps Canaveral is shown in at least three different locations. Henry Wilson was the first Postmaster in 1891.

Canaveral Pier & Fish Co. Supplies Jumbo Shrimp

According to the front page of the January 15, 1931, Cocoa Tribune, "C. L Daniels, Manager of the Canaveral Pier & Fishing Company, is the authority for the statement that the company had shipped to northern points by express and freight fish and shrimp in carload lots to the number of thirty since October. Shrimp caught at Canaveral are said to be the largest to be found anywhere and are called "Jumbo Shrimp....."[33]

Picture of Grace Shockey and Cape Fish Inc Truck, courtesy, Evie Grose

Visit to Lighthouse a must

In 1931, apparently the New York Herald-Tribune wrote an article about a road and driving trip in the Cocoa Florida area of Florida. From the Cocoa Tribune we find: "...Being a hub of such a fine system of roadways, Cocoa has become an important motoring center. It offers an excellent starting point for motor trips to many interesting parts of Florida. A visit to the Canaveral Lighthouse should not be omitted from the itinerary. The way may be wild and rough, but it is well worth while. The view from the top is wonderful."[34] It is only a bit easier to visit the Cape Canaveral Lighthouse today, free tours are conducted by the Patrick Air Force Base, Public Affairs Office.

Turtle watching at Cape Canaveral in 1931

Let us hope that environmentalists will forgive this entry. According to the Cocoa Tribune; "A diversion at Canaveral is turtle watching. They go to the beach in the evening to watch the huge turtles come out of the ocean, build their nests in the sand and lay their eggs. It is most interesting and many of the young people ride on the turtle's backs as they go back to their ocean home."[35]

Picture of Devil Ray, courtesy Florida Historical Commission

Devil Fish Causes Exciting Trip

Strange things sometimes happen on or near Cape Canaveral. Captain C. W. Jandreau, of Cape Canaveral, reported that a "devil ray[36] that was 25 feet in diameter, pulled his son, Eugene, and George Holmes who were working in their rowboat when they noticed that an anchored launch was traveling to the windward with no one in it, which they knew was strange.[37] Ya think? "The two lads rowed their boat, caught up with the launch and boarded it. They were then treated to a five hour, eight mile ride out into the Atlantic, courtesy of a Devil Ray before they released the anchor line and freed themselves."[38] The paper goes on: "several years ago a like instance occurred in the bight at Canaveral. But that time the devil ray was captured. It measured twenty feet across and soon after being killed, gave birth to a young devil ray, weighing several hundred pounds."[39] Now that's a fish story.

Picture of fishermen at pier, courtesy, Florida Historical Commission

Another Fish Story: 10 Fish weigh 3,000 lbs

On July 30, 1931, the Cocoa Tribune reported on the front page that "Ten fish that totaled 3,000 pounds were what a party of sportsmen caught at Canaveral. The largest was a Black Sea Bass which weighed 500 pounds."[40] Is there something that we should know about the waters around Cape Canaveral?

Keeper John B. Butler 1907 - 1930

It may be that Keeper Butler was on or served on The Mangrove. The picture here was provided in a collection from the Ponce Inlet Museum referenced as the Butler collection. The picture is of Butler and a throw ring from the Lighthouse Service Ship Mangrove.

Picture of Mangrove Courtesy
Ponce de Leon Inlet Historical Association

> "The MANGROVE was a patrol boat throughout World War I, being returned to the Lighthouse Service 1 July 1919. In 1922, she was assigned to a permanent station in the 6th LHD at Charleston, S.C. During World War II, Mangrove continued as a buoy tender (USCGC MANGROVE, WAGL 232) until 1 January 1946, when she returned to the Treasury Department. She was decommissioned 22 August 1946 and was sold 6 May 1947."[41]

Gas Prices in 1931

The Cocoa Tribune reports the price of a gallon of gas. "Gasoline sells for 13 cents in Duval County and 20 Cents in Starke."[42] Ah, for the good old days.

Airplanes Land on Cape Canaveral Beach

In 1932, "four young men in two Baby Veronica two cylinder airplanes on their way from the Miami Air Meet to Cincinnati,"[43] landed their planes, at high tide, near the Cape Canaveral Harbor. "It is claimed that these planes make twenty-two miles on a gallon of gas and hold only eight gallons. They took on gas at the Harbor and planned to make their next stop at Daytona."[44]

Revival at the Cape Canaveral School

More stuff happening in a school house at the Cape. In March 1933, "The Rev. Claude Bridges of Cocoa and T. E. Bush, the blind evangelist form Georgia, are holding revival meetings at the Canaveral School house."[45]

The Canaveral Ocean Golf Course (One of the earliest in Florida)

How about this for an amazing factoid?

"The Canaveral Ocean Golf course is about completed. It is nine holes covers nineteen hundred yards, and a par game of eighteen holes is estimated at sixty. The course is free to those desiring to use it."[46] A review of a 1942 aerial photograph of the area confirms that there may have been a golf course along the ocean in the Lansing Beach area, about 2 miles north of the lighthouse. When the Canaveral Ocean Golf Course was opened for play at Cape Canaveral in 1933, it was not the first in Florida. Darn!!

The first course in Florida was probably Temple Terrace:

In 1925, the "Temple Terrace Golf and Country Club" (still in existence) hosted the first ever Florida Open (billed as the Greatest Field Of Golfers Ever to Play in Florida). "Long" Jim Barnes was resident professional of the course at the time and every major golfer of the day competed in the event except Bobby Jones. Leo Diegel won the tournament. The golf course architect was Tom Bendelow who also designed Medinah #3 in Chicago. Temple Terrace is one of the first planned golf course communities in the United States (1921)"[47]

War Comes to Cape Canaveral - Pan-Massachusetts torpedoed off Cape Canaveral

"The first German U-boat attack along the Florida coast came on the afternoon of February 19, 1942."[48] The ship was owned by National Bulk Carriers, built in 1919 by Bethlehem S.B. Corp and had a gross weight of 8,202 tons. It was some 456 and powered by 833 n.h.p. turbine engines.

The Pan-Massachusetts was "sunk by German submarine U-128 about 20 miles

Picture of the Pan Massachusetts courtesy Rose Wooley

off Cape Canaveral, Florida, 28°27'N, 80°08'W; Coast Guard lighthouse tender Forward (WAGL-160) and British tanker Elizabeth Massey rescued 18 survivors from the 38-man crew."[49]

Cities Service Empire

Picture of the Cities Service Empire, courtesy, Rose Wooley

The German Sub must have been hanging around Cape Canaveral for several days because just three days after U-128 sank the Pan Massachusetts, it went after the Cities Service Empire. On the morning of February 22, 1942, at daybreak the tanker was approaching Cape Canaveral. At the same time, the German Submarine U-128 was sitting quietly in wait and sank the tanker about 25 miles south of Cape Canaveral, Florida, 28º 0'N, 80º 27' 14 crewmen died with 36 saved.[50]

The U.S. Coast Guard cutter USS Vigilant (WPC 154) reached the burning ship before midnight and saw three men at the bow of the tanker. The Vigilant nosed up to and boarded the burning tanker. They battled flames until they rescued two of the Empire's crew members. The tanker exploded igniting oil from bow to stern, broke in half and sank at a few minutes past midnight on February 23, 1942. The master, three armed guards and ten crewmen died. The 34 survivors on the rafts were later picked up by the USS Biddle (DD 151) and taken to Fort Pierce, Florida.[51]

Picture of Cities Service Empire's Gun Crew Courtesy World War II U.S. Navy Armed Guard and World War II U.S. Merchant Marine

USS Biddle (DD–151) was a Wickes Class destroyer in the United States Navy during World War II, later reclassified AG-114. She was the second ship named for Captain Nicholas Biddle. The Biddle was launched 3 October 1918 by William Cramp and Sons Ship and Engine Building Company, Philadelphia, Pennsylvania.[52]

Picture of The USS Biddle, courtesy, US Navy

LaPaz gets Torpedoed (Account from an Eye Witness)

The La Paz, a merchant ship, was hit by two torpedoes from the German submarine U-109 in shallow waters about 10 miles southeast of Cape Canaveral.[53]

An eye witness to the event was Ms. Flossie Holmes-Staton and provides the following:

The war years were both exciting and frightening for those of us who lived along the coast. The children weren't sensible enough to know what peril we were in but our parents took turns manning the spotting towers that were built up and down the beach, to look out for foreign aircraft or ships. I was on the Pier with a number of other people the night that U boats torpedoed a merchant ship, the LaPaz, and we watched the flares sent up from the ship. For the next few days the men in the neighborhood helped to rescue survivors, bring in the dead, and I presume the staff at Banana River NAIS arranged for the burial of those who had perished. A great deal of salvage work was needed for the LaPaz and again, the able bodied men of the area who were not already in the Armed Forces, were pressed into service.

Picture of The La Paz, courtesy, National Archives

My Father was one of the men who brought in the survivors of the LaPaz and discovered later that one of the men was an English cousin whom he had never met. His last name was Jenner. Small world.[54]

"U-109 was sunk on 4 May 1943 south of Ireland by 4 depth charges from a British Liberator aircraft, all hands lost."[55]

Wildlife Shortage

How about this for an interesting factoid, Frank Wilson was well ahead of the government. "The first official acknowledgement of the county's wildlife shortage came in 1945, when the legislature created a wildlife refuge on the lower Canaveral peninsula. A breeding ground of about 12 square miles was established for the protection of deer. For Canaveral residents, that act was long overdue. The numerous deer killed by hunters had already caused one resident to establish a deer park at the Cape. Frank Wilson purchased 800 pounds of wire to fence 40 acres for the protection of deer-in 1898!"[56] He was well ahead of his time.

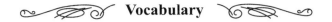

Here are just a few words that Lighthouse fanciers should know.

Alee - Away from the direction of the wind. Opposite of windward.

Anchorage - A place suitable for anchoring in relation to the wind, seas and bottom.

Bowline - A knot used to form a temporary loop in the end of a line.

Buoy - A floating minor aid to navigation, moored to the seabed. Some have been designed with lights, sirens, gongs, or bells to make them easier to locate at night or in bad weather. Usually used for marking a position on the water or a hazard or a shoal and for mooring.

Captain - Most masters of a ship or sailboat are referred to as Captain. The term is given to a Naval Officer or the Master of a ship. Lighthouse Keepers were called Captain.

Captain's daughter – The cat o'nine tails, (A Whip) which in principle is only used on board on the captain's (or a court martial's) personal orders.

Ebb - A receding current. An Ebb tide is a tide that is receding.

Fathom - Although a fathom is now a nautical unit of length equal to six feet, it was once defined by an act of Parliament as "the length of a man's arms around the object of his affections. The word derives from the Old English Faethm, which means "embracing arms."

Fresnel Lens - Invented by Augustin J. Fresnel in about 1865 -- a lens that has a surface consisting of a concentric series of simple lens sections so that a thin lens with a short focal length and large diameter is possible and that is used especially for spotlights.

Knot - A measure of speed equal to one nautical mile (6076 feet) per hour. To convert knots to statute mph, multiply by 1.14.

Lampest - A person hired by the Lighthouse Service to work on the Fresnel and earlier oil burning lamps. Wenslow Lewis was probably the most famous.

Lard oil - A form of animal-based oil used as a lamp fuel in the mid-to-late 1800s. It was cheaper than whale oil, but produced acrid fumes and often congealed in cold weather.

League - A unit of linear measure varying in different times and countries: in English-speaking countries it is usually about 3 statute miles or 3 nautical miles.

Lee - The side sheltered from the wind.

Lighthouse - a structure (as a tower) with a powerful light that gives a continuous or intermittent signal to navigators.

Mariner - A person who navigates or assist in the navigation of a ship.

Mineral Oil - Kerosene; A thin, distilled oil used for American lighthouse illumination in the late 1800s and early 1900s.

Nautical Mile - Any of various units of distance for sea and air navigation, in the US since 1959 an international unit of length equal to one minute of arc of a great circle of the earth or 6076.12 feet or 1.1508 miles.

Scuttlebutt - The cask of drinking water on ships was called a scuttlebutt and since Sailors exchanged gossip when they gathered at the scuttlebutt for a drink of water, scuttlebutt became U.S. Navy slang for gossip or rumors. A butt was a wooden cask which held water or other liquids; to scuttle is to drill a hole, as for tapping a cask.

Sheet - A rope used to control the setting of a sail in relation to the direction of the wind.

Under the weather - Serving a watch on the weather side of the ship, exposed to wind and spray.

White horses or whitecaps - Foam or spray on wave tops caused by stronger winds (usually above Force 4). Wind speed between 13 and 17 MPH.

[1]Maps Etc, (accessed April 30, 2009) <http://etc.usf.edu/maps/pages/5200/5283/5283.htm>

[2]Ibid, <http://fcit.usf.edu/florida/maps/pages/3500/f3584/f3584.htm>

[3]FloridaHistory101, (accessed June 6, 2002) <http://www.familyhistory101.com/maps/fl_cf.html>

[4]WikipediA, the free encyclopedia (accessed May 14, 2007) http://en.wikipedia.org/wiki/Lighthouse_of_Alexandria

[5]WikipediA, the free encyclopedia (accessed November 15, 2008) <http://en.wikipedia.org/wiki/Capture_of_HMS_Epervier>

[6]Today in Florida History, (accessed September 1, 2007), <http://www.floridahistory.net/month.htm>

[7]Ibid.

[8]Ibid.

[9]The Florida Star, January 24, 1901

[10]The Florida Star, April 26, 1888

[11]The Cocoa Tribune, August 13, 1931

[12]Robert Ransom, East Coast Florida Memories, (Port Salerno: Florida Classic Library) VI

[13]The Florida Star, Advertisement, Friday, January, 1900

[14]Ibid.

[15]Digger O'Dell Publications, Your place for Information on Old Bottles, (Accessed September 21, 2008) <http://www.bottlebooks.com/drkilmer.htm>

[16]Ibid.

[17]DR Bob's Medical Quackery, (Accessed September 21, 2008) <http://www.bobgroveauctions.com/drbob.html>

[18]Florida Star, Titusville, August 9, 1887

[19]The Florida Star, Ocean Drift Bottle, January 19, 1900

[20]Google Earth

[21]The Florida Star, Titusville, Latest News and Incidents, dated June 19, 1900

[22]Maps of Florida, The Rand-McNally indexed county and township pocket map and shippers guide of Florida showing all railroads, cities, towns, villages, post offices, lakes, rivers, etc. (accessed May 4, 2008) <http://fcit.usf.edu/florida/maps/1800c/cram99.htm>

[23]The Florida Star, Canaveral, June 29, 1900

[24]Stories of Early Life along Beautiful Indian River, Compiled by, Anna Pearl Leonard Newman, Printed by Stuart Daily News, Inc., Stuart, Florida, pg 15

[25]WikipediA.com

[26]The Florida Star, Titusville, Nathan, April 19, 1901

[27]Stories of Early Life along Beautiful Indian River, Compiled by, Anna Pearl Leonard Newman, Printed by Stuart Daily News, Inc., Stuart, Florida, pg 27

[28]Letter to the Lighthouse Board, dated April 28, 1906, Records Group 26 E 58, Box 16, National Archives, Washington, D.C.

[29]Clinton Honeywell, Letter to the Lighthouse Board, dated April 19, 1906, Records Group 26 E 58, Box 16, National Archives, Washington, D.C.

[30]Inspector 6th District, Letter to the Lighthouse Board, dated June 2, 1906, Records Group 26 E 58, Box 16, National Archives, Washington, D.C.

[31]East Coast Advocate, Titusville, Fla., January 10, 1913 TS

[32]Maps of Florida, 1890, Rand, McNally & Company map. Map Credit: Courtesy of the private collection of Roy Winkelman (accessed May 4, 2008) <http://fcit.usf.edu/florida/maps/1800c/rand90z.htm>

[33]The Cocoa Tribune, January 15, 1931

[34]The Cocoa Tribune, February 19, 1931

[35]The Cocoa Tribune, July 2, 1931

[36]WikipediA, the free encyclopedia; The devil fish (Mobula Mobular), also known as the giant devil ray, is an Eagle ray in the family Myliobatidae. (accessed March 24, 2008) http://en.wikipedia.org/wiki/Devil_Fish

[37]The Cocoa Tribune, July 30, 1931

[38]Ibid.

[39]The Cocoa Tribune, July 30, 1931, pg 5

[40]The Cocoa Tribune, September 3, 1931

[41]U.S. Coast Guard History, mangrove (accessed March 23, 2008) <http://wwwUSCoastGuard.mil>

[42]The Cocoa Tribune, August 8, 1931

[43]The Cocoa Tribune, January 14, 1932

[44]Ibid.

[45]The Cocoa Tribune, March 2, 1933

[46]Ibid.

[47]WikipediA, the free encyclopedia, Temple Terrace, Florida (accessed May 14, 2008) http://en.wikipedia.org/wiki/Temple_Terrace,_Florida

[48]Melissa Williford Euziere, FROM MOSQUITO CLOUDS TO WAR CLOUDS: Florida State University, College of Arts and Science, A thesis submitted, fall 2003, page 31

[49]Hyperwar The Official Cronology of the U.S. Navy in World War II, Chapter IV 1942; (accessed July 14, 2008) http://www.ibilio.org/hyperwar/usn/usn-chron/usn-chron-1942.html

[50]U-Boat Net, (accessed November 11, 2008) <http://www.uboat.net/allies/merchants/1364.html />

[51]Ibid.

[52]WikipediA, the free encyclopedia, (accessed May 9, 2009) <http://en.wikipedia.org/wiki/USS_Biddle_(DD-151)>

[53]U-Boat Net, (accessed July 15, 2008) <http://www.uboat.net/allies/merchants/1584.html>

[54]Flossie Staton, Eberwein/Holmes/Staton History, descendants recollections provided, June 2008

[55]U-Boat Net, (accessed July 15, 2008) <http://www.uboat.net/boats/u109.htm>

[56]Research by John Eriksen, Patrick Base Library; Chapter 23195, Laws of Florida, "AN ACT to Create and Establish A Breeding Ground of Area for Deer in a Part of Brevard County" filed June 11, 1945; To Start a Deer Park, Indian River Advocate, November 18, 1898

This chapter is dedicated to the wonderful hard working people who settled Cape Canaveral. Although I hope no one is missed, I know and fear that I will miss someone. For any omission, I apologize and ask for your forgiveness now. The U.S. Census will be our guide. Mrs. Rose Wooley and her work in tracking, protecting and preserving the memories of the Cape Canaveral settlers and their history is my inspiration for this chapter. Her book, <u>History of Cape Canaveral and the Early Settlers</u>, is used as a guideline in preparing for the first part of this chapter. We will the U.S. census and the 1926-1927 Brevard County Directory of Towns and Cities for Artesia and Cape Canaveral and other documents in an effort not to miss anyone. Again, I fear that I will miss someone and again I ask you understanding and forgiveness.

We find no definitive record of persons being on Cape Canaveral between the time of the Ais' Indians disappearance, which was between 1710 & 1750, and the time in 1847 when Mr. George Center was sent from St. Augustine to find a location for a lighthouse. Mr. Center's activities were documented in the Chapter III "The First Lighthouse." After the Ais, the first two settlers of Cape Canaveral were probably Nathaniel Scobie and Ora Carpenter. Both gentlemen were also discussed in Chapter III "The First Lighthouse."

At the time of the 1885 Census, seven families were living on Cape Canaveral. They were: Mills Olcott Burnham, Henry Wilson, George M. Quarteman, Oscar F. Quarterman, James Knight, John Hogen (must have been John Harvey Hogan) and Nathan Penny.[1] Although some have been written about in earlier chapters, we will visit each in this chapter, with the exception of Mills O. Burnham who has been thoroughly discussed in earlier chapters.

Henry Wilson: May 1, 1829 - April 14, 1917

Picture of Henry Wilson,
courtesy, Rose Wooley

Henry Wilson was discussed in an earlier chapter but his life and contribution to the settlement of Cape Canaveral deserves a bit more discussion. In 1847 he was sent to Florida to serve in Miami, and then sent to Ft. Dallas. Ft Dallas was established in 1836 as a U.S. Military Post and a prison during the Seminole Wars.[2] "It was named in honor of Commodore Alexander James Dallas, U.S. Navy, who commanded U.S. naval forces in the West Indies. Fort Dallas remained in Union hands during the American Civil War and was abandoned afterward."[3] While at Ft. Dallas, Henry Wilson was given the assignment of delivering 200 head of mules across the state to Ft. Brooke. It was about a six-week long round trip.[4] Fort Brooke was a military post located at the mouth of the Hillsborough River in present day Tampa. The Tampa Convention Center currently stands at the site.[5] "The fort was named after Col. George Mercer Brooke, who, on 10 January 1824, led four full companies of the U.S. 4th Infantry Regiment from Pensacola to Tampa Bay to establish a military post. The intent of building the wooden fort was to hinder illegal activity around the area. Fort Brooke would serve as a major outpost on Florida's Suncoast during all three Seminole Indian Wars and the Civil War. The fort also played a part in the development of the village of Tampa." [6]

Corporal Wilson also served at Forts Clinch[7] and Pierce. [8] "Fort Clinch is one of the most well-preserved 19th century forts in the country. Although no battles were fought here, it was garrisoned during both the Civil and Spanish-American wars."[9] "The second Seminole War began in 1835 and the U.S. Army established military posts throughout Florida. Lt. Col. Benjamin Kendrick Pierce, Commander of the 1st Regiment of Artillery, and brother of the future President Franklin Pierce, in January 1838, began to erect a block-house, much like many others, but this one was made from palmetto logs. After construction, it was named Fort Pierce for its' Commander."[10] The Officer put in Charge at Fort Pierce was none other than Lieutenant Tecumseh Sherman.

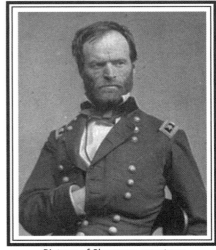
Picture of Sherman, courtesy, Shotgun's Home of the American Civil War

Yes, the very same General Sherman of Civil War fame. The General "entered West Point in June 1836 and four years later, in June 1840, graduated sixth in his class. He was commissioned a second lieutenant in the Artillery Corps. His first assignment was to Fort Pierce, Florida, where he was peripherally involved in the Second Seminole War. He was promoted to first lieutenant in November 1841 and transferred to St. Augustine, Florida."[11]

Corporal Wilson was given the assignment of delivering the mail from Ft. Pierce to New Smyrna. It was a three week long round trip, using two boats, one on the Indian River side of Haul Over Canal and one on the Ocean side. In about 1854, Corporal Henry Wilson was sent to Cape Canaveral, along with a Sergeant and another enlisted man, to protect the lighthouse community, namely Mills O. Burnham and his family, from the Indians.[12]

After resigning from the army, Henry returned to Cape Canaveral and married Frances A. Burnham on March 30, 1856. The wedding was held the Trinity Episcopal Church, St. Augustine, Florida and performed by Rev. Alfred Miller. The bride's father, Mills O. Burnham, gave the newlyweds a wedding gift of forty acres of Cape Canaveral land, and, his new son-in-law, a job as Assistant Lighthouse Keeper.[13]

Picture of the Wilsons, courtesy, Helen Tucker

On or about July 12, 1883 a post office was established at Cape Canaveral and Henry Wilson was the first Cape Canaveral Postmaster. The first mail was delivered to the new post office on July 13, 1883 by Mr. Sam Norton. Weekly deliveries were made to the newly opened Post Office starting with the July 19, 1883 delivery.[14] Henry Wilson was the Cape Canaveral Post Master for the next thirty-four years. He was succeeded by his eldest daughter's husband, Thomas J. Thompson.

Henry passed away on April 14, 1917 at age of 86. Frances passed away September 2, 1924 and is buried beside her husband in the Burnham Cemetery on Cape Canaveral.

The Wilson's had eight children, they were; Henrietta, Alfred Burnham, Francis Mills

(Frank M.) Delia, Mary Augusta, Gertrude, Agnes and Florence.

Henrietta Wilson: March 21, 1859 – January 18, 1922

Henrietta had been married to a person named Meyers, and had two daughters: Louise and Bessie Meyers. Bessie was born in 1882. Louise married Edward Praetorius; more on the Praetorius family later. Henrietta married First Sergeant Thomas Thompson on December 11, 1887. The couple had two more daughters, Henrietta in November of 1896, and Mabel on December 5, 1899.[15]

In January of 1922 a disaster happened at Cape Canaveral. "Mrs. Thompson was taken to a hospital where her leg was amputated just below the knee, but too late, it seems to prevent the spread of blood poisoning which had already set in. For weeks, Mrs. Thompson has lain at death's door."[16] She is buried next to her husband in the Burnham Cemetery on Cape Canaveral.

First Sergeant, Thomas J. Thompson: August 1852 - January 13, 1922

The First Sergeant was born in August of 1852 in Carroll County, Maryland. He enlisted into the United States Army as a soldier on December 17, 1877. He declared his occupation to be a butcher. The oath of enlistment was administered by 1st Lt. E. Crawford of the 3rd Calvary.[17]

At the time of enlistment, Thomas Thompson declared that he was 21 years old. He had blue eyes, brown hair, a fair complexion, and stood five feet eight inches tall. He was assigned to the Fourth Cavalry, and reached his regiment on February 26, 1878 and served in the war with Company D, reaching the rank of First Sergeant before his discharge on December 16, 1882 at Fort Stanton, New Mexico.[18]

A search of the internet reveals that Col Mackenzie and First Sergeant Thompson may have been in New Mexico together. Now that would be fun. Imagine John Wayne as Mackenzie and Ward Bond as First Sergeant Thompson. Now that would be just too good to be true.

Thomas J. Thompson was appointed Postmaster at Canaveral, in Brevard County, Florida on February 25, 1918 by Albert S. Burleson, Postmaster General of the United States.[19] First Sergeant Thompson was the second postmaster appointed to the Cape Canaveral Post Office.

On January 19, 1922, "The little community of Canaveral was shocked last Friday, the 13th inst., when Mr. Thomas Thompson, the postmaster, was found to have committed suicide that morning at about 6 o'clock by cutting his own throat, bleeding to death before help arrived. ...

Picture of Thomas & Henrietta Thompson Grave Markers, courtesy, Nancy D. Watts

Several months after Mrs. Thompson was attacked by a wild hog and being driven into a barbed wire enclosure from which she could not extricate herself, she was at the mercy of the angry beast which inflicted great gashes in the calf of Mrs. Thompson with its tusks. ... Mrs. Thompson was taken to a hospital where her leg was amputated just below the knee, but too late, it seems to prevent the spread of blood poisoning which had already set in. For weeks, Mrs. Thompson had lain at death's door... her suffering increasing daily. This sad state bore upon the mind of her husband, who took his life to escape the ordeal of witnessing her slow passing."[20]

Thomas Thompson is buried beside his wife, Henrietta, in a concrete fenced, two-grave plot that he built for his wife, Henrietta, in the Burnham Cemetery on Cape Canaveral.

Delia Wilson: February 26, 1867 – January 11, 1951

Picture of Grace Ranson, courtesy, Ancestry.com

Delia was born February 26, 1867 at Cape Canaveral. She married Robert Ranson on August 4, 1887. According to a search of Ancestry. com records, and the 1900 United States Census, the Ranson's had four children; Francis E. in 1889, Robert W. in 1891, Grace born November 28, 1892[21] and Marion Burnham Ranson who was born September 1, 1907 and passed away January 2, 1997.[22] The picture of Grace Ranson is a photograph that she used for a passport.

Comment about picture below: The picture is of Mary Burns, Bessie Meyers Burns, Catherine Burns and Delia Wilson Ranson. Her son, Robert, is pictured just behind and to the right of Delia. The lady to the far right is his wife.

Picture of Delia Ranson from the Burns Collection, courtesy, John Whitney

Robert Ranson, Sr. was born on May 10, 1859 at Ipswich, Suffolk County, England. Robert was author of the East Coast Florida Memories, 1837 to 1886 which is quoted a number of times throughout this book. He holds the distinction of being the first Town Clerk of Titusville.[23] He received title, Certificate # 13298, to: lots numbered one, two and four of Section twenty-nine in Township twenty-three South of Range thirty eight East of Tallahassee Meridian in Florida containing one hundred and fifty two hundredths acres and sixty two hundredths of an acre [24] at Cape Canaveral.

Ranson passed away in St. Augustine, Florida January 19, 1934 and is buried in the family plot in Evergreen Cemetery.[25] Delia passed away on January 11, 1951 in St. Augustine.[26]

Picture of Robert Ranson, courtesy, Rose Wooley

Mary Augusta Wilson: January 30, 1869 - April 17, 1965

Mary Augusta married Arthur Franklin of West Palm Beach, Florida on May 4, 1888. She is the grandmother of George Franklin.

Gertrude Wilson: July 11, 1870 - April 5, 1951

Gertrude Wilson married Clinton P. Honeywell who was born on June 24, 1860 in Baltimore, Maryland.[27] Captain Honeywell came to Florida in 1884. He was appointed 2nd Assistant Keeper of the Cape Canaveral Lighthouse on May 7, 1891 and appointed Keeper November 4, 1904. He retired as Lighthouse Keeper on 23 Jan 1930.[28]

Ms. Roz Foster interviewed Florence Honeywell Patrick on April 25, 2002. From that interview, we learn that Gertrude Wilson Honeywell actually lived in the keeper's home at the lighthouse while her aunt, Florence, lived in one of the assistant's homes. Counting the Honeywell kids and Assistant Keeper Butler's six children, the tiny school had a grand total of nine students. Between the Butler's and the Honeywell's they had enough kids to populate a school. So

Picture of Mary Augusta Wilson Franklin, courtesy, Evie Grose

Keeper Honeywell converted a store house into a school house. Among the first to teach at the school probably were Ms. Virgie Richardson and Mr. Sam Knutson.

Picture of Florence Honeywell Patrick, sister, Gertrude Swanson, and Raymond Swanson, courtesy, Yvonne Thornton

Gertrude made fans, baskets and hats out of Palmetto. Some of her hats were "sold out of a shop in New York."[29] Although life was somewhat sparse, the people of Cape Canaveral must have eaten reasonably well because; the Honeywell's had a "wonderful garden, and mother planted corn, beets, carrots and cabbages. We used cast nets to catch fish. Mother and Uncle would catch gopher turtle to eat."[30] Food was plentiful "cows and horses, panthers were around, black bear as well as ducks, huckleberries and sea grapes."[31]

Florence informs us that "a sternwheeler once (came up the river) and the captain was Mr. Cohen, and it would stop at Burn's dock. Mail came from Merritt Island in a boat and then was delivered to the post office, wherever it was at the time."[32] This last comment by Florence gives credence to the notion that the Cape Canaveral Post Office has been located at several places on Cape Canaveral. It is assumed that she was telling us that Captain Cohen brought the mail to the Cape via a sternwheeler.

Clinton Honeywell installed six flag poles at the lighthouse to be used to "test American flag material. Every morning he would hoist them up and take them down every night. He would test the materials to see how they stood up against the elements of wind and salt spray, etc."[33]

Both Clinton P. Honeywell and his wife Gertrude are buried in the Evergreen Cemetery at Cocoa, Florida.[34]

Agnes Wilson: December 29, 1875 - December 3, 1925

Agnes, a semi-invalid, lived on Cape Canaveral, with her mother and father, until her passing in December 1925.[35]

Florence Wilson: April 1, 1881 - November 15, 1971

Florence married Mr. Oscar Floyd Quarterman who was a year younger than her. The couple had three children.[36] O. F. Quarterman was appointed Keeper of the Cape Canaveral Lighthouse in 1930.[37] He was born in October 1882, and passed away February 28, 1951 and rests beside his wife Florence, in the Georgiana Graveyard, Merritt Island, Florida.[38]

Picture of Black Bear, courtesy, Helen Tucker

The following entries include names of families found in records and the 1926-1927 Brevard County Directory of Towns and Cities and other documents. Artesia with 18 people/families and Canaveral with 80 people/families. From the Directory:[39]

Artesia, on the Banana River, 7 miles north of Cocoa Beach. Mrs. Eliz. B. Eberwein, Postmaster. Artesia Public School Eliz J. Eberwein tchr Punctuation has been added for clarity.

Name	Occupation	Resides with	Name
Brown, A. H.	barber		
Chandler, Wilkinson	fisherman		
Chandler, Wyaat (Bernice)	fruit grower		

Picture of the Artesia School, courtesy, Flossie Station

Wyatt Chandler: May 1871 -

According to the 1900 U.S. Census, Wyatt E. Chandler was born the son of James E. and Emma E. Chandler, May 1871, in Hunter, South Carolina. Wyatt married Bernice Quarterman in 1898. Bernice was born at Cape Canaveral in November 1879.[40] Her parents were George and Anna Quarterman. Wyatt and Bernice had two children; George and Lorena.

Coulter, Geo M. (Brooke)   fruit grower

George M. Coulter: 1865 -

The 1920 Census has George and Brooke living in Canaveral near the Chandlers. George was born in about 1865 and Brooke in 1871 both in Indiana. The census indicated that he was 24 and she 19 when they were married. The 1930 census has them living in Artesia.[41]

Picture of the Wyatt Chandler Family, courtesy, Florida historical Society

Eberwein, Eliz B Mrs.	postmaster	r	John Eberwein
Eberwein, Eliz J.	teacher	r	John Eberwein
Eberwein, John (Eliz B.)	fruit grower		
Eberwein, Otto	fruit grower		
Eberwein, Philip	mech	r	John Eberwein
Eberwein, Wm	mech	r	John Eberwein

Eberwein/Holmes, 1895 - 1942

John Eberwein immigrated to the United States in 1883 from Bavaria.[42] He homesteaded the property that now includes much of the Port in 1895, as a single head of household.[43] He was a farmer and owner of an orange grove. Legend has it that, John Eberwein, took a buggy whip to a Mr. Beuhler who was the abusive husband of Elizabeth Beuhler.[44] Mr. Buehler left the Cape and was never heard from again.[45] Not sure about that because there is a John W. Buehler listed as a laborer in the 1920 U.S. Census for Precinct 13, Canaveral, Florida.[46] However, the 1926-1927 Brevard County Directory of Towns and Cities does not have the name Beuhler listed. Maybe it's true. I'm betting the legend is true.

Elizabeth, in due time, became Mrs. Eberwein and the couple raised two sons and a daughter, William, Philip and Elizabeth. Her three sons, from the first marriage, died in World War 1. There was also a daughter, Anna, who married a brewer in New York.

Elizabeth, became Artesia Postmaster in the 1920s, taking over the office from Col. Harvey Hogan. The Eberwein's lived on the river side of the county road and Col. Hogan was on the ocean. There was a footpath used to get to the beach, always known as Hogan's Trail. In December 1940, her daughter, Elizabeth Holmes took over the job as Postmaster at Artesia and served for the next 26 years. The Artesia Post Office became Port Canaveral in 1954. It may have been located at the Pier for some period of time and it is possible that it moved to the riverside in the late 1930s.

John Eberwein passed away in 1942, at the age of 92, from injuries resulting from falling into a fire that he had built to burn branches he had cut from the orange trees.[47]

Picture of Flossie and Elizabeth Holmes,
courtesy, Flossie Staton

Picture of John and Elizabeth Eberwein,
courtesy, Flossie Staton

Punctuation has been added for clarity.

Name	Occupation	Resides with	Name
Parker Wilson			
Praetorious, Albert M	student	r	Edward J Praetorius
Praetorious, Edw J	fruit grower		
Praetorious, Edw R	eng	r	Edward J Praetorius
Praetorious, Waas	fisherman		
Praetorious, Wm	fruit grower		

Edward J. Praetorious: January 16, 1869 - July 21, 1950

Edward J. Praetorious was appointed 2nd Assistant Lighthouse Keeper at Cape Canaveral November 1, 1904 and left that position September 1907.[48] He was born January 16, 1869 and passed away July 21, 1950, and is buried with his wife Barbara in the Georgiana Graveyard, Merritt Island, Florida.[49]

Mr. Allen H. Andrews and Paul Phillips visited Mrs. Praetorius and her nursery at Cape Canaveral on Nov 3, 1940. Of the nursery he makes the following observation:

"If there is one thing outstanding above another in the Praetorius plant collection it is begonias, of which she has one of the largest and finest collections that I have ever seen. She has a number of Maranta species with attractive markings. Among other oddities was a plant of true commercial ginger. Conspicuous for its showy coloring was a yellow bougainvillea, originated by Mrs Praetorius. I was surprised to note large bearing trees of not only mangoes, avacados (sic), papaya, guavas

and rose apples but rarer fruiting plants such as litchi, sugar apple, muntingea, cecropia, kaffir orange, star apple and Barbados cherry."[50]
A maranta is a red-veined prayer plant.

Another plant, the "Sacred Lily of India... ...is in full foliage at the present time. The foliage lasts for as long as one month and is an interesting sight and the bloom starts to form as soon as the foliage fades."[51]

"Mr. Praetorious is (was) a metal finisher by trade and later worked as a carpenter on most of the Flagler hotels that were constructed many years ago along the East Coast Railway."[52]

Picture of Al Praetorious & Shirley Tucker, courtesy, Rose Wooley

Punctuation has been added for clarity.

Name	Occupation	Resides with	Name
White, Alice			
White, Wm	manager		

Canaveral located between the Banana River and the ocean about 10 miles north of Cocoa Beach, Canaveral is one of the oldest settlements in this part of Florida. The government light house is located in this vicinity. A big and modern harbor is planned for Cape Canaveral. J. J. Jeffords, postmaster. Canaveral light house - Capt. Clinton P. Honeywell, keeper. Canaveral School - Eliz. F. Evrand, teacher.[53]

Picture of the Lighthouse School and possibly Elizabeth Evard, courtesy, the Burns Collection & Rose Wooley

Punctuation has been added for clarity.

Name	Occupation	Resides with	Name
Arton, Margt M. Mrs.			
Arton, Paul,	Laborer	r	Mrs. M. M. Arton
Atkinson, Quincey E.	Lighthouse Kpr	r	C. P. Honeywell
Breuning, L. F. (Laura)			
Burns, Kath	Student	r	R. C. Burns

| Burns, Edith | Student | r | R. C. Burns |
| Burns, Robt C. (Bessie M.) | Real est | | |

Elliot Judson Burns: March 17, 1854 - December 28, 1896

Elliot J. Burns helped build and develop the "neighborhood" of Cape Canaveral where he and wife Mary lived with three children Robert C., Isabelle and Edith A. Elliot J. Burns passed away December 28, 1896 his obituary in the Indian River Advocate read: "Mr. Burns passed and was returned to Eau Gallie on the schooner Edna and was taken to Canaveral by the steamer Spartan, for interment. He is buried in the Burnham Cemetery on Cape Canaveral."[54]

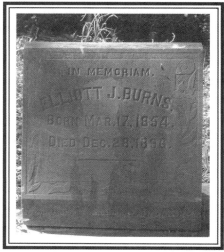

Picture of Elliot J. Burns grave, courtesy, the Burns Collection, John Whitney

The Burns family, led by Mary and oldest son Robert, made a significant contribution to the development of Cape Canaveral with their work in commercializing the Palmetto Berries that grow all over Cape Canaveral. From Tile and Till, February 1923, "Eli Lilly & Company are numbered among the saw palmetto berry customers of Mr. Burns."[55] This would have been Robert C. Burns.

The Tile and Till provides a peak into the perils of depending on making a sustained living from growing and harvesting Saw Palmetto Berries:

> All saw palmetto berries are not suitable for gathering. The bushes are subjected to at least one disease, called by local gatherers blight. It appears as a fungus only in the past ten years. It appears to be spreading and makes crop rather an uncertain quantity. Most of the damage occurs just before the ripening season and causes the berries to drop off. The pulp of this fruit is watery and is impossible to cure it with good results.[56]

The Tile and Till continues with a salute to R. C. Burns.

> It takes courage to be a gather of Saw Palmetto berries. A man must be brave enough to go into the bushes and trust to providence that a rattlesnake or a cottonmouth moccasin will not bite him. Last autumn forty-five or more were killed in the Canaveral section of Florida. There seems to be a fascination about the work, and while danger is always present and many narrow escapes are reported yet in a period of thirty-five years, since saw palmetto gathering first started in this section, there has been but one fatality. .... A mule was bitten by a huge rattler. The animal died in exactly one hour and thirty-five minutes after much suffering. The fang wounds were spaced two and a quarter inches apart.[57]

The picture here is of Mr. Burns holding up a Diamondback Rattlesnake. The same picture was published in the Tile and Till in 1923.

Robert Cleveland Burns:
November 17, 1882 - September 23, 1957

Robert married Bessie Benner Meyer at Titusville on December 30, 1903. Along with mother Mary Burns, Robert C. Burns, wife Bessie, son of Elliot Meyer, born July 28, 1914; daughters Meredith, born September 16, 1905; Catherine Benner, born July 27, 1908; and Mary Louise, born January 22, 1919, contributed to the development of fruit growing on the Cape by "demonstrating that avocado pears can be successfully grown on this side - the only draw-back being that occasionally it is cold enough to freeze them. But anyone wanting to go into raising them on a large scale could with a little capital, fire a grove in time of a freeze, and reap a rich reward."[58]

Picture of Burns holding a rattlesnake skin, courtesy, the Burns Collection, John Whitney

Mr. Burns must have been very proud of his school teacher daughter. According to the Cocoa Tribune, "Miss Katherine (Catherine) Burns, who is teaching in Eau Gallie, spent the weekend at the home of her father, R. C. Burns."[59] A politician? Why not? "R. C. (Bob) Burns, of Artesia, formally announced his candidacy for nomination as State Senator in April 1944.[60]

Robert passed away September 23, 1957. His funeral services were held on September 26, 1957 at Wylie Funeral Home Chapel in Cocoa, Interment was in Titusville."[61]

Picture of Mary Louise Burns, courtesy, the Burns Collection, John Whitney

Picture of Meredith, Elliot, and Mary Burns, courtesy, the Burns Collection and John Whitney

Directory Continues:

Name	Occupation	Resides with	Name
Canaveral Harbor Lodge	Mrs. Ruby Marks, Mgr.		
Canaveral Public School	Eliz F. Evarard teacher	r	C. P. Honeywell
Chaplain, Mary F.		r	Chas Lansing
Clapp, Glenn	laborer		
Coleman, Rufus (Margt)	farmer		

Albert B. Carter: 1862 - 1944
Rufus Henry Coleman: August 11, 1886 - March 9, 1973

Albert and Katherine Carter migrated from Minnesota to Florida in the 1880s. They had seven children: Lily, Walter, George, Margaret, Nathan, Rose, and Clayton most were born in Georgiana (south Merritt Island). Although a record cannot be found, Walter homesteaded at Cape Canaveral in the early 1900s. The 1920 United States Census shows an Albert B. Carter living at Cape Canaveral and with a father's birth place of Minnesota.[62] According to descendant, Shirley Kid, "the Homestead consisted to 40 acres just west of the Pier,"[63] placing the homestead near the turn where Pier Road turns north toward the lighthouse.

Margaret Adell Carter met and married Rufus Henry Coleman, who was born in South Carolina, on August 11, 1886.[64] He registered for World War I on June 5, 1917. On the registration form 596, he indicated that he had a wife and child to support and resided in Georgiana, Florida; meaning that he and Margaret Carter were married prior to June 1917.[65] The 1920 U.S. Census has the family living in Titusville.

By 1926, Rufus and Margaret Coleman had become residents of Cape Canaveral, possibly homesteading in 1924. They are listed in a "listing of Canaveral residents from 1926-1927."[66] His occupation is listed as "farmer." The listing does not mention a Carter family.

Upon arrival at Cape Canaveral, the family lived in two tents; one large tent and one small tent. They slept on camp cots. According Margaret Catherine Coleman, "We lived in the tents until we saw this huge, big rattlesnake crawl though the yard. So, he hurried and got the foundation and floor laid for the house, and put the tents on top of it

Picture of House, courtesy, Flossie Staton

'til he finished it (the house). The platform was built up approximately 4 feet above the ground on railroad ties because of the snakes and the low savannahs. The house had two large rooms and a little kitchen "shed" on the back and a tiny screen porch." The above would be Rufus Coleman.

Margaret tells of "an awful storm in the early 1920s. All the roads were out due to the savannahs, really low and no trees. When the storm hit, there was about 5 feet of water in the front yard. Also, it blew so hard that it took off the roof and the railroad ties the house was on were all leaning." That probably was the August 1928 hurricane that arrived at Cape Canaveral as a category 1 storm.[70]

By the 1930 U.S. census the Coleman's had moved back to the mainland Georgiana. Their family had grown to 14 year old, Catherine; 10 years old, Rheta (Reta); 7 years old, Ina; and 1 year old Henry C.[71]

Directory Continues:

Name	Occupation	Resides with	Name
Creel, Jessie B			
Crocker, Louis	carpenter	r	Jas Merchant
Crowder, Ivan (Iva)			

Ivan Crowder: - 1892

The Fifteenth (1930) U.S. Federal Census has an Ivan Crowder living at Cape Canaveral and his wife being born in 1892. His occupation is listed as Labor, Public Road. Both Crowders were born in California. Mr. Crowder lists his parents as having been born in Texas. Interestingly, an Emma Crowder is listed as a renter with her age at 72 years and her birth place as Texas. She was probably the mother of Ivan. The Crowder family may have lived in section 16 near current day Launch Pad 16 at Cape Canaveral.[71]

Davis, Frank	carpenter		
Davis, Leonard	carpenter	r	Frank Davis
Davis, Nora		r	Frank Davis

John L. Easterlin: May 17, 1881 - February 15, 1930

John Easterlin was born May 17, 1881 at High Springs, Alachua, Florida. He was the eldest son of Charles Brooks Easterlin, Sr. and Maria A. (Sissy) Jeffords. John's family home was in High Springs, but Charles Brooks Easterlin, Sr. worked for Alachua County as a Clerk in Gainesville.

John and Busie Julia Jeffords Greathouse were married in Jacksonville around 1920. Sam L. Jeffords gave the couple, as a wedding gift, property on the Cape where Space Launch Complex 14 is now located. John Whitney tells us that John and Busie were the only family on the Cape to have a maid.[72] How about that?

Now here's a story. John Easterlin owned a dump truck and made good money hauling gravel, etc for road beds. According to John Whitney, on the evening of the February 14, 1930, John arrived at the shell pit for his load. The foreman would not load him as it was after 5 P.M. John made a comment to the effect that "if I had my pearl handled pistol, you would load me."[73]

The next morning after getting a load of gravel, his truck went off the road in the soft shell rock, and turned over. He was taken to the hospital in Melbourne where he died later that day. John died on February 15, 1930, and is buried at Cape Canaveral. A white cross marks his grave.[74]

The Easterlin's sold forty acres of their property, some if not all, to Mr. E. W. Sweet of Kalamazoo, Michigan in April of

Picture of John Easterlin, courtesy the Letasky Collection, Darlene Kosko

1929. The Cocoa Tribune tells us: "The acreage comprises about 500 feet of ocean frontage. Mr. Sweet is a grower of blueberries and has about 400 plants put out on Merritt Island as a demonstration farm. He believes that Merritt Island will produce blueberries on an extensive scale that will make the industry grow here."[75]

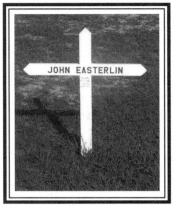

After John's death, Busie Easterlin married Guy Carlisle. Busie was born November 5, 1900 in Miami, Florida and passed away on December 7, 1937. She is buried at Cape Canaveral. Busie was survived by a daughter Mrs. A. E. Whitney, Brother Julius J. Jeffords, and sisters Elizabeth Jeffords, Bettie Mae Easterlin, and grand children Leonard (John) Whitney and Lawerence Whitney.[76]

Picture of John Easterlin's grave taken by author

From left: Busie Carlisle's grave stone taken by author, Bussie funeral, and Busie Julia Jeffords' grave, courtesy John Whitney

Directory Continues:

Name	Occupation	Resides with	Name
Erickson, M. W.	farmer		
Evrard, Eliz F.	teacher	Cape Canaveral School	

Evrard, Eliz. F.

Elizabeth F. Evrard was one of the first teachers at Cape Canaveral. She came to teach Assistant Keeper Butler's children in 1922. She was born in 1868 in Franklin, Missouri and lived with her father Francis, mother Emily, and sisters Mary W.; Lithe M.; Cora J.; Amelia Ann and brother Isaac. In the 1880 U.S. Census, Francis Evrard declared his occupation to be a physician and farmer.[77] See Chapter 6

Foley, Jos E. (Alice)   farmer

From the Cocoa Tribune dated March 29, 1929: "J. E. Foley has recently purchased some fine breeding rabbits for his rabbitry (don't know if that's a word). He intends to build up the rabbit industry to quite an extent here at Canaveral and put it on a substantial, profitable basis."[78]

Directory Continues:

Name	Occupation	Resides with		Name
Gerry, Wm L. (Irene G.)	salesman	Lansing & Stillman	h	Canaveral Beach
Greenlaw, Margt Mrs				

Margaret Greenlaw

The Greenlaw homestead may have been located near the present day Complex 14 or 16. The picture here, was taken in late 1925, in front of the Greenlaw homestead. From Left to right are Susan Robinson, Nellie Robinson, Maggie Greenlaw, Louise Robinson, Frank Robinson and baby Margaret. Margaret (Maggie) Greenlaw was Louise Robinson's mother.

Picture of Maggie Greenlaw and the Robinsons, courtesy, Rose Wooley

Godberg Gulbrandsen: December 11, 1863 - February 3, 1919
Marie Elizabeth Quarterman Gulbrandsen: 1875 - 1943

Picture of Godberg Gulbrandsen (Goody) courtesy, Memory Ancestry.com

The Gulbrandsen family originated from Egeberg, Buskerud, Norway. Two of the brothers, Andrew and Nils Gulbrandsen homesteaded at the Cape. Another brother, Godberg Gulbrandsen born December 11, 1863, married Marie Quarterman who was born in 1875, the daughter of Orlando and Catherine Quarterman. The couple had a son name Godberg, born May 1, 1919 and passed away April 5, 2001. He was called Goody. Marie Elizabeth Quarterman passed away in 1943.

While Andrew and Nils were homesteading at the Cape, Andrew died around the turn of the century from Tuberculosis and his homestead property was sold to Samuel Jeffords for the sum of one dollar. Sam Jeffords, in turn, gave an area of the land to be used as the cemetery where he and several others are buried. The cemetery is now known as the Cape Canaveral Community Cemetery. Nils Gulbrandsen left Florida for South Africa and was not heard from again.[79] See Appendix II.

Picture of the Gulbrandsen brothers, courtesy, Darlene Kosko

Directory Continues:

Name   Occupation   Resides with   Name

Hall, Frank A. (Ida)   farmer

Thomas Hardin: March 10, 1855 - November 12, 1937

Picture of Thomas Hardin and Addie, courtesy, Evie Grose

Thomas Hardin was born March 10, 1855 and Addie Bell Hardin was born May 14, 1865. Thomas and Addie were married on January 8, 1889 in Illinois. In 1900, they lived in Keithsburg City, Mercer, Illinois and had four children. At some point between 1900 and 1910 they and their five children moved to Kansas. There were two boys; Edward Lee and Glenn Raymond, and three girls; Verna Maude, Ida Viola, and Grace Henrietta Hardin. In 1926 the Hardin's left Kansas for sunny Palm Beach, Florida.

The Hurricane of 1928 and its destruction caused them to leave Palm Beach and relocate to Cape Canaveral in Artesia. The September 16, 1928 Hurricane was the deadliest storm in Florida History. It was a Category 4 monster packing winds of 150 miles per hour, killed over 2,300 people, caused catastrophic damage and left thousands homeless.[80]

Picture of Hardin's grave stone taken by Author

After coming to Cape Canaveral the Hardin's lived in the last house on Pier Road on Cape Canaveral. From there they started building boats and a commercial fishing business. Addie canned all their meats and vegetables and helped Ida Viola by watching her grandchildren while Ida worked. Ida took in laundry, baked fresh bread for the Hotel and later on worked for the Hotel. Ida Hardin Shockey helped run the hotel; she cleaned rooms, cooked meals and did anything that was needed to keep the Hotel in operation.[81]

Addie Hardin died July 24, 1932 and Thomas passed away November 12, 1937. The Hardin's are buried side by side in the Cape Canaveral Community Cemetery.

John Harvey Hogan: November 19, 1832 - July 14, 1922

John Harvey Hogan was born in "Dublin, Ireland November 19, 1832 and came to America when he was a very young man. He joined the Union Army during the Civil War, and was promoted to the rank of Colonel."[82] He came to America in about 1847 and arrived in Florida in 1880 along with his wife Louisa. "Mrs. Hogan was born in Germany and came to the United States when she was five years old and settled in New York. She met and married Colonel Hogan in St Louis, Missouri."[83] The couple settled in Artesia. Artesia was a small community located just a bit north of where Port Canaveral now exists. At some point in time, in the late 1890s or early 1900s, a Post Office was established at Artesia.

"Col John Harvey Hogan was the first Post Master of Artesia in the late 1890s and a man named Wise was appointed Post Master for a short time after Col Hogan, then Elizabeth Eberwein took over the Post Master duties in 1911 and served until 1940."[84]

According to the 1920 U.S. Federal Census, John H. Hogan lived at Canaveral, Florida was married to Louisa and had three other people in the household: Mary M. Schaeffler age 62; James H. Kempton age 8 and Elizabeth Kempton age 5.[85] Mary Schaeffer was Mrs. Hogan's sister.[86]

Little more is known about the family. Colonel Hogan had been in declining health for some time before he passed away. "He is buried in the Georgiana Cemetery"[87] Mrs. Hogan passed away in November of 1937 and is buried in Pinecrest Cemetery.[88]

Directory Continues:

Name	Occupation	Resides with		Name
Holmes Beatrice	student	r	H. L. Holmes	(See Eberwein)
Holmes, Howard L.	farmer			

Howard L. Holmes: 1871

The 1930 Census has Mr. Holmes being born in about 1871 and living at Cape Canaveral with his daughter Beatrice. His occupation was listed as farmer, citrus grower. He listed his birthplace as Ohio. Beatrice was born in about 1912.

Honeywell, Clinton P. Capt (Gertrude) lighthouse keeper
Clinton P. Honeywell has been written about in earlier Chapters and in the Keepers of the light.

Honeywell, Clinton P. Jr	student	r	C. P. Honeywell
Honeywell, Florence	student	r	C. P. Honeywell
Jandreaux, Chas (Vida)	farmer		
Jandreaux, Nicholas	r	Chas Jandreaux	

Charles William Jandreau: September 27, 1884 - January 1937

Captain Charles W. Jandreau was born on September 27, 1884 in Madison, South Dakota. He was widely known as a guide and a deep sea fisherman. He married Vida Kate King of Shell Pond, Florida on April 10, 1904 in Vero Beach.

"Charles W. Jandreau moved to Vero Beach after the railroad. For a while, Henry Gifford was offering land free to anyone who would come and build a 10-by-10-foot shack. Jandreau was the only one who took advantage of the offer. In 1905, Jandreau was building his house on the riverfront property."[89]

"Charles W. Jandreau passed away in the Marine Hospital at Savannah, Georgia. He was 52 years old and had been ill for several months.[90] The Captain is buried at Canaveral."

Picture of Jandreau grave stone
taken by Author

Vida Kate (King) Jandreau: July 10, 1883 - September 11, 1942

Vida Kate King was born at Shell Pond in Levy County, Florida, July 10, 1883. She was the first of eight children born to Mary Jane Patrick Tuten King and Nicholas King. Vida Kate married Charles Jandreau, and their children are: Charles Lawrence, Nicholas, Julia Yola, Eugene Jerome, and Ernest Israel.[91] They made their home at Canaveral for about 15 years.

Vida Kate passed away on September 11, 1942 and is buried in the Cape Canaveral Cemetery beside her husband.

Nicholas N. Jandreau: September 13, 1909 - June 17, 1931

Picture of Nicholas Jandreau's grave stone taken by Author

Nicholas Jandreau, was the second son of Mr. and Mrs. Charles Jandreau. His death was caused by measles following a bad case of pneumonia. "Nick, as all his friends called him, was a quiet, home loving young man, and his father's constant companion. He was upright and liked by all who knew him. Funeral services were held at the grave site, Canaveral Cemetery."[92]

Directory Continues:

Name	Occupation	Resides with	Name
Jandreaux, Lawrence		r	Chas Jandreaux
Jeffords, Julius J (Florence A.)	post master		
Jeffords, Saml L (Kath)			

Samuel L. Jeffords: September 18, 1857 - November 11, 1941

Samuel L. Jeffords (Julius Samuel LaLare Jeffords), now that's a name for you, was born September 18, 1857 at Bluffton, Beaufort, South Carolina. Jeffords bought his first property at Cape Canaveral in 1885. Although he never spoke with Capt. Burnham, he did continue a practice that

Picture of Sam Jeffords grave stone taken by author

Burnham perfected. When Samuel's daughters would marry, he gave each a piece of land on Cape Canaveral. Marry a daughter and get land at Cape Canaveral, sounds like he took a page from Burnham's play book. When Busie Julia Jeffords married John L. Easterlin, the couple was given the property at the Cape Canaveral where Space Launch Complex 14 is now located.[93]

Samuel Jeffords participated in the construction of the Canaveral Pier and served as Post Master for the Cape Canaveral Post Office from September 4, 1913 - December 22, 1917. Sam bought the piece of property now know as the Cape Canaveral Community Cemetery from Nils Gulbrandsen for one dollar and donated it to the people that lived on the Cape.[94] Sam passed away November 11, 1941 and is buried next to his fist wife, son, Joseph, and daughter Busie at the

Canaveral Cemetery.[95] Busie, passed away December 7, 1937. See Appendix I.

Directory Continues:

Name	Occupation	Resides with	Name
Joselin, Wm		r	G. N. Kimble
Knight, Edw L (Lorten)			
Kimble, Geo			
Kincaid, Bert W. (Bertha)			

Bert W. Kincaid: 1870

The 1935 Florida State Census has a Bert Kincaid born in 1870 in Massachusetts living at Cape Canaveral.[96] Even though the directory, above, had him married to a lady named Bertha the census had him listed as a widower.

King, Thomas Y	carpenter	(See Tuten/King)
King, Waneta		r
Chas Jandreaux		

Samuel Knutson: December 1, 1884 - September 1967

Picture of Sam Knutson, courtesy, Rose Wooley

Samuel L. and Lorena Knutson, along with daughter Nonie, lived on the Banana River side of Cape Canaveral. They fished the river for mullet and the ocean for shrimp. Once caught, the shrimp were "beheaded" at the pier, packed in ice and shipped to market. They planted groves of oranges, grapefruit, tangerines, even planted banana, mulberry and lemon trees.[97] The 1930 Census has them listed as living at Artesia with daughter Noni and 69 year old Anna Quarteman.

On Nonie's fifth birthday, her father, Sam Knutson gave her a birthday party that made the paper. "Little Miss Nona Knutson celebrated her fifth birthday on Wednesday and had as her guests, Misses Billey Chandler, Betty and Frances Carter, Milton Jergenson, Mrs. Wyatt Chandler, Mrs. T. G. Carter and Mrs. O. H. Chandler."[98]

Samuel L. Knutson was among the first school teachers to teach in the Cape Canaveral Lighthouse School when Keeper Honeywell converted one of the storage buildings into a school house.[99] He also served a Port Canaveral Commissioner before it was dredged. His home was in Artesia, but he maintained a real estate office in Cocoa.[100]

The Knutson's raised chickens to eat or sell and farmed. With help from Wyatt Chandler, Lorena's father, Sam and Lorena planted a three acre vegetable farm. Wild deer, quail, even an occasional black bear provided food for the families.[101]

Sam Knutson must have enjoyed life because on "Saturday, November 20, 1915 he entertained a select party of friends from Artesia, Courtney and Canaveral at the Light-House. Dancing in the shade of the tower to the strains of "Meet me in the Shadows" rendered by a Victrola, was the order of the day. Knutson and Quarterman won their way into the hearts of those present with their impersonation of "Castles" in their swing waltz, foxtrot and one-step canter. Everyone voted it the greatest social event since the erection of the tower in 1864.[102] The tower was erected a bit later, see chapter on the Iron Lighthouse for the date. Okay, what the heck, it was 1868 and relocated in 1894.

Directory Continues:

Name	Occupation	Resides with	Name
Lansing, Chas (Mabel; Lansing & Stillman, Cocoa)			

Charles Lansing: March 23, 1872 - January 15, 1944

Captain Lansing was born in Plattsburg, New York, March 23, 1872. He was educated at the Plattsburg Academy and at Columbia University. He was the last of a long line of newspaper publishers and when barley of age succeeded his grandfather, Wendell Lansing, as editor and publisher of the Essex County Republican.[103]

"Newspaper editor Wendell Lansing was a well-known abolitionist. In 1839, when he was 30 years old, Lansing founded the Essex County Republican, a Whig newspaper published in Keese-ville. He was forced out of the paper in 1846 when he was not allowed to use it as a platform for his staunchly abolition-ist views. From 1846 to 1854 he lived in exile in Wilmington, doing odd jobs around the community, until he was called back to start a new abolitionist paper in Keeseville, which later merged with the Republican. Lansing died in 1887."[104]

In 1917, Charles Lansing was commissioned as Captain in the U.S. Army and in April 1919, he was given command of a force of 285 Coast Artillery troops and ordered to France. There he joined the 54th Coast Artillery near Rheims France.[105] On October 21, 1918, while on special duty at the front, Captain Lansing was gassed and wounded at Bradant-sur-Meuse, and sent to an army hospital. He was under treatment for seven months and finally was sent home on a hospital ship in 1919.[106]

Picture of Wendell Lansing, courtesy, Lake Placid News

"Capt. Lansing came to Canaveral in about 1924, and served as secretary of the Cocoa Chamber of Commerce for a time. Later he developed Canaveral Beach Park at Canaveral a real estate development." Capt Lansing played a major role in the attempt to commercialize Cape Canaveral in 1929 with the construction of

Picture of Lansing Home at Canaveral Beach from advertisement by Apollo.

the Harbor Inn, Hotel.

Mr. Leigh Chamberlin, who lived on Cape Canaveral for four years 1930 -1942, recounted in an interview with Bob Hudson and reported in the Florida Today April 18, 2001 that "his father served in World War I under a man by the name of Capt. Lansing who told him about a town being built on Cape Canaveral." In 1938 the **Chamberlin family** moved to Cape Canaveral for health reasons and occupied the only house ever built on the extreme east end of the Cape.[109]

Picture of home at east end of the Cape, courtesy, The Seidel Collection

William Letasky: January 10, 1919 - February 14, 1983

Picture of William and Betty May, courtesy, Darlene Kosko

William Adam Letasky, was born January 10, 1919 in Ohio. He enlisted as a Private in the in the U.S. Army, on August 1, 1942, at Little Rock, Arkansas.[110] William Letasky, in 1943, met Betty Mae (Jeffords) of Cape Canaveral and married her in Palm Beach, Florida. Note: ancestry.com records indicate that the name of the bride was Betty Mae Tucker.[111] The 1945 Florida Census has the couple living in Duval County in 1945.[112] Betty Mae was born Elizabeth Mae Atkinson, but her name was changed when she was adopted by Julius J. Jeffords because he already had a daughter named Elizabeth.

William Adam and Betty Mae must have moved to Cape in or about 1945 and lived in the north part of Cape Canaveral and were blessed with five children William Emre (1944), John Stephen (1944) Margarette Elizabeth, and Darlene Letasky Kosko (1950).

"Their home was moved to along the Banana River on North Merritt Island when the government purchased the property in the 1950s. Both the Jeffords and Letasky's lived there until the government bought that land for what was then called the NASA Launch Operations Center, now known as Kennedy Space Center. Their homes were again literally picked up and moved across the Indian River to the mainland of Cocoa. When William Adam Letasky left the service, he went to work for the Port Canaveral fishing fleet. Betty was a homemaker."[113]

Margarette Elizabeth Letasky: 1945 - February 10, 1948

A white cross marking a tiny grave is the only visual

Picture of Margarette Letasky's grave taken by Author

reminder that 3 year old Margarette Letasky lived at Cape Canaveral. At the time of her death, she was the only daughter in this family of five.

Obituary: "Baby Letasky, Margaret (Sic) Elizabeth Letasky, 3 year old daughter of Mr. and Mrs. Wm. A. Letasky, of Artesia, passed away at the local hospital at 5:40 a.m. Thursday. Funeral services were held Saturday morning, Feb. 12, at 10:30 at the Koon-Wylie Chapel with Father Michael Reynolds, of St. Mary's Catholic Church, officiating. Interment was at Canaveral. Besides the parents, the little girl is survived by two brothers, Wm. Emory and John Steven, of Artesia."[114]

Directory Continues:

Name	Occupation	Resides with	Name
Lewis, Wm B.	mechanic		
Lohr, Ernest			
Marks, Ruby (wid B.O.)	mgr Canaveral Harbor Inn		

William Makowsky: May 12, 1861 - August 25, 1947

Picture of William Makowsky's grave stone taken by Author

William Makowsky immigrated to this country from Germany. He and his wife Clara came to Cape Canaveral in about 1926. The Makowsky's had a son that attended the University of Florida. "William Makowsky who is a student at the University of Florida, at Gainesville, is spending his spring vacation with his father and at the Harbor."[115]

He passed away in his residence at Merritt Island, Florida on August 25, 1947. Graveside services were held at the Canaveral Cemetery, Artesia, Father Mark McLaughlin of Melbourne Catholic Church officiated.[116]

Many thought that Mrs. Makowsky was buried next to her husband.. The following may put that to rest: "Mrs. Clara E. Makowsky, 84, formerly of Merritt Island, passed away in April 1955 at a St. Petersburg rest home. The remains were sent to Philadelphia where funeral services and interment will occur."[117]

Directory Continues:

Name	Occupation	Resides with	Name
Merchant, Jas W. (Hazel)	farmer		

Merchant, Jas W.

The Cocoa Tribune reported that the "Adventist Church has received a gift from Mrs. James Merchant of her former home on the county road."[118] The "county road" would be the present day Samuel L. Phillips Parkway. "The present church at Whidden Center will be taken down and used to remodel this building, which will become the future home as the Canaveral Adventist Church."[119]

Directory Continues:

Name	Occupation	Resides with	Name
Miller, Wm F.		r	E. L. Knight
Moore, Chas M. (Phyllis)	farmer		

Chas. M. Moore

According to the 1930 US Census, Charles Moore was a renter, born in about 1880. His wife Phyllis was born in about 1887, and both were born in Georgia and married in about 1907. Mr. Moore has his occupation listed as Laborer, Public Roads. Children living with them were daughter, Muriel 19; son Keith 18, with a listed occupation of Fisherman River. Daughters Mildred 16; Martha 14; and Carol age 5. Assuming the Census data is correct the family moved from Georgia to Cape Canaveral in 1925.[120] They may have lived in Section 12, which would be south of the Nathan Penny Homestead.[121]

Moore, Wm H (Mary C.)
Morgan, Kath
Norrell, Percy R. (Martha)   farmer

Percy R. Norrell

There is a Russell Norrell with a wife named Martha listed in the 1930 U.S. Census for Cape Canaveral. The 1910 Census has Mr. Norrell being born in Georgia in 1885 the son of Robert and Odelonia Norrell.[122] Martha was born in Georgia in about 1890. The 1930 Census has the age at marriage for Russell at 17 and Martha age 35. That would be impossible. Apparently a Thomas C. Fowler and Walter Fowler were boarders with the Norrell's at Cape Canaveral in 1930.[123]

Norseworthy, Wm (Mary)   carpenter
See Chapter 6 for information about William A. Norsworthy.

Post Office J. J. Jeffords   post master
Quarterman, Oscar F (Florence)   lighthouse keeper

Picture of
Verginia W. Quarterman's
grave stone taken by Author

William G. M. Quarterman: September 6, 1816 - December 25, 1869

William George Middleton Quarterman and his wife Mary A. Thomas were both born in Georgia. W. G. M. was born in 1816 and Mary A. was born on May 26, 1817. They were married in about 1838. The couple had seven children: Fanny A, born 1839; Margaret born 1840; Emma W. born 1842; Robert T. born in 1845; Orlando Adolphus born in 1848; Nette A. born in 1851; and George M. born in 1856.[124] William G. M. Quarterman was a teacher and Margaret was an assistant teacher.[125]

Mary A. Quarterman passed away on March 15, 1878. She is buried in one of the two

Picture of Quarterman graves
taken by Author

Picture of W. G. M. Quarterman's grave stone
taken by Author

Quarteman cemeteries beside her husband and a grandchild, Verginia W. Quarterman (July 17, 1888 - October 24, 1888) at Cape Canaveral.

George M. Quarterman lived on Cape Canaveral and married Anna Dummet Burnham in the 1880s. They had three children: Oscar Floyd, born at Cape Canaveral in October 1882; George, January 1880; and Bernice, March 1887.[126]

George M. Quarterman would become Keeper of the Cape Canaveral Lighthouse when his father-in-law, Mills O. Burnham passed away in 1886. Eventually his son, Oscar Floyd Quarterman, would become an Assistant Keeper. They lived in a nice home located on just off the Banana River.

Oscar Floyd Quarterman married Florence Wilson, daughter of Henry and Frances Burnham Wilson, who was born April 1, 1881. They had three children. Oscar Floyd became Assistant Keeper of the Cape Canaveral Lighthouse August 1, 1923 and Keeper on January 23, 1930.[127]

Picture of Ann D. Quarterman, courtesy, the Memory Project, Florida Archives

George M: 1856 - 1923 and Anna D.: 1860 - February 12, 1945 are buried in their family cemetery on Cape Canaveral. White crosses mark their graves.

Nathan N. Penny: 1828 -- February 11, 1911

Nathan N. Penny was born on Long Island, New York. He was the first child of Nathan and Hannah Penny. Nathan N. Penny came to Cape Canaveral in 1878[128] and on June 13, 1884, he was issued Homestead Certificate no. 4304 "for lots one, two and three of section twelve in township twenty three, south of range thirty seven ease of Tallahassee Meridian in Florida, containing eighty-eight acres and eighty six hundredths of an acre."[129]

According to the 1900 Census, Nathan and Maria must have had three children: Nathan O.; born July 3, 1877,[130] Fanny M.; born September 1878, and Rosalind; born February 1880. Maria Penny

Picture of
Nathan N. Penny's grave
taken by author

Picture of
Maria Penny's grave
taken by author

passed away on July 1, 1890 and is buried on Cape Canaveral.[131] At some time after Maria passed away Nathan married a lady named Lovina or Leorna E. Washburne; little is known about her.[132]

Nathan Penny grew grapefruits on 60 acres of land on Cape Canaveral. Well how about this? Between 1891-1899 the town of Nathan was located on the east side of the Banana River and is assumed to have began as a steamboat landing near the Penny Homestead. Looks like Nathan Penny took a note from Henry Titus. The town of Nathan only lasted only a few years and is shown on Cape Canaveral in an 1899 map.[133]

Picture of Nathan O. Penny in car, courtesy, Rose Wooley

The first automobile in Vero Beach was an Orient Buckboard. Shown in the picture are Mr. and Mrs. Nathan O. Penny and their children. Mrs. Penny, the former Ruby Sarah Gifford, was the sister of Charles Gifford. She was just three years old when in 1888, she and her brother moved to Vero Beach to live with their parents. The automobile was brought in by boat and was assembled in Vero Beach.[134]

Between 1903 and 1908 they made approximately 2,500 Orient Buckboard Cars at the Waltham Manufacturing Company on Rumford Avenue in Boston. The cars were sold all over the world and today they are a big part of America's history on cars. Recently a survey was taken throughout the world of all Orient Buckboards in existence today. There are a total of 57 Orient Buckboard owners today; 45 are in the United States and, of course, one of these is at the Waltham Museum.[135]

Captain Penny passed away on February 11, 1911[136] and is buried beside Maria. Captain Penny's grave went unmarked for over ninety years until a white cross bearing his name was placed at his grave in 2004.

Picture of Frank Robinson, courtesy, Rose Wooley

Directory Continues:

Name	Occupation	Resides with	Name
Rasmussen, Marie Mrs.			
Robinson, Marie Mrs.			

Robinson and Greenlaw

The Robinson's and Greenlaw's may have had homesteads near the present day Complex 14.

Siskind, Marcus

Spies, John   mail carrier

The 1930 US Census lists John Spies as born in 1897 in New York; and living with him is wife Hazel age 34, also born in New York; his six year old daughter, Dorothy, and a Brother-in Law, Jason Clapp at Cape Canaveral. Jason's employment is listed as barber.[137]

Picture of Hubert Wensley Syfertt's grave, photo taken by author

Stewart, John C.

Swanson, Ralph (Gertrude)   artist   r   O. F. Quarterman

Syfret, Nellie   student   r   David Syfret

David Syfrett (Syfret)

David and Elizabeth Syfertt came to Cape Canaveral in 1926 and purchased land from Samuel Jeffords. According to the 1930 United States Census, the Syfrett family consisted of David and Elizabeth, Kenneth, 17; De Veland, 15 and Glendee age 13.[138]

Mrs. Rose Wooley writes that "Lillian Syfrett would eventually become the third wife of Samuel Jeffords."[139] Hubert Wensley Syfertt was born August 27, 1929 and died December 31, 1931 and is buried in the Cape Canaveral Community at Cape Canaveral.[140] Hurbert was not listed in the 1930 Census.

Picture of the Terryn House/Store, courtesy, the Brevard Historical Commission

Charles A. Terryn: September 4, 1891 - January 12, 1949

Charles Terryn arrived in the United States on October 6, 1903. He was a 13 years old when he left Antwerp, Belgium on a ship named the Finland.[141] He moved from Chicago, Illinois to Cape Canaveral along with the Whidden family in the late 1920s.

Charles married Aline Mask in

Picture of Terryn grave stone, taken by author

1937, and started a family at Canaveral with the birth of their first daughter Myrtice in 1938, son Charles was born in 1939, followed by Hazel in 1942 and then Shirley in 1943.[142]

Charles homesteaded approximately 25 acres close to the river, on the east side of the Cape Road, now known as Phillips Parkway, where he built a home for his family. In 1942, with the help of Robert Mask, who came to the Cape in 1933, Charles built a house with a storefront for his mother, Prudence Ardelia, and sister Charlotte. The house was approximately 30 feet long and 24 feet wide, constructed of heart pine lumber and sat on concrete block piers stacked two high. The approximately 700 square foot house consisted of a living room across the front, two bedrooms and one bathroom on the left side, a small kitchen and a screened porch across the back. A 10 foot x 10 foot store was built onto the front of the house that sat on a concrete slab foundation at ground level.[143]

Prudence Terryn opened Terryn's Store and sold snacks such as candies, cheese and crackers, peanut crackers, and a variety of chewing gum: Black Jack, Clove, Cinnamon, Juicy Fruit and Cokes. She also sold Gulf gasoline and kerosene. If milk, bread, canned goods, and other staples, were needed, they could be purchased at Tolly Whidden's Store. Both places were on Pier Road.[144]

School bus drivers Dixie and Ben Lewis transported the six children that lived at Canaveral to school in Cocoa. Children played games, climbed trees, and young Charles played - butt head with the goats, which was done very gently.[145]

Charlie Terryn was engaged in the palmetto berry business on the Cape. He built drying frames four feet high from the ground for the berries, which were harvested in the fall. It was hard work - from dawn to dusk - cutting stalks of berries, stripping the berries into hampers, and hauling them to the drying frames. By spring the berries would be dry and ready to pack into burlap sacks and transport, by truck, to the Cocoa train station and shipped to various pharmaceutical companies. Charlie died in 1949, and is buried at the Cape Canaveral cemetery.[146]

Picture of William and Flora Tucker, courtesy, Rose Wooley

Directory Continues:

Name	Occupation	Resides with	Name
Tucker, Elmo	laborer	r	W. A. Tucker

Picture of the Tuckers, courtesy, Rose Wooley

William A. Tucker: January 25, 1879 - April 18, 1957

William Andrew Tucker met Ms. Flora Haygood Anderson, January 2, 1888 - 1955, from Manatee County, Florida and they were married on February 19, 1906 in Fort Christmas, Florida. In about 1921 - 1922, William and Flora Tucker, with their four boys, moved to Cape Canaveral. One of the boys William Andrew, Jr. was born January 9, 1907 and from that day forward was known as W.A. Three girls would

Picture of Melvin Tucker,
courtesy, Rose Wooley

be born to the couple while they lived at the Cape: Buelah Jean on September 7 1922, Canaveral Rose on May 27, 1925, and Iona Belle on May 27, 1929.[147]

The Tucker's moved to the Cape in a wagon drawn by two oxen. The oxen, Mott and Brindle, swam across the river but the wagon was brought over in pieces by boat. They homesteaded 160 acres about two miles north of the lighthouse and about a quarter of a mile off the ocean. Mr. Tucker and the boys built a large home using gathered wood and lumber that they found on the beach. They used Mott and Brindie to clear the land and grew gardens for food. This was called proving up the homestead.

The Tuckers found plenty of work when Captain Charles Lansing arrived and started to clear land and build houses. Lansing had a tractor and hired the Tucker boys to clear land north of the lighthouse and just south of the Tuckers homestead. This caused an influx of people who needed services and places to live or visit. The center of population was shifting from the river to the beach area causing the Canaveral Post Office to be moved to Lansing Beach.[148] Lansing Beach was to become a community of the future and even had a school.

"Helen Wilson married W. A. Tucker, Jr. on September 16, 1929 at the justice of the peace in Titusville, Florida. The proud father-in-law gave them eleven acres next to him on the Banana River as a wedding gift."[149] The couple would be blessed with sons Melvin Wilson, 1931; Kelvin Lowell, 1937; Vernon Andrew, all born on Cape Canaveral and delivered by mid-wife Lena Whidden. The tuckers were moved off Cape Canaveral on September 5, 1950.[150]

Tuten and King

The Kings and the Tutens were neighbors. That's how Mary Jane Patrick Tuten and Nicholas King met. They were married on May 7, 1882 by the Rev. John Penny at the residence of Nicholas' father William John King, Jr. The area where Mary Jane (always known as 'Minnie') and Nicholas King lived was then known as Shell Pond.

Nicholas and Mary Jane King bought land at Artesia on Cape Canaveral and moved their family to the Cape. According to a homestead map prepared by descendants, the Kings lived in the north central part of Cape Canaveral near Nathan Penny's place. Nicholas and Mary started a family with Lela Belle King born March 11, 1893; Luba Edna December 11, 1895; William Curtis King August 14, 1898 and Anderson Jennings King, March 18, 1900. The family moved to Vero Beach, Florida where they owned a rooming house, and Nicholas operated a delivery wagon.[151]

Directory Continues:

Name	Occupation	Resides with	Name
Turner, Martha D.	student	r	Mrs. Ruby Marks
Turner, Regna E.	student	r	Mrs. Ruby Marks
Wakefield, Anna			
Wakefield, Gailand		r	Anna Wakefield
Wakefield, Hazel		r	Anna Wakefield
Wakefield, Rosa Mrs		r	Anna Wakefield
West, Thomas	Rev		

Whidden

The Whidden's arrived at "Cape Canaveral in early 1923, possibly February."[152] Their home was "about two hundred feet north of the Post Office, Julius Jeffords was the postmaster."[153] In a listing of Canaveral residents from 1926 - 1927 Julius J. Jeffords is listed as Postmaster.[154]

The Whidden's moved away from the Jeffords place to create a place called Whidden Center.[155] The move was just in time for "the July 28, 1926 Hurricane that brought 80 miles per hour winds."[156] Three Whidden cousins took up homesteads at Whidden Center.

Picture of Widden's Store, courtesy, Rose Wooley

Cousin, Eugene Whidden, a medical doctor, built a little grocery store and sold Sinclair Gasoline. "The building is to be of stucco finish on the outside while the interior will be conveniently arranged to meet the needs of a store of this kind."[157] The store was on Pier Road about half way between the Cape Road and the Hotel. "He would take care of all the illness and medical emergencies. They had a lot of broken arms. The old model T Ford was responsible for many broken arms and wrists from the crank kick back."[158]

Allee Whidden: February 1, 1899 - October 13, 1945

Allee came to Cape Canaveral from Pensacola in the 1920s. He had served in the Merchant Marines and held the rank of Lt. Colonel. He also served in World War I with the Merchant Marines. He and wife Grace had three children: Allee Jr., Kenneth, and Gloria. According to the Cocoa Tribune, "Allee Whidden was the successful bidder of the mail route of Canaveral to Cocoa and will make his first trip July 1st, 1931."[159]

Picture of Allee Whidden's grave stone taken by Author

Mr. Whidden died at the Marine Hospital in New York. He is buried in the Cape Canaveral Community Cemetery.[160]

Directory Continues:
Name   Occupation   Resides with   Name
Wiig, Howard
Williams, Jennie
Wilson, Alfred B.
Wilson Frank M. (Henrietta) farmer

Alfred B. Wilson: February 20, 1861 – June 24, 1940

Alfred B. enlisted in the United States Navy as a Seaman on May 4, 1898. In 1903, he applied for service with the Light-House Establishment and was assigned as a third Mate on the Light-House supply-vessel U.S.S. Armeria. He served onboard the Armeria during

Picture of Alfred B. Wilson, courtesy, Florida Memory Project

the Spanish American War and attained the Rank of Chief Master at Arms.[161] He was paid $50.00 per month. In 1908, he was appointed as a Deckhand in the service of Department of Water, Supply, Gas and Electricity, City of New York, his pay was to be $2.50 per day. The letter of appointment was signed by John H. O'Brien, Commissioner.[162] Alfred B. Wilson was awarded the New York State Decoration for Service in War, citation No 1677, signed at Albany on February 5, 1916 by the Adjutant General.[163] Records from Ancestry.com indicate that Alfred B. Wilson married Maggie Commerford in 1897 in Brooklyn, Kings, New York.[164]

Picture of Frank and Henrietta, courtesy, Helen Tucker, Descendant

The Department of the Interior took his request for pension under consideration on August 29, 1923, Claim Number 1438714.[165] He passed away on June 24, 1942 and is buried beside his brother, Frank, in a cemetery on Cape Canaveral just north of the Burnham Family Cemetery.

Francis Mills (Frank M.) Wilson: August 11, 1865 – November 6, 1940

Although very little is known about Frank Wilson, we do know that he was born at Cape Canaveral on August 11, 1865. Frank owned 160 acres of land on Cape Canaveral and was appointed 2nd Assistant Keeper at the Cape Canaveral Lighthouse on July 23, 1894. He held that job until July, 1902.[166]

According to Helen Tucker, "Frank met Henrietta Weitzel in the summer of 1911 at the pier on Cape Canaveral. Later that year Frank asked the father, Charles Witzel for permission to marry his daughter. Mr. Witzel said yes."[167] Please note the different spellings of the name. Wonder if they met at Reba's Place. Frank married Henrietta Witzel of South Carolina. On Dec. 13, 1913 a daughter, Helen, and the only child was born to the couple. In about 1926, Helen Wilson married W. A. Tucker.[168]

Dixie Pauline Whidden: November 15, 1928 - April 19, 1929

Little Paulina Whidden passed away on Friday, April 19, at the Canaveral home of her grandmother, Mrs. Margaret M. Orton. This tiny five month's old baby was the only child of Mr. and Mrs. L. A. Whidden, and was greatly loved by all who knew her. She was a very playful, happy little girl and had made for herself a very large place in our hearts. Besides her parents she leaves to mourn her loss, her grandmother, Mrs. M. M. Orton, her great-grandmother, Mrs. E. A. Crowder, her great-uncle and aunt, Mr. and Mrs. J. I. Crowder. Miss Lena Whidden, Mr. and Mrs. Archie Whidden and children, all residing on Canaveral. There are other aunts, uncles and cousins

Picture of Dixie Pauline Whidden's grave stone, taken by Author

residing in other states who will grieve over the loss of this dear little girl.[169]

To Pauline Whidden

Baby Girl with eyes of blue
All our hearts are full of you,
Tho you've gone far from our sight
We can see you day and night.
We can see you smile and coo,
And all the cunning ways of you.

Baby Girl, with nut brown hair
You are happy "Over There"
Tho our hearts are sad and alone
Since our Bit O'Sunshine's gone,
We must bow unto His will
Trusting in His mercy still.

Baby Girl, we love you so
We are sad to let you go.
Empty is our house, and still
But He's promised that we will
Some glad day in that far land
Kiss again your baby hand.

--Contributed.[170]

Life was so very hard on the very young people that lived and then died on Cape Canaveral. They and their families are the true heroes. Their hard work and sacrifice to settle Florida is all but forgotten. I love and respect every one of them. Sonny Witt

[1]1885 US Census, provided by Rose Wooley

[2]WikipediA, the free encyclopedia: (accessed January 12, 2007) http://en.wikipedia.org/wiki/Fort_Dallas

[3]Ibid.

[4]Robert Ranson, East Coast Florida Memories, (Port Salerno: Florida Classic Library) Appendix I, II

[5]WikipediA, the free encyclopedia: (accessed January 12, 2007) <http://en.wikipedia.org/wiki/Fort_Brooke>

[6]Ibid.

[7]Florida Online Park Guide, Fort Clinch, (accessed October 19, 2008) <http://www.floridastateparks.org/fortclinch/>

[8]St. Lucie Historical Society, Inc., Saint Lucie County History, (accessed October 19, 2008) <http://www.stluciehistoricalsociety.org/slcohistory.htm>

[9]Ibid.

[10]Ibid.

[11]Wondering Lizard, William Tecumseh Sherman, (accessed October 19, 2008) <http://www.inn-california.com/Articles/biographic/shermanwt.html>

[12]Robert Ranson, East Coast Florida Memories, Port Salerno: Florida Classic Library

[13]Rose Wooley, History of Cape Canaveral and the Early Settlers, (Compiled by Mrs Rose Wooley), Titusville, Florida, 1998, page 12

[14]Florida Star, Titusville, Florida; July 12, 1883, July 19, 1883

[15]Rose Wooley, History of Cape Canaveral and the Early Settlers, (Compiled by Mrs Rose Wooley), Titusville, Florida, 1998, page 13

[16]Cocoa Tribune, January 1922

[17]K. Denise Donovan, Grand Daughter, Mechanicsville, Virginia, copy of Form A.G.O. No.73, Oath of Enlistment and Allegiance.

[18]William Van Horn, Researcher, USCMRL, cavalry@flinthills.com

[19]K. Denise Donovan, Grand Daughter, Mechanicsville, Virginia, Copy of appointment certificate

[20]The Cocoa Tribune, SUICIDE of P.M. AT CANAVERAL, January 19, 1922

[21]ancestry.com, US Passport Application, 1795-1925, Passport issue date July 28, 1920, (accessed January 8, 2009) <http://www.ancestry.com/>

[22]ancestry.com, Florida Death Index, 1877-1998, (accessed January 8, 2009) < http://www.ancestry.com/>

[23]Rose Wooley, History of Cape Canaveral and the Early Settlers, (Compiled by Mrs Rose Wooley), Titusville, Florida, 1998, pg 14

[24]ancestry.com, Database, U.S. General Land Office Records, 1796-1907, (accessed January 9, 2009) <http://www.ancestry.com/>

[25]Rose Wooley, History of Cape Canaveral and the Early Settlers, (Compiled by Mrs Rose Wooley), Titusville, Florida, 1998, pg 14

[26]Ibid.

[27]Yvonne Thornton, Grand Daughter, Merritt Island, Florida

[28]A. Parks Honeywell, Editor, Honeywell Heritage, Vol. 4, No. 2, Spring 1997

[29]Roz Foster, Interview of Florence Honeywell Patrick, April 25, 2002

[30]Ibid.

[31]Ibid.

[32]Ibid.

[33]Ibid.

[34]Yvonne Thornton, Grand Daughter, Merritt Island, Florida

[35]Helen Wilson Tucker, Daughter of Frank and Henrietta Wilson, Information in hand-written form "The Story of Cape Canaveral as long as I have lived on it."

[36]Ibid.

[37] Neil Hurley, Keepers of Florida Lighthouses, An Illustrated CD-ROM database

[38]USGenWeb Archives by Ruth, (accessed January 22, 2007) <rootsweb.ancestry.com/pub/usgenweb/fl/brevard/cemetery/georgiana.txt>

[39]Ada Edmiston Parrish, A. Clyde Field, George Leland "Speedy" Harrell, Images of America Merritt Island and Cocoa Beach, Arcadia Publishing, Charleston, S.C.

[40]ancestry.com, 1900 U.S. Federal Census, (accessed January 4, 2009) http://www.ancestry.com/

[41]ancestry.com, 1920 & 1930 U.S. Federal Census, (accessed May 17, 2009) http://www.ancestry.com/

[42]ancestry.com, 1920 U.S. Federal Census, (accessed January 4, 2009) http://www.ancestry.com/

[43]US Census, 1900, Canaveral, Precinct 15

[44]Flossie Staton, Direct Descendant

[45]Ibid.

[46]Fourteenth Census of the U.S.: 1920 - Population, Township Precinct 13 - Canaveral

[47]Flossie Staton, Direct Descendant

[48]Inspector 6th District, Letter to The Lighthouse Board, Apr 15, 1907, Records Group 26 E 58 Box 16, National Archives, Washington D.C.

[49]USGenWeb Archives by Ruth, (accessed January 22, 2007) <rootsweb.ancestry.com/pub/usgenweb/fl/brevard/cemetery/georgiana.txt>

[50]Allen H. Andrews, A YANK PIONEER IN FLORIDA, Recounting the Adventures of a City Chap Who Came to the Wilds of South Florida in 1890s and Remained to Grow Up With the Country, Jacksonville, Florida, Douglas Printing Co., 1950

[51]The Cocoa Tribune, Canaveral, Thursday, July 7, 1932

[52]Allen H. Andrews, A YANK PIONEER IN FLORIDA, Recounting the Adventures of a City Chap Who Came to the Wilds of South Florida in 1890s and Remained to Grow Up With the Country, Jacksonville, Florida, Douglas Printing Co., 1950

[53]Ada Edmiston Parrish, A. Clyde Field, George Leland "Speedy" Harrell, Images of America Merritt Island and Cocoa Beach, Arcadia Publishing, Charleston, S.C.

[54]Indian River Advocate, Obituary, January 1, 1897

[55]Tile and Till, THE STORY of SAW PALMETTO BERRIES, 1923

[56]Ibid.

[57]Ibid.

[58]The Cocoa Tribune, September 20, 1917

[59]The Cocoa Tribune, March 17, 1932

[60]The Cocoa Tribune, April 20, 1944

[61]Star Advocate Obituary, September 27, 1957

[62]ancestry.com, 1920 United States Federal Census, (accessed February 28, 2009) Rufus Henry Coleman 1920 Census

[63]Shirley J. Sellers Kidd, from an oral interview with her mother, April 30, 2008

[64]ancestry.com, World war I Draft Registration (accessed February 28, 2009) <http/search.ancestry.com/cgi-bin/sse.dll?rank=1&new=1&msav-0&mst-1&gsfn=Rufus+Henry+Coleman>

[65]Ibid.

[66]Ada Edmiston Parrish, A. Clyde Field, George Leland "Speedy" Harrell, Images of America Merritt Island and Cocoa Beach, Arcadia Publishing, Charleston, S.C., pg 100-101

[67]ancestry.com, 1920 United States Federal Census, (accessed February 28, 2009) Rufus Henry Coleman 1920 Census

[68]Shirley J. Sellers Kidd, from an oral interview with her mother, April 30, 2008

[69]Ibid.

[70]South Carolina State Climatology Office, (accessed March 1, 2009) <http://www.dnr.gov/climate/sco/tropics/past/Tracks/Hurr1_1928.php>

[71]ancestry.com, 1930 United States Federal Census, (accessed May 24, 2009) Ivan C. Crowder

[72]John Whitney, Descendant, Merritt Island, FL

[73]Ibid.

[74]Ibid.

[75]The Cocoa Tribune, April 11, 1929

[76]Rose Wooley, History of Cape Canaveral and the Early Settlers, (Compiled by Mrs Rose Wooley), Titusville, Florida, 1998, pg 19

[77]ancestry.com, 1880 Census (accessed February 28, 2009) <http://www.ancestry.com>

[78]The Cocoa Tribune, March 29, 1929

[79]Terry Dalegowski, Direct Descendant, Cleveland, TN

[80]Palm Beach Dailey News.com, (accessed February 22, 2009) http://www.palmbeachdailynews.com/news/content/specialsections/HURRICANE1928page.html

[81]Evelyn Grose, Direct Descendant

[82]The Cocoa Tribune, Mr. John Harvey Hogan, Obituary, July 13, 1922

[83] The Cocoa Tribune, Mrs Louisa Hogan Dies, November 4, 1937

[84] Flossie Staton, Direct Descendant

[85] ancestry.com, 1920 United States Census, (accessed January 4, 2009) Http://search.ancestry.com/cgi-bin/sse.dll?rank=1&new=1&MSAV=0&msT=1angs-i&gsfn

[86] The Cocoa Tribune, Mrs. Louisa Hogan Dies, November 4, 1937

[87] The Cocoa Tribune, Mr. John Harvey Hogan Dies, July 13,1922

[88] The Cocoa Tribune, Mrs. Louisa Hogan Dies, November 4, 1937

[89] Indian River County, History Column: Old, New Vero Joined as One city, (accessed April 30, 2009) <http://www.tcpalm.com/news/2009/jan/24/history-column-old-new-vero-joined-together-one-ci/>

[90] Titusville Star Advocate, Obituary, January 7, 1937

[91] Eula Mae Jones Anderson, Descendant, Vero Beach, Florida

[92] Rose Wooley, History of Cape Canaveral and the Early Settlers, (Compiled by Mrs Rose Wooley), Titusville, Florida, 1998, pg 24

[93] John Whitney, Direct Descendant, Merritt Island, FL

[94] Terry Dalegowski, Direct Descendant, Cleveland, TN

[95] Ibid.

[96] ancestry.com, 1935 Florida State Census, (accessed May 18, 2009) < http://www.ancestry.com/>

[97] Provided by Nonie Fox, Descandant

[98] The Cocoa Tribune, Canaveral, Thursday, July 7, 1932

[99] Roz Foster, Interview of Florence Honeywell Patrick, April 25, 2002

[100] Ada Edmiston Parrish, A. Clyde Field, George Leland "Speedy" Harrell, Images of America Merritt Island and Cocoa Beach, Arcadia Publishing, Charleston, S.C.

[101] Provided by Nonie Fox, Descandant

[102] Florida Star Titusville, Canaveral, December 3, 1915

[103] The Cocoa Tribune, Capt Charles Lansing Dies, January 20, 1944

[104] Lake Placid News, Adirondack Underground Railroad ties, Lee Manchester, February 6, 2004 (accessed April 20, 2009) <http://www.aarch.org/archives/leeman/040206%20VLP%20UGR%20in%20ADKs%20article.pdf>

[105] Ibid.

[106] Ibid.

[107] The Cocoa Tribune, Obituary, January 20, 1944

[108] Florida Today, Bob Hudson, April 18, 2001

[109] Ibid.

[110] ancestry.com, Florida Marriage Collection, (accessed January 4, 2009) < http://www.ancestry.com/>

[111] Ibid.

[112] ancestry.com, Florida State Census, 1867-1945, (accessed January 4, 2009) < http://www.ancestry.com/>

[113] Darlene Letasky Kosko, Sister

[114] The Cocoa Tribune, February 12, 1948

[115] The Cocoa Tribune, Canaveral, April 14, 1932

[116] Rose Wooley, History of Cape Canaveral and the Early Settlers, (Compiled by Mrs Rose Wooley), Titusville, Florida, 1998

[117] The Cocoa Tribune, April 19, 1955

[118] The Cocoa Tribune, February 9, 1933

[119] Ibid.

[120] ancestry.com, 1930 United States Census, (accessed May 4, 2009) <http://search.ancestry.com/>

[121] Cape Canaveral Homesteader's Map, Holley Tucker

[122] ancestry.com, 1910 United States Census, (accessed May 22, 2009) <http://search.ancestry.com/>

[123] ancestry.com, 1930 United States Census, (accessed May 22, 2009) <http://search.ancestry.com/>

[124] Rose Wooley, History of Cape Canaveral and the Early Settlers, (Compiled by Mrs Rose Wooley), Titusville, Florida, 1998, pg 15

[125] ancestry.com, 1920 United States Census, (accessed January 4, 2009) <http://search.ancestry.com/>

[126] Rose Wooley, History of Cape Canaveral and the Early Settlers, (Compiled by Mrs Rose Wooley), Titusville, Florida, 1998

[127] Neil Hurley, Keepers of Florida Lighthouses, An Illustrated CD-ROM database

[128] Rose Wooley, History of Cape Canaveral and the Early Settlers, (Compiled by Mrs Rose Wooley), 1998, Titusville,

Florida

[129]ancestry.com, Certificate 4304, (accessed May 14, 2009) <http://www.ancestry.com>

[130]ancestry.com, Nathan O. Penny, passport, (accessed May 14, 2099) <http://www.ancestry.com>

[131]Rose Wooley, History of Cape Canaveral and the Early Settlers, (Compiled by Mrs Rose Wooley), Titusville, Florida, 1998, pg 26

[132]Ibid.

[133]University of South Florida, Exploring Florida, (accessed November 29, 2008) <http://fcit.usf.edu/FLORIDA/maps/countgal/cram99/05cram99.htm>

[134]Anna Pearl Leonard Newman, Stories of Early Life Along Beautiful Indian River, Compiled 1953, Printed by Stuart Daily News, Inc., Stuart, FL

[135]Waltham Automobiles (accessed April 26, 2009) <http://www.walthammuseum.com/autos.htm>

[136]Florida Star, Nathan, April 19, 1911 - Indian River Chronicle, January 27, 1911

[137]ancestry.com (accessed May 18, 2009) John Spies, 1930 Census <http://www.ancestry.com>

[138]ancestry.com (accessed February 26, 2009) <http://www.ancestry.com>

[139]Rose Wooley, History of Cape Canaveral and the Early Settlers, (Compiled by Mrs Rose Wooley), Titusville, Florida, 1998, pg 19

[140]Ibid.

[141]ancestry.com, New York Passenger List, 1820 - 1957 (accessed January 11, 2009) <http://www.ancestry.com/>

[142]Roz Foster, The Terryn House, The Indian River Journal, Volume VII, Number 1, Spring/Summer 2008

[143]Ibid.

[144]Ibid.

[145]Ibid.

[146]Ibid.

[147]Thomas L. Tucker, Florida Pioneers, The Tucker & Wilson Story, pg 16, n.s. 2003

[148]Hellen Wilson Tucker, The Story of Cape Canaveral as Long as I have Lived on it, In her own words and hand-written, undated

[149]Thomas L. Tucker, Florida Pioneers, The Tucker & Wilson Story, pg 58, n.s. 2003

[150]Hellen Wilson Tucker, The Story of Cape Canaveral as Long as I have Lived on it, In her own words and hand-written, undated

[151]Carolyn McNeil, Descendant, Mansfield, Mass, October 27, 2008

[152]Woodrow Whidden, The Life and Times of Woodrow Whidden, as Told by Himself, Transcribed by G. A. Jones, pg 2

[153]Woodrow Whidden, The Life and Times of Woodrow Whidden, as Told by Himself, Transcribed by G. A. Jones, pg 11

[154]Ada Edmiston Parrish, Alma Clyde, Fiels, George Leland "Speedy" Harrell, Images of America Merritt Island and Cocoa Beach, pgs 100 - 101, Arcadia Publishing, Charleston, S.C. 2001

[155]Woodrow Whidden, The Life and Times of Woodrow Whidden, as Told by Himself, Transcribed by G. A. Jones, pg 11

[156]Cape Canaveral's History with Tropical Systems, accessed October 29, 2008) <http://www.hurricanecity.com/city/capecanaveral.htm>

[157]The Cocoa Tribune, Canaveral, March 29, 1929

[158]Woodrow Whidden, The Life and Times of Woodrow Whidden, as Told by Himself, Transcribed by G. A. Jones

[159]Cocoa Tribune, Canaveral, June 30, 1932

[160]Rose Wooley, History of Cape Canaveral and the Early Settlers, (Compiled by Mrs Rose Wooley), Titusville, Florida, 1998, pg 20

[161]Rose Wooley, History of Cape Canaveral and the Early Settlers, (Compiled by Mrs Rose Wooley), Titusville, Florida, 1998, pg 13

[162]Rose Wooley, Copy of letter of appointment

[163]Ibid.

[164]New York City Marriages, 1600-1800s, ancestry.com, provided by Rose Wooley, May 27, 2008

[165]Rose Wooley, Copy of form 3-837

[166]Letter appointing Asst Keeper, July 23, 1894, Records Group 26, National Archives, Washington D.C.: Lighthouse Keepers payroll record

[167]Thomas L. Tucker, Florida Pioneers, The Tucker & Wilson Story, pg 57, n.s. 2003

[168]Helen Wilson Tucker, Daughter of Frank and Henrietta Wilson, <u>The Story of Cape Canaveral as long as I have lived on it</u>, Information in hand-written form.
[169]The Cocoa Tribune, Canaveral, April 25, 1929
[170]Ibid.

The following is simply a list of Cape Canaveral Lighthouse Keepers and Assistant Keepers by year as we know them today. The names and dates have been compiled using Pay Records, Keepers lists, letters, data from works done by Rose Wooley, Historian, author of "History of Cape Canaveral and the Early Settlers, 1998", and friend, as well as documents found in the National Archives which are referenced in endnotes.

A special acknowledgement must go to Neil E. Hurley, the recognized authority on the subject of Florida Lighthouses. Neil is a Commander in the U.S. Coast Guard Reserve, and author of An Illustrated History of Cape Florida Lighthouse, Keepers of Florida Lighthouses 1820-1939, Lighthouses of the Dry Tortugas, co-author of a CD-ROM book entitled "Lighthouses of Egmont Key". A number of references within this page and others in this book are attributed to him.

KEEPERS	ASSIGNED	REASON FOR LEAVING	DATE
Nathaniel Scobie	27 Jan 1848	Resigned	11 Oct 1849[1]
Ora Carpenter	27 Feb 1850	Replaced	1853
Mills O. Burnham	30 Jul 1853	Passed away	17 April 1886
G. M. Quarterman	27 Apr 1886	Resigned	19 Mar 1887[2]
James M. Knight	10 Aug 1887	Removed	15 May 1893[3]
John L. Stuck	1 Jun 1893	Resigned	30 Sep 1904[4]
Clinton P. Honeywell	4 Nov 1904	Retired	1930
Oscar F. Quarterman	23 Jan 1930[5]	Retired	1 Jul 1939[6]
T. L. Willis	1 Jul 1939	Retired	30 Jun 1941[7]
L. G. Owens (USCG)	3 Jul 1939[8]		

ASSISTANTS	ASSIGNED	REASON FOR LEAVING	DATE
Frances A. Burnham	Early 1850s[9]	No pay	No record
Alexander R. Rose	1 Oct 1851	Resigned	5 Jun 1868
Henry Wilson	12 Mar 1855	Resigned	1861 - 1866
F.O.F Dunham	5 Jun 1868	Resigned	5 Mar 1870[10]
Richard Jones	5 Mar 1870	Resigned	23 Apr 1872

FIRST ASSISTANTS	ASSIGNED	REASON FOR LEAVING	DATE
Alfred H. Taffard	2 Feb 1876	Resigned	13 Mar 1876
G. M. Quarterman	21 Apr 1877	Promoted	21 Dec 1886
James M. Knight	19 Mar 1886	Removed	17 May 1887[11]
John L. Stuck	23 Mar 1887	Promoted	1 Jun 1893
Clinton P. Honeywell	2 Jun 1893	Promoted	1 Nov 1904
Thomas Knight	1 Nov 1904	Transferred	24 Aug 1911[12]
John B. Butler	11 Aug 1911	Transferred	18 Jul 1923[13]
Oscar F. Quarterman	1 Aug 1923	Promoted	23 Jan, 1930[14]
Arthur F. Hodges	Jul 1930	Unknown	29 Jan 1936[15]
Benjamin F Stone[16]	Sep 1936	Transferred	1 Jan 1936
T. L Willis	8 Jan 1937	Promoted	30 Jun 1939[17]

SECOND ASSISTANTS	ASSIGNED	REASON FOR LEAVING	DATE
Alfred H. Traffard	23 Apr 1872	Resigned	1873
Levi Butler	10 Dec 1873	Resigned	1876
G. M. Quarterman	2 Feb 1876	Promoted	27 Dec 1877[18]
John M. Meyer	27 Dec 1876	Resigned	1 Oct 1877[19]
Daniel S. Brightman	4 Mar 1878	Resigned	18 Jan 1879
J. Brady Bonner	18 Jan 1879	Removed	17 Apr 1880[20]
James M. Knight	21 May 1880	Promoted	21 Apr 1886[21]
Mills D. Cottrell	3 Jan 1886	Resigned	23 Dec 1887[22]
John Abbott	23 Dec 1887	Transferred	12 Aug 1890[23]
Thomas H. Ferguson	22 Oct 1890	Resigned	3 Mar 1891[24]
Clinton P. Honeywell	7 May 1891	Promoted	1 Nov 1893
Ludwell C. Demaree	25 Sep 1893	Transferred	1 Dec 1893
Frank M. Wilson	23 Jul 1894	Resigned	31 Jan 1902[25]
Wilbur Scott	1 Feb 1902	Transferred	16 Apr 1902[26]
Thomas Knight	16 Apr 1902	Promoted	1904
Edw. J. Praetorius	1 Nov 1904	Resigned	30 Apr 1907[27]
John B. Butler	7 Jun 1907[28]	Promoted	1911
O. F. Quarterman	1 Sep 1909	Promoted	1 Aug 1923[29]
Oscar William Rust[30]	1 May 1907	No show	
John W. Griffin	1 Aug 1923	Transferred	16 May 1925
Quincy E. Atkinson	15 April 1925	Transferred	Apr 1935[31]
Julius J. Jeffords	17 Dec 1929	Transferred	24 Feb 1930[32]

KEEPER'S PICTURES

Mills Olcott Burnham
Keeper
July 30, 1853 - April 17, 1886, Passed Away

Picture, courtesy, Florida Memory Project

George M. Quarterman
Keeper
April 27 1886 - March 19, 1887, Resigned

First Assistant
April 21, 1877 - December 21, 1886, Promoted

Second Assistant
February 2, 1876 - December 27, 1877, Promoted

Picture, courtesy, Rose Wooley

John Stuck
Keeper
June 1, 1893 - September 30, 1904, Resigned

First Assistant
March 23, 1887 - June 1, 1893, Promoted

Picture, courtesy, Florida Memory Project

Clinton P. Honeywell
Keeper
November 4, 1904 - 1930, Retired

First Assistant
June 2, 1893 - November 4, 1904, Promoted

Second Assistant
May 7, 1891 - November 1, 1904, Promoted

Picture, courtesy, descendant Yvonne Thornton

Oscar Floyd Quarterman
Keeper
January 23, 1930 - July 1, 1939, Retired

First Assistant
August 1, 1923 - January 23, 1930, Promoted

Second Assistant
September 1, 1909 - August 1, 1923, Promoted

Picture, courtesy, Rose Wooley

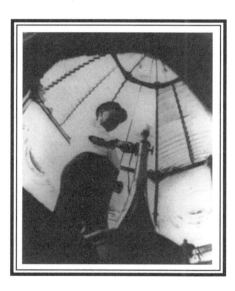

T. L. Willis
Keeper
July 1, 1939 - June 30, 1941, Retired

First Assistant
January 8, 1937 - June 30, 1939, Promoted

Picture, courtesy, Rose Wooley

Frances A. Burnham
Assistant Keeper
Early 1850s - No pay - No record
Assisted her Father

Picture, courtesy, the Florida Memory Project

Henry Wilson
Assistant Keeper
March 12, 1855 - 1861, Resigned

Picture, courtesy, the Florida Memory Project

John Belton Butler
First Assistant Keeper
August 11, 1911 - July 18, 1923

Picture, courtesy, the Ponce de Leon Lighthouse Preservation Association

Arthur Franklin Hodges
First Assistant Keeper
July 1930 - January 29, 1936

Picture, courtesy, the Ponce de Leon Lighthouse Preservation Association

Benjamin F. Stone
First Assistant Keeper
September 1936 - 1 January 1936, Transferred

Picture, courtesy, Neil Hurley

John M. Meyer
Second Assistant Keeper
27 December 1876 - 1 October 1877, Resigned

Picture, courtesy, the Ponce de Leon Lighthouse
Preservation Association

Frank M. Wilson
Second Assistant Keeper
23 July 1894 - 31 January 1902, Resigned

Picture provided by Helen Tucker from a tintype.

Quincy E. Atkinson
Second Assistant Keeper
15 April 1925 - April 1935, Transferred

Picture, courtesy, Neil Hurley

Julius J. Jeffords
Second Assistant Keeper
17 December 1929 - 24 February 1930, Transferred

Picture, courtesy, John Whitney

[1]Stephen Pleasonton, Letter to William Meredith, Secretary of the Treasury, dated 11 Oct 1849, Records Group 26, National Archives, Washington D.C.

[2]Neil Hurley, Keepers of Florida Lighthouses, An Illustrated CD-ROM database

[3]R. D. Evans, Letter recommending Immediate Dismissal, 15 May 1893, Records Group 26 E 31, National Archives, Washington D.C.

[4]Letter dated 1 October 1904 from Launeuce O. Murray, Acting Secretary of the Department of Commerce and Labor to The Light-House Board accepting resignation of Keeper Stuck, Records Group 26 E 31, National Archives, Washington D.C.

[5]Neil Hurley, Keepers of Florida Lighthouses, An Illustrated CD-ROM database

[6]Journal of Light Station at Cape Canaveral, Records Group 26, National Archives, Washington D.C., entry dated July 1, 1939

[7]Neil Hurley, Keepers of Florida Lighthouses, An Illustrated CD-ROM database

[8]Journal of Light Station at Cape Canaveral, Records Group 26, National Archives, Washington D.C., entry dated July 3, 1939

[9]Neil Hurley, Keepers of Florida Lighthouses, An Illustrated CD-ROM database

[10]Neil Hurley, Keepers of Florida Lighthouses, An Illustrated CD-ROM database

[11]Neil Hurley, Keepers of Florida Lighthouses, An Illustrated CD-ROM database

[12]Neil Hurley, Keepers of Florida Lighthouses, An Illustrated CD-ROM database

[13]Neil Hurley, Keepers of Florida Lighthouses, An Illustrated CD-ROM database

[14]Neil Hurley, Keepers of Florida Lighthouses, An Illustrated CD-ROM database

[15]Neil Hurley, Keepers of Florida Lighthouses, An Illustrated CD-ROM database

[16]Neil Hurley, Keepers of Florida Lighthouses, An Illustrated CD-ROM database

[17]Journal of Light Station at Cape Canaveral, Records Group 26, National Archives, Washington D.C., entry dated July 3, 1939

[18]Neil Hurley, Keepers of Florida Lighthouses, An Illustrated CD-ROM database

[19]Neil Hurley, Keepers of Florida Lighthouses, An Illustrated CD-ROM database

[20]Neil Hurley, Keepers of Florida Lighthouses, An Illustrated CD-ROM database

[21]Neil Hurley, Keepers of Florida Lighthouses, An Illustrated CD-ROM database

[22]Neil Hurley, Keepers of Florida Lighthouses, An Illustrated CD-ROM database

[23]Letter dated 12 August 1890 Transferring to Mosquito Inlet, to replace Mr L. G. Stringfellow, Records Group 26 E 31, National Archives, Washington D.C.

[24]Neil Hurley, Keepers of Florida Lighthouses, An Illustrated CD-ROM database

[25]Copy of letter dated 8 January 1902 from Frank M. Wilson to Lighthouse Inspector 6th District, Records Group 26 E 48, file 1049 National Archives, Washington D.C.

[26]Letter dated 16 Apr 1902 Transferring to Mosquito Inlet, Records Group 26 E 31, National Archives, Washington D.C.

[27]Inspector 6th District, Letter to The lighthouse Board, Apr 15, 1907, Records Group 26 E 58 Box 16, National Archives, Washington D.C.

[28]Inspector 6th District, Letter to The lighthouse Board, Jun 8, 1907, Records Group 26 E 58 Box 16, National Archives, Washington D.C.

[29]Neil Hurley, Keepers of Florida Lighthouses, An Illustrated CD-ROM database

[30]Letter from Inspector 6th District to The lighthouse Board dated Apr 15, 1907, Records Group 26 E 58 Box 16, National Archives, Washington D.C.

[31]Neil Hurley, Keepers of Florida Lighthouses, An Illustrated CD-ROM database

[32]Neil Hurley, Keepers of Florida Lighthouses, An Illustrated CD-ROM database, Jeffords is shown as 2nd Assistant at Ponce de Leon Inlet on 24 Feb 1930

In 1880 Benjamin age 62, and Minerva age 55 and their five sons were living in Kenithburg, Mercer Township, Illinois. The sons were, John age 30; Alvis age 28; Thomas age 25; Larry age 22; Frank age 14; and a servant Nellie Dish age 20. Benjamin's occupation is listed as farmer.

Pictures of Benjamin and Minerva Hardin, courtesy, Evie Grosse

Picture of Willie Butler, courtesy, Ponce de Leon Lighthouse Preservation Society

Wee Winsome Willie Butler has some great watermelons in front of the 1st Assistant Keeper's home showing the Cape Canaveral Lighthouse in the background.

Addie Belle and Thomas L Hardin pictured here. Thomas Lawrence Hardin was born in Illinois on March 10, 1855 and died November 11, 1937. Addie Belle Sheckel Hardin, was born in Indiana on May 14, 1865 and she died July 24, 1932: The Hardin's are buried in Cape Canaveral Community Cemetery at Cape Canaveral, Florida.

Picture of Addie Belle and Thomas Hardin, courtesy, Evie Grosse

Picture of Carolyn Agnes Fournier
courtesy, John Whitney

Picture, courtesy, Roz Foster from the
John Whitney Collection

Maria A. Jeffords, her son John L. Easterlin holding baby, Busie Julia Jeffords Easterlin, and in front is Bernice Greathouse.

John and Busie Julia Jeffords Greathouse were married in Jacksonville around 1920. Sam L. Jeffords gave the couple, as a wedding gift, property on the Cape where Space Launch Complex 14 is now located.

Looks like Bernice Greathouse and Uncle Julius J. Jeffords are checking for honey.

Picture, courtesy, Roz Foster from the
John Whitney Collection

William Adam and Betty Mae must have moved to the Cape in or about 1945 and lived in the north part of Cape Canaveral. Here we have Betty Mae Jeffords holding Jimmy Tucker.

Picture, courtesy, John Whitney

Bessie Meyers, Albert Praetorius, Mary L Burns, Louise Meyer Praetorius are all fishing for clams at Cape Canaveral.

Picture, courtesy, Rose Wooley

Picture, courtesy, Roz Foster and the John Whitney Collection

Front row: Betty, Bernice, Busie Julia Jeffords Easterlin and Pauline

Back row: Juluis J. Jeffords, Augusta Jeffords and John Easterlin

Could this lighthouse school class be made up of the Butler and Honeywell kids? The picture was taken at the Cape Canaveral Lighthouse. Here we may possibly have Ms. Elizabeth Ervard teacher captured in the picture. She taught there in about 1922.

Picture, courtesy, Rose Wooley

The Cape Canaveral Lighthouse getting painted. The painter may have been Mr. Ringo of Cocoa, Florida.

Picture, courtesy, Rose Wooley

Marion Ranson (pictured) is the grandson of Robert Ranson a very early settler of Cape Canaveral.

Picture, courtesy,
the Burns Collection

The Burns Reo decked out with ducks.

Picture from the Burns Collection, John Whitney

Picture provided by the Florida
Historical Society Mosquito
Beaters Collection

Papayas still grow near the Quarterman homestead and near the ocean in the area once known as Lansing Beach.

Picture of Mrs. Wilma Hodges, wife of First Assistant Keeper, Arthur Franklin Hodges.

Picture provided by the Ponce de
Leon Lighthouse
Preservation Association

Margarette and William E. Letasky. Margarette is getting away from the car. Guess she knew that William may have a problem with driving. Just getting in the car could be somewhat difficult.

Picture, courtesy,
the Letasky Collection, John Whitney

Picture, courtesy,
the Letasky Collection, John Whitney

Margarette with four or five puppies. What a beautiful little girl.

John Eberwein, Mrs. Eberwein and Mr. Howard Snyder, a visitor from Michigan. John came to the United States in 1883 from Bavaria.

He homesteaded in the area that now includes much of the Port Canaveral in 1895, as a single head of household. He was a farmer and owner of an orange grove.

Picture, courtesy, Flossie Staton

Johnny Beuhler, from Mrs Eberwein's first marriage, with sister Elizabeth Eberwein.

Picture, courtesy, Flossie Staton

Picture, courtesy, Flossie Staton

Elizabeth and her dog. Elizabeth Holmes took over the job as Postmaster at Artesia and served in that position for 26 years. The Artesia Post Office became Port Canaveral in 1954. It may have been located at the Pier for some period of time and it is possible that it moved to the riverside in the late 1930s.

Here we have Otto Eberwein and John Eberwein. Otto was born in Germany in 1862. He lived in Artesia in 1920 a neighbor of John Eberwein. His occupation is listed as farmer, citrus grove.

Picture, courtesy, Flossie Staton

Son William, Mrs Eberwein and daughter Elizabeth riding on a donkey.

Picture, courtesy, Flossie Staton

Picture, courtesy, Flossie Staton

Phillip Eberwein was a mechanic and as fisherman at Canaveral Harbor.

The Eberwein Home.

Picture, courtesy, Flossie Staton

Clinton Honeywell installed six flag poles at the lighthouse to be used to "test American flag material. Every morning he would hoist them up and take them down every night. He would test the materials to see how they stood up against the elements of wind and salt spray.

The 1930 U.S. Census has Albert M. Praetorius, born in 1911, boarding with a George W. Burgess and 19 years old. His occupation is listed as Assistant Manager Hotel. It is presumed it was the Harbor Inn.

Vida Kate married Charles Jandreau: The Jandreau and King kids.

The Butler children John B. 1904; Myrtle V. 1906; Charles W. 1902; Grace E. 1909; James H. 1911; William E. 1913

They lived at the Cape Canaveral Lighthouse.

Picture, courtesy, the Ponce de Leon Lighthouse Preservation Association

Picture, courtesy, Rose Wooley and the Seidel Collection

Charles Lansing, Alice Seidel, Bert Kincaid, ?, ?, Mabel Lansing.

Albert and Grace Taylor along with friends from Cocoa visit the lighthouse. Albert came to the area and founded the Brevard County State Bank in 1889. He was also the President of the first town council of Cocoa and mayor in 1898.

Picture, courtesy, the Brevard Museum of History and Natural Science

Charles Taylor and his sister pose at the Cape Canaveral Lighthouse.

Picture, courtesy, the Brevard Museum of History and Natural Science

Picture, courtesy, the Florida Memory Project

Alfred Burnham Wilson as an adult. He served on board the Armeria during the Spanish American War and attained the Rank of Chief Master at Arms.

Clinton P. Honeywell may have been the first biker on The Cape. He is setting on what is believed to be a 1916 Harley. Also, notice that he and the Harley are in front of where the door is now located. This picture was taken in about 1919.

Here is a picture of the George M. Quarterman home with a detached summer kitchen to the right.

Picture, courtesy, the Florida Historical Society

The Jandreau brothers: Ernest I., born in October 1922, and Eugene J., born October 14, 1915; sons of Charles and Vida Kate Jandreau.

Picture, courtesy, John Whitney

Picture, courtesy, Evie Grosse

Grandpa Tucker, Guy, W A, Elmo, Holley, and Degene, 1937

When the Tucker's moved to the Cape, they brought with them a wagon and two oxen. The oxen, Mott and Brindle, swam across the river but the wagon was brought over in pieces by boat.

Sam and Catherine Syfrett Jeffords. Not sure but, the remains of this vehicle may have been found several years ago in 2002 by the author. If it is wouldn't that be a hoot?

Picture, courtesy, John Whitney

Florence Jeffords and sister & Thelma (Jamie) Franklin

Picture, courtesy, Roz Foster
from the John Whitney
Collection

Lizzie Jeffords Sanders Brickell

Picture, courtesy, John Whitney

Howard Lexinton Holmes was born in Ohio in 1871. For the 1930 Census he was listed as a widower and his occupation was Farmer -Citrus Grove. His Beatrice lived with his Cape Canaveral in 1930.

Picture, courtesy, Flossie Staton

163

Picture, courtesy, Flossie Staton

Picture of William, Mrs Eberwein, Elizabeth and Phillip taking time to rest after clamming and a bit of hunting or is that gun for protection.

This picture is of a young lady sitting on the wall of a cistern. This cistern may be located just north of the old Lighthouse Road. Cisterns have been used to catch and store water for thousands of years.

Picture, courtesy, Yvonne Thornton

Picture of Phillip Eberwein with a deer, courtesy, Flossie Staton

Phillip Eberwein with a deer.

Grace Shockey and friend Arnold.

Post Master of Artesia Post Office, Mrs. Moore, (Flossie Staton's mother)

Here we have a picture: Front Row; Oscar F. Quarterman, possibly John W. Griffin and son, Lansing, Alice Seidel, (do not know the person on far right).

On the back row are Elinor Seidel, Hason, Alice Seidel.

This picture was probably taken between 1923 and 1925, Notice no entry door on the left.
Cape Canaveral School, 1948

1st row: Jessie Hill, Donna Jandreau,
Lee Chamberlin, Freddie Jandreau, Patsy Evans
2nd row: Ira Hill, Roger Dobson, Benjie Lewis,
Delores Morgan, Florence Holmes
3rd row: Dorita Evans, Melvin Tucker,
Gloria Whidden, Beverly Dobson
4th row: Noni Knutson, Katheryn Morgan (Mask),
Tommy Willis
5th row: Jane Lewis, Jack Mask,
Mr. Evans (Teacher), Betty Mae Jeffords

Picture, courtesy of Lansing Beach
School, Flossie Staton

Picture, courtesy, Yvonne Thornton

Keeper Clinton Honeywell and a bunch of visitors to the lighthouse and notice again, that it appears the door is not cut in the bottom.

Virgina Sanders, Pauline Bair, Catherine Jeffords, Lizzie Sanders and Samuel Jeffords.

Picture, courtesy, John Whitney

CHAPTER ELEVEN
The Descendants. In Their Own Words

The Butlers

This is a synopsis of the history of John Belton Butler: John Belton Butler was born on October 18, 1871, in Charleston, S.C. On April 4, 1899 he joined the Light House Establishment serving as a seaman on the lighthouse launch "Snowdrop" based in Charleston.

On June 7, 1907 he was appointed second assistant keeper at the Cape Canaveral Light Station for a short while and then he returned to Charleston. In 1911 he was promoted to first assistant keeper at the Cape Canaveral light station replacing Thomas Knight who had been promoted to principal keeper at the Hillsboro Inlet Light Station.

John Butler did not get along very well with the principal keeper, Clinton Honeywell. However, they worked together for 12 years. During Butler's service at the Cape Canaveral Light he received several commendations for services in saving ship-wrecked people.

John B. Butler married Mamie Wilhelmina Witzel in May of 1902 at Charleston. The Butler's had four children, two boys and two girls, when they came to Cape Canaveral.

In August 1926 John Butler was transferred to the Mosquito Inlet Light Station. The name has since changed to Ponce Inlet Light Station. The Butlers moved to Mosquito Inlet Light Station with their six children:

Daughters:	Myrtle	b. October 30, 1904	
	Grace	b. January 16, 1908	
Sons:	John Jr.	b. April 6, 1903	
	Charles W.	b. July 24, 1906	
	William E.	b. March 11, 1912	
	James H.	b. June 13, 1910	
	Harold W.	b. June 8, 1914	d. August 13, 1914

Harold Witzel Butler was born at Cape Canaveral and is buried in Burnham Cemetery.

John Butler retired from the Lighthouse Service in June, 1937 and bought a farm near Hawthorne, Florida. He died November 5, 1948 at Hawthorne, Fl
Provided by Rose Wooley, Titusville, Florida

The Carter Family

Albert and Katherine Carter came to Florida from Minnesota in the 1880's. They had several children: Lily, Walter, George, Margaret, Nathan, Rose, and Clayton most which were born in Georgianna (south Merritt Island). After his enlistment in the service, Walter homesteaded in Canaveral and subsequently his sister (Margaret Adelle Carter Coleman) and her family.

As part of a family oral history project, I interviewed by mother (Margaret Catherine Coleman Sellers) while driving from Merritt Island to Jacksonville on July 11, 1994. During this process, she recalled her family's stay in Canaveral. The following account are excerpts of that discussion.

Rufus and Margaret Coleman and their three daughters, Margaret Catherine, Rheta Dell, and Ina Mae moved from Titusville to the Carter homestead in approximately 1924. The homestead consisted of approximately 40 acres and was located west of the pier. Rufus Coleman was a carpenter and worked on some sort of building project. Per my mother, it was a "subdivision."

At the beginning, they lived in two tents; one large tent and one small tent. They slept on camp cots. According to my mother: "We lived in the tents until we saw this huge, big rattlesnake crawl though the yard. So, he (her father) hurried and got the foundation and floor laid for the house, and put the tents on top of it 'til he finished it (the house)." The platform was built up approximately 4 feet above the ground on railroad ties "because of the snakes and the low savannahs." As a child, they used to play under the platform. The house had two large rooms and a little kitchen "shed" on the back and a tiny screen porch.

She recalled that there was "an awful storm" in the early 1920's. All the roads were out due to the savannahs (really low) and no trees. When the storm hit, there was about 5 feet of water in the front yard. Also "it blew so hard that it took off the roof and the railroad ties the house was on were all leaning."

She started third grade in Canaveral. Miss "Everon" was the teacher. She taught all levels in the same schoolhouse and it wasn't far from where they lived. Her father had to take her and pick her up each day. Her father had a "stripped down" car that he drove. There were no seats, so her father had to sit on a box to drive! She estimated that there were approximately 20 to 25 children at the school.

Eventually they started running a bus that went "up north" to a school that was back of the lighthouse. It had two rooms and was for all grades. As she recalls, she went there thru the 9th grade. She said they had a married couple that taught there. From Canaveral, they moved from the homestead back to Georgiana (south Merritt Island).

Compiled by Descendant: Shirley J. Sellers Kidd, Merritt Island, Florida

Eberwein/Holmes/Staton History

Family history has it that my Grandfather, John Eberwein, took a buggy whip to my grandmother's abusive first husband, Mr. Beuhler, and Mr. Beuhler as the story goes, was never heard from again. In due time, my Grandmother, Elizabeth, became Mrs. Eberwein and produced two sons, William and Philip, and my Mother, Elizabeth. Her three sons from the first marriage died in World War 1. There was also a daughter, Anna, who was married to a brewer in New York.

My Grandfather, who homesteaded the property that now includes much of the Port in 1895, was a farmer and owner of an orange grove and my Grandmother became Postmaster in the 1920s, taking over the office from Colonel Harvey Hogan. The Eberwein's lived on the river side of the county road and Colonel Hogan was on the ocean. There was a footpath that we used to get to the beach, always known as Hogan's Trail.

Upon my Grandmother's death in December of 1940, my Mother, Elizabeth Holmes, took over the job as Postmaster, a position she held for 26 years. My Grandfather died in 1942, at the age of 92, as a result of falling into a fire that he had built to burn branches he had cut from the orange trees.

Granny always kept a vegetable garden, growing the vegetables used by the family, canning the surplus fruit and vegetables, or making jams. They grew several varieties of grapes from which table wines were made. These grew on the wire fence that surrounded a large chicken yard. The chickens and guineas, ducks and turkeys produced the eggs used in baking and some of the birds became dinner. My uncles hunted and fished to put meat on the table, contributing venison and wild ducks and fish of all sorts. The family also kept bees, extracted the honey and sold it. Nothing was wasted nor was any opportunity left unexplored!

I was born in 1932 and attended Canaveral School for about a year and a half until it was closed and we were transferred to Cocoa. There were only two of us going to school at Canaveral at the time. Some residents had moved and others had already enrolled their children in Cocoa schools. The school bus picked us up around 7:30 or 8, after which we picked up Cocoa Beach kids and the ones who lived on Banana River Naval Air Station. We then went across the wooden bridge (at the foot of what is now Minutemen Causeway in Cocoa Beach) to pick up students in Angel City. We then crossed what was known as Humpback bridge and a long wooden drawbridge from Merritt Island to Cocoa.

The war years were both exciting and frightening for those of us who lived along the coast. The children weren't sensible enough to know what peril we were in but our parents took turns manning the spotting towers that were built up and down the beach, to look out for foreign aircraft or ships. I was on the Pier with a number of other people the night that U boats torpedoed a merchant ship, the LaPaz, and we watched the flares sent up from the ship. For the next few days the men in the neighborhood helped to rescue survivors, bring in the dead, and I presume the staff at Banana River NAIS arranged for the burial of those who had perished. A great deal of salvage work was needed for the LaPaz and again, the able bodied men of the area who were not already in the Armed Forces, were pressed into service.

What I remember most vividly about the war years was that my feet were growing. We had coupons for everything sugar, coffee, meat and shoes. My feet needed shoes more often than coupons were issued, so my Uncle Philip who was a fisherman and more often seen in rubber boots than shoes, gave me his coupons and he always told that he never had a new pair of shoes during the entire war.

A trip to Titusville was a real adventure. My father's parents lived there and I often went to stay with them for a weekend. Several times my Mother put me on the train so that I could have the experience of riding on one. I was either met at the other end or I walked the few short blocks to the house. Occasionally my Dad or my Uncle Frank would take me to a baseball game, but when they and my Uncle Sam went into the service I more often had to rely on the other children who lived in the neighborhood for entertainment.

It seems as though we had just recovered from one catastrophic period when along came another.. this time in the form of notices that my Mother's land was needed to build a missile base and all the residents of Canaveral and Artesia were to be bought out. A few of the residents were satisfied to go elsewhere, but those of us who had lived on the Cape our entire lives and whose livelihood depended on it were not well pleased. About that time the Port came into being. The south side of the Port goes thru land that was my Grandfather's orange grove. The tank farm is also on property that was family owned. The house I was raised in was on the North side of the cut and my Mother was given the opportunity to buy back our house and move it, which she did, onto property that had been family land and was now owned jointly by her and her two brothers. The wooden post office was moved to the front of that same property and my Mother replaced it with a small block building soon after. When Artesia became Port Canaveral and then incorporated and became Cape Canaveral, our little post office was too small to handle the volume of mail and the

Post Office Dept. decided we needed a larger facility. At that time my Mother was ready to retire and she asked to go into the new office as a clerk instead of Postmaster. She retired shortly after the office was built and died in 1964.

My childhood was happy. We were poor but so was just about everybody else. I had no near neighbors, nor siblings, but I had the river and a rowboat and hours of free time in the summer and on weekends. What more could one ask? We went into Cocoa for groceries at the A&P or Piggly Wiggly on weekends and I generally was allowed to go to the movie at the State Theater always a double feature on Saturday and if you were under eleven the price was 9 cents. Traveling to Cocoa at that time was more complicated and time consuming, but after the advent of the 520 causeway that connected the beach with Merritt Island and Cocoa it became a bit easier.

I graduated from Cocoa High School in 1950 in a class of 40 and continued my education at Florida State University, where I met and married my husband, Roy Staton. After graduation, and three years in the Air Force, we came back to Cape Canaveral and Roy went to work at the Cape for General Electric. I have a son, a daughter and one grandchild, a girl named Elizabeth.

Our high school class was small but mighty. There are still a number of us in the area and we are close, having dinner together every three months as a group. Including spouses and significant others, there are usually around 22 of us, which is pretty good considering we are all in our mid 70s. A group of the 'girls' go out to breakfast together the second Wednesday of every month. There is much to be said for the close ties of kids who grow up together in a small town.
Provided by Descendant, Flossie Station, Cocoa, Florida

The Gulbrandsens

The Gulbrandsen family originated from Eiker Township, Buskerud, Norway. It is surmised that the four brothers: Andrew, Nils, John and Godberg came to the United States to avoid the compulsory draft into the Military. The state religion at that time was Lutheran and it is believed the Gulbrandsen's were of the Quaker faith according to my grandmother Hazel Payne Gul brandsen; who shared with me that her husband Carl Gulbrandsen, who also held Quaker beliefs, was brought up by his father, John Gulbrandsen.

The four brothers and later one sister, ventured to this country and landed in New York. After a year or two, the brothers went out west, but not liking it, returned to New York. After hearing about land openings in Florida, they headed south, arriving at Cape Canaveral. Two of the brothers, Andrew and Nils Gulbrandsen, homesteaded at the Cape, while another brother, John Gulbrandsen, who was more interested in boats rather than farming; took an interest in the eldest daughter of Samuel L Jeffords and Julia B Thompson, and followed Captain Jeffords down from Canaveral to the new town of Miami and married Harriet Elizabeth Jeffords. This union produced an only son, Carl Gulbrandsen, who had many memories of the Cape while growing up and visiting his grandparents and numerous aunts, uncles and cousins. Godberg, yet another Gulbrandsen brother, married Marie Quarterman also of Cape Canaveral and the daughter of Orlando and Kate Quarterman. This marriage produced another only son they named Godberg Gulbrandsen Jr. and who married Constance Brown Clokey.

While Andrew and Nils were homesteading at the Cape, Andrew died around the turn of the century from Tuberculosis and his homestead property was sold to Samuel Jeffords for the sum of one dollar. Sam Jeffords, in turn, gave an area of the land to be used as the cemetery where he and several others are buried. Nils Gulbrandsen left Florida for South Africa and was not heard from again.

Provided by Descendant, Terry Dalegowski, Cleveland, TN

The Hardins

T homas Lawrence Hardin was born in Illinois on March 10, 1855 and died November 11, 1937. Addie Belle Sheckel Hardin, my (Great, Great, Grand Mother) Thomas Hardins wife was born in Indiana on May 14, 1865 and she died July 24, 1932: The Hardins were buried in Samuel Jeffords Cemetery at Cape Canaveral, Florida. Thomas and Addie Hardin were married on January 8, 1889 in Illinois. After Thomas and Addie were married, they moved to Colony, Kansas and started a family. Their first two children were boys; their names were Edward Lee and Glenn Raymond, soon after they had three girls named Verna Maude, Ida Viola, and Grace Henrietta Hardin. Ida Viola Hardin was my great grandmother.

The Hardin family were farmers and hunted for a living. They were not wealthy people, but they made due with what they had. Addie and Thomas Hardin were getting a little tired of farming, so they decided they needed a change of climate and work. They knew they were getting older and could not work their land anymore, so, in 1926 the Hardin family decided to move to Florida for warmer weather and for my great grandmother (Ida Violas) health and their health too. Ida Viola Hardin was Addie's fourth child, she was born with Respiratory issues and she suffered with her health problems continually. The move to Florida hopefully would be just what the doctor ordered for her and the whole family.

Ida Viola was married in 1917, and one year later (1918), she gave birth to a son (William). William died at the age of four from Pneumonia and was buried in Kansas. Ida and her husband Commodore had two other children, and one the way when their parents asked them to move to Florida with them. Ida and her husband (Commodore Grant Shockey), talked it over and agreed to help her parents and move with them. The Hardin family packed up their belongings and made their way to Florida (Palm Beach, County). Ida's children; Edith Belle, Grace Marie (my grandmother) where very young and the traveling was very difficult for Ida Viola Hardin Shockey because she was pregnant. As the family traveled from Kansas, they slept on the side of the road and rested very often due to my great grandmother Ida's condition.

They finally arrived in Palm Beach County, Florida and the family loved it! They made Palm Beach County their home. My great uncle Glenn was born not to long after they arrived in Florida, he was born in February, 1926. My great grandfather (Commodore Grant Shockey) and great uncle Edward Lee and great uncle Glenn Raymond Hardin earned a living by learning a trade in the fishing industry and how to build boats. They sold and used the boats for commercial fishing. The boats had big nets for catching fish, crabs and all other seafood. The Hardin men made a good living at this trade because the town catered to the tourist industry.

The Hardin family lived in Palm Beach County, Florida for two years or so until one of the worst hurricanes ever hit. This terrible day happened in September of 1928. They did not name hurricanes as we do now so, it was just called the 1928 Hurricane. It hit with all its furry! The people did not have any warning at all and from what I read, the Governor and politicians of the town did not want anyone to know of the destruction that the hurricane caused because Palm Beach County was a big tourist town and they did not want to lose any business. This storm flattened houses to the ground. The flood from this hurricane killed more than 2,000 people. Some were never found so the count was higher than 2,000. The hurricane of 1928 tore up most of the East Coast. My great grandmother (Ida Viola) was injured in this storm and the Red Cross helped her and her children by sending them back to Kansas to a hospital for my great grandmother to get medical help. She had lost her eye due to an infection and had some other health issues that the hospital took care of, and then when she was better, she moved back to Florida with her kids only to find out she could not find her husband. She then decided to move in with her parents (Thomas and Addie Belle Hardin) and her brothers; Glenn Raymond and Edward Lee Hardin, which had moved to Cape Canaveral, Florida or what they used to call Artesia.

They lived on Pier Road at the Cape. Ida's brothers; Edward and Glenn Hardin, started the family business up once again. The Hardin men started building their boats and continued commercial fishing once again. While Thomas Hardin hunted, Addie tended to a small garden. Addie canned all their meats and vegetables and helped Ida Viola by watching her grandchildren while Ida worked. Ida, my great grandmother took in laundry, baked fresh bread for the Hotel in Artesia and later on worked for the Hotel. Ida Hardin Shockey helped run the hotel; she cleaned rooms, cooked meals and anything that was needed to keep the Hotel in operating fashion.

My grandmother (Grace Shockey Howard) told the family many stories about living in Artesia as a young girl. She said it was the best time of her life. The sand was as white as snow. Grace Marie Shockey my (grandmother) told many stories about going to school at the Cape (Artesia) at the time there were only two teachers; a man and his wife, that taught first thru sixth grade. After sixth grade, she was to attend Junior High and High School in Cocoa, Florida. This meant they had to travel by bus to school every day on a rough and rippled road of coquina rocks and shells from the beach. The road was about 30 miles one direction.

The route started at the Cape or Artesia, then south of Cocoa Beach, then turned west where the Surf Restaurant is at the Banana River. There was an old wooden bridge; when you crossed the bridge you were on South Banana River Drive. The school bus kept going until they came to what is known as Kelly Park. The bus driver picked the children up for school and then headed back toward the 520 Causeway. They drove over another wooden bridge, which was the 520 bridge, then turned down North Florida Avenue to reach Cocoa Junior and Senior High Schools. Grace Marie Shockey (my grandmother) mentioned things about the living conditions in Artesia. She said the mosquitoes were unbearable and people put kerosene on their screens to keep the bugs away. The bugs never bothered my grandmother Grace and her brother Glenn Shockey; they would place their hands on the screen door of their house to attract the mosquitoes, and when they took their hands off, there would be an outline of their hands on the screen door. They made a game out of everything. My grandmother, Grace Shockey loved living at the Cape. Grace Shockey, my grandmother told me many stories. One time her brother Glenn and my grandmother Grace Shockey went swimming on this one particular day, they both decided to go swimming under the pier and a shark tried to get them by mistaking them for fish scraps. Men that were fishing were throwing fish scraps into the ocean from their boats and this was causing the fish to surface to get a free meal. Grace and Glenn Shockey were having a grand time swimming until they were mistaken for the fish scraps. They both learned a lesson that day!

Grace and Glenn Shockey had many friends while growing up in Artesia, but they were very close friends with the lighthouse Keeper and his children; they played all the time together. My grandmother Grace and her brother Glenn Shockey played games with their friends by climbing up and down the lighthouse stairs to see who would tire out the fastest. I would imagine that my grandmother Grace and her brother Glenn Shockey played all the time together, they were very close. The people that lived in Artesia or the Cape had to be very careful of wild animals. There were Bob Cats, Rattlesnakes six to ten feet long, and any other wild animal you could think of. I have told all I know of how my family, the Hardins became a part of the history of the Cape (Artesia) and how they came to Florida. I do know one thing to be true, that my grandmother, Grace Marie Shockey Howard loved living at the Cape as a child.

In 1997, our family placed a beautiful granite head stone at the Samuel Jeffords Cemetery in honor of Addie Belle and Thomas Lawrence Hardin. Just after the Descendants Day celebration of this year, 2008, my grandmother, Grace Marie Shockey Howard died. She died at home on the third of June, 2008 from Alzheimer's disease. She will be deeply missed by all. Grace's brother, my great uncle, Glenn Shockey is the only one left of my grandmother's siblings. He moved back to Kansas to live some years ago, and that is where he lives today.

Provided by Descendant, Evelyn Grose, granddaughter of Grace Hardin

The Jeffords

Sam L. Jeffords (Julius Samuel LaLare Jeffords), was born September 18, 1857 at Bluffton, Beaufort, South Carolina, the second son of Thomas Jones Jeffords and Elizabeth Winningham. His family were large land owners who lost their holdings in the Civil War. Sam married Julia Busie Thompson on December 6, 1876 at the Seaman's Home in Charleston, South Carolina. Over the next 14 years, they produced 6 girls and 2 boys, all but one living to adulthood.

In January of 1885, Sam came to the Gainesville, Florida Land Office and purchased his first piece of property at Canaveral. In March of that year, he brought his wife and three daughters to Cocoa and purchased a dirt floor cabin on Harrison Street and lived there for several years until their home on the Banana River in Canaveral was completed.

Sam was instrumental in constructing the Canaveral Pier and engaged in farming, orange groves, harvesting palmetto berries, shark fishing (He boiled the oil from the shark livers) and other agricultural pursuits that provided a good living for his family. He also served as Post Master at Artesia for several years, a post his son Julius would later fill.

During the Spanish American War, he served as Quartermaster at Fort Dallas in Miami. While in Miami, the family lived on a houseboat in Biscayne Bay, where Busie Julia Jeffords was born. At the close of the war the family returned to Canaveral.

By June of 1921, all the children were married and living in various parts of the state. In July, Sam's wife Julia B. Thompson died of a stroke at the family home at age 59. In 1922, Sam married Ida L. Kennelly, a widow from Jacksonville. This marriage was annulled for "failure to consummate". In 1924, Sam went to Sopchoppy, Wakulla County, Florida to marry Lillian Catherine Syfrett and brought her to Canaveral. (Note: Sam was age 66 and Lillian age 21) Sam would later bring Lillian's family to Canaveral. One child, Elizabeth Jeffords was born to this marriage.

Like many, Sam lost his money in the crash of 1929. Over the next few years, he sold property to maintain his family. Finally, the family homestead was sold and he moved to the seven acres he owned in Indian River City, between the Florida East Coast Railway and the Indian River. There he suffered a stroke in 1941, and passed away in November of that year at age 84. Sam is buried next to his first wife, son Joseph, and daughter Busie at the Canaveral Cemetery. Near them are buried other relatives; Margarette Elizabeth Letasky, Wesley Syfrett, and a son-in-law, John L.

Easterlin.

When Sam's daughters would marry, he would give them parcels of land on Cape Canaveral. When Busie Julia Jeffords married John L. Easterlin, they were given the property where launch complex 14 is now located. Sam also donated to the Canaveral Community, the property where the Canaveral Cemetery is located. It is believed his son Joseph E. Jeffords was the first burial there in December 1894.

As Julius James Jeffords had no children, (he and his wife did adopt a daughter) the Jeffords name is not passed on in this line. However, we, his descendants, honor Sam L. Jeffords, his pioneer spirit, and his love of family. To quote a Russian proverb, "We live as long as we are remembered."

Provided by Descendant, John L. Whitney, Rockledge, Florida

The Tuckers

MY CANAVERAL
By Canaveral Rose (Tucker) Koontz

Wherever I'd go, whomever I'd meet, For years, it was always the same!
A look of surprise and pity combined Whenever I'd tell them my name!

"Where in the world did you get such a name?" It seemed they thought it from space!
When told I was named for where I was born, They never had heard of the place!

Now, who is responsible-who can I thank For giving Canaveral its fame?
For now it easy for me to say, Canaveral Rose is my name.

Family and friends called me Canaveral Rose, but if anyone wanted my attention in a hurry, it sounded more like, "Canavarose. "In our Spanish-English dictionary, "canavera" is a common reed grass, and "canaveral" is a plantation of sugarcane. A Cuban doctor, while drawing stalks of sugarcane on his note pad, told me, "You not just one tree; you many trees! You very sweet!

Well, you'd think! Having such a sweet name to inspire me, and having been told I was born in the honey-house! (The honey-house was built a little way from the main house for the purpose of extracting and storing barrels of honey.) Furthermore, because my mother insisted on my drinking a glass of milk with each meal, and in order to down that much milk, I had to eat many biscuits sopped in butter and honey!

One of the chores I was permitted to do as a child was to churn butter. All I had to do was to turn a little crank, vigorously at first then gradually more slowly as the flecks of butter began to collect on the wooden paddles in the big glass jar. "Beauty" was our Jersey cow. Her milk was plentiful and very rich, but, until we moved inland, we never realized how salty it was from grazing in a pasture close to the ocean.

Our family consisted of Papa (Will Tucker), Mama (Flora Tucker) and their ten children. The names of their children listed from oldest to youngest are as follows: W. A., Elmo, Shirley, Flossie Mae, Holley, DeGene, Daisy, Buelah Jean, Canaveral Rose, and Iona Belle. W.A., the oldest child and my now deceased brother, was twenty-two years older than Iona Belle, who is the youngest child.

Since we had such a large family, our canned-goods were bought by the case. Our peanut butter came in a tub (2 gal. size). Our pantry shelf divided the kitchen from the feed-room. Sometimes I slipped in through the feed-room and scooped out a handful of peanut butter. My mother must have seen the evidence, but she never said anything.

Dorothy Speece had a darling little playhouse built on the back of her parent's store, which was between the school and the beach. My playhouse was a tall wooden crate with one shelf to hold the "Mothers Oats" dishes, which were plentiful because our big family used a lot of oatmeal. Then, one day, I saw our dog, Trixie, disappear into the scrub-oak thicket, just off from the mallard duck pen. I crawled on my hands and knees through the hole where she had disappeared. To my surprise, I found a large private room! There was no undergrowth, because 'the sun had to stay outside.' From then on, that was my playhouse!

For most of the year, the ocean was our playground and bathtub. I both feared and loved the waves of the ocean, just as I both feared and loved the height of the lighthouse! For my surf-board, I used ironing-board shaped boards used for stretching animal hides. There were several sizes, so as I grew, there were larger boards to fit my size. The straight-end of the board was placed at my waist, and the tapered-end was held and guided by my hands. Just before the waves broke, I jumped as high as possible and the waves took me all the way in and up on the sand!

We could not go in the ocean unless Papa was standing at the edge to watch out for sharks. But, I practically lived in my bathing suit, so that whenever someone would say, "Let's go swimming!", I was ready to go! Once in the ocean, I never wanted to come out!

The older siblings played out beyond the breakers. So many times, I tried to reach them, but unless someone had mercy on me and carried me out there, the waves just knocked me down and tumbled me over and over until it seemed I would drown! Then, one day, I found I could go to my knees and lean forward into the base of the wave and then come up on the other side! That was a great break-through to freedom!

BOB UP ON THE OTHER SIDE
By Canaveral Rose Koontz

When I was a child and used to play
the waves along the shore,
So many times they knocked me down
And tumbled me o'er and o'er!
One day, I learned to bend my knees,
Let the waves roll over my head,
Then I'd bob up on the other side,
There was nothing more to dread!

Now, when the waves of trouble roll
And tower above your head,
Don't try to stand in your own strength,
But bend your knees instead!
Just learn to pray and trust the Lord,
Fear not the rolling tide! Just bend your knees,
let the troubles roll by, And bob up on the other side!

Though the ocean was a great place to play, there were many other games to play and books to read. My favorite game was croquet, and, for a long time, the only recreational books I would read were western novels. Then, one day, Mama bribed me with a five-dollar bill to read, "Little Lord Fauntleroy." From then on, my tastes for reading was not as limited.

We needed a bus for our big family, but only had a Model-A Sports Roadster with a rumble seat. Around Canaveral, we could all climb aboard with some of us on the fenders and running board. However, half of us went to church one Sunday, and the other half went the next. We traveled up the sandy beach road to Titusville, and took picnic lunches so we could spend the day and attend the evening services.

Every other Saturday, Papa and Mama took turns traveling to Cocoa to do the shopping, and we kids would take turns traveling with them. Beaulah Jean was my movie-going partner, and Daisy, being the oldest sister still at home, went with Iona Belle, the baby of the family. The brothers, Holley and DeGene, paid our way, but we were not allowed to sit with them, because it would "cramp their style." On the Saturdays we missed, Holley would relate and act out the movies and it was almost as good as being there. W. A. and his family, lived on the Banana River side of Canaveral. There was another whole big list of fun things to do at their home!

Shirley was away much of the time, working on a drag line and building roads. He sent money to Mama so she could order our school clothes from Sears Roebuck and Montgomery Ward catalogs.

Flossie Mae married and left home when I was eight. I just couldn't imagine why? She was my "second mother," because Mama nearly died with the flu when I was born, which was the reason for my being born in the honey house. I was the only one of ten children beginning life on Eagle Brand condensed milk.

The first Christmas of my memory, Flossie Mae gave baby dolls to Beaulah Jean and me, which she bought with her baby-sitting money. My doll had a pink organdy dress and bonnet, and Beaulah Jean's doll had a blue dress and bonnet. Also, Flossie Mae taught me to read the first grade primer before I started to school.

Daisy (Annie), 6 years older than me, would hold my ankles with one hand, and let me hang head first down her back, grab my wrists with her other hand and pull me through and up between her legs without my touching the ground. She could also, while standing, put one knee forward, pull me over and spank me! Why? Well, one thing I remember was that I insisted on chasing the rooster away from "fighting" the hens.

When I got older and started portrait sketching, Daisy used to take my turn at pumping and bringing to Mama a bucket of water. Mama wouldn't even call on me for anything if I happened to be practicing on the piano. She tried to teach me to read notes, but I played mostly by ear.

One summer, after grubbing roots, Elmo went in the ocean, which was chilled by melting icebergs brought in from a current from up North. He got rheumatic fever and nearly died! But when the doctor gave up on him, prayer pulled him through.

When Elmo was able to walk with crutches, Trixie and I would go with him to sun on the beach. Trixie would take turns chasing sand pipers and sitting by me while we observed the pelicans fishing and cruising the surf. One day I found a wrinkled, dried up, and seemingly petrified young sea turtle. I thought him dead, but Elmo told me to take him down to the water and massage him. This I did until he resurrected and swam away from me into the waves!

There was another animal I was able to save. One day, while out walking, I saw a baby rabbit that wasn't able to run from me, because four big fat leeches had all but buried themselves into his stomach. I carried him home, and with a large safety pin, removed the leeches. I kept him in a box and fed him till he got big enough to hop out of the box. I had hoped to have him for a pet, but, like the turtle, he set out to seek his own fortune.

Trixie was half coonhound and half coyote. You'd never see the coyote in her unless you happened to step on her. She'd bare her teeth and growl ferociously, but, if you'd quickly say "Poor Trixie! Poor Trixie!" all would be forgiven! One day, Iona Belle stood up in her highchair, over balanced it, and fell on top of Trixie! But it was all right, because, on her way down, she quickly called out, "Poor Trixie! Poor Trixie!"

The lighthouse children were driven to school in cars. The harbor and Riverside children rode the school bus, but since we lived just within two miles North of the school we had to walk. The brothers drove the car to work too early for us to ride with them. When we were obedient (and we usually were, because the palmetto switches were so handy!), we walked on the beach where we were not so apt to encounter alligators, snakes and wildcats.

One day, we planned to take the Sunset Road as far as the County Road, then, cut across to the ocean. Just before reaching the County Road, we encountered a six-foot rattlesnake! He was there stretched completely across the rutted road-possibly sunning or sleeping. I know there had to have been snakes under six-foot, but I never saw one! There was no getting around him! If we went back by the school, we'd be getting home too late! There was nothing to do but pray and make irritating noises until the snake moved on--and we did too.

Some days later, we got brave enough to try going home that way, again. The snake was there again just like before, but this time, our prayers and irritating sounds didn't budge him! The mailman came along and shot the snake with his pistol. Saved again! We never tried that same way again, but we did reach the County Road by another road nearer to the beach. No snake this time--just a yellow jacket nest, in the middle of the road! Iona Belle got stung! We didn't get by that time without a stern rebuke, because Papa knew exactly where the yellow jacket nest was! We decided that God really meant what He said! "Be sure your sins will find you out." It seemed that God was always on the side of our parents! Even when I only thought to have an "attitude," I'd mash my finger, stump my toe, or step on a nail-each pain worse than the one before until I changed my attitude! It didn't take me long to catch on!

Although we didn't have the luxury of riding to school, we found a lot of neat things to do after school. I enjoyed climbing the flag pole and swaying in the breeze while looking over the country side. One time after school, the teacher failed to throw out the pine-sol mop water. I laid the jump board down on the ground, poured on the mop-water, took a running start and slid from one end of the board to the other, standing up! When that got tame, I propped one end of the board up on the wall of the porch and slid down still standing! That was something Papa hadn't thought to forbid me to do!

I overheard Mrs. Chandler, who was one of the teachers, saying to the principal, "Iona Belle is a nice quiet child, but that Canaveral Rose--!" I don't remember what she said about me, but I reckon I deserved it.

I never did anything mean or destructive, just silly things. Like the time everyone had been talking too much and Mr. Harnley thought to punish us by having us write a story using all the words he had written on the blackboard. They were all words that everyone needed to look up in a dictionary. But there was one word that I knew-¬"flicker". So I wrote a story about the life of a flicker woodpecker, and without using the dictionary, sprinkled in all the other words. I turned in my paper and sat back to watch him read. His face got redder and redder until finally, he burst out into laughter! I had no idea why he found it so funny, but it put him in such a good humor that the rest of the students were excused from finishing their stories. Mr. Harnley said, "I ought to whip you!" One of the students, Eulah Lee Morgan, said, "Mr. Harnley, you hadn't ought to whip her, because if it weren't for her, we wouldn't have anything to laugh about!" To which he replied, "That's all that saves her!"

It seemed that the school principles, who were all men, hardly ever lasted more than a year. However, Mrs. Chandler, a teacher who filled in when needed, was made of 'sterner stuff.' Sometimes she had charge of the whole school, and you couldn't hand her any 'junk!'

Sometimes, we went to the post office after school, and waited for the mailman to come and for the postmistress to sort the mail. We could watch Squire Kincaid, who lived above the post office, as he fed the scrub jays that flocked around the upstairs porch. One of the lighthouse keepers had a little dog that he would throw a ball to and the dog would run to catch it about thirty feet away before it hit the ground. He'd bring it back to the starting place and do the same thing over and over again! That was a delight to see!

We observed the manners and speech of the retired northern people from the Lansing Beach Community. Then, we'd go home and imitate them. I'm sure our manner and speech was just as novel to them! I appreciated Mr. Lansing's trying to bring culture to the community. He even came to school, one day, and tried to teach us all how to do the waltz and the fox trot. I never told Papa about this! Since becoming a Baptist, he had given up dancing. We were told he had once been quite good at doing the buck dance, but he would never let us see him, no matter how much we begged him! He did show us that he could jump up and click his heels three times before landing, a thing I never could do no matter how much I tried! It seemed wise, to me, not to let him hear my "Delightful Florida Waltz" song.

THE DELIGHTFUL FLORIDA WALTZ
By Canaveral Rose Koontz

We were waltzing, so gaily waltzing
To the delightful Florida Waltz!
Sea breezes playing, palm branches swaying
To the delightful Florida Waltz!
The moon shed beams and led us to dreamland,
Dreams only meant for you and for me!
Softly I kissed you, couldn't resist you!
Heaven on earth beside the blue sea!

My heart breathed a sigh and
My! But I felt so awfully proud!
When you whispered, "I love you!"
Dear, we were dancing up on a cloud!

Now you are mine and I am thine and
We are so glad our vows were not false,
Those vows we made while they played
The delightful Florida Waltz!

There was another dance Papa did when he was a young man! He told us that he and his uncle, Whitis Cox, equally young, entered into a Seminole Indian camp and began dancing like they were dancing, and imitating their sounds! They got by with it for some time, then one of the Indians walked up to them and said, "White man go home now." And so they did!

Mr. Lancing built some interesting buildings adjacent to and near the post office. There was an arched driveway between the post office and another office used for odd and sundry purposes-sometimes for voting. The county road workers drove "Mack" and "Maggie" (Mack and Model-T flat-bed trucks) through the arched driveway and parked them in the huge garage behind the offices along with other odd and sundry road-building equipment. On the east side of the office was a paved walkway and concrete benches built around a pool with a fountain statue. Past the pool was a round tower-like structure used for a library. These things, also, made waiting for the mail a pleasant pastime.

On the other side of the office and walkway was a theater building for stage plays. I only attended one of them. But the retired northerners, the sailors from the harbor, and people throughout Canaveral graciously attended all our plays at school. Along with the plays put on by the whole school, Betty Mae Jeffords and I did some humorous skits. This was a lot of fun! Also, Betty Mae, Holley and I played our harmonicas in a "black-face minstrel" show that Mr. Lansing wrote and starred in.

The Indian shell-mound was our richest garden spot. (The Indian shell-mounds were made of broken shells and pottery, and was not a burial ground.) A spring well was dug in the savanna by the mound. We worked together to carry water to the garden. The size of the water bucket depended on the size of the child. Papa was always careful to see that we didn't carry anything too heavy, and that we rested from one to two hours after eating before working or playing. I only remember using bailed lard-buckets. Between loads of water, I often took time to play leap-frog over the tall clumps of switch grass. I never cleared the tops, but, being pushed over, they made a soft cushion for my three-point landing!

We had two tidal waves during the time I lived at the Cape. One which I barely remember, when I was four; the other, after I was old enough to be in school. At the end of one school day, Papa met us with our wading shoes. The waves were still over-flowing the banks and finding a place in the savanna behind our house. The winds were still blowing hard, so, with a square of cloth held over my head, I made myself into a sail. When the wind carried me across the yard, I felt like Elijah with the hand of the Lord on him to make him run faster than horses and chariots! The ducks had fun too! We herded the mallards, muscovies and big white Peking ducks into the water-filled savanna for the time of their life! The only pool they had been used to was a water-filled drag-line scoop.

Of all the poultry we had, guinea fowls, Rhode Island Reds, etc., the turkeys were my favorite audience when I stood on my "soap box" to speak. They gathered quietly around and listened intently until I paused for a moment. Then they all began yelping loudly and profusely. But as soon as I resumed speaking, they were "all ears" again. Was that an "easy room" or what? No I wasn't trying to be a comedian. Because of my being a female, I knew I could never be a preacher but I had things to say. I guess that's why I began writing songs. Women can write songs even if they are preachy songs. But who listens? Where are my turkeys?

Beach combing was one of our favorite pastimes or way of life. There was no end to the neat things you could find washed ashore. I even found a suitcase with two nice suits. Papa wore one to church and Holley wore the other.

Besides the pretty seashells there were odd and curious things. I found a string of tough coin-shaped eggs attached to each other at the center. In each egg were what looked like tiny baby conk shells.

I especially remember a huge red bean, which I'd kept for years, till one day, I decided to plant it and see what would come up. What came up was a thorny bush that grew higher than a man's head and was greedy to take over the whole backyard if something wasn't done about it. Mama said that since I was the one that planted it, I must be the one to get rid of it! So with a huge machete, used for cutting sugar cane, I began hacking away. It was like the seeds of sin we sow that cost us more that we are willing to pay.

When Beaulah Jean (3 years older than I) started going to school at Cocoa, W. A. was her school bus driver. He allowed Iona Belle and me to ride as far as his place, then, we'd get on the Canaveral school bus with Melvin CW. A.'s son). Uncle Alfred Wilson (the uncle of W.A.'s wife, Helen) waited with us at the road to protect us. It was fun and easier than walking nearly two miles to school on cold and rainy days.

Another thing that made our life easier, was when Papa and the boys rigged up chains and pulleys in the garage and took the roadster body off our car and put in its place a 4-door sedan body with plush seats and headliners. I loved to sit in it even when there was no place to go. It made a warm, quiet reading place on cold days. Of course, riding in the rumble seat or on the fender was fun, but you can't have everything. By this time the size of our family had already dwindled by half.

These days, when a storm causes our house lights to go out and we have to light the kerosene lamps, I think, "How did we ever manage to read all those years with such dim lights?" But they were a tremendous blessing when that was the only light we had! We never felt deprived of air-conditioning when there was no such thing.

My Canaveral Lighthouse
By Canaveral Rose (Tucker) Koontz

My Canaveral lighthouse, keep shining for me
And bring back the mem'ries of my used-to-be.
Like a guar . an angel to ships out at sea,
You led me _ dream-land and watched over me.

At night on my pillow I'd never count sheep.
I'd just count your beams and go right off to sleep.
But the place of my childhood is closed now to me.
So, Canaveral lighthouse keep shining for me.

I wonder, do the strangers who now keep your light
Love to watch while you're sending your beams through the night,
Like the slow-turning spokes of a gigantic wheel?
Do they watch with the reverence that I used to feel?

Since the rockets and missiles have come to your shore,
Am I never to climb up your stairs anymore?
You are all that is left of a fond memory.
So, Canaveral Lighthouse, keep shining for me.

Provided by Descendant, Canaveral Rose Tucker Koontz, Orlando, Florida

The Tutens and Kings

T he Kings and the Tutens were neighbors. That's how Mary Jane Patrick Tuten and Nicholas King met. They were married on May 7th, 1882 by the Rev. John Penny at the residence of Nicholas' father, William John King, Jr. The area where Mary Jane (always known as 'Minnie') and Nicholas King lived was then known as Shell Pond. At that time they must have traveled to Willis Mills to be counted in the Census. I don't know. Willis Mills may have been the beginning of Williston. Further research is required to find out.

Having such a close-knit community was a wonderful thing. At Shell Pond, they had a school house that was also used on Sundays as a meeting house for worship services that were conducted by Circuit Riding preachers. Weddings, dances, community affairs meetings were also held there.

Patrick Howell Tuten died on July 5, 1864 at Shell Pond while on leave from Co. F, 2nd Florida Cavalry. He had contracted typhoid fever and had come home to the birth of his child and died when she was three weeks old. Three years later, Mary Ann, his widow, married James P. Moson. He stayed around long enough to get her assets in his own name and left...supposedly to take 300 head of cattle to market in Jacksonville. He was never seen again by any of the family. This caused very dire circumstances for her and her children, the oldest one still a young teenager.

Mary Ann Tuten Moson's Bauknight brothers lived in the area around Ocala and Micanopy. One brother, Carey, moved back to South Carolina for a time and then came back to Florida and purchased property in Titusville. It was at his home that she died on October 10, 1900. She was taken back to their old home place about two miles west of Micanopy for burial in the Bauknight family cemetery.

With the families expanding every year, land must have been becoming depleted, or so they thought, because they were accustomed to having so much of it. They started drifting apart - going to different areas of the State. Nicholas and Mary Jane King bought land at Artesia on Cape Canaveral and brought their family there. For the sake of history, I must state that Vida Kate King was born at Shell Pond, Levy Co, Fla, on July 10, 1883. Adeline Muller King was born on March 6, 1885 also at Shell Pond. The next two, Drucilla Maude King born on April 23, 1887 and Minnie Myrtle King born on September 22, 1888 were both born at or near Dorchester, Georgia. Then at Artesia, Florida were born: Lela Belle King, March 11, 1893; Luba Edna King, December 11, 1895; William Curtis King, August 14, 1898, and Anderson Jennings King, March 18, 1900.

My mother, Myrtle King, always talked about the wonderful childhood they had growing up at Artesia. She said the oak trees were so big and the grape vines so big and strong that they had a great place to play. The grapevines were as big as their wrists and they would climb up in the trees, grab a vine and swing out like Tarzan...complete with his yell! But they had it first! The Atlantic Ocean was not too far away to walk, but the Banana River was close by, too. They always had plenty of fish and oysters, to say nothing about the beautiful gardens they grew for vegetables, many fruit trees and all they could want. Of course, they had their own chickens and beef.

In 1905, they moved to Vero in St. Lucie County which was another town just starting up. They built the second house in Vero to live in and were directly across the street from the Charlie Gifford family. Mrs. Fanny Gifford was a Penny and related to Captain Penny at Cape Canaveral.

There again they planted citrus and guavas, avocados, had plenty of wild huckleberries, sea grapes for jelly and swamp cabbage. Life was good. There was a schooner that plied the waters of the Indian River and that schooner was their supply ship fabrics, thread, buttons and other sewing notions, barrels of flour, cornmeal, grits, and sugar were usually brought. There was lard, feed for the animals and many other supplies. People living today would probably think this life primitive, but think of the many times we still want to go camping! These families were all good God-fearing, Bible reading people who loved life and appreciated everything they had and were always willing to share with the less fortunate. God blessed them.

Provided by Descendant, Eula Mae Jones Andresen, Vero Beach, Florida

The Kings

Wm. John King Sr., born 1790, married Martha Cooper in McIntosh County, Ga. Wm. John King Jr. 1823, was born in Harris Neck Plantation, McIntosh County, Ga.

He married Caroline Beckley Peck, 1833, she was born in Canaan, Litchfield County, Conn. where her parents owned an Inn.

Caroline was a school teacher on the plantation. She met and married William John King Jr. He had a delivery boat on the ocean. We were told during the war that Caroline took the children elsewhere until the finish of the war. They were eating dinner when a Yankee ship sent a cannonball right through the dining room, into the mantel, while they were eating. My mother and my son went and saw the house and the cannonball. William John King was taken prisoner, during the Civil War, to Maryland.

Caroline and William King Jr. had a son, Nicholas King 1855. He was born in Harris Neck Plantation in McIntosh County Georgia. He married Mary Jane Tuten, 1864: She was born in Shell Pond, Archer, Levy County, Fl.

The story was she was going with a fellow that left the area to make money for them to marry. She never heard from him. She eventually met and married Nicholas King. She was home in Archer, Levy County, Florida, when her past beau came to the house. He had made enough money for them to marry. He asked her why she never answered all his letters. It turned out her mother, MaryAnn Bauknight, Tuten intercepted them, and Mary Jane never new he had written her, or this story of characters would have been different.

MaryAnn was married to Patrick Howell Tuten. He was captured during the Civil War, and when he came home, ill, he lived to see his daughter born 9 months later, MaryJane in 1864. He died a week later from Cholera. MaryAnn named her daughter, MaryJane Patrick Tuten.

Nicholas King and MaryJane Tuten had Vida Kate King, Adeline Muller King, at Shell Pond, Fl. (Drucilla Maude, born and died 4 months later, in Liberty County, Ga.) then Minnie Myrtle was born in Liberty County, Ga.

*Then the family moved to Artesia, Cape Canaveral, Brevard County, Florida, and they had the following children; Lela Belle King, born, 3-11-1893; Luba Edna King Roberts, 12-11-1895; William Curtis King, 8-14-1898; Anderson Jennings King, 3-18-1900: they were all born in Artesia, Cape Canaveral, Brevard, County, Florida. From there the family moved to Vero Beach, Fla. They owned a rooming house, and Nicholas had a delivery wagon. Ernest Jandreau still lives in Cape Canaveral, Fla. he is the son of Vida Kate. He has some wonderful stories to tell of the time and area.

Provided by Descendant: Carolyn McNeil, Mansfield, Mass

Today the recognized area of Cape Canaveral consists of approximately 16,000 acres, is about 15 miles long, and about five miles wide. It is bordered by the Atlantic Ocean to the east, the Banana River on the West, Merritt Island to the north and Port Canaveral on the south. In 1946, the Army, after capturing German rockets and getting Dr. Wernher von Braun to teach them how to launch rockets, was already looking for a new launch location. Locations under consideration were: El Centro, California; Aleutian Islands; Alaska; and the Banana River Naval Air Station, now known as Patrick Air Force Base, Florida with launches from the bombing range at Cape Canaveral.

In 1947, the Army, with Dr. Von Braun's help, was launching rockets at White Sands, New Mexico, when a V2 rocket made a U-turn and headed south, instead of north. It flew over El Paso, Texas and crashed landed in the Tepeyac Cemetery, Juarez, Mexico. The crash dug a hole some 50 feet wide and about 30 feet deep. This accident caused an international incident and ended any chance of using El Centro as a launch site.

The bombing range at Cape Canaveral would not work for the Army, but the area near the lighthouse was owned by the U.S. Coast Guard and would work. On May 11, 1949, President Harry S. Truman signed legislation entitled Public Law 60 establishing the Joint Long Range Proving Ground at Cape Canaveral.

Although all of the original buildings on Cape Canaveral at the time the military took up residence have long since vanished, signs of the first Cape residents, the Ais and homesteaders, include ten preserved grave sites, home sites, a number of orange and grapefruit groves, gardens, flowers and of course the historic Cape Canaveral Lighthouse.

My final thoughts: Wonderful and hard working people came to Cape Canaveral to live mostly because the lighthouse offered jobs and a home. Had not the Lighthouse Establishment and the Coast Guard reserved the land around the lighthouse, it would have been filled with homes, hotels, shops and many, many people, therefore the Army probably would never have brought rockets to Cape Canaveral. ...so, it was the lighthouse which first brought settlers to Cape Canaveral and, in the end, it was the very thing that caused them to be removed.

May their memories never be lost.

APPENDIX I

All documents published in the appendix are copies of originals as found in records Group 26 and 365, National Archives. The drawing of the foundation was from the U.S. Coast Guard and is in the Florida Historical Commission's archives.

A number of the following letters, advertisements and drawings have been used as a reference in the earlier text. We have tried to lay the letters out in chronological order.

Stephen Pleasonton sent George Center to Cape Canaveral to pick a place to build a Lighthouse in this March 12, 1847 letter.

May 30, 1847 letter from George Center to Pleasonton. Site Selected.

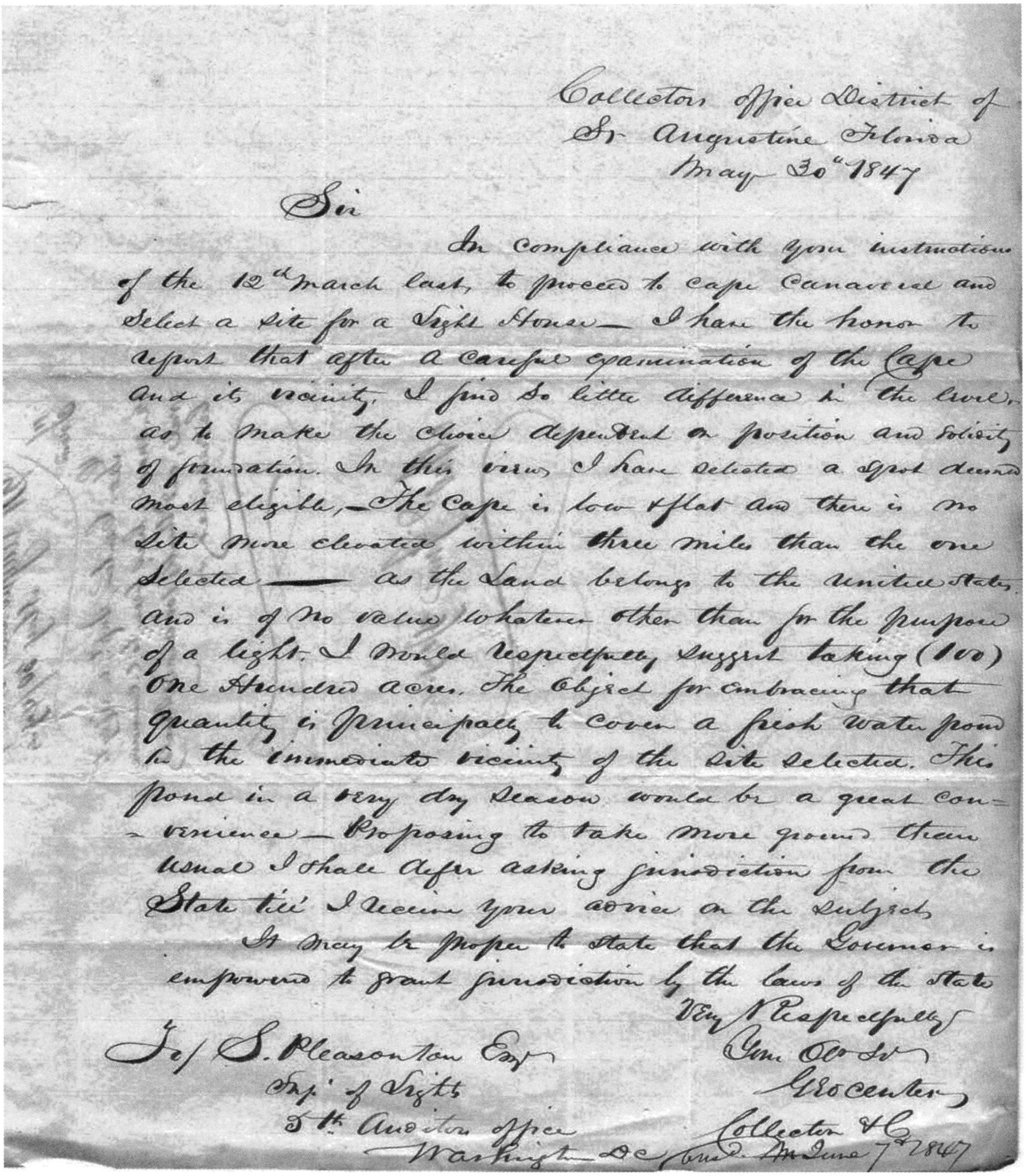

Collector Office District of
St Augustine Florida
May 30" 1847

Sir

In compliance with your instructions
of the 12th March last, to proceed to Cape Canaveral and
Select a site for a Light House — I have the honor to
report that after a careful examination of the Cape
and its vicinity, I find so little difference in the level,
as to make the choice dependent on position and solidity
of foundation. In this view I have selected a Spot deemed
most eligible, — The Cape is low & flat and there is no
Site more elevated within three miles than the one
Selected —— As the Land belongs to the United States,
and is of no value whatever other than for the purpose
of a light. I would respectfully suggest taking (100)
One Hundred acres. The Object for embracing that
quantity is principally to cover a fresh water pond
in the immediate vicinity of the site selected. This
pond in a very dry season would be a great con-
venience — Proposing to take more ground than
usual I shall defer asking jurisdiction from the
State till I receive your advice on the subject

It may be proper to state that the Governor is
empowered to grant jurisdiction by the laws of the State
Very Respectfully
Your Obt Sv
Geo Center
Collector &c

To S. Pleasonton Esq
Supt of Lights
5th Auditor Office
Washington DC

recd An June 7 1847

186

No time was wasted between site selection and the posting of the request for proposals. The below proposals were posted on July 7, 1847 for the first lighthouse in a Boston newspaper.

PROPOSALS.

COLLECTOR'S OFFICE,
Boston, July 7, 1847

PROPOSALS will be received at this office until the 19th July inst., at 12 o'clock, M., for finding materials and building a light-house and keeper's dwelling on Cape Carnaveral, Florida, agreeably to the following specifications, viz:

The tower to be of hard brick. Form, round. Foundation to be sunk as low as may be required to make the whole fabric secure. Height of tower to be 55 feet from the surface of the ground to the top of the stone deck. Diameter at the base 20 feet, at the top 12 feet. The thickness of the walls at the base 4 feet, regularly graduated to 2 feet at the top, where there is to be an arch turned, on which is to be laid a soapstone deck 14 feet diameter; outside course 4 inches thick, and to run two inches inside the sashes of the lantern. Through the arch to be a scuttle to enter the lantern 24 by 26 inches. Scuttle door, an iron frame to shut into rabbets, covered with copper. The foundation and the walls to be laid solid with the best Rosendale cement. The exterior to be well plastered with the same, and white washed. The area of the tower to be filled up two feet above the surface of the ground, then paved over with hard brick laid in cement. To be a door 6 feet 6 inches high, by 3 feet. Stone door post and cap 10 inches square, with rabbets to receive the door and lock. Door-sill, stone, 20 inches wide, 4 inches thick. Door, a strong iron frame, covered with iron ¼ inch thick, strong hinges and latch. Lintel over the door, mica slate, to run through the thickness of the walls.

To be three windows in the tower, 12 lights, 8 by 10, each glazed with strong glass; sashes wrought iron, upper and lower ones secured into the brick work. The middle one hung with hinges. Stone jambs 6 inches square, with rabbets to receive the sash. Hook 18 inches long to keep the sash open, with fastenings to keep it shut. Window cap and sills, mica slate, to run through the thickness of the walls. Circular iron stairs from the paved floor to within 6 feet of the entrance of the scuttle in the arch; stairs 4 feet long, 10 inches wide, 9 inches rise, connected with an iron tube in the centre, 11 inches diameter in the hollow, for the clock weight to run down. An opening on one side of this tube 12 inches wide, 3 feet long, 4 feet from the bottom. An iron hand railing the whole length of the stairs. At the head of the stairs to be an iron platform ¾ inch thick, forming a quarter circle; the apex on the centre tube and upper stair to run 4 inches into the brick wall. On the apex to be an iron standard 3 feet high, on which is to be secured one end of an iron rail, the other end to go into the wall. An iron ladder 22 inches wide; steps 2 inches wide, ¾ thick. To go from the platform into the scuttle of the arch.

LANTERN.

On the soap-stone deck to be a wrought iron octagon lantern, sufficient height and diameter for the sash in each octagon to contain six lights, 28 by 22, and one copper pane 22 by 12. Post of the lantern two inches square, to run down four feet into the wall. The top to be a dome formed by sixteen iron rafters, concentrating in an iron hoop at the top, 5 inches wide, 12 inches diameter, there secured with nuts and screws. The dome to be covered with copper, 32 oz. to the foot, to come down, turn over the hoop of the lantern, and rivet on the top of the sash, which must be three inches wide. On the top of the dome to be an iron framed traversing ventilator and vane; ventilator 16 inches diameter, 24 inches high; vane 30 inches long, 12 inches wide, secured to the ventilator. In one of the octagons to be an iron-framed door, covered with copper, to shut tight into rabbets ¾ inch deep, with two strong turn buttons and handle; rabbets of the sashes ¾ inch deep; bearing of the glass ¼ inch. Lantern glazed with best French plate glass; no plate to be less than 3-16ths of an inch thick, well bedded in putty, secured in with twelve lead pins to each pane. The lower tier of panes in each sash to be filled with 24 oz. copper, with a stud in the centre to rivet the copper to, secured in with lead pins. In four of the octagons to be a ventilator in one of the copper panes, made so as to regulate the draught of air, and keep out the wet. Around the lantern to be an iron railing. Post 1¼ inch square, the foot to go two inches into the stone deck, two inches from the outer edge; to run up five feet, then turn in and secured through the lantern post with nut and screw. To be two railings ¾ inch iron. All the iron and copper work to be painted two coats. Lantern white inside, black outside. To be a copper electrical rod, ¾ inch diameter, to run up one foot above the vane, and down to the foundation of the tower, there turn off four feet, secured to the tower with copper staples.

DWELLING HOUSE.

35 by 20 feet; foundation hard brick; wall one foot thick, laid 18 inches below the surface of the ground and carried up 2 feet above; on which is to be laid a frame building, sills 8 inches square; posts eleven feet high, 4 by 8, braced above and below; lower flooring joist 2 inches by 8, eighteen inches apart, bridged; chamber floor joist 2 by 6, fifteen inches apart, to be laid so that the rooms finish 8 feet; 6 inches roof, ⅓ pitch, rafters 4 by 4 inches; sides, end, and roof boarded by good seasoned pine boards and shingled with the best pine or cedar shingles, laid not more than four inches to the weather on the roof, or more than five inches at the sides and ends; house to be divided into two rooms, with an entry between, 7 feet wide; a chimney in each end of the house, with fireplace in each parlor, with three windows in each, twelve lights 12 by 9. The stairs to lead from the entry into the attic; closet back of the stairs; attic divided into two chambers, with an entry between 7 feet wide; one of the chambers to be sub-divided into two; a luthern window in the entry between the chambers, ten lights 8 by 10, collared with lead, as well as both the chimnies; doors in front and back of the entry, one into each parlor, to each chamber, and the closet, the doors to be four pannelled, 1 inch thick, except the front and back door, which are to be 1¼ inch. The front with frieze lights, with a good lock; a bolt on back door; the doors hung with good hinges and latches; a window in each chamber, 12 lights 8 by 10. Parlors, chambers, entry below and in the attic, and closet lathed and plastered, finished in a plain decent manner; gutters back and front of the house, with trunks to lead off the water; and opening in the brick foundation each side of the house 12 by 8 inches; piazza on the front side of the house 8 feet wide, floor to be six inches below the sill of the door, the roof shingled; all the wood work, except the roof painted two coats; all the floors in the house to be laid double.

At a convenient distance from the dwelling house to be a frame kitchen, 15 feet by 12, to stand on six brick pillars, 2 feet from the ground; 7 feet post, boarded and shingled; roof ½ pitch; two windows, 12 lights, 8 by 10; and one door; a chimney, with a suitable fire place for cooking, with crane, tramel, and hooks; the floor laid double; attic floor single and matched; one window in the attic; compact stairs or steps to go into the attic.

A well to be dug, at a convenient distance, sufficiently deep to obtain a supply of good water, bricked up, with a curb windlass, chain and bucket.

If good water cannot be procured at a reasonable expense, to be a brick cistern to hold 1200 gallons, sides and bottom hard brick, 12 inches thick, laid in cement, and well plastered inside with the same.

No payment to be made to the contractor for the above work until it shall have been completed, and the same inspected and approved by the collector and superintendent of lights at St. Augustine, or such person as he shall appoint for the purpose; the whole to be completed, in a workmanlike manner, on or before the first day of January next.

j8 epist19th

When the request for proposals went out, it was actually for two lighthouses, one at Egmont Key, the other at Cape Canaveral. Page 1 of this July 20, 1847 letter announces that F.A. Gibbons was the winner of the bid for Egmont Key.

Custom House, Boston,
Collector's Office, July 20, 1847.

Sir:

In accordance with your letter of the 1st inst., I invited proposals for building Light Houses at Cape Canaveral and Egmont Key, in Florida; and, herewith, I send you a list of the several bids, which were opened and recorded, at this office, yesterday, the 19th instant, at 12 O'clock, M., — viz:

For Egmont Key Light House.

No. 1.	Thos. C. Hammond,	of Mattapoisett,	$7,495.
" 2	Winslow Lewis,	" Boston,	8,234.
" 3	S. Hazelton & Co.	" "	11,000
" 4	David Cary,	" Fall River,	14,300
" 5	D. D. Tarbox, J. P. Hobart &		
	C. G. Gilman,	of Charlestown,	66,000
" 6	F. A. Gibbons,	" Baltimore,	6,250 x
" 7	N. C. Sturtevant & J. R. Tarbox,	Mattapoisett,	7,850
" 8	W. H. Powell,	of Brooklyn, N.Y.	8,350
" 9	W. S. Whitney,	" New York,	8,250
" 10	Thos. Butler	" "	9,150

188

This is page 2 of the July 20, 1847 letter announcing the winner of the bid for Cape Canaveral - Thomas C Hammond

For Cape Canaviral Light House.

No 1.	Thos. C. Hammond,	$ 8,495. x
2.	D. Hazelton &c.,	13,000.
3.	David Carey,	19,175.
4.	S. S. Tarbox + others,	69,000
5.	F. A. Gibbons,	8,700.
6.	Sturtevant & Tarbox,	11,950.
7.	Thos. Butler,	10,250
8.	W. H. Powell,	9,850.
9.	W. S. Whitney,	9,500.

This morning, (the 20th,) I received a letter from Washington, a copy of which I enclose, marked A., in relation to their proposals; but as it was not received here, within the time specified in the advertisements, I have not recorded it with the other ~~bids~~ letters relating to the bids.

You will observe that Thomas C. Hammond, of Mattapoisett, in this state, is the lowest bidder for Cape Canaviral Light House &c.; and F. A. Gibbons, of Baltimore, is the lowest for Egmont Key Light House. I shall write Mr. Gibbons by this day's mail, of the result of his bid; and I shall wait for further advice from you, before I conclude

This is page 3 of the July 20, 1847 letter announcing the winner of the bids for the Egmont Key and Cape Canaveral lighthouses.

the Contracts. If the Contracts are executed at this office, shall I require bonds for the faithful execution of the work?

Proposals were asked from Mess. Hooper & Co. and from W. Lewis, for lighting the two Light Houses. No bid was received from Hooper & Co. — W. Lewis bid $2,794 for Cape Canaveral, and $1,330 for Egmont Key.

Mr. Hammond was present when the proposals were opened & declared, and was notified that his offer for Cape Canaveral was the lowest.

I am, very respectfully,
Your obdt. Servant,

Marcus Morton Supdt.

Hon. S. Pleasanton.
Fifth Auditor &c.
Washington.
D. C.

Nathaniel Scobie's January 29, 1848 certification of completion of work on the first lighthouse.

Cape Canaveral, January 29th 1848.

This is to certify that on this day Mr. J. C. Hammond has completed this Contract on Cape Canaveral in a substantial and workmanlike manner, with the exception of furnishing granite stone in place of mica slate as the Contract calls for, notwithstanding I consider the Granite a good Building material for a Fire proof Building.

Nathaniel C Scobie

To George Centes Esqr
Collector St. Augustine.

Stephen Pleasonton wrote this August 1, 1849 letter requesting help and voiced Keeper Scobie's concern for indian attacks. Keeper Scobie asked for army protection and Pleasonton seems to be sympathetic. Notice however, that he was not offering lighthouse establishment funds.

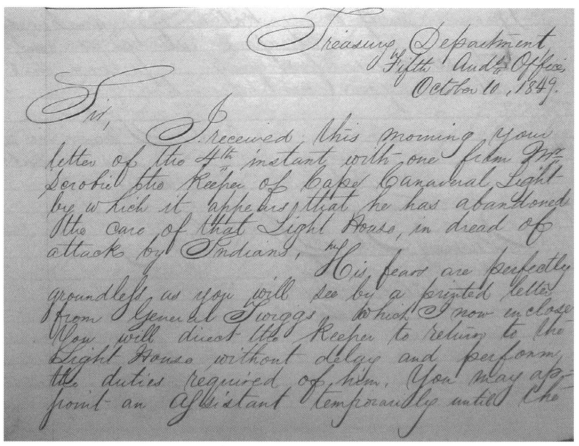

Treasury Department
Fifth Audr Office,
October 10, 1849.

Sir,

I received this morning your letter of the 4th instant with one from Mr Scobie the Keeper of Cape Canaveral Light by which it appears that he has abandoned the care of that Light House, in dread of attack by Indians, His fears are perfectly groundless, as you will see by a printed letter from General Twiggs, which I now inclose. You will direct the Keeper to return to the Light House without delay and perform the duties required of him. You may appoint an Assistant temporarily until the

466.

Secretary of the Treasury can be consulted, to whom you may allow 30 Dollars a month. Should the Keeper decline to return you will send some other suitable man as an Assistant, and nominate him to the Secretary for the appointment. Let me hear from you on this subject as soon as possible.

I have &c &c,
S. Pleasonton

417
558

James R. Sanchez Esq,
Supt of Lights,
St Augustine, Florida.

By 1860, a new keeper was in place and it was determined that the brick lighthouse was too short. Hartman Bache, in this January 19, 1860 letter recommends that an Iron tower be constructed at Cape Canaveral.

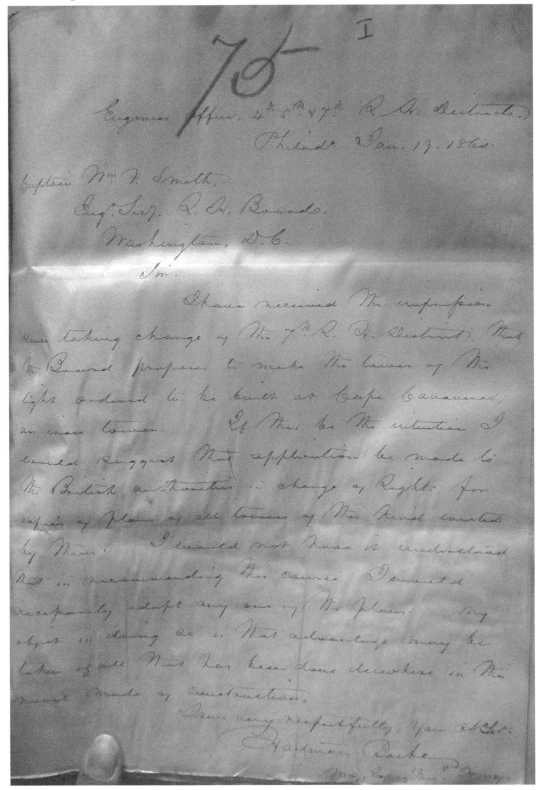

This is the drawing of the foundation for the Cape Canaveral Iron Lighthouse.

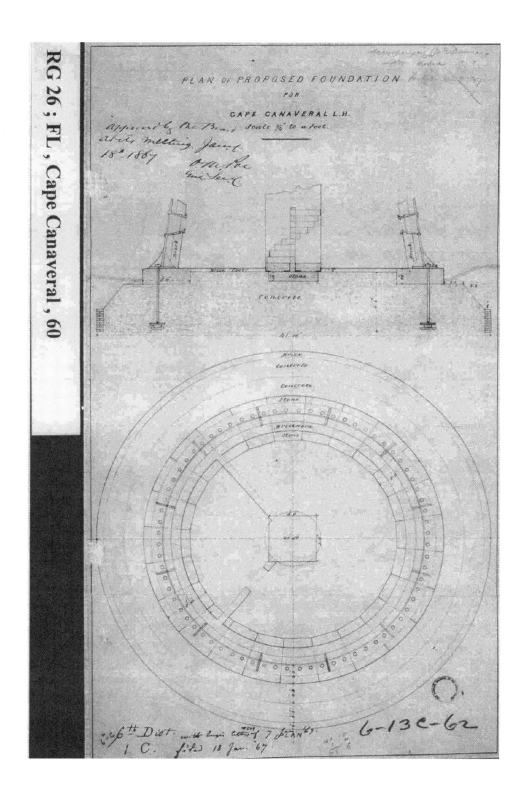

The December 3, 1860 letter announcing West Point Foundry as the winner of bids for the Iron Lighthouse. pg 1

Washington D.C.
Monday Dec. 3 1860

The Board met in pursuance of the Act of to organization of August 31st 1852

Present Commodore Shubrick (chairman) Prof Bache Prof Henry, Capt Tilton and the two Secretaries.

The minutes of the proceedings of the last meeting were read and approved

This being the day appointed for the opening of the bids for the construction of an iron lighthouse for Cape Canaveral Fla. the following bids were opened viz

Sage Warner & Whitney	Nashua N.H.	$ 69600 .~
Jas Bogardus	N York	65756 .~
People's Works	Philada	63800 .~
Denio & Roberts	Boston	57000 .~
J.G. McPheeters	St Louis	55521.87
Globe Locomotive Works	Boston	55000 .~
Wm Adams & Co	"	52932 .~
Pusey, Jones & Co	Wilmington	49500 .~
Henry Steele & Son	Jersey City	47440 .~
Atlantic Works	Boston	45000 .~
Wm M. Ellis & Bro	Washington	45000 .~
J P Morris & Co	Philada	45000 .~
Kittinger Cook & Co	Charlestown Mass	44900 .~
Hayehurst & Co	Baltimore	39900 .~
Ira Winn	Portland Me	39556 .~
Trenton Loco. & Mach Manufg Co	Trenton	39450 .~
Poole & Hunt	Baltimore	35550 .~
Knap. Rudd & Co	Pittsburg	32000 .~
J Morton Poole & Co	Wilmington	31985 .~
West Point Foundry	Cold Spring N.Y.	28000 .~

196

December 3, 1860 letter announcing the winner of bids for the Iron Lighthouse. pg 2

584

It appearing that the bid of R. P. Parrott was the lowest viz in the sum of $28000.– the contract was awarded to him.

The Question of appointing a 3rd Asst Keeper for the Minots Ledge Lt House was then taken up – and considered and it was Ordered That the Secretary of the Treasury be requested to authorise the appointment of said Assistant Keeper, and that he be also requested to recommend to Congress, a reduction of the present salarys of the Keeper and Assistant Keepers of that light house so that the aggregate amount of pay of a keeper and three Assistants will not exceed the amount now allowed & paid to a keeper and two Assistants

A list of balances of appropriations sent to the Board from the Office of the Register of the Treasury, was referred to the Committee on Finance, to report what balances if any, may be dispensed with, and thus be ~~reduced~~ returned into the Treasury

There being no further business before the Board it adjourned

W B Shubrick
Chairman

R. Semmes
Wm. F. Smith } Secretaries

September 7, 1861 receipt for $326.50 to Douglas Dummett for transferring the Cape Canaveral Lighthouse lamps from Canaveral to St. Augustine.

February 15, 1867 letter announcing the foundation stones are ready for shipment at Saco, Maine.

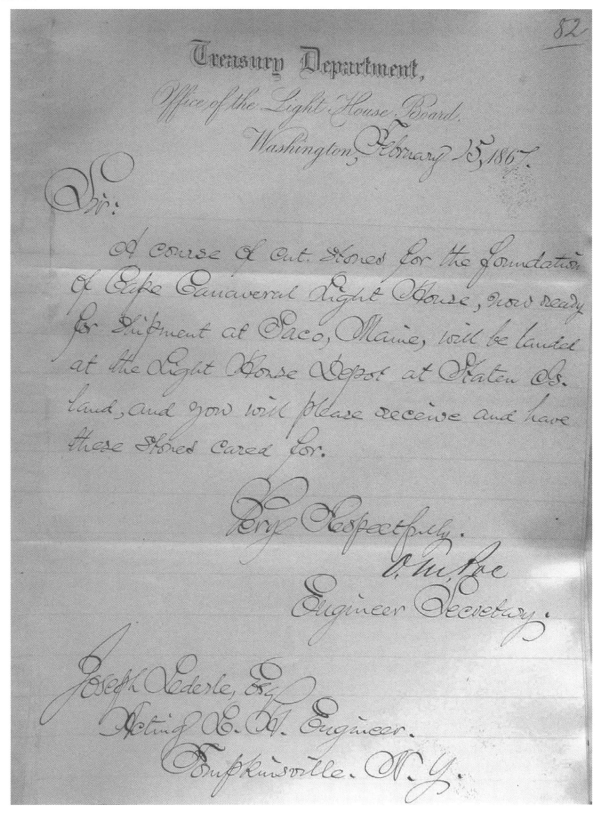

To Mr. Smith, secretary of the commission of the Lighthouses of the
United States

Sir,
I did receive the letter that you wrote me this past January 20 in which you order a
gilt-edged machine (of the best quality) for the lighthouse of Cape Canaveral, as well
as the drawing and the note related to the form and the height of the column forming the
pedestal.

We conform ourselves exactly to the information contained in these instructions and we
will ship everything toward the coming month of June.

It would have been desirable to know what arc of the horizon must be lit but I suppose,
since it is not specied, that this machine must light the whole horizon.

Since February 1 of this year 1860, the cost of making glass having been reduced, the
optical part of the equipment has undergone a ten per cent reduction which I hurry to
bring to your attention. Here is the estimate of the value of the equipment that we are
going to build for Cape Canaveral.

Gilt-edged equipment with stationary light lightning 360 degrees:
    8 lenticular dioptric panels at 1,400 francs each
    8 superior catadioptric panels at 1,500 francs each
      Charge to be carried forward
          11200 francs
          12000 francs
          23200 francs

Translation of French letter, by Hervé le Guilloux, a French Teacher at Trinity Prep in Winter
Park, Florida and Bridgett R. Griffin of Titusville, Florida.

French letter to Mr. Smith, Secretary of the Lighthouse Commission of the United States acknowledging Mr. Smith's letter of January, 1860 ordering a gilt-edged machine for Canaveral lighthouse.

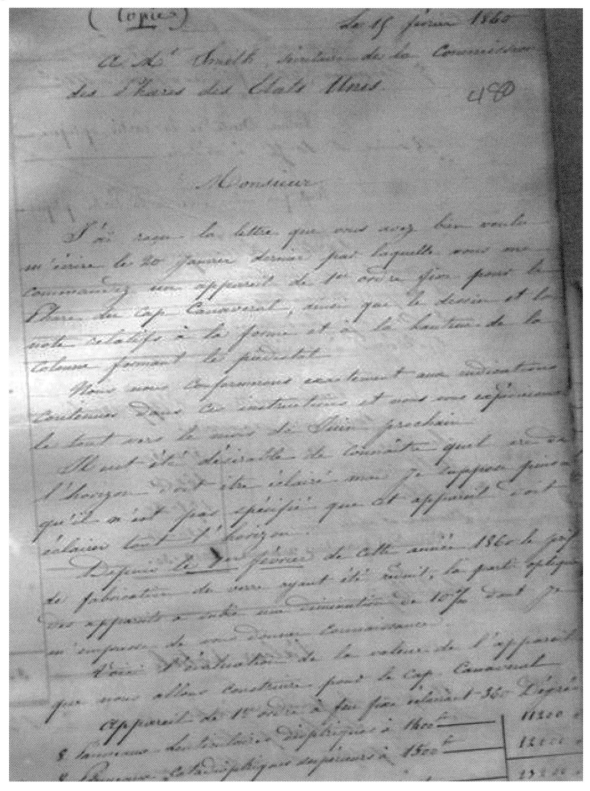

The Iron Lighthouse daymark was announced in this June, 1873 Draft Notice to Mariners.
Notice it was black and white alternating stripes with white stripe ending next to the lamp room.
Notice the burn marks. Most of the lighthouse records were destroyed in a 1926 fire.

July 21, 1876, letter charging Mills O Burnham with 1: absent from station, 2: not standing watch, 3: selling a boat belonging to the U. S. Government. pg 1.

July 21st 6

Sir,

Referring to the Board's letter of May 5th, 1876, I have respectfully to make the following report on the charges against Mills O Burnham Keeper of Cape Canaveral Light, contained in the letter of Mr Benjamin Hall of Ocean View Fla.

Charge first: that he (Burnham) is absent from the Station a large portion of his time, is disproved by both of the present, and one former Assistant Keepers.

Charge second; not standing his regular Watch, is admitted by Burnham and seems to have been an arrangement made among

July 21, 1876, letter charging Mills O Burnham with 1: absent from station, 2: not standing watch, 3: selling a boat belonging to the U. S. Government. pg 2

the Keepers

Charge third, selling a boat belonging to the United States and making no returns It is claimed by Burnham that the boat in question, which was one that had been used in landing Materials for the new tower, was given to him by the Engineer, Mr. Couvier, to dispose of as he pleased. There is no evidence on file in this Office to show that the Station was furnished with a boat by the Engineer. One was supplied by the Inspector which was destroyed in the hurricane of 1871

Charge fourth, decreasing the number of wicks in the lamp, is disproved by the testimony of the Assistant Engineer.

July 21, 1876, letter charging Mills O Burnham with 1: absent from station, 2: not standing watch, 3: selling a boat belonging to the U. S. Government. pg 3

Charge fifth, not lighting the lamp at the proper time, is disproved by the assistants. As Mrs Hall's place of residence is about ten miles from the Station it is hardly possible that he could determine the exact time of lighting.

Charge sixth, spending a large portion of his time away from the station drinking, loafing &c is not proved.

The affidavits and letters bearing on the case are herewith enclosed.

Very respectfully
Your obt Servt

A Cd Bache
Captain USN Inspector

Professor
Joseph Henry, L.L.D.
Chairman L.H. Board
Washington, D.C.

February 19,1887 investigation report of charges against Keeper Burnham. pg 1

February 19th

Sir,

In compliance with your orders of January 4th I have investigated the charges against Mills O. Burnham, Keeper of Canaveral Light, contained in the affidavit of J. H. Meyers, backed by the testimony of Alexander Rose and Betsy Thomas.

Of the 1st Charge: Neither Meyers or Betsy Thomas had any personal knowledge, although they had testified to its truth, and the only shadow of evidence in its support is that of Rose, who asserts, that during the time he served as assistant small quantities of refuse oil were taken by Burnham to burn in his kitchen at his orange grove

Burnham on the other hand shows

that he had oil of his own — and there was therefore, no occasion for him to use even refuse oil. All the charges relative to neglect or mismanagement of lamp and revolving machinery are entirely disproved by Quarterman the 1st Assistant and also by Rose. It is true that the lamp and burner are not usually changed oftener than once a quarter provided they work well, but the oil is drawn off, the plunger removed and both lamp and burner thoroughly cleaned every fortnight.

The revolving machinery is cleaned quarterly and for over a year has been running two fast instead of slow as charged.

There is no evidence to sustain the charge of false entries having been made in the "Expenditure book" by the Keeper.

The charge relating to building the

February 19,1887 investigation report of charges against Keeper Burnham. pg 3

store house is not true.

The 1st Assistant emphatically denies that he ever gave any instruction about carrying the flame lower than required. It is proved that Burnham did not stand a regular watch, but this was by agreement among the Keepers which was evidently satisfactory to Meyers as he made no complaint when the station was inspected. I do not consider that this matter require any further action

Very respectfully
Your Obt Servt
A. E. K. Benham
Captain U.S.N. L.H. Inspector

Professor
Joseph Henry, LL.D.
Chairman L.H. Board
Washington, D.C.

The move of the Cape Canaveral Lighthouse was approved in the following February 18, 1893 letter to Capt Eric Bergland, Engineer, 6th Light-House District.

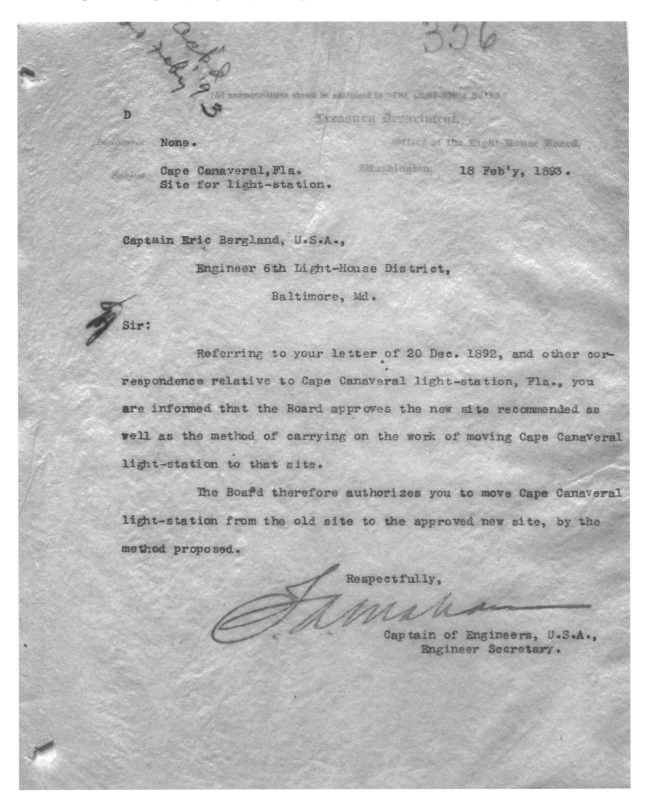

(All communications should be addressed to "THE LIGHT-HOUSE BOARD.")

D

None.

Cape Canaveral, Fla.
Site for light-station.

Treasury Department,

Office of the Light-House Board.

Washington, 18 Feb'y, 1893.

Captain Eric Bergland, U.S.A.,

Engineer 6th Light-House District,

Baltimore, Md.

Sir:

Referring to your letter of 20 Dec. 1892, and other correspondence relative to Cape Canaveral light-station, Fla., you are informed that the Board approves the new site recommended as well as the method of carrying on the work of moving Cape Canaveral light-station to that site.

The Board therefore authorizes you to move Cape Canaveral light-station from the old site to the approved new site, by the method proposed.

Respectfully,

Captain of Engineers, U.S.A.,
Engineer Secretary.

John Mew was approved to supervise the lighthouse move in this March 7, 1893 letter. His pay
was to be $150.00 per month.

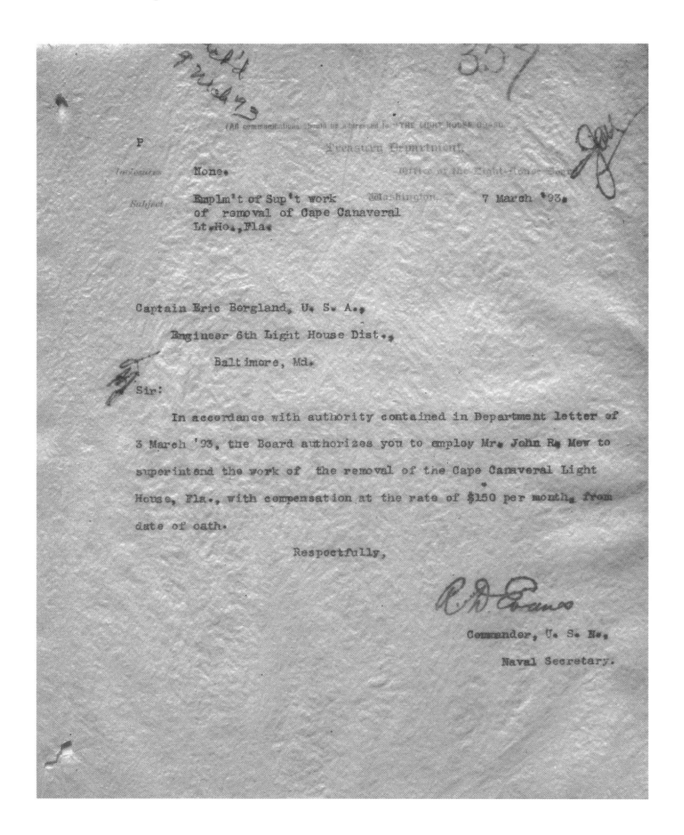

June 29, 1894 Notice to Mariners of relighting after the move. See the keeper's log for the exact time.

ESH

1 inclosure.

Washington   29 June '94.

Captain Eric Bergland, U. S. A.,

   Engineer 6th Lighthouse District,

      Baltimore, Md.

Sir:

   Inclosed is transmitted a copy of Notice to Mariners, No. 79 of 1894, giving notice that, on or about 25 July '94, the first-order light at Cape Canaveral light-station, Fla., will be reestablished in the tower recently reerected about 5,200 feet to the southward and westward of its former position.

   The Board requests you to have the new tower in readiness for the exhibtion of the light on the date specified in the notice.

                              Respectfully,

                              R. D. Evans

                              Captain, U. S. N.,

                              Naval Secretary.

March 11, 1889, Executive Order reserving land for the new site of the Cape Canaveral Lighthouse.

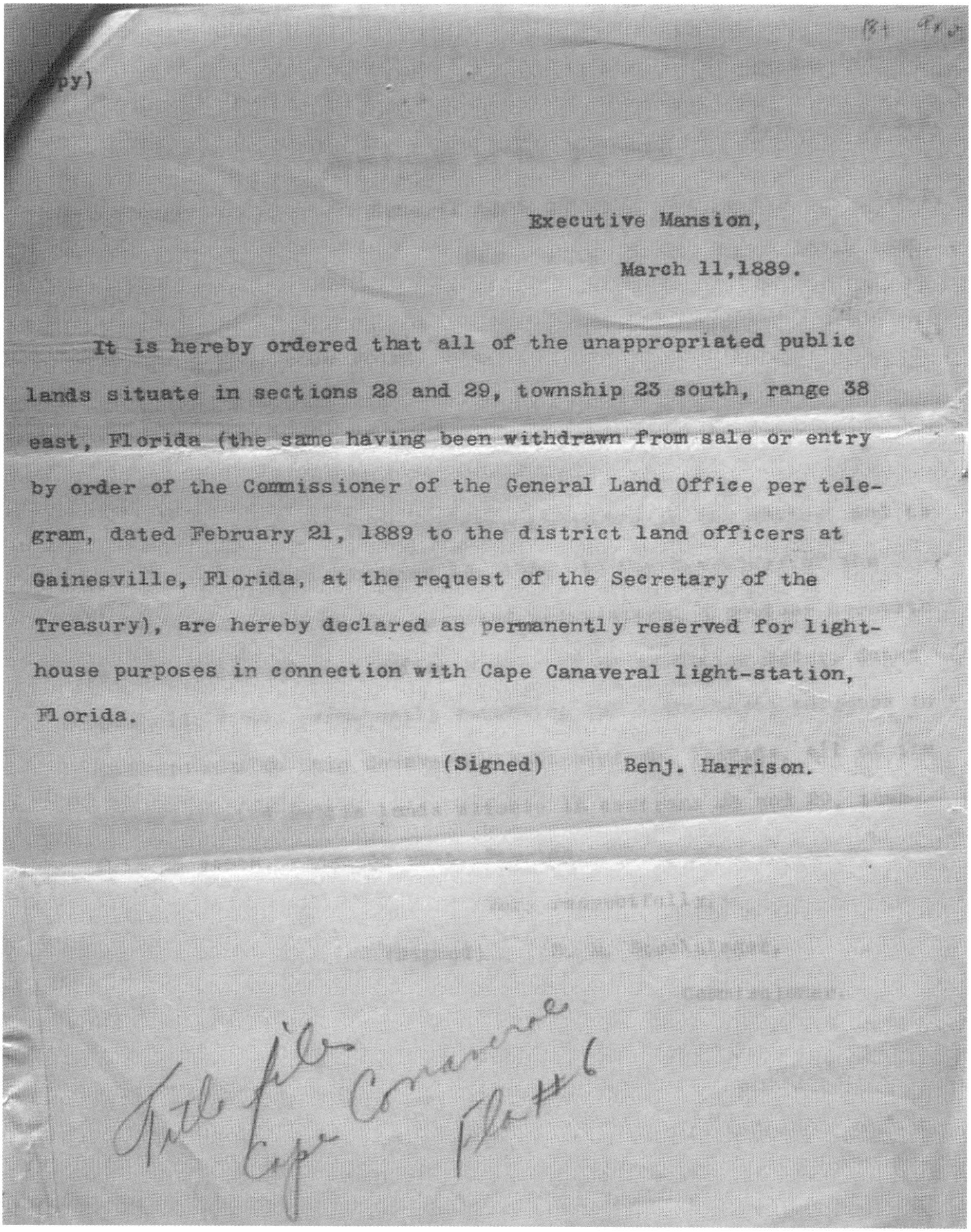

py)

Executive Mansion,

March 11,1889.

It is hereby ordered that all of the unappropriated public lands situate in sections 28 and 29, township 23 south, range 38 east, Florida (the same having been withdrawn from sale or entry by order of the Commissioner of the General Land Office per telegram, dated February 21, 1889 to the district land officers at Gainesville, Florida, at the request of the Secretary of the Treasury), are hereby declared as permanently reserved for lighthouse purposes in connection with Cape Canaveral light-station, Florida.

(Signed) Benj. Harrison.

Title file
Cape Canaveral
Fla #6

February 18, 1893 letter approving the move of the Cape Canaveral Lighthouse.

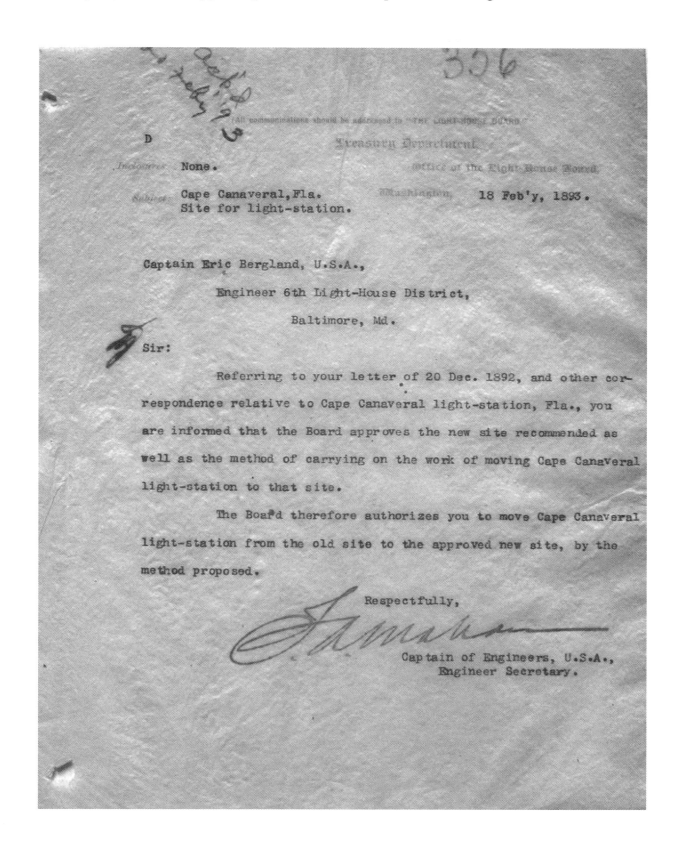

336

All communications should be addressed to "THE LIGHT-HOUSE BOARD."

Treasury Department.

D

Inclosures None.   Office of the Light-House Board.

Subject Cape Canaveral, Fla.   Washington,   18 Feb'y, 1893.
          Site for light-station.

Captain Eric Bergland, U.S.A.,

            Engineer 6th Light-House District,

                  Baltimore, Md.

Sir:

            Referring to your letter of 20 Dec. 1892, and other cor-
respondence relative to Cape Canaveral light-station, Fla., you
are informed that the Board approves the new site recommended as
well as the method of carrying on the work of moving Cape Canaveral
light-station to that site.

            The Board therefore authorizes you to move Cape Canaveral
light-station from the old site to the approved new site, by the
method proposed.

                              Respectfully,

                              Captain of Engineers, U.S.A.,
                              Engineer Secretary.

April 28, 1906 letter discussing the fate of the lighthouse mule that pulled the iron pieces of the lighthouse to its current location. pg 1 - Note the mule was a she.

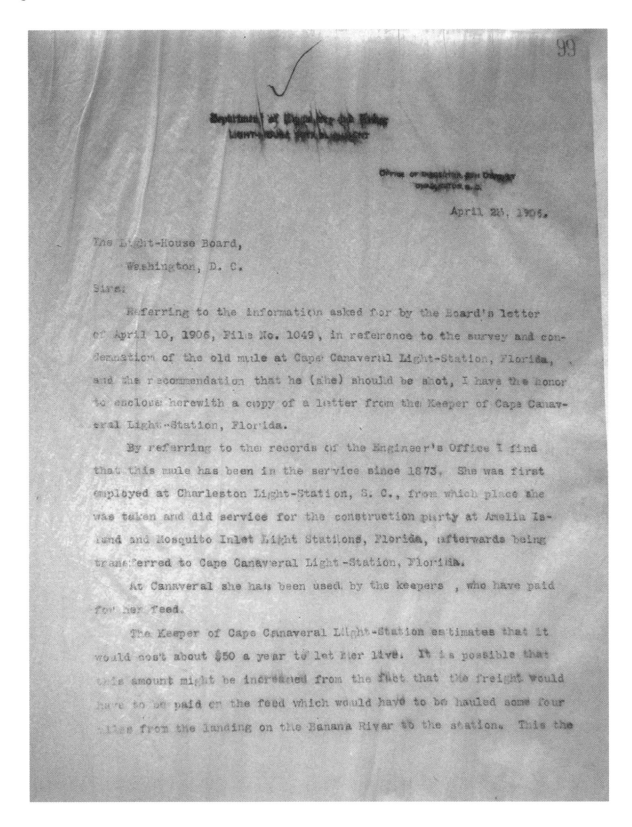

Department of Commerce and Labor
LIGHT-HOUSE ESTABLISHMENT

Office of Inspector, 6th District
Charleston, S. C.

April 28, 1906.

The Light-House Board,

Washington, D. C.

Sir:

Referring to the information asked for by the Board's letter of April 10, 1906, File No. 1049, in reference to the survey and condemnation of the old mule at Cape Canaveral Light-Station, Florida, and the recommendation that he (she) should be shot, I have the honor to enclose herewith a copy of a letter from the Keeper of Cape Canaveral Light-Station, Florida.

By referring to the records of the Engineer's Office I find that this mule has been in the service since 1873. She was first employed at Charleston Light-Station, S. C., from which place she was taken and did service for the construction party at Amelia Island and Mosquito Inlet Light Stations, Florida, afterwards being transferred to Cape Canaveral Light-Station, Florida.

At Canaveral she has been used by the keepers, who have paid for her feed.

The Keeper of Cape Canaveral Light-Station estimates that it would cost about $50 a year to let her live. It is possible that this amount might be increased from the fact that the freight would have to be paid on the feed which would have to be hauled some four miles from the landing on the Banana River to the station. This the

April 28, 1906 letter discussing the fate of the lighthouse mule that pulled the iron pieces of the lighthouse to its current location. pg 2.

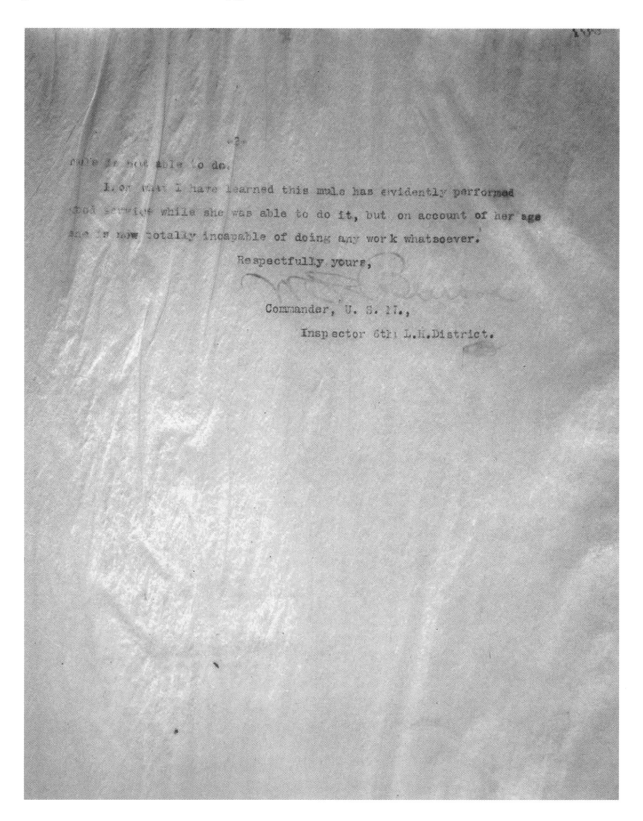

-2-

mule is not able to do.

From what I have learned this mule has evidently performed good service while she was able to do it, but on account of her age she is now totally incapable of doing any work whatsoever.

Respectfully yours,

Commander, U. S. N.,

Inspector 6th L.H.District.

April 9, 1906 letter from Clinton P. Honeywell, Keeper of the Cape Canaveral Lighthouse, requesting an artesian well.

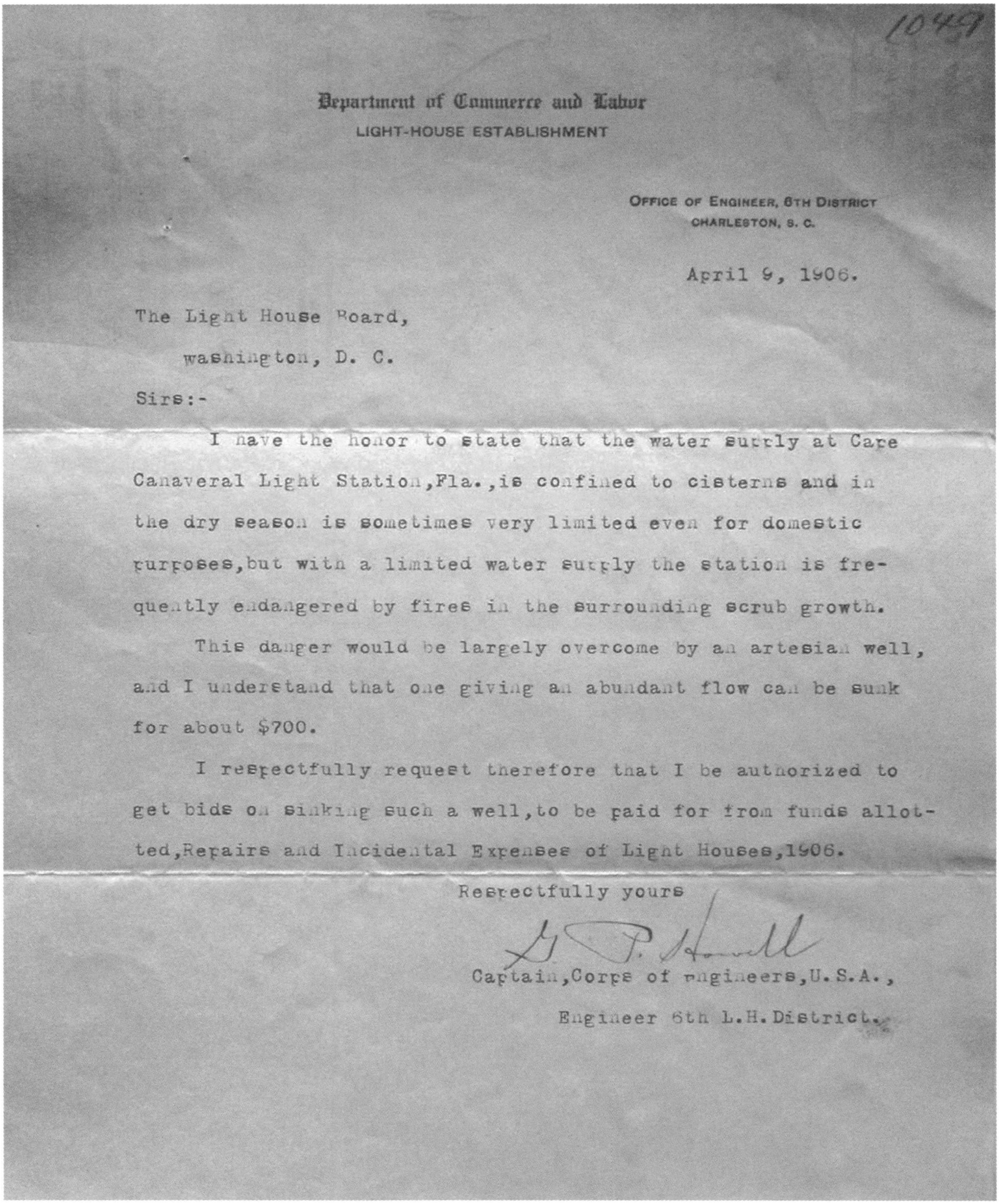

Department of Commerce and Labor
LIGHT-HOUSE ESTABLISHMENT

OFFICE OF ENGINEER, 6TH DISTRICT
CHARLESTON, S. C.

April 9, 1906.

The Light House Board,

washington, D. C.

Sirs:-

I have the honor to state that the water supply at Cape Canaveral Light Station,Fla.,is confined to cisterns and in the dry season is sometimes very limited even for domestic purposes,but with a limited water supply the station is frequently endangered by fires in the surrounding scrub growth.

This danger would be largely overcome by an artesian well, and I understand that one giving an abundant flow can be sunk for about $700.

I respectfully request therefore that I be authorized to get bids on sinking such a well,to be paid for from funds allotted,Repairs and Incidental Expenses of Light Houses,1906.

Respectfully yours

Captain,Corps of Engineers,U.S.A.,

Engineer 6th L.H.District.

November 9, 1906 letter approving the well and authorizing Alex Near of Eau Gallie to do the work.

Department of Commerce and Labor
LIGHT-HOUSE BOARD
Washington

ML
File No. 1049.
THREE Enclosures.

9 Nov., '06.

... that the person named be employed to sink the well ...

... without formal contract, that being the most advantageous and the
The Honorable, ... to the Government of having the work done.

The Secretary of Commerce and Labor.,

Sir:

The Board has the honor to state that only one bid was received in response to invitation by posters and circular letters for sinking an artesian well at the Cape Canaveral Light-Station, Fla., as follows:-

                    Mr. Alex Near,
                              Eau Gallie, Fla........$625.00

This bid was publicly opened at the Office of the Engineer of the Sixth Light-House District, at Charleston, S. C., on 10 May, '06, that being the date fixed therefor in the advertisement.

Posters, copy herewith, were displayed at the Post Offices at St. Augustine, Daytona, Eau Gallie and Titusville, Fla.

Proposals were requested from Mr. Alex Near, of Eau Gallie, Fla., and Mr. Fox, of Haiti, Fla., who it was thought might tender a bid.

The bid of Mr. Alex Near, of Eau Gallie, Fla., being the only one received, is reasonable, advantageous to the Government and not in excess of current market rates, for doing the work specified.

The Board, therefore, recommends that this bid be accepted,

June 4, 1906 hand-written letter from Samuel Jeffords requesting a lease for use of Lighthouse land. pg 1

Canaveral Fla
June, 4th 06.

Hon. J. P. Taliaferro
    Dear Sir:—
Knowing of your many kind acts
for the benefit of the working
man in your official capicity,
causes me to write you asking a
special favor. Allow me to
introduce my-self to you, by
refering you to a few of my many
friends who would indorse any
partition if nessacerry.
Hon. Minor Jones
Judge Gaulden, Judge Penny, and
Capt James Pritchard,
Pres
Credit, Indian River State Bank.
Hon P. A. Mac, Millan of Eau Gallie
and I would say the majority of
leading men in Brevard and

June 4, 1906 hand-written letter from Samuel Jeffords requesting a lease for use of Lighthouse land. pg 2

2.

Dade Co. My present buisness is fishing. I have lived here at Canaveral and in this vacinity for the last 20 years and is well known as a Licenced steam boat piolot on the Indian River. My partition would ask you to secure for me, special permission from the goverment to use 10 acres of land at Cape Canaveral for a fishing site, The said land to be returned to the goverment at any time in case of actual need for war or other purposes. Further that there will not be built no large houses, or other signs that will in any way affect appearance of Canaveral light. If granted the

June 4, 1906 hand-written letter from Samuel Jeffords requesting a lease for use of Lighthouse land. pg 3

5.

County and a great help to fisher-men in this section.

Please find inclose a map describing land in question. In securing this grant, you will do me a great kindness and service.

Very Respectfully Yours

Samuel L. Jeffords.

APPENDIX II

This Appendix is devoted to selected records that have been referenced within the text and to provide a sampling of the records for the reader's enjoyment and use.

The chart here is a copy of the third page of the 1850 "Schedule of Free Inhabitants in the 18th Division in the County of St. Lucie State of Florida enumerated by me, on the 9th day of Decbr: 1850. Geo L Tahnbauer (/) ASST Marshal 223" The Assistant Marshal signs and certification at the bottom of the page and then adds the following written statement: "N.B. The Inhabitants of the County were driven from it on acct of the Indian hostilities and only a few of them have as yet returned." It is signed with the initials "G. L. T." Chart Courtesy Ancestry.com.

Keeper's Journal, December 1885 - May 1886 - Notice the entry dated, April 17, 1886.

JOURNAL of Light-house Station at *Cape Canaveral*

1885 MONTH.	DAY.	RECORD OF IMPORTANT EVENTS AT THE STATION, BAD WEATHER, &c.

December 31st — The U.S. Steamer *McHarg* Capt Brown Master landed Capt B.P. Lamberton U.S. Navy and Inspector 6th Light District — and also landed Paint and Oil for Painting Tower and after Inspecting the Light Capt Lamberton left same day in his Steamer for Charleston

Mills O. Burnham
Keeper

1886

March 25 — Capt B.P. Lamberton Insp. visited the Light Station and inspected the light and left the Same day via Titusville

April 17 — The Keeper of Station Mills O. Burnham died at the Station this day at 4 P.M. after an illness of several weeks

17 — The Inspector B.P. Lamberton visited the Station and inspected the Light & was present at the death of the Keeper Mills O. Burnham and attended the funeral. and returned by the way of Titusville on the 19th Apl

May 7 — Jacked up and took off rollers and cleaned truck of Lens.

May 11 — Changed the burner of Lantern at sunset on account of rivet which jamming

223

JOURNAL of Light-house Station at

1886 MONTH.	DAY.	RECORD OF IMPORTANT EVENTS AT THE STATION, BAD WEATHER, &c.
May	12	Cleaned out the basin and float cha—
	13	Painted the Lantern sash on outside
	15	Painted dome on inside. Rail & Wall
	17	Painted outside Deck of Lantern
July	23	The Schooner Pharos Landed Lumber For the Light Station and Colonel R.R. Light and Buildings and Returned to The Schooner Remaining to Anchor
August	7	Mr. R.P. Haines Superintendent The Breakwater and started to which Remained to Anchor in the
August	23	Cleaned out the Lamp and Float
August	31	at 9.30 P.M. Experianced quite a Shock as to shake out quite alot of putty Time piece in the Tower and the about two Minutes weather Clear
September	3	at 10.40 P.M. Experianced a slight Shock in Caused by an Earth Quake the
September	20	Expended Two Barrels of Lime outer Buildings
Nov	24	Jacked up the Lens and taken
Dec	15	Capt. R.P. Lamberton Inspector Light Inspection and Returned to Charleston

224

Keeper's Journal, May - December 1886 - Right Side - Earthquake: see fifth entry

with Strong hot Soap Suds

on outside

For Bulding a brake water and the Rations
Smith Assistant Engineer and he inspected the
Charleston on the 25. By the way of Titusville
in the Bight

---

of the Brakewater Completed the work on
Charleston in the U.S. Schooner Pharos
Bight until the work was Completed.

Chamber.

Causing the Lens and Tower to shake so much
out of the frame of the Lens and stoping the
one in the Dwelling. Duration of Shock
with Light S.W. wind.

---

the Tower and Dwelling supposed to be
same as the above

---

and whitewashed the fence and all the

---

off the Collar and Cleaned the Tracks

House District Visited the Station and made his
Dec 16th by the way of Titusville

This June schedule of inhabitants in Cape Canaveral in the county of Brevard in the State of Florida enumerated in June 1885, verifies the seven families that lived at Canaveral at that time. It appears that the enumeration is signed by one, W. R. Sanders.

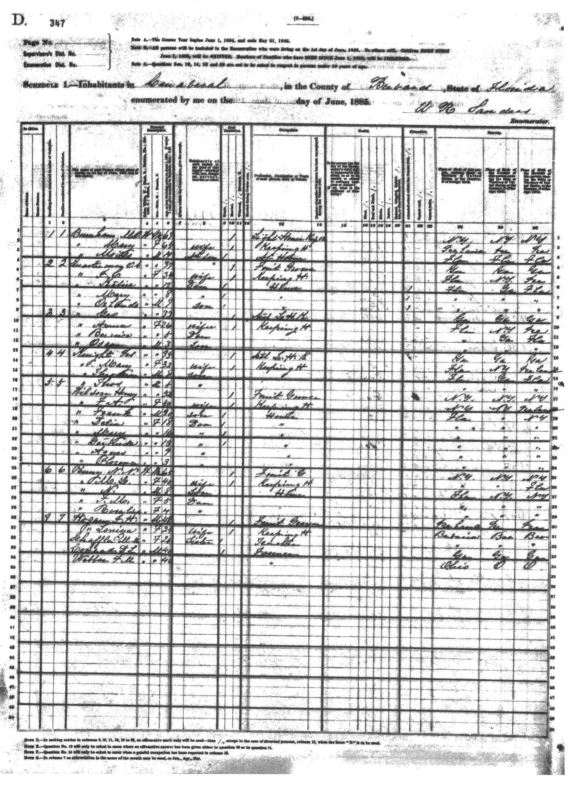

December 25, 1887 - Christmas

JOURNAL of Light-house Station at *Cape Canaveral*

1887 MONTH.	DAY.	RECORD OF IMPORTANT EVENTS AT THE STATION, BAD WEATHER, &c.
December	18th	Supply vessel Fern capt. William Master landed Light House Supplyes and Rations capt. Merrill Miller U.S. Navy inspector 6th L.H. Dist visited the Station and inspected the Light in company with capt Lamberton the New Inspector leaving the Station on the 19th for Charleston via Titusville
December	25th Christmas	Hoisted Oil up to oil Room Bbls Six
March	20th	Hoisted 5 Bbls oil up to oil room and deposited Same in Bulk
May	12	Heavy hale Storm commencing East and Shifting to South East then to South and South West and wind blowing very heavy banking up the hale Stones against the buildings any fences ten inches in thickness many of which were three inches in diamater which broke thirteen lights of Glass in the dwellings and kitchen.

George M. Quarterman turned over the lighthouse to James M. Knight in April 1887.

1887. MONTH.	DAY.	RECORD OF IMPORTANT EVENTS AT THE STATION, BAD WEATHER, &c.
April	1st	George M Quarterman Resignation Tendered on March 14th AD 1887 Took effect this Day James M Knight Succeeding To The Position of Keeper George M Quarterman Turned over all the Property Belonging to the Light House Establishment to James M Knight taken his Receipt Therefor Wrote By George M Quarterman
	10	Jettys broke of 20 fathom water and
	11	we opened 1 can of inside white and comenced painting the inside of the Lantorn
	12	I opened 2 Cans of Tink 20 lbs and one can of inside white
May	3	I opened 1 cane of Inside White to Cover the stones on in eided Tower
	5	Finished Covering the noty ehots in the Towe to day
	24	I cleard out the Lamp & Note chamber
May	26	Schooner Thomp Capt Anderson Master anchored in the Bell and camensed Landing material for the repars of this Station
June	6	Capt G G Anderson Sailed for Charleston at 4 oclock after making all neasary Repares at this Station

JOURNAL of Light-house Station at

1888 MONTH.	DAY.	RECORD OF IMPORTANT EVENTS AT THE STATION, BAD WEATHER, &c.
Mch	26	Nibb Conner special agent General Land Office DeFuniak Springs Fla
April	23	Schooner Pharos Capt Anderson finished the Breakwater at this Station and made Anchor at 11.35 A M and sailed for Charleston
June	15	Visited + inspected the Station and found Everything in very good order B.P. Lamberton Comd U.S.N. S.L. Ho. Inspr.
July	14	Inspected 6.30 a.m. Everything in Excellent order. R. White Lt. J.G. Comd. L.H. Inspr.
August	21	one mile N. of the Light came ashore one Bottlenose Whale 20 feet Long
		Oct 11/88 to Schr You wall Frying Pan Lot Ship WSW 7 mile wind N E G E overcast and moderate John Cony Jr 516 Linden St Camden N J
Dec	8	the Keeper's Son found the above note

Here is the left side of the September 1893 Keeper's Journal. Please note, that the date was not changed to 1893, still reads 187. We are interested in the right side entry of September 26th on the next page.

187 . MONTH.	DAY.	RECORD OF IMPORTANT EVENTS AT THE STATION, BAD WEATHER, &c.
September	1	Cloudy — — — — Wind Light S E
"	2	" " Rain "
"	3	" " Rain " S W
"	4	" " " N W
"	5	Clear — " N E
"	6	" " Fresh
"	7	Cloudy Rain " E
"	8	" " Light S E
"	9	Clear — "
"	10	" " S W
"	11	Cloudy Rain " S W
"	12	" " "
"	13	" " "
"	14	Clear "
"	15	" " "
"	16	" " N W
"	17	" " W
"	18	" " N E
"	19	" " S W
"	20	" " N W
"	21	" " N E
"	22	" "
"	23	" "
"	24	" "
"	25	" "
"	26	" " S E
"	27	" " Fresh "
"	28	" " E
"	29	" " N E
"	30	" "

Keeper's Journal, September 1893 - Right Side. Note: 26 lines down tells us the date the Brick Lighthouse was blown up.

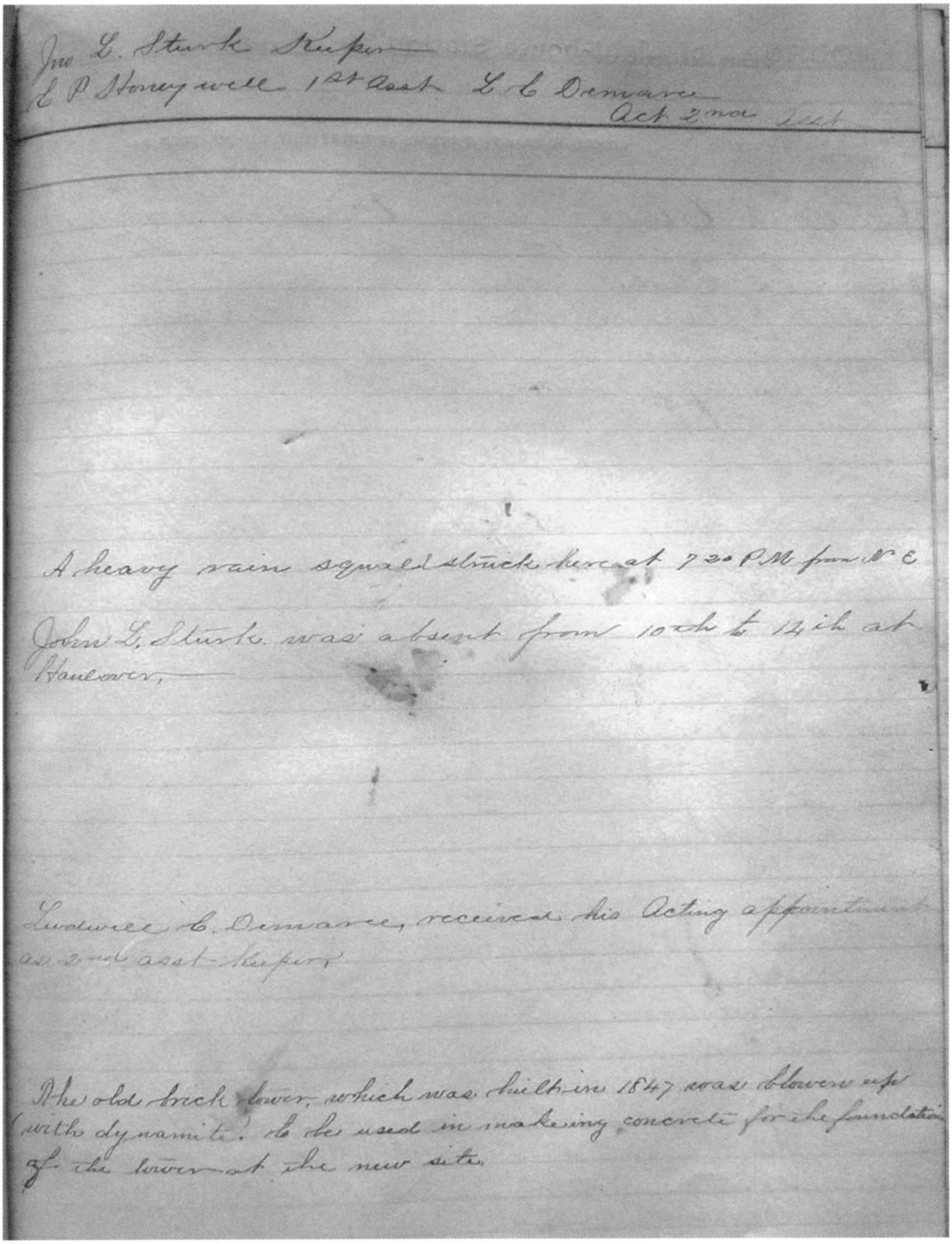

Jno L. Sturk Keeper

E P Honeywell 1st Asst   L C Demare

Act 2nd 114

A heavy rain squall struck here at 7 20 P M from N E

John L. Sturk was absent from 10th to 14th at Haulover,

Ludwice C. Demare, received his Acting appointment as 2nd Asst-Keeper

The old brick tower, which was built in 1847 was blown up with dynamite. to be used in makeing concrete for the foundation of the tower at the new site.

Keeper's Journal, April 11, 1931 - Light gets electrified

1931 MONTH	DAY	STATE WORK PERFORMED BY KEEPERS REGARDING UPKEEP OF STATION, AND RECORD OF IMPORTANT EVENTS, WEATHER CONDITIONS, ETC.
March	26	Clear. Worked with Radio Engineer
	27	Clear. Worked with Radio Eng.
	28	Rain. " " " "
	29	Sunday. Clear. Cleaned Points in Engine.
	30	Clear. Worked Charging Battery
	31	" " " "
April	1	Clear. Mr. Mc. Lee Went to Jupiter.
	2	" Cleaned and iled clock
	3	" Went to Petersville for supplies
	4	" Cleaned plate glass
	5	Rain. Sunday.
	6	Clear. Polished Brass
	7	" Painted Engine room
	8	" " Radio Room and floor
	9	" Went to Cocoa filed lens
	10	Cloudy. Cleaned and oiled leaders
	11	" Charged Battery to Test Light in Tower.
	12	Sunday. clear.
April 11 '31		The Electric light was put in Lead for regular operation on April 11th 1931 at 6 45 PM.
	13	Cleaned clock and repaired governor, Charged battery
	14	Charged Battery painted Weather cloudy.
	15	Put Rags on the Charged Bats. and painted

232

1892 Eberwein Land Map

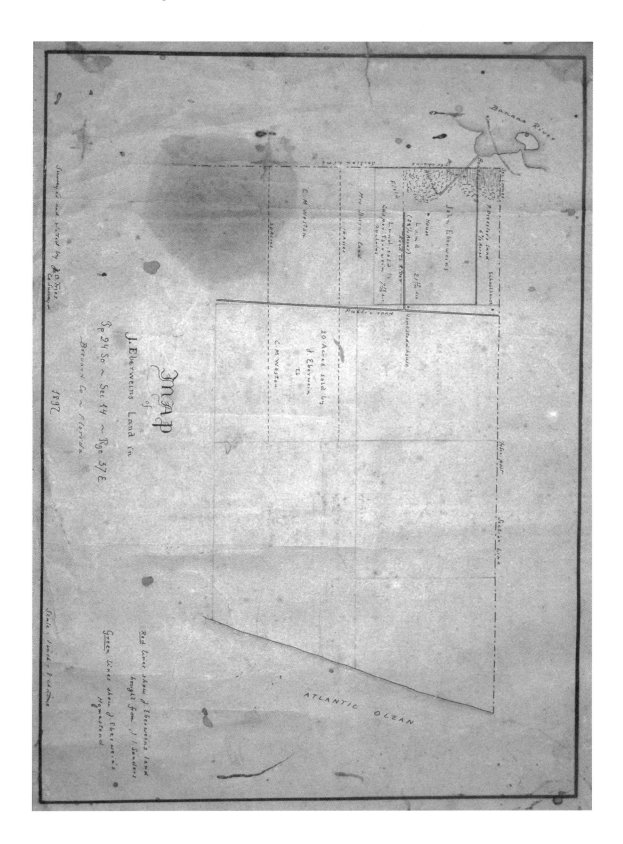

Jeffords' Map of Land lease request. Jeffords drew this map of land he wanted to lease from the Lighthouse Service. Please notice the map shows two wharfs, (one Jeffords' the other the U.S. Government's). The two wharfs, when added with the pier at the hotel and the one built by the Cape Fishing Company, account for four piers that existed at Cape Canaveral. Another mystery solved!

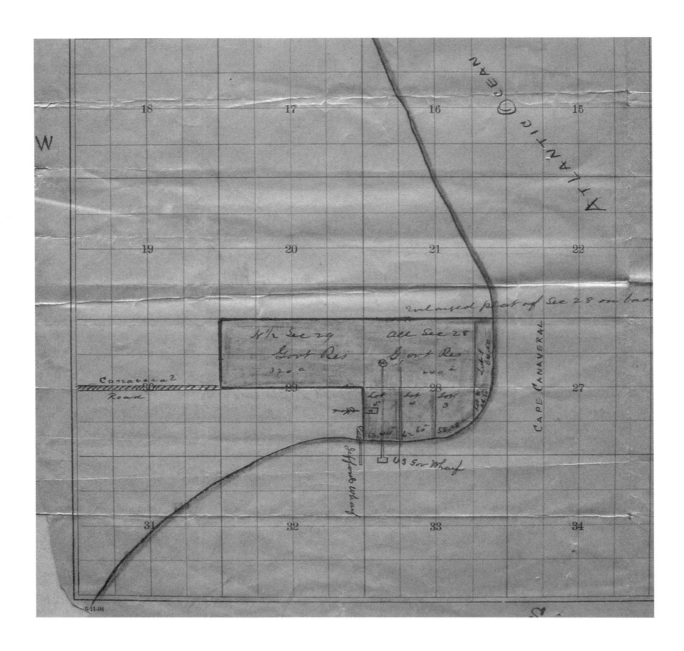

This is a hand-drawn depiction of the Cape Canaveral Pier by Glenn Shockey. The drawing supports an earlier statement of Reba's Place and the dance hall.

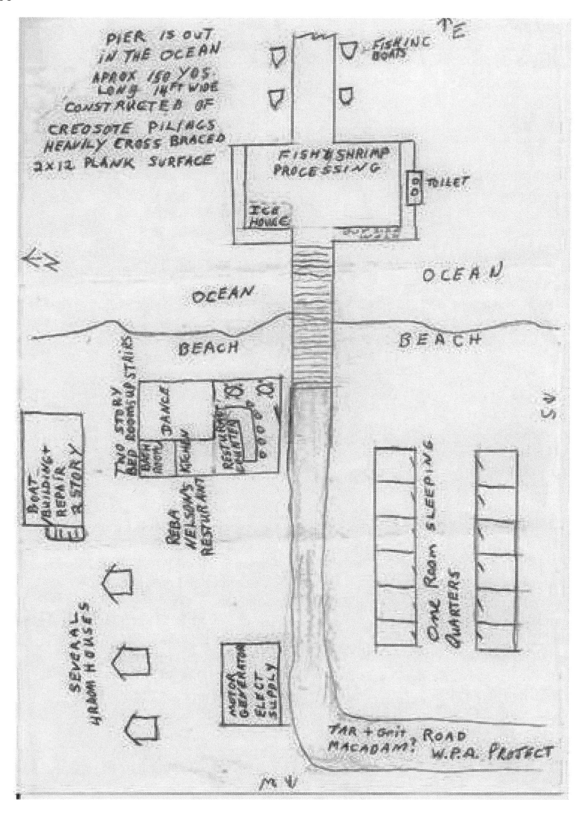

Memminger, C.G., 38-39
Mendez, 6
Mew, J. R., 59, 59, 71
Miller, Alfred, Rev, 108
Moore, Chas M., 129
Move, Lighthouse, 61-66
Mule, 59

N

Nancy Hanks, 60, 97
Nathan, Florida, 40, 96
Nathan Post Office, 41
Nelson, Reba, 84
Newfound Harbor, 15
Norrell, Percy R., 129
Norsworthy, William A., 86
Note in a bottle, 96

O

Oakland Cemetery, 17
Ocean Drive, 85
Oil House, 71
Orient Buckboard, 131
Orlando-Canaveral Harbor Rail Road Co., 83
Orton, Margaret M., 136
Oslo, florida, 97
Osceola, Chief, 13
Osman, Harry, 60, 81
Owens, L. G., 89, 143

P

Pacetti, B. J., 59
Packard's Transfer, 89
Palmetto Hats, 111
Pan-Massachusetts torpedoed, 101
Parrott, Robert P., 37
Peck, Samuel H. Colonel 13
Pedestal for Lens short, 45
Penny, N. Nathan, 18, 129
Penny, Fanny, 97
Penny, Nathan O., 97, 130, 131
Pharos, 51, 71

Pharos of Alexandria, 93
Praetorious, Al, 84, 159
Praetorious, Edward J., 114, 144
Phone to lighthouse, 82
Pier, 84
Pier Road, 85
Pleasonton, Stephen, 20-25, 31
Poe, O. M., 43
Ponce de Leon, 12
Ponce de Leon Lighthouse, 57
Port Canaveral, 114
Praetorious, Edward G., 18, 114

Q

Quarterman, Ann Dummett, 130
Quarterman, George M., 18, 48, 145
Quarterman (home), 162
Quarterman, Orlando A., 18
Quarterman, William G. M., 18, 49, 129, 143
Quarterman, Oscar Floyd, 60, 89, 130, 143
Quarterman, Virgenia, 129

R

Radio expert, 87
Ranson, Marion, 154
Ranson, Robert, 110
Ranson, Grace, 110
Reba's Restaurant, 84
Reed, Samuel, Colonel, 12
"Reo de Ais", 7
Request for Proposal, 187
Reynolds, Michael, Father, 128
Ringo, Mr., 154
Robinson, Frank, 121, 131
Robinson Susan, 121
Roosevelt, President, 88
Rose, Alexander, 31, 143
Rust, Oscar William, 144

S

Sacco Main, foundation stones, 42, 192
Sacred Lily of India, 115